WHAT BOOKS PRESS

AN IMPRINT OF

THE GLASS TABLE

COLLECTIVE

LOS ANGELES

ALSO BY CHUCK ROSENTHAL

*Loop's Progress*

*Experiments With Life and Deaf*

*Loop's End*

*Elena of the Stars*

*Avatar Angel: The Last Novel of Jack Kerouac*

*Never Let Me Go*
MEMOIR

*My Mistress, Humanity*

*The Heart of Mars*

*Are We Not There Yet? Travels in
Nepal, North India, and Bhutan*
MAGIC JOURNALISM

# COYOTE O'DONOHUGHE'S HISTORY OF TEXAS

## CHUCK ROSENTHAL

LOS ANGELES

Publisher's Cataloging-In-Publication Data

Rosenthal, Chuck, 1951-
   Coyote O'Donohughe's history of Texas / Chuck Rosenthal.

     p. ; cm.

   ISBN-13: 978-0-9823542-9-2
   ISBN-10: 0-9823542-9-0

   1. Indians--Mixed descent--Fiction. 2. Mexicans--Texas--Fiction. 3. Shapeshifting--Fiction. 4. Texas--History--Republic, 1836-1846--Fiction. 5. Picaresque literature, American. I. Title.

PS3568.08368 .C69 2010
813.54                        2010928212

What Books Press
23371 Mulholland Drive, no. 118
Los Angeles, CA 91364

WHATBOOKSPRESS.COM

Cover art: Gronk, *untitled*, mixed media on paper, 2010
Book design by Ashlee Goodwin, Fleuron Press.

# COYOTE O'DONOHUGHE'S
# HISTORY OF TEXAS

For Gail, my Morning Star

It must have happened something like this.

Roberto Bolaño, *Distant Star*

# INTRODUCTION

I AM COYOTE O'DONOHUGHE, Comanche shaman and shape shifter, warrior, intellectual, secretary to William B. Travis, traveling companion of General Antonio López de Santa Ana, Harvard man. I fought against Texans on the Great Plains, fought with them at the Alamo; fought with the San Patricio Battalion in the Mexican War, fought for both the North and the South in New Mexico; I fought with Cochise and I fought against him.

During my sojourn at Harvard I spent time with a bunch called the Metaphysical Club. One of them believed that everything was in our own minds and another didn't believe in the mind. One believed that the whole world was based on mathematics and another that reality was just a bunch of signs and symbols. They could argue all night. It was after one of those meetings, sharing a cigar and rye whiskey with the notorious James brothers, William and Henry, that Billy James tried to convince me to write down my life.

"The Comanche don't write things down," I said.

"Only because they don't write," said Billy.

"Neither do they teach at Harvard and speak seven languages," said Henry.

"My mother spoke five," I said.

"An exception that proves the rule," said Henry James.

These Harvard types were crazy about the exception that proved the rule. Everything proved the rule including the exception and then where were you?

My mother was a language shaman, among other things. Aside from Comanche, she taught me Nahuatl, English, Spanish, and French. I learned Latin and ancient Greek from the Jesuits down in Mexico City, all before I ever came to Harvard.

"You've experienced so many unique things," said Billy James.

"Let me offer you a syllogism," I said to those James boys. "A Harvard man is to ideas as a Comanche is to horses. You love ideas. We love horses. You ride ideas. We ride horses. I could go on, but I'll end with we steal horses and you steal ideas."

"Preposterous," said Henry James.

"I'd love to steal your ideas," said Billy James.

You had to like Billy James, he was open-minded.

So I sat down and wrote this book. I wrote another one, too. My life, from birth to Harvard. Then I let those two James brothers take a look.

"Reads like Twain," said Henry James.

"Is that a compliment?"

"No," said Billy.

"I don't care for his style," said Henry. He took a long puff on his cigar, let out a bunch of smoke. "Nor his metaphysics."

"I think it's fantastic," said Billy.

"Precisely," said Henry. "Unbelievable."

"Do Indians really talk to each other like that?" said Billy.

"Comanche speak to each other in Comanche. I got as close as I could get."

"Anyway, you saved me a trip to Texas," said Henry James.

"Let me keep these," said Billy James. "I'd like to show them to my editor."

"These are the only copies?" I said. I was worried he'd already done a word raid.

"For now," said Billy James.

"Give me the night to think about it," I told him.

That night I packed up a few things, including these manuscripts, got on my horse and headed for Texas. In not much longer, you won't be able do something like that anymore. When I get there, I'm going to bury this first book on the plains where I buried the heart and liver of my first horse. I'll put the second one under a cottonwood tree. Then I'm going to join Quanah Parker and the Quahada Comanche for their last stand against William Tecumseh Sherman and Ranald MacKenzie's 4th Cavalry. So I don't imagine anyone will ever read this, but if you do, well, it's a miracle.

# Part One

1

THERE WAS TOO MUCH inexperience all around. Our war chief, Turkey Feathers, was twenty-two years old and didn't have a half-dozen scalps on his lance. I was sixteen. The only one of us who'd ever ridden out in front of a party before was seventeen year old Wind Sister, though she'd been doing it since she was ten. But we were Comanche and everybody was afraid of us, as well they should have been. We weren't even chasing Apaches, who could be trouble on occasion. We were young and mischievous. And with the Mexicans and Texans busy fussing at each other over land that wasn't even theirs, something that would soon lead to that massacre at the Alamo, we figured we might romp around the plains unmolested.

We thought we'd just ride into some Caddo village and take coup, which for a lot of us would be our first. Caddoans fought poorly and their scalps were hardly worth the time to take them. We didn't use them for slaves because they didn't ride well and so were worthless for travel. Even if you wanted to sell them in Santa Fe to the Spanish or Navajo it would take you a half month to get them there and by that time they'd be scrawny and completely in despair and worth nothing. Maybe a priest would buy one just for the price of his soul, but you'd be surprised how little a soul is worth, just in terms of corn and beans. The Apache and Wichita say that the Caddos are good eating, but a Comanche would have to be pretty hungry to eat a Caddo. In general we didn't eat pigs, birds, fish, horses, white folks' cattle, or people if we could help it, which included Caddoans. Who needs the soul of a farmer inside of you? They were just good practice for young warriors. The British would call it sparring.

We took all our weapons: lance, bow, arrows, shield, hatchet, knife, war club. Some of the older raiders, like Turkey, even had a musket, but in truth we just planned on running through the Caddo village and clubbing the men on their heads. Some of those Caddo braves had been whacked by Comanche so many times that they'd traded half their winter food supply for those leather helmets the Spanish wore. They ran out of their mud huts with those things on their heads and knelt down and took their medicine. It was a way of protecting the rest of the family. They knew we could only hit them twice and two different warriors had to do it. After that it didn't count anymore. Lesser people, like the Cheyenne for instance, will count coup on the same person till he's been slapped silly. There's no dignity in that. But neither is it brave to walk out and take it with a helmet on. It can get you mad enough to stick a spear through somebody.

Wind Sister once told me that the Caddos knew that, too, so the risk made them brave. I told her you couldn't think about it that much. In general, we Comanche, particularly the men, were not thinkers. We didn't like politics or religion. Didn't go in much for ceremonies, rules or philosophy. We liked riding and fighting. Hunting was good. Love, that was good, too, but it was more exacting.

Our little band had ridden for a week. We'd finished off our pemican, picked up and broke some mustangs on the way. We took down an elk, which we were lucky to find that close to the southern plains that time of the year, when things were so dry. Then two of our scouts, Fat Otter and Twin Cub, spotted the Caddos camped by a stream. Their fields of beans and corn and squash surrounded the encampment, their few horses were tied up next to their grass lodges.

Most of these bands built barricades around their camps when they came in for the fall harvest, set some sharpened poles on top, dug a ditch around it, kept lookouts while the workers were in the fields. If you were inclined toward humiliation, you could arrive at the crops in late summer and just wait there like a puma at a gopher hole. We'd done that to the Apache a few times, and the Pawnee, because they'd fight for their crops. These Caddos would just get very sad, do a lot of wailing and go off and spend the winter eating bugs and roots. Half of them would starve and that would be bad medicine for us.

We dismounted our ponies behind a hill, downwind, and examined the village. This camp didn't have a ditch around it yet, but most of us were too young and itching to fight to be suspicious. We figured maybe they'd got to the harvest a little late and hadn't set up their defenses yet.

"Then why haven't they started the wall?" said Wind Sister.

"They just got here," said Turkey Feathers. "Like us."

"That's right," said Twin Cub. He was Turkey Feather's friend and agreed with everything Turkey said.

"Yet their huts are already built," said Wind Sister.

"We're pretty far south," I said. "Maybe they think they're safe."

"Safe from whom?" said Sister,

"From us!" Turkey said

"They aren't safe from us!" Wind Sister said.

"Yes! That's right!" said Turkey Feathers.

"That is right," said Twin Cub.

"After this," said Sister, "I will not ride with young boys." She was clearly exasperated. It was the price of thinking things through.

But Turkey Feathers just wanted a fight. He didn't care about the odds. He didn't care about anything, not against Caddos. Wind Sister was a woman and women cared about unfigurable things. Anyways, in the end it would depend on who wanted to go and who didn't because no Comanche was in charge of any other Comanche at any time except in the absolute heat of battle. Then you listened to your war chief without exception until the moment the battle was over.

Of all the people in the Plains, we were the best horseback riders, and the fiercest and the quietest, if not the most refined. A Comanche could ride up from behind you and steal your horse and take your scalp faster than a Spaniard can say *oro.*

We camped that night without fires. We opened our medicine pouches, parfleche bags made out of buffalo intestines, and lay our luck in front of us. We smelled the wind and watched the sky. A full moon had risen at sunset, a pretty good sign even if we planned for it. And though it was the season for falling stars, none fell that night, which meant bad luck for somebody, though it was hard to tell for whom. That was the thing about omens and why some of us didn't take much stock in them unless they were good omens.

I smoked tobacco with Fat Otter and asked for my power. At the time my official power came from the Rabbit, which was not the greatest warrior medicine, but it was medicine and I'd achieved it and earned the name when I was very young. Since then, a shaman, Little Owl, had brought Coyote to me, and my mother, a shaman as well, taught me to call on Coyote when I needed him. In fact, part of the reason I was on this escapade was to earn my new name.

Not that your power was always your name. Fat Otter was a skilled rider and bowman and his power came from the Badger, which was fierce medicine. Wind Sister had the Eagle, which was very powerful, though Turkey Feathers, well, the Comanche respected turkeys more than most.

There were only twenty-four of us and Twin Cub estimated that the Caddos had a good one hundred men who could fight, not counting the women who would fight too. We all gathered together again in the middle of the night.

"I have been listening to the ponies," said Turkey Feathers, "and they are anxious to free their brothers from a miserable life among the Caddos."

Sure, it was a joke, but Turkey thrived on leadership, a born war chief, and he knew how to get Comanche blood flowing. Any talk of stealing horses went right to our bones.

"We will fly through the Caddo like wild birds." He passed his hand through the air like a wing. "We will strike like lightning!" That wing of his stiffened into a fist. He sought everyone's eyes as he lit his elk bone pipe. Turkey had loyal followers among us, and for good reason. He came from strong blood and all that, not like me, a half- breed. His father, Dark Eagle, had scalped Spaniards and even Texans and, as you can see, Turkey Feathers had his poetic side and anybody that knows anything knows that war is what poetry is all about and vice versa.

"They have no horses worth stealing," said Wind Sister. She took the pipe from Turkey and smoked it. Unlike Turkey Feathers, she stared out at nobody. When Sister stared out at nobody and spoke, it gave her an aura of spiritual power. She was a well-built and powerful girl, dark, smooth skin, hair so thick and black that war chiefs begged her for shavings to weave into their own. She lowered her lids slowly toward me because being the youngest and a half-breed I'd be riding out in front of the party with her to prove I was the equal of the rest. She rode out first because having a virgin warrior leading your raid brought exceptional luck.

It wasn't my right to speak that early in the meeting, though in the end my vote counted for me and was worth as much as I was. If me and Sister chose not to come, that left two fewer raiders, less luck, and they'd have to choose somebody else to ride out front. There were twenty-two other young warriors there, one of them, Wind Sister's friend, Soft As Doe Skin, was a girl only a few months older than me. The rest of the boys were teen-agers too. Doe Skin wasn't permitted to ride out front because she was known as the pleasure seeking sort. She'd visited too many beds in too many tipis, and it didn't matter to her whether you were male or female. Not that anyone in the tribe was bothered by that, unless they felt left out. In fact she got her name because of how good she felt next to you, not that I'd had the privilege, but you couldn't have those kinds of habits and ride out in front of a war party, it just went without saying.

We were a bunch of kids, young, wild Indians, playing at it as much as anybody ever did, itching to paint up and get on the back of a horse and ride like hell, half serious and half not—except for Turkey and Sister, we didn't really have a clue. The adults would never have let us out of camp if we hadn't headed south where all we'd run into was poor Mexican farmers and disheartened Indians.

I saw the war chiefs lining up as we rode out, smoking rolled tobacco, shaking their heads, some of them smiling out the sides of their mouths. The mothers were more worried. They didn't even come out to see us off, though they knew there were two girls with us and probably hoped two female brains were enough to keep us roughnecks from losing our lives.

"Sister," said Turkey Feathers, "some of these boys are young and have never taken coup." He made his wing motion again with his hand and smiled, a real diplomat.

That's when Big Like A White's Horse spoke out. He was extremely tall and had light colored hair because he'd been adopted. I guessed he was a German or a Swede, though that would have meant nothing to most Comanche. His legs were so long they almost touched the ground when he rode his war pony. At one point his father even stole him an American cavalry horse to better fit him, but the thing was too fat and pampered to keep up with our mustangs. That explains a little about his name, too. He used horse tails and women's hair, when he could, to braid into his own, which gave him the look of a big, mottled dog. He wanted Mottled Dog for a name, but he wasn't going to get it until he accumulated some coup. That being the case, he had a lot to prove.

"If we come back with our ponies empty, it will be a disgrace," said White's Horse. Being adopted, White's Horse considered himself an expert on disgrace.

"Raiding a bunch of defenseless Caddos is a disgrace," I said, less because I believed it than I had a crush on Wind Sister.

Everybody got quiet. I'd spoken out of turn and though I'd spoken to White's Horse, I'd challenged everybody's bravery, especially Turkey's, when we all knew that no Comanche ever picked a fight he thought he'd lose.

"Rabbit," Turkey Feathers said to me, "you are too smart to be a warrior."

He didn't think that up. It was an old Comanche insult which meant that thinking made you a coward. We stood insult to insult, though his insult meant more because he was more important than me and he'd used an old insult. In a debate, Comanches gave extra credit for older curses.

"I'll ride," Wind Sister said, ending it, "though this will come to a bad end or nothing."

So we got all painted up and put what few feathers we'd earned into our hair. Saddled and painted our war ponies. We didn't use the same horse for day riding as we did for battle. Your dearest horse was your war pony who you trained on to do all your tricks. I had a bay mare I named FireBlood. You'll hear that Comanche only rode geldings into battle, but that's not true. A gelding tended to be a steady, trusting beast, often noble enough but seldom fierce. An animal that kept its sex maintained an alertness and wildness inside. It knew love and passion and jealousy. Wind Sister rode a gray stallion.

We smoked together again as the sky lightened. We unwrapped our war arrows and placed them in our quivers, took our shields from their shield bags. Many of our shields held strong enough medicine to block the flight of bullets. Everybody was a brother or sister by that point, for as long as the battle lasted. Turkey, his body and face painted half black and half red, grabbed each of us by the hand and pressed our fists to his chest. I painted myself red everywhere. Just red. Sister had yellow and black stripes on her face and arms. You could paint yourself however you wanted. It was up to you.

"When the sun rises," said Turkey Feathers, "we will have more men among us than when the sun set." That boy sure wanted to be a leader. I wish he'd had more of a chance.

When I was among white folk I heard a lot of tales about when the Comanche liked to attack; whether it was at dawn or sunset or under the moon. It's said that we didn't like to attack at night because we were afraid our souls would get lost in the dark if we were slain. Well, some Comanche were afraid of that, others weren't. For the most part we attacked whenever we pleased. You don't have to think about it too hard. It's a damn Indian raid, not a train schedule. And we didn't go in whooping and hollering unless it gained us some psychological advantage from the enemy knowing we'd arrived. One thing I can tell you, there's nothing like galloping into battle.

That morning we came over the hill just before sunrise, in the gray of light. First the Caddoan dogs started up, and then their horses. By the time we hit the edge of the camp, spreading out so we would come in from as many angles as possible, a few of the Caddo men had already emerged from their huts. I rode in and hit one square on the side of the helmet, my first coup, and Sister was there to mark it. He rolled, got up, and Sister came in behind me and laid her war lance on his back the way you'd tickle a lover with a feather.

The Caddo turned, baffled, and there she was, staring down on him, her lance at his chest. Whatever stories Caddos told about facing our wrath, Sister wasn't going to let him take an anonymous beating and turn it into medicine. No, that girl understood humiliation.

We ran the perimeter of the village, ritually knocking the helmets off Caddos, a rout in no uncertain terms. Even White's Horse got coup on a follow up. He spread out and yelled so loud his toes touched the ground from the top of his pony. Even though we were just a bunch of kids, we weren't going to get much of a fight out of these farmers.

The plan had been to hit them there at the edge of their camp and then race through the center of the village, gathering horses and heading out, but there were so few horses and so little resistance we decided to see what booty we could take. Sometimes they kept their best horses with them in their huts. Often enough the Caddos scraped together enough furs to trade the French for a pot or a metal blade, which, if you didn't want to pound it into an arrowhead, was a nice thing to bring back and give to your mother.

Turkey Feathers dismounted and ran into one of the sod huts, but he was out fast, looking around wildly. By that time a few of us had already been in and out of the Caddo homes and found the same thing. Nothing. Wind Sister was racing through the edge of the village, calling out to everybody to mount up. It took a little while for us to realize that the only noise was our own celebrating and as soon as we quieted down that village sounded like a burial ground.

But it's not that easy to gather up a bunch of wild Indians in the middle of a battle. White's Horse had already charged into the second line of homes. He made a wonderful dismount, being so long, and just slid off the back of his pony on the run. His horse came to a skid, turned, and waited while White's Horse ran into the hut, his avaricious howl the only sound in the world.

Until a bang roared out so loud you'd swear the sky came apart. White's Horse backed out, a circle of blood on his back as big as his shield. He turned to us. I saw the look in his eyes. He wasn't coming home. He was dead before he fell to his knees.

Turkey Feathers let out a blood curling yell, but I could hardly hear it over the din of guns. From the second ring of Caddo shanties, white men emerged with long rifles and in the next explosion Turkey Feather's best friend, Twin Cub, went down.

It only made sense for us to turn tail, but not before picking up our casualties. You could come back empty handed from a war party and feel ashamed, but to come back having left your wounded or dead could put you in disgrace for life.

We rode into our circle. Depending on our prey, we might tighten the circle slowly, but in this case it was defensive. We needed to consolidate so we could sweep in for our dead. And now was the time to act because it took a while for a man to reload his rifle and in that time a good archer could get off ten arrows outside the accuracy range of a pistol.

Twin Cub gave his signal that he was alive, twitching his left foot, and we tightened the circle, some of the boys dropping down on the outside of their ponies and firing arrows under their necks, a tactic that worked well enough around Indians, because the honor of a coup is to take the rider, not the horse. Besides, a horse is too valuable to kill. But a white man will just shoot your horse out from under you. A white man will shoot at anything, even dead things.

As me and Turkey Feathers approached at a gallop, Cub sat up quickly and raised his arms. We snatched him on the run, one of us on each side, and he swung quickly to the back of my pony. His shoulder was blown up badly, but another brave had gathered his horse and he made the transfer in an instant. White's Horse would be more difficult. For one, he was dead, and a dead man is no help. Worse, he'd fallen among the whites and two of them stood over his body now, pistols and knives drawn. I surmised they were Texans if they knew we had to collect him or be disgraced. Texans were quick to learn our ways so they could kill us better.

You hear a lot about great Indian fighters, particularly Texans, but to be honest they were not at their best when they had to move. They liked to sit still and pick you off or get you hand to hand with a Bowie knife. Most Texans came from Tennessee, Kentucky, Pennsylvania, places where the men were committed to long rifles, good for hunting or sniping at long range, if they had plenty of time to reload. But like most folks these frontier types wanted one answer for every circumstance, so they used long rifles for everything, even when it didn't make any sense, like on a horse, for instance. For all the talk about their marksmanship, and all that's been written about them since, no Comanche was afraid of a Texan as long as we were on horseback.

Though it was pretty clear to me, as we started unloading our arrows on the run, that they had the first part of this trap they'd laid pretty well thought out. They knew we wouldn't leave our dead and they were paired off in those Caddo huts, one stepping out and firing while the second stepped inside to reload. We put a few arrows in a number of them, but when white men were fortified and ready for you they were tough to lick.

I rode up beside Turkey Feathers and told him. "Let's get White's Horse and get out of here!"

Well there are smart ways to do things and stupid ways. Contrary to what you might think, we had prescribed strategies for dealing with these kinds of problems. I won't discuss them now, because we didn't use any of them. Instead, Turkey Feathers, our young war chief, let out his war cry and took it upon himself to make a battle charge. He headed straight in at the two men standing over White's Horse. Maybe he thought I'd insulted him, it's hard to say, but his medicine was good. He deflected one shot with his shield, perfectly angled to deflect the ball, fired his own musket and took the man down. He had his war pony shot out from under him by the other, but used his falling horse to launch himself and his war lance. He even had the presence of mind to turn his blade so it pierced the Texan's rib cage. The spear came out the other side with the Texan's heart fat on the tip of the blade.

Fat Otter rode in with Wind Sister and plucked White's Horse from the ground, dragging him between them as they galloped off, but Turkey Feathers lingered to get his scalps and took a musket ball in the guts before he could finish the second.

I came in for him as he struggled to his knees.

"I will not be eaten by Caddos," said Turkey Feathers. He grimaced. I could see he was trying to show a sense a humor, because seeing as we didn't have a doctor in our war party, he was as good as dead. He picked up his knife and used both hands to finish the scalping, letting his guts spill out and not tucking them back in till he was done.

Doe Skin came in with another pony for Turkey, but as she did one of the whites, a huge man, grabbed her little horse by the tail and pulled them both down. He took her head off with his Bowie knife in a single swipe.

I put my spear in his chest, but I didn't get the blade turned and it stuck in his ribs. He grabbed the damn thing and cracked it in two, almost pulled me off my horse. I hit him on the head with my war club, to no avail. He grabbed me by the chest. Turkey Feathers knifed him and those two went down together like a boy wrestling a bear, but by then I had four arrows in the man's back, which didn't stop him until I put the fifth in his neck underneath his skull. In all of this, you'd think somebody would have shot me, but my medicine was good that day. I took my first scalp, a blond one, though it would be hollow because of the deaths, and helped Fat Otter gather up Doe Skin. Turkey Feathers, covered in blood, slipped onto his new pony and we fled.

2

IF YOU RUN AWAY from a white man, he'll follow you. It took us a while to learn that because it's something that doesn't make any sense to an Indian. For us, if somebody runs away, great, that's the point. We moved back through our camp and picked up our extra ponies, changing horses on the fly without dismounting. We tied the dead into their saddles, including the headless Doe Skin, though I had her skull, hair intact, in my parfleche bag. Despite our predicament, and failures, we'd left no dead to be mutilated by the Texans or eaten by the Caddos, lost no scalps, and taken several. We were on the run, but even in Caddo territory we were at the advantage on the move, which we could continue without rest, without camping, without sleep.

I could hear the Texans behind us, thundering on their heavy horses, shooting and shouting, wasting their energy, ammunition and, thank the Great Everywhere Mystery, time.

Once we were off, our quickness raised a gap again between us and them and we began our first, methodical splitting, the party dividing in two. But our pursuers divided, too.

We ran from them all day, though not as you might think. No horse can run constantly, even unburdened. The first thing to go is their lungs. You have to change horses often and you have to break up the speeds of their canters. You've got to alternate your galloping with slow and fast trots. Sometimes you even have to get off and walk. You must save your horses. Your horses are life. Your horses are everything.

We wove among each other's tracks as we broke speed to obscure the prints of our ponies' hooves, not to disguise our path, that would be impossible, but to erase the distance between the hoof prints and destroy the depth of their marks in the dust; this to confuse the Texans as to the speed of our riding and the number of our party. Late in the day we divided again, chasing the sun. I was with Fat Otter, Wind Sister, the wounded Twin Cub and dying Turkey Feathers when we divided again. The Texans divided once again, too.

Had they chosen not to match us when we split up, we would eventually divide up completely, leaving the whole of them in pursuit of a single warrior who, if he could not elude them, would turn on them and attack, taking as many as he could, robbing them of vengeance and torture while letting the rest of us escape.

But these were dogged pursuers, the new kind of Yankees we'd heard about, Rangers, bred to fight and kill us and take our buffalo and land. The war chiefs had talked about them in councils. It was a new fighting that had no honor, no code, no sense, that understood nothing but annihilation.

Wind Sister knew it. "Rangers," she said as we broke to a trot. "It will be a long day and a long night."

"We will outrun them," I said

"They will track us," said Fat Otter.

"If they camp, we can double back on them," said Twin Cub.

"They are too smart for that," said Sister

"No one can run with us," I said.

"They will follow," said Sister.

"If you can make it to our land," gasped Turkey Feathers. He held his stomach. It was easier to ride at a smooth lope, and the jerky trot of his pony wrenched his guts. His face no longer held any blood and his stoicism was frightening.

"Each of you give me a feather," he said. "Let them get close enough so they will see I am the chief."

"You're a chief," I said. "Not the chief."

"Do not quibble," he said. He was as authoritative as he'd ever been in his life. "We will take the bodies. Let the dead fly. Let the dead follow the dead."

We didn't have to listen to him, he was just in charge. But he'd beat me to the punch again with a famous saying. Let the dead follow the dead. The Cheyenne liked to say, It is a good day to die, and later on it got so popular out on the plains it became a kind of joke. Hell, there's no good day to die, any Indian knows that, that's why it was said. But by the end you even had white people saying it. Personally, and I say this having been educated by Spaniards and Yankees alike, both in Mexico City and up at Harvard, we should never even have started talking to whites.

Turkey Feathers was half dead and half right. As much as Texans came to know about us, they were still white people, and white people, among others, overestimated the importance of being in charge. They probably would chase him. We'd have to divide up again anyways before we started doubling back, using our speed to regroup and outnumber one batch of pursuers before the other batch could catch up.

We gave him our feathers, then Turkey and Twin Cub slowed and split off, taking the bodies of White's Horse and Doe Skin with them as the sun went down. We had to slow down ourselves for a bit until the moon came up to give us light to run in. We changed horses again, still saving our war ponies, and Otter and I put on shirts. We were lucky in that the wind came up behind us, a warm wind that would carry the sounds and smells of the Texans if they got close.

Otter rode ahead. He was superstitious. He was caught between riding off with the dead and near dead, or a girl and a fledgling Coyote with a severed head in his parfleche. I'd forgotten to give Doe Skin's head to Turkey and Cub and that was a big blunder. Dividing up somebody's remains was bad medicine. Anybody could understand that.

"If only I could see the future like I see the past," said Fat Otter. Crisis and doom brought out a lot of famous sayings among our people. It reminded us that the spirits hadn't wasted their time thinking up any new, depressing situations we hadn't been in before.

"I saw this," Wind Sister quietly said to me. "I told Turkey Feathers, but it didn't do any good."

"We were already in the middle of it," I told her. "We couldn't turn back."

"Even before that," she said.

"Well Turkey doesn't listen," I told her. "It would have been worse without you. You're good luck."

"No," she said.

Even a kid like me understood what she meant when she said, no.

"We rode each other's dreams," she said.

"You and Turkey?"

"The night before leaving. To call it off would have been to admit it. Now I have doomed us."

More than doomed us, she was breaking my heart. I was tempted to ask her if Turkey was a good lover, but a woman like Sister, she could read your mind.

"I saw in him what you saw today. I wanted that in me. A man cannot do that for himself. Only a woman can let a man live beyond death."

There was nothing like having done something wrong to get a Comanche preaching. Virtuous people, Indian or white, keep their mouths shut.

"Don't say anything to Otter," I said to her. "He already feels bad enough."

"The future came to me like a buffalo calf. I killed him and drank his mother's milk, still warm in his belly."

Worse than preaching were visions. When Comanche thought they were going to die, they started seeing and singing.

"Don't start singing your medicine yet," I said to Wind Sister. "If you think about what you're saying, then either you or Turkey have to survive this. Besides, you don't want to die with me around, I'm a horrible singer."

She laughed, an honest laugh, not a death grimace like Turkey's, and that was good.

"A good, practical Coyote," she said.

"That's right," I said.

"And how are your powers under this moon and sun?"

"My powers are fine," I said. "Under this moon. Under this sun."

She was asking me if I could go it alone when we divided up for the last time at dawn. Otter was older. It was protocol that she go with him, besides, he had a decent musket, a percussion rifle at that. And if truth be told, I had slippery medicine, for one, the gift of tongues, Spanish, from my father who was a Spanish Creole, and a bit of Nahuatl, which is Aztec and pretty close to Comanche. My mother, a shaman, spoke Spanish and Nahuatl, as well as English and French. Knowing I'd need special skills as a half-breed, she made me learn them. I knew a little Latin and ancient Greek, too, but all that's another story. Along with the sign language of the plains, I could pretty much get by anywhere. You'd be surprised what a man can accomplish with the right language and a change of clothing.

As the dawn approached we pulled up. Everything told us the Texans were still coming. The tremor of the earth, our mother, spoke them. The wind carried the smell of their buckskin and horses. Our war ponies, trained to signal the approach of buffalo, predators, and enemies, tipped their ears far forward, the sign for white men on horseback. So Turkey's ruse had failed.

"As I said," muttered Wind Sister.

Otter had his ear to the ground. "They travel with plenty of horses," he said.

"You wouldn't want to go through all this trouble and not steal their horses, would you?" I said.

Otter got up and went to his medicine bag, re-applying his war paint. "It is time to fight, not joke," he said.

"We'll ride our fastest horses now," said Sister.

She and Otter would try to put some distance between them and their trackers and come back against the wind when the sun was high. I'd push my slowest horse, allowing whoever followed me to close the gap. When Sister and Otter circled back, we'd have my pursuer briefly outnumbered and we'd dispose of him before lying in wait for the others. Then we'd head back again for Turkey and Twin Cub.

Fat Otter put my fist to his chest. "Live to be a warrior," he said.

I took his fist. "Lose some weight," I said.

Wind Sister cut a lock of her hair and wove it into mine. "May I see you in battle," she said to me.

"Don't be so formal," I said. I mounted my second pony, Gray Lout, and tethered FireBlood. "I'll save you a scalp." Then I kicked that old gelding and headed for the river.

3

ON THE OTHER SIDE of the Cross Timbers lay Béjar-San Antonio, Goliad-La Bahia, San Felipe de Austin. We'd originally thought that by sweeping north of them, before heading down into Caddo land, we'd avoided trouble with whites. We never stayed long down here ourselves because the buffalo didn't venture into the wetlands. The plains here were too broken by rivers and streams, stands of forest and grass taller than a man on a horse. Common sense might tell you it's better territory for hiding, but in fact it's easier to track a rider through vegetation because he can't move as fast and he leaves the signs of his passage everywhere.

I reached the River of Mud, Colorado the whites call it, and kept to its southern bank till it forked. Then I ran between the banks of both rivers before crossing again; to the west, after an open plain, there'd be canyons where I could hold out, if I had to, until Otter and Sister doubled back.

Once into the plains it was easy to spot my enemy as he closed in on me, pushing one horse hard underneath him. Now that we had each other in sight, I ran my fat gelding out to the escarpment of the canyon, pulling up under a bowl of rocks that sat up high enough to give me a view of the plain and would collect the wind, carrying his sounds and smells to me but denying mine to him. Had I a gun I could have ended the chase quickly. This he must have known. And I knew he'd prefer that I turned and charged him so he could shoot my pony with his rifle and put me away with his hand guns. But braver men than me are dead.

I locked my war spear into the stirrup of FireBlood so it stood straight up. I took poor Doe Skin's head out of the parfleche and mounted it on top the spear, then I told that mare to stay put and moved off to the other side of the rocks with Gray Lout. I'd have preferred to have left Gray Lout there and had FireBlood to ride, but I knew she was smart enough to listen to me if she chose and I couldn't count on Lout for much of anything. I put him behind a boulder and snuck up while the Texan came on like a wind devil. I whispered Fireblood forward a few feet until Doe Skin's head popped up over the rock. The Texan pulled up and I let loose an arrow.

Somebody good with a bow could have put an arrow through his throat from fifty yards or more, but not me; I managed to hit his horse in the neck near his shoulder where it would stun him, though he'd recover. I'd want the horse if I could get him. But that Texan panicked and pulled the animal down and slit his throat so there was no chance he'd get up and run away. He barricaded himself behind the beast's body. Texan's loved to do that. It demonstrated, to their minds, that they were ruthless and brave; to our minds that they were wasteful and stupid. I guess he figured that after he finished me off he could walk to San Felipe de Austin.

Now I was supposed to be as wasteful and stupid as him and run my war pony down the barrels of his loaded guns. Not me. If I could have got out of there without coming in the range of his rifle, I'd have just rode off to meet Otter and Sister. As I thought of it, I'd probably taken down his horse too early. If I'd have let him take a shot at Doe Skin's head I could have hightailed it before he got reloaded. I couldn't hit him with an arrow while he crouched behind that horse, either. Then I began to worry about abusing the body part of one of my own people. In another circumstance I might call it bad medicine.

I put a shakiness into my voice and threw it against the dome so it sounded like it was coming from Doe Skin's head.

"Why have you come here pale one?" I said. From what I could see of him, he looked young, maybe the age of Turkey.

"Who's talking there?"

"What do you want?"

"You're speaking English."

"Would you like it another language? *Allez*! *Vite*! Go away!" I said.

"Who are you?"

"I'm the spirit of this mountain."

"You're not."

"I am."

"You are not!"

"I am!" I said. "This is my home, such as it is."

"It is not."

"It is!"

"Is not."

"Who the hell do you think I am then?"

"You're a damn Indian who's got my uncle's scalp."

"I do not," I said.

"You do, too."

"I killed the Indian who did that and sent him far away," I told him. "I'm going to do the same to you if you don't get out of here."

He hesitated for a little bit. Just my luck I'd get a talker. It's harder to kill somebody after you get to know them. "Where'd you learn English?" he said.

"That's none of your business. I'm a spirit and I know lots of stuff." I tried to listen for Sister and Otter, but it was too difficult. The wind came from the direction of the Texan and the escarpment behind me blocked sound from the other direction. The sun wasn't quite high enough anyway, and being Comanche they'd probably be late. I looked at FireBlood's ears. They stood up, motionless.

"Go away, before I kill you," I yelled.

"Why were you picking on those innocent Caddos?" he said.

"We were just having some fun," I said.

"Thought you were the mountain spirit."

"Mountain spirits can have fun. What the hell were you doing there?"

"Trading."

"Trading my ass. That was a trap and you and your uncle killed a bunch of kids."

"A bunch of Comanche devils."

"Nope, innocent kids. You're bad people," I said. "You're really, really bad. But I'll let you live if you go away and tell your friends that they are bad people and they should leave us alone."

"You're no damn ghost," said that young Texan.

"Well shoot me, then," I told him. This was becoming an explicit demonstration of why people should just shut up and shoot each other right off. "Shoot me. I dare you."

"I goddamn will!" he said.

"Go ahead, shoot, you jackass."

Well, it was too much encouragement. He was getting suspicious. He poked his long rifle over the body of that poor, dead horse and peered at Doe Skin's head. He rotated his own head slightly, right, then left. If nothing else, things were mysterious enough for him. I figured if he were smarter he'd be more scared.

"Your mother is a jackass," I said.

That got to him. He fired off. Damn good shot, too. He knocked poor Doe Skin's head clean off the spear. I sent a few arrows toward the Texan and scrambled over for what was left of her head. I mounted FireBlood, but I was scared sick over the bad medicine of abusing Doe Skin's head just to save my life. It is a fact that Coyotes get in trouble, with the People, with the spirits, even with the best of intentions. I was swiftly contemplating all of this during my hasty departure when I saw the dust rising off in the distance to the east. FireBlood lay her ears down forward and flat. White men.

# 4

I GUESS THOSE TEXANS knew us pretty well. When we split up they obviously chased Otter and Sister just long enough before cutting out in my direction. Now they had me outnumbered and they could polish me off before circling back for Sister and Otter. Sad days. They even had extra horses.

They came into the basin and circled far behind the kid. Maybe they were worried that they figured wrong and a whole mess of us had him pinned down. Texans were notorious for overestimating the number of their enemy and even worse at calculating enemy dead. Before these Rangers were done they'd probably cut me up into pieces and count me and Doe Skin's head as thirty dead Comanche.

I cantered back and forth behind the rocks and let off a flurry of arrows, hoping to confuse them as to my numbers and keep my young friend pinned down. Of course, that depleted my arrow supply and it was just a matter of time before they checked the ground and figured out there were only two horses that headed into my fortifications. They started yelling to my new friend, his name was Henry Wax Karnes Jr., who told them I was a devil because he'd already shot my head off and there it was, back again where, of course, in the meantime, I'd returned it to my body.

I got back on Gray Lout, taking Doe Skin with me, because I figured I might need FireBlood beneath me when things really heated up. I could hear everything pretty good because I had that wall of rock behind me catching their voices. These new men were older and were skeptical of the ghost thing, so I figured to jump to what little advantage I had while I had it.

"He's right," I yelled out in plain English. "I'm a dangerous and powerful spirit, but there are dozens of wild Comanche waiting behind these rocks. I can only protect you for so long. You better just go away."

"He speaks lots of languages!" Henry Wax Karnes Jr. yelled to his friends.

"*Exactamente!*" I shouted. "*Hablo español! Je parle française! Veni, Vidi, Vici!* The whole kit and caboodle. So you better clear out."

"You see?" yelled Henry Wax Karnes Jr.

"You wouldn't know a different language from snake shit," yelled the oldest of the bunch to Henry Wax Karnes Jr. "And what's he going to do, talk us to death?"

"I might," I said. "I'm very powerful."

The other one knelt down with his long rifle and kablooie, off went Doe Skin's head again. It made me feel just horrible. But I retrieved it and stuck it back on the spear.

"Don't get me mad!" I yelled.

At that point they took to strategy, not knowing I could hear them as clear as my own heart. The older man, who had a full beard and a floppy hat, was named John and the sharpshooter, in buckskins, was Erastus. Henry Wax Karnes Jr., it seemed, was the son of Henry Wax Karnes who I guess was the leader of this bunch, off now chasing Turkey and Twin Cub. And I had Henry Wax Karnes's brother's, Big Dan Karnes, scalp right there on my saddle. It's amazing what will bring people together when you're out in the wilderness.

The Texans planned to sweep in on me from opposite directions, firing alternately, first their rifles and then both of their pistols, as worthless as any of that would be at fifty yards on horseback, and meet at Henry Wax Karnes Jr. Each of them would take in an extra horse, in case I shot the first one. Then they'd ride back to their position and reload. By then all us Comanche back here in the rocks would have fired off our weapons and exposed our numbers and armament.

"John, that plan will never work," I yelled out.

"What the hell!" said John.

"I told you I was powerful," I said. "Junior, you can just walk back to your friends. We don't care what you do as long as you stay away from these holy rocks."

That was a mistake. As befuddled as they were, you don't tell white men that there's one thing they can't do, because they'll be sure to try and do it. The first story in the Bible will show you that. It's the whole point of the Bible to my mind.

Erastus went to his knee again and I got Doe Skin's head down just in time to avoid another sacrilege. "Remember I did that," I whispered. I knew her spirit was somewhere out there between her head and the rest of her and it wouldn't depart until I got all her pieces united and properly given back to the Mother.

I put her head back up. "Boo!" I said.

"That's enough of this damn Injun hocus-pocus," said John, and in they came, firing and hollering. They swept in and got Henry Wax Karnes Jr. on a horse and rode back to their position. All the while I didn't bother to fire a single arrow. To my mind the situation had transcended guns and arrows.

The sun had climbed to the top of the sky and still no sign of Sister and Fat Otter. It would have made perfect sense for them to take off for home once they discovered they weren't being followed. Then they could gather a war party and return.

Erastus and John and Henry Wax Karnes Jr. reloaded their weapons. I heard them clicking and clattering out in the basin like a flock of birds. They took out their Bowie knives and let them glitter in the sunlight so I could get a good look at them, then sheathed them again. You get more than two white men together for any length of time and they start behaving like a drum and bugle corps. I'm surprised they didn't raise a flag and send in the fife and drums.

Old John sent Erastus and Henry Wax Karnes Jr. far out to his left and right. They stopped there and signaled to each other, rifles pointed in the air. I guess they just weren't afraid of ghosts that much. We'd see. They signaled to each other, spurred their horses, and began galloping in, heading right for me, guns out, full of bluster and doom.

5

It was time for Fat Otter and Wind Sister to show up. I never was one of those types who put on his war paint and rode out bravely to his death with the objective of taking out as many enemy as possible. That always struck me as kind of a last resort, and last resorts should come last, if at all. I simply hated the prospect of death.

I took down Doe Skin's head and led the horses to the back of the dome, as far away from the excitement as possible. Then I gathered up some rocks and stuffed them under my shirt, across my shoulders and arms. I pulled my leather shirt up over my head and set Doe Skin's head right there on top of my own, leaving a little opening at the neck of my shirt where I could see out. Then I found a boulder in the shade and sat down in front of it, right out in the open where they could find me. I didn't want to surprise a pack of trigger happy fools who might be stupid enough to shoot a ghost and end up killing me in spite of themselves. Nor did I want them seeing too good; I needed them to be standing in the sun and staring into the dark.

They came roaring up to the escarpment, screaming and shooting like all hell. I just lay there firing my last arrows into the air so they'd think there was somebody back there fighting them. They dismounted and ducked behind the rocks, reloading their guns. One popped up, fired, BANG, then ducked. Another fired and the first moved up to a closer rock. I sent an arrow out, yelling, "Ahk-hea!" our coup yell; that's as close as I can reproduce it in English.

They fired off and moved closer. They were having a hell of a battle. They were even winning. I looked back to FireBlood to see if maybe she heard Sister and Otter, but she just gave me a long, sorrowful gaze. She was contemplating what it was going to be like being owned by a white man.

"You'll be lucky if they don't shoot you, you traitor," I said to her.

She nickered and put her ears forward, then gave them a little wriggle. It meant white men were coming on foot.

"You're a big help," I said and she nodded, reminding me of some famous Comanche wisdom. Don't expect your horse to take care of you. Being a clever individual, and not a wise one, it frightened me to find myself thinking wise things. If I wasn't doomed, there had to be ghosts nearby.

The Texans came up to the rim of rocks around the dome now, so close I heard the shuffle of their feet. They fired wildly into the area, their balls ricocheting off the rocks. It was time to call up my power. I brought the white of my bones forward through my skin and let the stench of death flow from my pores. I called upon the dead who walk among us. The blackness of the shade darkened and the sunlight brightened around it as the gunfire quieted and the Texans, finally, John, Erastus, and Henry Wax Karnes Jr., came forward from behind the rocks to stare at my remains.

# 6

"WHAT IS IT?" whispered Erastus.

"I don't know," said John. "Keep your gun on it."

"I don't like this," said Henry Wax Karnes Jr.

"We haven't seen any bodies," said Erastus. He glanced around.

"There's one right here," said John. He peered hard at the darkness. "There aren't many horse tracks."

"And no other bodies," said Erastus. "And it was a hell of a battle."

"I don't like this," said Henry Wax Karnes Jr. "We already killed this one several times."

Old John sneered. "There's a body to plunder here."

"Maybe it's a trap," said young Henry Wax Karnes Jr.

"Well let's just put a half dozen more bullets in him," said Erastus,

That was my cue to stand up. I must have looked frightening enough because they all backed up a little.

"This is a trap," I said.

"Holy Jesus!" cried Henry Wax Karnes Jr.

"I am Coyote, spirit of this mountain!"

But old John raised his rifle to his shoulder. "What a load of crap," he said through his teeth. "This ain't even a goddamn mountain."

"Let's get out," pleaded Henry Wax Karnes Jr. "I can't shoot him anymore."

I needed a few more of him around and a fewer of old John. Erastus, the sharpshooter, was somewhere in between the two of them and stood with his gun half raised.

"Leave!" I said. I reached up and took off my head. I grabbed Doe Skin's bloody head by the hair and shook it at them.

But things just didn't go as I expected. It was Henry Wax Karnes Jr., his skin yellow with fright, who fired his gun and without thinking I threw my spear into his throat. Erastus didn't even shoot at me, he shot at Doe Skin's head and hit it again. I tried to spin away from old John, the rocks on my shoulders falling into my shirt as I scrambled, but he had me dead to rights and put a ball into my chest. I fell back, stunned, but quickly realized I was all right. The thing had hit one of the stones and shattered it against me, but the rocks had blocked the bullet.

For the first time old John came up short, his jaw dropping loose like Doe Skin's. Erastus pulled his pistol out of his belt, but I reached inside poor Doe Skin's head and grabbed a hunk of what was left of her brains and threw it in the sharpshooter's face. You never know what's going to stop a man. His eyes went horrible. His knees buckled and he fell back and ran.

By that time old John had recovered. He looked me in the chest, or the eyes, depending. He had both his pistols out and I had nothing left but my war club and knife and Doe Skin's head, which didn't even have any brains left in it.

"I'd like to kill you real slow," said John.

Well that was not my idea of a good time. I thought about trying to speak some Latin to him, but most of these Texans were Methodists, he'd just get madder. As little as I liked the idea, it was time for the last resort.

"Do you surrender?" I said.

"You son-of-a-bitch," said old John.

I screamed out my lungs, lunging at him, but when he discharged his pistols he didn't fire them at me but slightly to my right. I reached him with my knife and gutted him. He was a tough old man, but I had him, pushing the blade up under his rib cage and into his heart. I got up elbow deep in his guts till he stopped squirming. Then I pulled the blade out, up to my shoulders in his blood. I sat up. My breath disappeared in that quiet wind that carries the souls of the dead. There stood Doe Skin, headless, the bullet holes from the Texan's guns open in her chest. I knew what I'd done and what I had to do.

I retrieved her poor, mutilated head and put it on her. Vultures circled above us in the morbid air.

"You have called up the dead, Coyote," she said to me. "You asked for the aid of the dead."

"I didn't know I could," I said. Already the Texan's blood was drying on my arms, like deadly paint.

"Now you are an ally of the dead."

I knew what she was telling me. An ally of the dead had no friend among the living. She turned away and walked behind the rocks, the hot wind devils swirling, the cries of the ravens like children dying. Fireblood whinnied from the back of the bowl, pinning her ears: Comanche on horseback.

# 7

SISTER AND OTTER RODE up to the escarpment and into the bowl of my defense.

"Good timing," I said.

"When we discovered they had stopped following, we came back for you," said Sister. "Now it is time to recover Turkey Feathers and Twin Cub." She was a very serious girl.

Otter dismounted and pulled my spear from Henry Wax Karnes Jr.'s throat. He gave a war cry. "It is a great day of victory for you," he said.

"Oh, it's not," I said. "Otter, it really is a very bad day."

But Fat Otter wasn't the kind of Comanche who could understand the subtleties of spiritual doom, not that many could, particularly among the men.

"You must claim your coup," said Otter

"One of them got away," I said.

"He will pass your legend among the whites," said Sister from atop her stallion.

"That's just wonderful," I said.

I went to Henry Wax Karnes Jr. I picked up his rifle and gave it to Wind Sister.

I gave Fat Otter his Bowie knife. He had some money, silver, which I threw away, and a golden locket with his mother's name on it, Edna Dokes Karnes, with love to her son, Henry. Though we could use silver for trade in Pecos or Santa Fe, we didn't tend to take money because we didn't kill for money. We

42

wanted to keep that clear to the whites. Fat Otter wanted the locket, but I wouldn't let him have it.

"It's from his mother," I said. "It should go back to the earth who is his mother and mine as well."

Otter knew enough to back off. Comanche aren't religious types, so when one gets spiritual his comrades know enough to leave him alone. I took Henry Wax Karnes Jr.'s scalp because to leave it would be to dishonor him. Sister pointed to an engraving on the musket stock.

"This is the rifle's name," she said.

"No, it's the owner's name. Henry Wax Karnes Jr."

I gave her the powder and ammunition.

"Karnes is a great Texas warrior," she said solemnly.

"Don't tell me," I said. "Besides, Junior means son."

"Then you've earned a great enemy."

"I'm elated," I said.

I claimed old John's musty scalp, took his rifle and knife for myself and took his hat for my step-father. John's last name was McKenzie, one of the famous McKenzie brothers, notorious Indian fighters.

"Holy white man's God," I said.

"I am jealous of you, brother," said Fat Otter. And he had a right to be. He was twice the warrior I was, a better rider and better with the bow and arrow. He could barely walk or talk if he wasn't on a horse. I suppose I could have offered him the coup, but he'd be a coward not to take it, and who needed the reputation I'd just earned? Not a boy, like me, or even like Fat Otter, but a very great warrior.

FireBlood came forward, ears rotating like she was surrounded by Comanches.

"Silly horse," I said.

"Your parfleche is empty," said Wind Sister.

"That's not the half of it," I said. "I've got a hunch we'll find all of Doe Skin when we run into Twin and Turkey."

"You are strange, but you are powerful," said Fat Otter.

We were straightforward people and he was being as gracious as a Comanche could be.

"I am really depressed," I said.

"As I said," said Otter.

"Mount up," said Wind Sister. "We have our own dead to care for."

8

WE FOUND TWIN CUB and Turkey Feathers up near Yegua Creek. They'd crossed over and tried to make their stand there, figuring to front up while the Texans struggled to cross. Any good Apache or Kiowa would just have given up the battle at that point, or come on across if they had the numbers, but Texans don't think that way. They more than likely just pulled up on the opposite bank and shot Turkey and Twin out of their seats. From the number of hooves and footprints left in the area it looked like the majority of the Texans had indeed followed these two, so they got their chief, even if he was only two years out of his teens.

Texas Rangers were bounty hunters and mutilators. They couldn't take a scalp without hacking half a head off, and they cut off their victim's penis and testicles and stuffed them into his mouth. If you were lucky you died before they did it. I don't care to supply any more details than that. As a Comanche you got used to seeing pretty grizzly stuff, but I never got used to the Rangers. They thought they were doing what we did, only worse, and that would intimidate us, but they never had a damn clue what we were about.

We gathered up the parts of our comrades: Turkey Feathers, White's Horse, and Twin Cub. Sister wept over Turkey Feathers. She didn't even wait to get back to camp, but cut off her hair and slit her forearms right there. She wrapped him in her long hair. She let her blood rain on him.

Otter and I found Doe Skin a short lope back from the dead boys, head in place, the wounds on her face barely visible, like the ground after a wind storm.

"I might not ride with you again, Coyote," Otter said to me.

"I know that," I said. This kind of medicine could not be controlled, not even by a powerful shaman, let alone a boy. But we can't always choose these things. Some people ask for power and get none. Others receive too much.

Mounting the dead left us no extra horses. The Texans had no use for Twin Cub's and Turkey Feather's ponies, so they just shot them. Some of the vultures who'd showed up a little too early, hell, they'd shot them, too. Everything in the range of a long rifle around there was dead. I guess it made them feel safe. Finally, we mounted too.

Unbeknownst to us, we had just fought what in Texas history is known as the Battle of Peach Creek. If you read about it, you'll learn that a hundred Comanche warriors attacked a dozen or so Texas buffalo hunters who'd been peacefully at trade with the Caddoans and that the Texans killed over thirty of us and we wounded one of them. The fact is, about forty Texas Rangers and a village of Caddos set a trap for a couple dozen Comanche teenagers and a bunch of Texans got sent to hell without their hair. The scalps I took that day from Henry Wax Karnes Jr., old John McKenzie, and the big blond, a man named Ben Hooker, are accounted for in separate Texas legends where they went down in ambushes, horribly outnumbered, guns blazing. In fact they say Hooker was at the Alamo, though I know better because I was there. Whites had no honor when it came to counting enemy dead, and nobody can exaggerate like a Texan.

For our account, we were still three nights away from our tribe, the Honey Eaters, and our particular band, The HorseSleepers, were camped north of them, in the area on the River of Virgins. It would be a hard ride, especially carrying our dead with us. The rest of the raiding party had split west, toward home, and with luck they reached camp ahead of us. We'd arrive with our families already in mourning.

# 9

MY MOTHER, MANY POWERS, always said that the world was upside down. It's the fault of the men, she said. You men are standing on your heads. This feeling of your feet flying and dirt in your hair gives you the notion that you are walking in the sky. When men finally get up on their feet and shake the dirt out of their hair, she said, when they look around, things don't look right to them. They pray for medicine. They go out looking for a fight. If you're lucky they come back with a buffalo. This goes on until somebody gets killed. Then the women bury him in the sky. And have more babies.

One morning, after all the burials, the women come out of their tipis and they see the men and boys. The men are teaching the little boys how to plant their heads in the earth, their feet flying. Their horses are muttering around them, waiting for them to get up and go off to war.

"Mother," I asked, "what does it mean?"

"It means you don't have to stand upside down before you go off to war," she said to me.

My mother taught me that most men will put their lives on the line for any reason, so most men's lives aren't worth much. My mother, a brave woman, said that between the brave man and the coward stands a man foolish enough to be anything. All of this in one man. Love makes us cowards and madness makes us brave. The trick was to stand in between yourself, foolish, mad, in love, brave, all at once, all and none.

Like Wind Sister, Many Powers ran in front of war parties before she married my father, Many Wounds, Hermano O'Donohughe. The People, as any Indian calls his tribe, were already coming to her for Medicine while she was still raising me. Most women didn't become shamans until they were grandmothers.

Among us a person has many names, all earned, whether deservedly or not. My step-father was known in the tribe as Arrow Hits. He added the Always. And when my mother spoke to him she dropped both the Arrow and the Always and simply called him Hits. "Old Hits," she'd say to me. "One day, when you're older, I'll teach you something about the arrow and how it should hit." Birds and bees.

Before any of that I was educated in Mexico City by Jesuits who were hiding out from the Spanish regime who threw them out of the New World for educating Indians and turning a profit. The Jesuits were the coyotes of the Catholic Church. In fact, the Jesuits who educated me were pretending, among other things, to be Franciscans. Later, much later, I went to Harvard and pretended to be a Protestant.

I was not an adopted Comanche, as many people have later written. My real father was Hermano O'Donohughe. He said it was spelled O'Donoju in the original Spanish and that he was a full-blooded Spanish Creole, a Mexican soldier for Spain. Of course if you know anything then you know that O'Donoju is not a Spanish name, nor a Mexican one, if ever it was anybody's name, and neither is Hermano, which just means brother. So from the start I was half Comanche and half made up.

Hermano got caught up in an expedition out of Santa Fe that the Lipan Apache and Tankawa cooked up. Those tribes tended to ally themselves with the Spanish, though the Spaniards still wouldn't sell them guns. We were allies of the Spanish then, too, in our way. We even traded in Santa Fe. But when we needed rifles we rode east toward Louisiana and got them from French traders who were happy to have us use them against the Spanish. In that way, they were no different from us. When we needed horses we stole them from anyone we pleased.

When the buffalo move, you have to move. When everything you eat, wear, and carry comes from buffalo there's no way around it. And if the People had to go farther south or farther east or farther west to hunt them, we did. That's how the Comanche ended up on the southern plains in the first place. So when the buffalo ran to the sunset, we raided the Apaches and Utes. When they ran to the sunrise, we stole horses from the Caddo and the Wichita. When the herds ran in the land of winter, our enemies were Kiowa, Pawnee, and Cheyenne. It's been going on for countless years, or numberless moons as whites would have us say and where they got that from I don't know.

The Caddo and Wichita are not good fighters. It's just not in their nature. The Cheyenne have too many rules to think on their feet. The Kiowa do not ride well. The Utes were once our brothers. Family makes for fierce enemies. The Pawnee are devils.

The Apache are pretty good fighters as Indians go, and decent riders, too. But they're crazy idiots. You have to respect them because they're wild idiots and they can be dangerous. But they fear death and in battle it's a severe disadvantage to fear death. They even fear their own dead so as to not speak their names.

Years back, when things got bad between the Apache and us, they'd ride into Santa Fe and complain about us. They'd get baptized. They'd promise to start growing crops and live in mud huts or whatever other madness the Spanish padres could cook up. The Apache spent a few weeks going to church and getting married and then the good Franciscans would convince the soldiers to march out into the plains and protect them all.

When everything went its idiot way, and it often did, the Spanish got all hot and talked about settling this Comanche thing once and for all by teaching us Comanche a lesson. Then our war chiefs would get all hot and talk about eliminating the Apache and the Spanish. Like anybody ever eliminated anybody and if you did you'd just have to go eliminate somebody else. You'd have to be crazy to believe any of it from either side, at least more than once or twice, but more often than not, it worked. It's still working. As my mother, Many Powers, said, men are either itching to fight or they aren't.

The problem for the Spanish was that they never really liked it this far north. They didn't like the desert or the plains. They hated the weather, the seasons, the snow, the cold. The Spanish like to have big ranches in warm places. They like dances and naps. They like to conquer other empires and make love. So they didn't like us horse Indians at all, who prided ourselves on being mobile and unruly.

Over to the west, the Pueblo and Zuni and Navajo, even if they didn't have gold and silver, at the very least they had villages. They were city Indians even if they didn't have big cities like the Aztecs. And the Spanish, being conquerors, liked having cities to conquer, it almost goes without saying. Conquerors like to have something worth conquering. And they marched up and down Texas, too, conquering everything in sight. They conquered until they ran out of crosses, corpses, and flags. But when they were done they had nothing to show for it, just a lot of buffalo and bushes and wild Indians who wouldn't sit still.

The Spaniards were always worried that if they weren't up here conquering around, conquering here and conquering there, conquering this and conquering that, then the French would be here conquering, or worse, Russians or non-Catholics like the English or Dutch. It's hard to make much sense out of it, even with my white education, but it's my opinion that our inability to understand this whole conquering thing, and cut it off early, proved disastrous for us Indians.

So the Spanish sent the padres out to save Indian souls and sent the soldiers out to protect the padres and the next thing you'd know they'd build a mission, and then a little fort, a presidio as they called them, and filled it full of people who didn't want to be in it. It made them nasty, that's the simplest way to see it. And they didn't send the best soldiers into Texas. Generally the Spanish soldiers in the north were riffraff: criminals and slaves, pacified Indians who'd come to the mission for protection and ended up getting sent back out to fight the wild Indians they came in to hide from, and half-breeds which for the Spanish was a kind of crime; it only made sense to punish some raped woman's child. The most unforgivable sins, like Original Sin, as far as the Spanish were concerned, occurred before you were born, and the less responsible you were, the more trouble you were in. Such subtle thinking was inconceivable to primitive minds like ours.

How my father, supposedly a full-blooded Spaniard born in Mexico, ended up involved with a questionable bunch like that, I don't know, though my mother had her opinions. By Spanish thinking it would somehow be my fault.

In any regard, one day what had happened a hundred times, under a thousand moons, so to speak, happened again. The Spanish governor gathered up his army and marched down to Pecos Pueblo and declared war on the Comanche. The governor and his army, for lack of a better term, sat up in the foothills, looking out, and the People sat down in the woods keeping an eye on them. Then, after a few weeks of everybody watching each other, they came out after the People. The

Comanche saw them and ran away. Who needs to fight a bunch of angry men with guns? There's no advantage in it.

Usually after a few days the Spanish got tired of following us and went home and declared a great victory. In fact if you listened to Spanish accounts you'd come to believe that they never lost a battle with Indians, not a fair one anyway. It's a great irony, to my mind, that white people, who hold themselves to be the most scientific of all races, can't count.

Now this was the early days when we didn't really understand that if you ran away from one of the European tribes, they'd follow you. It's crazy and it took us a long time to really take that seriously. But once we figured it out we'd have fun enough just letting them follow, as long as the buffalo held out. If things got boring some of us would just turn around and take coup, maybe steal a few horses, though that would increase the chances that they'd get upset and follow all the hotter. But a bunch of armored Spanish and walking Indians is not going to catch a band of mounted Comanches. Never happened and never will.

It was on one such occasion, before I was born, that my father came out to Pecos with the Governor to chase down our band of the People, the People Who Sleep with their Horses, or HorseSleepers, because of some horse thievery.

From how I've heard it, it was all a big accident, but during a trading festival in Santa Fe some Apache horses seemed to have gotten away. Always Hits was really young then and, as he tells it, there were a lot of horses there, most of them Comanche, because we are the horse people and horses our business. Horses are herd animals and like to hang around with other horses, anybody knows that. So when the Comanche left Santa Fe, well, lots of horses that weren't tied down or penned up left with them.

Now we'd taken the southern plains away from the Apache farther back than anyone could remember, so they were always looking for an excuse to gather up some allies and get back in the buffalo hunt. As for the Spanish, they could do some conquering and get the Apache out of their hair too if they could get rid of us. The other buddies of the Spaniards, the Tonkawa, were opportunists and driven by what they could steal.

So they made a big alliance and followed the HorseSleepers out toward Pecos and the whole thing unraveled as it usually did. After weeks of waiting the Spanish marched out of Pecos after the HorseSleepers and the HorseSleepers ran away. During the march the Tonkawa got bored and walked back to Mexico. The Apache got scared when the Tonkawa left and the Spanish horses, poorly conditioned and carrying too much Spanish armor and supplies, started dropping from the heat. The Governor, my father in tow, planted a flag, declared a great victory, and turned back for Pecos while they still had horses.

That's when the odds were good enough and the HorseSleepers attacked. Of course, the Governor took his few Spanish-born officers and ran away, saving the pure blood of Spain, and left my Creole father, the highest ranking non-commissioned officer, with the riffraff to hold off the Comanche hordes.

Even they could have just put down their goods and walked away, but they didn't. They did their stupid duty to Spain. And as Always Hits said, what can you do with a bunch of poorly armed, horseless soldiers who decide to fight you in the middle of the desert? You have to kill them. So they did. My father, Hermano O'Donohughe, stood, the last man among the bodies of the dead, an arrow through his shoulder, as the HorseSleeper warriors lined up to face him.

Now the Comanche do this kind of thing in an honorable way. You just don't go riding in, twenty against one, and hack somebody's head off. There's no glory in that. So my natural father, Hermano O'Donohughe, stood there while two dozen Comanche warriors quibbled about who got first crack at taking him out. I would have loved to have been alive then just to hear that discussion which, in its dark way, would make anyone laugh.

Once that was settled, Hermano took down the first warrior. The second put a war lance in his side and an arrow in his leg. By this time he was out of ammunition and had to do what he could using his rifle as a club. Several other braves made their passes, but with one spear and a year's worth of arrows in him, my father was still standing. That's when the old war chief, Black Bird, who was Dark Eagle's father, rode up to Hermano O'Donohughe and said, "You are a great warrior. Join us."

Needless to say, there were some translation problems. The Spanish didn't tend to make a hobby of learning Plains Indian languages, and the Comanche, we were the Lords of the Plains and if you didn't speak Comanche you were worse off for it. But it was a lucky day. My father knew some Nahuatl, or Aztec, which is similar in ways to Comanche. He recognized the hand sign for peace and read the circumstance. Despite what he'd heard about the cruelty of the Comanche, he surrendered.

Unfortunately, at times we are a cruel people. So the HorseSleepers took my father back with them to the land of our tribe, the Honey Eaters, and when his wounds healed up some they tortured him for a couple weeks. When he survived that, they made him a slave of Dark Eagle's wife, Likes Sleep. But once he learned to ride well enough they took him on some raiding parties and eventually got out the drums, danced around some, smoked their pipes and adopted him. There are a few people around who say they've witnessed the Comanche adoption ceremony, but from the inside I can tell you it was a pretty loose affair.

My father, for his part, and only in private of course, claimed he'd slain at least three Comanche braves that day in the desert, though the older he got the more he claimed to have killed. The People, who named him Many Wounds, just said he was a good fighter. He fell in love with Too Young To Have So Much Power, who became Many Powers, and that's when I came along. Many Wounds and Many Powers, that's what made me.

It was great being a Comanche kid. There were few rules, nobody ever punished you, and you learned to ride before you learned to walk. Always Hits, who was one of the few braves who didn't ride down on my father the day he was captured, became a close friend of Many Wounds O'Donohughe and soon they became brothers.

Always Hits was good with horses. A lot of the tribe just stole what they needed, or captured them, and we all did some of that because for us horses were wealth, that simple. But Always Hits was a breeder and believed a war pony should keep its sex and be bonded to its rider at birth. When his mare, Morning Fire, had her foal, Always Hits rushed to our tipi in the middle of the night. He knew Many Powers wanted me to ride a mare, and he'd been talking to that foal in the womb, getting her ready for me.

It was a cold spring night. Always Hits came through the tipi flap so fast our dogs hadn't yet stirred, and he swept me off my pallet. "It is time," he said, tucking me under his arm. With the blood and juices of Morning Fire still liquid on his skin, hot and steamy in the cold air, I thought he was some kind of ghost. We were on his stallion and off again before I could yell, and when we got to his pen he plopped me down right on top that foal.

"You must bond before she stands, so she will think she could not have stood without you," he said.

It was a hot, sweaty mess in there, but Always Hits showed me what to do. You had to be in every crevice of that animal, be all over it before it knew a damn thing different—ears, nose, mouth, butt, you name it—bend their legs, knock them on the hoofs, hug them around their chest and belly. By the time she stood up, little FireBlood thought she and I were the same animal, and so did Morning Fire, who tried to nuzzle us both over to her nipples. Of course not knowing any better I was open to the suggestion, but that's when Always Hits grabbed me by the hair and pulled me away.

"That is where we stop," he said. "You are not a horse."

Many Wounds gave Always Hits three geldings for that foal, and Many Powers gave him a scent that if applied after bathing in a hot spring would make him irresistible to women.

"Then I will wait to use it," said Always Hits. And he did. Hits was a patient and true man, which comes from seeing the world as a horse does, steady, stubborn, and ready to fly. He found his true love, a gorgeous, well, princess, for lack of a better word, from the Kiowa, Strangely Woman, who made the most exquisite buffalo robes. But she died when the cholera came through, another white gift. Many Powers lost both her parents then, too.

Comanche fathers were not affectionate with their sons and Many Wounds took to that aspect of tribal life remarkably well. So without grandparents, who usually filled that gap, I spent much of my time with Always Hits, training FireBlood and riding his geldings. By the time I was seven I could spend all day in a herd of ponies lassoing one from the back of another, hopping on the back of a new one and looking for the next.

The biggest day in the life of a boy is his first buffalo hunt, and because Many Wounds didn't know squash about hunting buffalo from horseback, I was working Always Hits for my chance to hunt buffalo before I knew the difference between the flint and the hock of an arrow. What my father could do was fire a muzzle loader and he taught everybody how to do that. He also won a lot of horses in musket shooting contests because Comanche men liked to gamble and often cared less what the odds were.

I had a happy life. I spent my days training FireBlood, riding ponies, playing bear hunt and hoop and stick with Turkey Feathers and Twin Cub, Wind Sister and Doe Skin, and Fat Otter who taught me what he could about the bow and arrow. I was waiting for the day I'd get my power and FireBlood would be old enough to ride out on the hunt. Then one day Talks Peace, one of our big peace chiefs, got the idea that we were due for a trip over to Santa Fe.

It went the usual way. Talks Peace said he noticed that the buffalo were putting on extra fur a little early. The next night he had a dream that came in on a cold breeze from the Land of Always Winter. His favorite pony walked out onto a river of ice and fell in. A white buffalo, chest deep in snow, offered to help pull the horse out if Talks Peace would travel the path of the sun and trade ponies. He took that dream to Thick Robes and without a word being said, the next day all of the women were making pemmican for the trip. By the time it went to the council, a tipi full of warriors and shamans where everybody smoked and aired their feelings, the women were already packing for Santa Fe.

The decision had already been made, word of mouth, in the secret language of the women—a big winter was coming, let's trade some ponies for corn so we'll have some food when things get tight. Besides, the women liked the market.

So the men decided it was a good idea to go to Santa Fe, each of them, individually, within his total self authority. According to my mother, who brought me into her tipi to have a discussion, the trip wasn't even Talks Peace's idea in the first place, it was his wife, Thick Robes, who while scraping buffalo skins noticed that the new hides were thicker.

"Humm," said Talks Peace.

"Time for a dream," said Thick Robes.

So, as with a lot of things, it was all timing.

My mother was already powerful and independent-minded, even back then, and kept her own tipi. She sat at the back of her lodge, a striking woman, tall for a Comanche, with a broad, clear forehead and a straight nose. She wore a deerskin tunic with long fringe, always did, right up till the end. You would never catch Many Powers in cotton or gingham, not even to tie her hair.

I entered her tipi ritually, as always, circling to my left, the west. She brought me to her breast and then let me sit next to her. Back then I was just a Comanche kid and thought my dad was a regular Comanche dad, more aloof than some, a good gambler and a good shot with a muzzle loader, not so handy on a horse with the bow and arrow though he had his share of scalps. He was okay.

"Ask your father why he will not return from Santa Fe," said Many Powers. "Tell him it is time for his story."

"Many Wounds doesn't tell stories," I said.

"Ask him if he plans to take you to Mexico."

"On a raid?" I said.

"Mexico City."

I didn't even know what a city was, let alone Mexico City.

"Did you have a dream, Mother?" I said.

"No," she said. "Not yet. Go tell him."

"Now?" I said.

"Now," said Many Powers.

I trudged around and finally found him over in Dark Eagle's tipi throwing sticks. I stood at the door and yelled in. "Many Wounds!" I yelled.

"Go away," said Dark Eagle.

"Many Powers sent me!"

"Is it a love message?" said my father.

"It might be. I don't know," I said.

He came out, squinting in the sun. He was a tall man, more slender than most Comanches, and he had to pluck his face of whiskers more often than most. Sometimes he even scraped his face with a blade, though when he could get one he preferred the edge of a sharp shell, which you could trade for in Santa Fe or get from the Karankawa who lived by the sea.

"It's okay," he said. "I was losing."

"Many Powers says you won't return from Santa Fe," I told him.

"Did she have a dream?" he asked.

"Not yet. She said you're taking me to Mexico City."

"Do you want to go?"

"No," I said. "What is it?"

He didn't answer me. He mounted his pony and he headed for Many Powers' tipi. I waited outside with his horse while he went in there and the two of them smoked, then made earth and sky. Those two used any excuse—mourning, celebration, fights—it was their bond, so to speak, and though most warriors, even the powerful chiefs, shared a lodge with their wife, or wives, Many Powers would have none of that. She had her own tipi and she was Many Wounds' one and only, and Many Wounds grew to like it that way. But Many Wounds was his own man, too. It wasn't that you couldn't kick him, as Many Powers said, it was that you couldn't kick him around. He just took what she had and went his own way. When they were done in there Many Wounds came out in just his breech cloth and stood in the sun. Then he sent me to get a runner to tell everybody to meet that night at a fire outside his lodge.

# 10

MANY WOUNDS DISAPPEARED for several hours and shot two turkeys and an elk. We'd been in that camp long enough to have a sweat lodge, so when he got back he set my aunts to making a bonfire and cooking up the meat while he rode over to the lodge and sweated away the end of the afternoon. Then he went back to his tipi and put on his finest eagle feathers and buckskin, emerging into the dusk with his finery as everybody gathered around the fire for his feast, the smells of seared turkey and roasted elk wafting through the smoke. The elk meat was skewered on sticks and placed into the flames—Many Wounds had already eaten the heart and liver at the sight of the kill—and the turkeys just thrown in feathers and all; when they were done my aunts just made a slit down the belly and popped them right out of their skins.

People started showing up, mostly kids and mothers and young warriors at first, mingling and dancing haphazardly as Many Wounds shared his meat. Many Powers showed up a little later, with the other power figures: shaman, medicine folk, singers, healers, peace chiefs and war chiefs. There was hardly anybody over the age of thirty who wasn't something or another; a delicate balance of responsibilities and duties, a free separation of power and authority which kept the band in good medicine.

Amid the log pounding and flute playing, Fat Otter's father, White Calf, broke into a travel song:

We are going away,
Where the sun sets.
We are going together.
We will return happy.
With many horses
To the land of honey and buffalo.


It seemed a happy occasion. But after a while Many Wounds called Council and all the power holders followed him into his lodge, moving left from the door and circling like the sun to the right of the entryway until the place was pretty much filled up. We had quite a crowd. I sat to my father's right, opposite the entrance. I'd tried to plop down in Many Power's lap, but she pushed me between her and Many Wounds.

Many Wounds lit and smoked from his pipe, then passed it left. It couldn't cross the mouth of the entrance, so it had to come all the way back around to get to Talks Peace, who sat opposite Many Wounds, just inside the opening. All that smoking and pipe passing took enough time to put me to sleep, but that was one thing about the People, this kind of thing was done with great deliberation and solemnity without regard to time.

Finally, everybody had smoked and Many Wounds began to speak.

"My People," he said. "You know how the buffalo leave and return, how the birds make their way in the seasons, how the sun chooses its ever-path. This is the way of all living things. And so it is with some of you HorseSleepers who come from other bands, other tribes of the People. Often you visit your first families, and often you return, here to the center of the world that moves like the great herds of black horned buffalo. Everything changes and moves and returns. With this no one argues." He paused there, making sure everybody was going to accept that undeniable reasoning before he moved on.

"As you know, before I had my great luck to become a HorseSleeper, I was like a traveling star who fed himself on the black sky. I burned brightly, but lived nowhere until I came among you, because my own people did not own the land where they buried their ancestors, but gave everything to a great, white chief across the sea."

"The Chief of the Spanish," said Many Powers, "who is not Mexican." You could see that Many Wounds had been working all afternoon in the sweat lodge on his speech, but he was getting too flowery and obscure to figure out head from tail, so Many Powers stepped in.

"Thank you," he said begrudgingly to my mother.

"But now, my own first people, the Mexicans, have taken back their land. So, too, is it in our land, the land of the People. After the great black horned herds have gone, after the yellow winged locusts have eaten everything, then the grass, the child of the earth, takes the plains again and stretches to the sky. The buffalo return to eat it so we may eat them. This is the way of things."

"Are you saying we have to eat the Spanish if they return?" said Talks Peace.

"The Mexicans have thrown the Spanish out," said my mother.

"We have heard of this," said Always Hits. "So we eat Mexicans instead of buffalo? Why not say it plainly?"

Contrary to what you might think, we Indians had a pretty far-reaching system of communication. We knew pretty much what went on from earth to sky and sea to sea. We knew that the Cherokee were currently being thrown out of their land by the Americans, as well, though we weren't quite clear what that meant for everybody else yet.

"Maybe it is time for us to throw somebody out of somewhere," said Always Hits.

"Maybe," said Talks Peace, "but it isn't the time to discuss it."

None of this stopped Many Wounds, who surveyed the circle and started off again. He went on and on in his fashion for a long time before coming to his inevitable conclusion.

"I must return and be a great chief among my first people," he said. "I must take my son to show them what great people ride in this land that runs forever from the mountains. My heart is filled with great sorrow and commotion, like the wind when it turns itself on its head and sweeps everything away."

"He means like a tornado," said Many Powers, because, in truth, we were all puzzled.

My father stood now, his arms outstretched, his face turned up to the smoke hole, before he gazed down again and searched the eyes of each woman and brave.

"It is with deep sadness that I must ask you to let me go," he said. He paused, head hung down in front of that full, silent, council tipi.

Finally, Talks Peace spoke again. "Are you done?" he said.

My father, Many Wounds nodded sullenly.

"Are you going with them?" Thick Robes asked Many Powers.

"They can go. I'm staying," said Many Powers.

"Is there more food?" said Dark Eagle.

"Yes," said my father.

"Then let's eat," said Talks Peace.

Talks Peace got up and everybody filed out. Soon we were banging and whistling again outside the tipi as the band finished off the turkeys and elk. White Calf sang:

We're eating Many Wounds' food.
 It's pretty good.
We'll stay till it's done.

Alone with me and Many Powers, my father looked sadder.

"You expected more resistance," Many Powers said to him.

Many Wounds burned some bitter roots and left the tipi.

"After he's gone I will change his name to Thought He Knew Everything," said Many Powers. She put her arm on my shoulder. "Go with him now," she said.

I went outside where he'd mounted his pony and I stood next to him. He put down his hand, lifting me up in one swift motion, and we rode back to the sweat lodge.

# 11

LITTLE OWL WAS once known as a vicious warrior, but now he was old, his braided hair gray, his eyes folded into his brow. His head was like a walnut. He met us at the sweat lodge.

"When I heard of your leaving I knew you would need me," he said to Many Wounds. He was a mystical type now and led many boys to their first animal spirit.

"How did you hear?" asked Many Wounds.

"There were birds perched near your smoke hole," said Little Owl.

News traveled fast. Little Owl put his wrinkled hand on my forehead. "He's a little young. He will need power to live among the whites, though the Mexicans are better than most," he said.

It was already dark, the sky exceptionally bright with stars, the sliver of moon had followed the sun across the sky all day, not that I'd noticed it, but Little Owl pointed it out.

The sun eagle was well past Longest Day and heading for Always Winter. His little sister, the moon, today a sliver like the wing of a dove, followed. Had I watched the sky, said Little Owl, I'd have known I was leaving.

"What if other people watched the sky?" I said to him. "What would they know?"

"That someone was leaving and someone was following," he said.

"How would they know the signs were meant for me?"

"They wouldn't. It was for you to know." He turned to Many Wounds. "After this, he shuts up," he said. "All right now, listening only," he said to me, stripping off my clothes. He burned some sweet grass and passed the smoke over me. "A child's body," he said. "You'll need strong medicine."

I followed Many Wounds into the sweat lodge. That was it for two days. No talking. No eating. In intervals Little Owl brought us water, or took us out to the stream to rinse, then led us back in. On the third night he wiped me down in a foul ointment and gave me a little fuzzy button of a plant to eat, then led me out naked under the stars.

"Come back whenever you want to," he said.

He turned and I immediately began to follow him back. He stopped me with a glance. "You're a funny kid," he said. He stood there and I stood there with him. I began to shiver, then I felt hot. Little Owl's face turned into a gray moon, then disappeared. I began to walk toward the lodge again, but the stars were raining down in streams of light making a cage around me. Dumbfounded, I sat until the night ran its course, but in the morning I was weak and immobile, the sun eagle painting me like a shadow onto the earth as the sliver moon sang behind him in the sky, tipping one way, then another. I saw then that everything, the trees, the grass, the rocks and mountains, was alive, everything alive and whole, in peace, in pain.

Late the next night, when the great sky warrior climbed out of the east, the rabbit running beneath his feet fell toward me, two star dogs at its heels. Everything around me filled up with white, white-laden like after a snow, and the star animals ran black like shadows against the white ground, the stars of their outlines bursting out in blue light like the sparks from a fire. Then the long-eared hare called out to me. "Save me!" it said in the voice of a girl, as the star animals ran about me, circling, sucking me up into a whirlwind of blackness and starlight.

"What good are you?" I said to her. "You are the food of the world."

"And food for the world beyond," she said. "But not as foolish as these loyal dogs."

"A rabbit has no power," I said, as the dogs nipped at her starry legs.

"In battle," she said, "more wolves have died than rabbits."

"How can I tell my father that a rabbit is my power animal?"

"How can you tell him anything else?" said the jackrabbit. She ran behind me and the dogs stopped short, snarling at me with their sparkling teeth.

"Let us have her!" they said.

"And what will you give me?"

"Let us have her," they growled, "and we'll share her bones when we scatter them across the night."

"They are cowards," said the rabbit behind me. "Test them and I will give you quickness."

I raised my arms as you would do to scatter any dogs and the two hounds fled, again falling behind the heels of the striding sky warrior. I heard them begging him for scraps from his next kill.

Then the rabbit came forward. "Feed me," she whispered.

I gave her pieces of my fingernails and hair. I plucked blades of grass from the great sky path for her. She ate everything I gave her and then came into my arms. But when I tried to hold her she leapt from me with such force that her claws ravaged my chest as I fell backward to earth.

At dawn I arose painfully and trudged back to the sweat lodge where Many Wounds and Little Owl waited. I rinsed in the stream.

"Well?" said my father.

"A bunny," I said. "My power is a bunny."

"A rabbit. Power is power," said Little Owl.

My father, who was visited by both Buffalo and Hawk, squinted his eyes. He did not say, My son, the bunny, he kept it to himself.

"He is a child," said Little Owl. He spit on his hands and ran his fingertips over my chest, tracing his saliva on the red claw marks which bled at his touch. "He is very lucky to have power at all. Rabbit will serve him." He washed me and my father and offered both of us pemican, then he spoke directly to Many Wounds. "Wait here one more day. It's time now for the two of you to talk."

My father had never been much of a talker, not to me, only when he spoke nonsense at council, and we sweated well into the day before he even looked at me. When he finally began, he spoke not to me, but into the air, muttering his story about the Spanish expedition against the People out of Santa Fe. He was nearly at the end before I figured out he was talking about himself.

"I don't want to be white," I said when he was done. Till then I'd never seen a white man, except for my father, I suppose.

"Whites have great cities and great weapons. They have learned to control the earth spirits and make the earth work for them instead of working at the earth and begging it for bounty. They own the land and do not rove about looking for food, but have the earth bring food to them. They dress in fine clothes and have huge families. Their women listen to them."

"They don't ride so good," I said.

"They ride well enough. They sail the oceans by catching the wind. They have one, powerful God who rules everything. Among them, in Mexico, when I claim my inheritance, I will be a rich man, and you will be the son of a rich man."

"Can I bring FireBlood?" I asked.

My father finally turned to me. He said, "No."

# 12

"A RABBIT," said my mother, Many Powers.

"The dogs didn't want me. Except maybe to eat."

"Power is power," she said. "There hasn't been a Rabbit in this band for a long time. Besides, it's a good sign that more powers will be coming to you."

"Not in Mexico City," I said.

"Maybe not in Mexico City, but all things change."

It was my last night in her tipi. Usually a child stayed in his mother's tipi, which was in most cases his father's, too, until he became a man, or if a girl, until she married. But though I wasn't a true hunter yet or a warrior, I'd received power and was leaving the tribe with my father. From then on I'd be sleeping in his lodge until I earned my own.

"Many Wounds says the whites have the most powerful medicine, and the Spanish are the greatest of the whites," I said to my mother.

"Then how did the Mexicans kick them out?" said my mother.

"He says they have great cities and weapons."

"Do you know what a city is?" she said.

"I don't know."

"Then how do you know they're so great?"

"Do you know what a city is?" I asked her.

"Yes," she said. "Suddenly you want to know things, Rabbit."

"What's a city?" I said.

"It is like Santa Fe, only much larger, with lodges made of stone like mountains. Water, food, everything is brought to it. It sucks the land and its people forget the earth is their mother. Men take over and worship only the sun and rain, making living things their slaves, growing plants and animals only to eat them. The real world is forgotten. People forget to watch the stars and become afraid of the night. They light up the ground around them so much that they cannot see the stars at all. They come to believe that the moon rises when the sun goes down. The men begin to eat each other and grow so afraid of other men that they keep their own wives captive inside their homes. Soon, they are eating their own gods. It is not just the whites. The People who lived where the sun passes, they lived that way, too, until the Spanish conquered them. Up here, the People were smart, and gave up cities uncountable years ago. Their ruins are everywhere."

I guess I'd asked for it. I never realized Many Powers knew so much and was so opinionated.

"Why does Many Wounds want to go back?" I said.

"He is a man. A sane woman never goes back to the whites." Many Powers brought me to her breast. "Men think they are brave," she said, "but they will never know the bravery of sending a husband to war or the heartbreak of saying goodbye to the child who once shared her body."

"Come with us," I whispered to her. I held back my tears.

"I am far too sane," she said. "But for you to go, it will change everything. If the crazy medicine of the whites doesn't kill you, you could return with great power, and then I will teach you the things no man has known, my Rabbit. The world will come inside you and your eyes will cross time."

# 13

ONE THING ABOUT where we lived, there were trees. The Wasp Band were our neighbors, as were the Timber People. Whites get confused about Indian names in general because they're so literal minded. Among Christians, for example, people name their sons Peter, which if you trace back through the Aramaic, means The Rock, you know, Thou art Peter and upon this Rock I will build my Church. But that doesn't mean that people think their kid is named after a darn rock. You could go on and on about it, that's one thing I learned at Harvard, you can go on and on about anything, even make a living at it, without having one significant effect on the world at large. In that regard my mother was right. White people were crazy. The only things they loved more than ideas were gold and machines.

Anyway, there were trees where we lived, and therefore bees, so we packed up plenty of honey combs in our pouches to trade with farther west, along with elk pemican and elk horns, pecans, mesquite beans, anything peculiar to our region that might be of value over there in the desert. It would take the band more than a half month to get there, including a stop at the Antelope encampment on the western edge of the Comanchería, the last place we could hunt buffalo.

For me it was a pretty dull trip, only to get worse. FireBlood wasn't ready for riding and I wasn't permitted on any buffalo hunts. We didn't raid anybody because we were on our way to a peaceful trade gathering and mostly the trip went through Comanche territories. Some of the younger boys would go out hunting jackrabbits but, you know, my power was new to me and I had some emotional confusion about rabbit hunting. Worse, I had to spend time with my dad who, I learned, spent a lot of his time thinking about himself. It was Many Powers, in fact, who had the foresight, when I saw her, to make sure I perfected my sign language and began teaching me Spanish, too.

It was a late summer day, still hot, the treeless plains stretching for miles before us. The tribe wouldn't return to the Timbers east of the great plateau until the first moon of the dry grass. When I could escape my father, I rode my pony next to Many Powers and her travois horses, one who pulled along her tipi and belongings and the other who pulled along the possessions of Many Wounds. Independent though she was, she was still Many Wounds' wife and she controlled all things domestic.

"Your father speaks some Aztec, which is like our tongue," said my mother. "Make him speak it so you can learn."

"Always Hits says there is only one tongue anyone needs to know," I said.

"He speaks the language of horses and doesn't even know he does it," said Many Powers. "If you live your life on the tips of your arrow heads, then that's all you need to know. But you are not a wolf, or an eagle or a bear."

"I'm a bunny," I said.

My mother laughed. "Do you think I am powerful?" she said.

"Yes."

"Even more powerful than the wives of war chiefs or peace chiefs?"

"Yes," I said. "Almost everyone comes to you. You have more power than many of the chiefs and medicine people."

"But I did not lead you to your animal power. I let you go to Little Owl."

"That's what he does," I said.

"That's right," she said. "Am I a woman or a man?"

"Don't be silly," I said to her.

"You don't be silly. I am a woman and do not try to be a man."

"You wouldn't prefer to be a man?"

"I'm not a man. I don't prefer. Whose idea was it for us to go to Santa Fe?"

"Talks Peace," I said.

"No," said my mother. "Thick Robes."

"Talks Peace decided to go," I said.

"Everyone decided to go. Those who didn't want to go, could stay."

"So Talks Peace is a bunny?" I said.

"You are witty," said Many Powers. "Talks Peace got his medicine from a bear. The bear is a powerful, fierce animal, but it will eat berries and roots as well as meat. A rabbit will never eat meat. It will fight to the death if it cannot run, if it thinks it can win, or to protect her young. The path of death is always there. Don't be a fool and run to it."

"You're saying warriors are fools," I said to her.

"Every man and woman is a warrior and some warriors are fools."

Now you see why Many Powers was so powerful. One of her powers was to talk with you till you felt like a snake that had tied itself into a knot.

"Learn the languages of the white tribes," said my mother, "and when you choose your death you will not die a fool."

# 14

THE COMANCHE WERE unceremonious. We didn't have a ritual for a one thing. Certainly not for leaving the tribe. Just east of Pecos, where the band was to spend a little time trading before heading into Santa Fe, my father gathered up a few things from his travois. He trotted up to Many Powers, put his hand gently on her neck, turned and rode off. I stood there in the dust between them, believing for the first time that we really were leaving. Not one Comanche in that damn tribe, including my mother, turned their head, though I felt Many Powers' eyes lean to me as her horses went by. Then they looked forward again, her posture gesturing to me. "Be a man about this. Go. Do not make me cry."

So I turned my travel pony away from my mother, Many Powers, away from my war pony, FireBlood, my tribe, the HorseSleepers band of the Honey Eaters, my People, in our language, the *Nuhrmuhnuh*, the Comanche. And I followed my father off to be a white man.

Outside Santa Fe we stopped near a stream and my father opened a parfleche. He took off his breech cloth and put on a cloth shirt and trousers. Where he'd hidden them all these years, I don't know. He cut off our hair with his knife. He made me put on my buckskins, hot as it was, so he wouldn't be seen riding next to a naked savage when we entered town.

"I am Hermano O'Donohughe," he said to me in Comanche. "You are to call me Padre."

"It's okay," I said to him in Spanish. "I can speak this white tribe's tongue."

"Spanish. From the nation, not tribe, of Spain. But now we are Mexican."

"I know all of this," I said, though I didn't have a clue what much of it meant.

"Your mother—" he began, but then stopped. I could have said it for him. He was crazy to leave her. Of course right then I was viewing him like we were both still Comanche, where a woman's power was respected and not feared. As a Spaniard or Mexican or whatever the hell we were becoming, Many Powers probably scared the hell out of him.

"What is your name?" my father asked. I guess he'd been thinking so hard about our future he'd forgotten.

"Rabbit," I said.

"Roberto," he said. "Roberto O'Donohughe."

So Hermano and Roberto O'Donohughe saddled up and made their triumphant entry into Santa Fe. We must have looked unusual enough, a Spaniard and a half-breed child clopping in on our Comanche ponies, though as a commercial crossroads they saw plenty of strange sights there. Santa Fe was a trading center for all of the Plains and Pueblo tribes, long before even the Spanish came. The village Indians brought goods and stories from the tribes who lived near the sunset on the Sea Where The Sun Bathes, and the Plains tribes traded in the east with the tribes from The Great Forest That Runs To The Sea On The Other Side Of The World. When the Aztecs, who I found out called themselves the Mexica—it was whites who called them Aztecs—were strong, before the Spanish, they came this far north to trade obsidian for ochre.

In Santa Fe the Spanish had been kicking butt for three hundred years. They conquered, got run out, and came back again. Most of the Indians who stayed around there were pretty depressed. The Mexicans took over and made a lot of noise about changing things, including an end to subjugating the Indian population, but though the majority of Mexicans were of some conquered Indian tribe themselves, or at least half-Indian, the ones in charge were full-blooded Spanish like my father, or at least claimed to be, who just happened to have been born in New Spain instead of Old Spain. Like most revolutions, they just replaced one pack of greedy wolves with another.

But Santa Fe wasn't any closer to Mexico City now that it was Mexican. There weren't many Mexicans in New Mexico, but there were still plenty of belligerent Navajo, Apache, Utes, and Comanche. It kept the situation workable.

My father knew Santa Fe. We rode into the town plaza and up to the Palace of the Governor where my father woke up the guard and presented his papers. Looking back, I don't think the guy could read any better than me, meaning not at all, but he seemed impressed that somebody was showing him papers and he took us right in.

I'd been in Santa Fe once before when I was really little. Most of the trading took place right there in the plaza, so I'd seen white folks' buildings before, but I'd never been inside one. My first impression was that they put a lot of emphasis on keeping their bodies away from the ground. They put stones or wood on the floor so their feet wouldn't touch the earth and built what looked to me like little trees to keep their butts in the air while they sat. The walls and beams were brightly colored—some Indian must have done it—but there were a lot of paintings which looked peculiarly real—I didn't feel any medicine in them at all—and a lot of bleeding statues of people wearing round, gold hats while being tortured.

I stood in the lobby with my father until a man came out who looked like a rather fine, plump, flightless bird. He shook Hermano's hand. He said his name, González, and then my father's. My father said mine. Then we followed Governor González deeper into that dark, white people's interior where he sat down behind a huge wooden barrier with my father's papers. I refused to sit in one of those trees and my father explained to the Governor the sadness of my odd and unfortunate circumstance.

"You are a brave man, Señor O'Donohughe," said González. "We need your type of man here."

That began a long discussion. Not much of Comanche life prepared me for life as a Mexican, but the fact that Comanche children were taught to sit silently for long periods of time got me through plenty. My father did a lot of talking about how important it was that he get back to the capital to claim his inheritance as a pure blooded Spanish-Mexican, as well as the property due to him in the division of Old Spanish lands. Further, it was essential that he get his poor, savage son, yours truly, to a good school where he could get a civilized, Catholic education. While in the City he would be sure to let everyone know what an excellent job the governor was doing and recommend to all who would listen that González be returned to Mexico City where his exquisite administrative skills could best be used.

"But your son," said Governor González. "He is half savage."

"My wife among the Comanche," said my father, his face growing pitiful in its stoicism, "she, too, was a captive. A Creole. My son has pure blood." A tear formed in the corner of Hermano O'Donohughe's eye and rolled down his impassive face. "She perished," he whispered, "during our escape."

"It has been very difficult, I am sure," responded the Governor in an equally measured tone. You'd think the two of them were talking about some me who wasn't there. "But he was not spawned in a Christian marriage."

"We were all born under a sin we did not commit," said my father. "He will be better off, like all of us, in a civilized place."

That wasn't the first nor the last time I heard my father speak a lot of hooey, but it was interesting to find out that all of this had come about solely for my benefit. I knew he just wanted the hell out of Santa Fe before the HorseSleepers showed up and began treating him like the white man he now was. Anybody, white or Indian, is dangerous when they believe their own bullshit. But I remembered what Many Powers told me about learning all of Hermano-Many Wounds' languages and I set my mind to learning.

The governor set us up with four good horses in addition to our ponies, plenty of food, and a couple of pack mules. We headed south along the Rio Bravo del Norte, as it was known to the Mexicans, the Rio Grande to Texans. We followed the El Camino Real, the Royal Road, which was neither road nor royal, the irony compounded by the fact that every damn road the Spanish had, well, built, for lack of a better word, was called El Camino Real. Every path wider then twelve inches was an El Camino Real to them.

Even sillier, their El Camino Real left the river and ran right through their Jornada del Muerte, Journey of Death, so named because it was a wide, desert canyon between two mountain ranges, ninety miles of nothing but sand, mesquite trees, and creosote bushes, and it sat atop a desert valley that ran all the way from Mexico City to Santa Fe. If you lacked the aptitude to feed yourself on desert flora and fauna, didn't like to drink mud, thought 110 degrees was too hot or twenty below zero too cold, and you weren't fond of getting ambushed by Apaches, then you'd be likely to find yourself depressed in Jorndada del Muerte. The alternative was to keep following the river and spend a month trudging through deep arroyos filled with jungle vines, twenty foot snakes, and jaguars. Compared to that, you could make it through the Journey of Death in three or four days, if you made it.

Of course we could have decided to abandon the idea of road travel and barter our way back across the plains, but Hermano didn't want to run into any Comanche and besides, we were white people now and white people used roads.

I didn't speak much with old Hermano O'Donohughe during that trip, but I did express my disappointment over this whole Camino Real-Jornada del Muerte thing just as we entered the desert.

"This is better," he said. "No one likes it here. We will run into few Apache and no Comanche."

"It's not better," I said.

"It is better."

"And now I'm a bastard," I said to him. "I heard."

"Better a Spanish bastard," he said.

And all those years I thought he'd been having a good time.

# 15

SO YOU CAN IMAGINE how delighted I was to see a band of Apaches come thundering out of the hills. Hermano looked shocked, like this was a real imposition, a real violation of the proceedings.

"We must run for it!" he yelled.

"How can we outrun them?"

"Then we will fight!"

"We're outnumbered twenty to two!" I yelled at him. It was amazing how fast he'd become a white man. There'd be no honor in killing us unless we fought, so they'd probably just steal all our stuff, leave Hermano half dead and take me as a slave. They were more likely to carve up Spanish or Mexicans. Enemies as we were as Comanche, having chased them out of the best buffalo hunting grounds and into the desert, our best bet would still be to deal with them as Indians.

"Let's go behind those rocks and undress," I said.

"Our short hair," said my father.

"'They know the HorseSleepers are trading in Santa Fe. They'll recognize our ponies and maybe they won't want trouble."

As a precocious child I preferred talking over fighting, especially when the odds were ten to one. I knew a little about the Apache because of Many Powers. They were to the low desert now what we were to the high plains.

Given our location now and where they came out of, I was banking on this
bunch being Chiricahua. They liked to hit and run and unlike us they didn't
enjoy fighting for fighting's sake. They had a tendency to seek the easy way out.
As Always Hits taught me, most people, unless they're absolutely crazy like the
Comanche, are like horses, motivated by laziness and the desire to avoid pain.

Once behind the rocks my father said the Act of Contrition to the white God,
then started his Comanche Death Song. I picked up some desert dirt and spit
into it. I'd never tried this before, except in children's games, but I put the
concoction over my face. Many Powers had said that I had more medicine than
just the Rabbit, and just then I felt it, as if it filled me, entering my feet from
the ground and my hands from the sky. I prayed.

Power of the Great Everywhere Mystery
Come to me
Give me the face of honesty
Give me cunning
I will thank you later.

Then I stripped and put a white rag on Hermano's musket and we walked out
in front of the rocks, horses and all, so the Apaches wouldn't think we were up
to anything. The band of Apaches pulled up within an arrow's shot. Any Indian
will stop short if you wave a rag at them, they're just honorable people. They sat in
a line and watched me for a while before a brave rode forward to talk. He had a
strong, handsome face, you know, that hawk-nose like the Apache have. He only
wore a breech cloth and he didn't have a gun, just his lance, club, bow and arrows.
It was tough to get guns from the Spanish. I figured he was less than twenty,
which meant this wasn't an experienced bunch. He jabbered in Apache, probably
something like, "Now that we've acknowledged your flag we're going to kill you."
The Apache are always saying that they're going to kill you and sometimes they do.

They didn't speak in anything even close our tongue, so I signed to him.
"Greetings to the Chiricahua, Lords of the Desert," I said. "I am Rabbit and
this is my father, Many Wounds, who does not speak in signs. By our ponies,
you can tell we are Comanche."

"I am Cochise," he said. "I would like a Comanche pony, even a Comanche
scalp though yours are puny."

I accepted that kind of talk as formality. Even as a kid I knew that if he wanted scalps that bad he'd have taken them already.

"Cochise," I said. "Even I, a child, have heard of you. You are already a legend. I thought you would be much older."

"I should kill you right now," he said.

Well, don't ever say you can't flatter an Apache.

"We were captured by the Spanish who cut our hair and made us slaves to the padres, nursing the white-scabbed ones." He'd know I meant small pox. "But we escaped."

"You do not have white scabs or scars," he said.

I leaned over to my father and told him to start pretending he was telling me what to say.

"I will tell you what to say," he said. "Tell them to leave now or the Great Chief of the Mexican tribe will send his armies to crush them."

"The desert sun, the Father of the Apache," I said to Cochise, "has healed us and we are offering these mules to him. You probably know the proper place to make our offering."

Cochise eyed us up and down. I'd given him his chance to think he might out-think us. He wouldn't care if we were lying to him as long as he felt he read the lie. In that way, all Indians were completely honest. "Wait here," he said, and rode back to his raiding party.

"You see," my father said. "You must play with a strong fist."

It was a damn good thing he was too arrogant to ever learn sign language. It was remarkable to me how he could be so diplomatic in front of the Governor of Santa Fe and turn into a head of stone in front of Apache warriors.

Cochise rode back. He nodded slyly. "My medicine man says that the mules are not enough for such a big cure. Our Father will need all of the mules and horses, the supplies, and the gun."

"What did he say?" said Hermano.

"He said he loves the King of Spain and President of Mexico and would love to give them gifts, but they are poor, desert Apaches and have nothing."

"My father says that it is an honor to be among such great warriors and generous people. He wishes that you would guide us to the closest watering place. There you can have all of our horses, supplies, and the gun if you leave us two mules and some bows and arrows."

The good thing about Indians in general was, like any other normal animal, they needed a good reason to kill you, though being human they were perfectly capable of making one up. But unlike civilized, white folk, if you took away an Indian's reason for killing you, you got him to hesitate if not negotiate.

Cochise rode back to his band and they agreed to our terms, so to speak. There wasn't enough coup to go around for the twenty of them anyway. Then Cochise rode back.

"You may ride with us," he said in sign language. "Follow."

We followed them easterly, into the white hills. They kept those horses at a walk in the heat. As we moved into the afternoon, I knew I'd have to get back to work in order to reconcile the deal that Cochise thought he'd worked out with my father, so I rode up beside him.

"Rabbit of the Comanche wishes to offer you his admiration," I signed. "It is not often we meet warriors as smart and brave."

He turned to me and made a little smile, almost a sneer, but gentler. "I speak the Spanish tribe's tongue," he said in Spanish. "The English, too."

I responded to him in Spanish. "*Entiendo*," I said. I understand. "Then if you are still going to give us our lives, it's best if we sleep tonight without finding a watering hole and you take our gifts while my father is sleeping."

That made him laugh. "If I thought you were truly of Comanche blood, you would be dead," he said. "But you are too smart for a Comanche and your build and face are Kiowa-Apache. Do you remember when you were taken captive?"

"No," I said. It was my first inkling that I actually had the capacity to change my appearance, though at the time I just took it as confusion and luck. But out there in the wilderness, the improbable mixing of blood through circumstance was as common as horse flies.

"Is the Spaniard your father?" Cochise asked.

"Yes, but he's Mexican now."

"I've heard of the change, though there doesn't seem to be much difference. Where the sun rises, they say the Americans are worse than the English or the French. We will see about the Mexicans."

We rode quietly for a while. Except for his mistaking me as Apache, it was completely his game.

"Do you wish to ride with us?" Cochise finally said.

I signed to him in Plains Indian. "I will stay with my father."

Well, Apache or no, Cochise was all right.

"In the morning," he said, "look into the shadows of the hills. You will see them bleed. Life goes to water. Follow it. Your mule will smell it before you do." He told me which toads needed mud to breed and sleep and how to follow the darkening color of plants to a water source. He pointed out the cactuses that stored water. "Take only a leaf," he said. "Leave enough to grow again for the next brother who comes along."

"What did you talk about?" asked my father when I rode back to him.

"We won't find water till morning," I said.

That night the Apache roasted jackrabbits and we shared some of our mesquite cakes and pemican. My father, suspicious, slept with his rifle, and though the Apache band slipped off in the night with most of everything else but the mules, they left him the musket, and left me a good hunting bow, wrapped thick and strong with antelope sinew, and a quiver of straight, Chiricahua arrows.

Hermano was enraged when we awoke at sunrise, but the hills were bleeding for us only an arrow shot away.

# 16

I THOUGHT MANY WOUNDS was an inattentive Comanche father, but he was downright doting compared to Hermano O'Donohughe who dropped me off at a monastery school in Mexico City faster than the Pawnee left their dead. He shook hands with a chubby monk, dressed much like the padres up in Santa Fe, and then came over and shook my hand.

"I was worried in the desert," he said to me. "You looked so much like an Indian."

"But I look Spanish now," I said.

"Mexican," he said. That was the new egalitarianism, as I was to learn. We were all Mexicans, though some people were more Mexican than others. Thinking like a Spaniard, the more Mexican, that is, Indian, you were, the less Mexican you could be. If you were a Spaniard like Hermano, that is barely Mexican at all, well then you were at the top of the Mexican heap.

"Learn," said Hermano, "and I will build an empire for your sons."

He gave me a nice slap on the cheek and he was gone.

One of the hardest things getting used to about being a white man and a Christian was you had to wear clothes everywhere and all the time, no matter how hot. In every way describable the natural world was a threat, something we were doomed, as fallen angels, to endure for the length of our miserable lives due to the fact that the Almighty Father was punishing our asses for being what he made us. Suffice it to say, that sacred mystery the Holy Trinity, whatever else you wanted to make of it, lacked a female principle and all three of those heavenly spirits resented the human race for having sex and reproducing. The mystery to me was how they created anything, let alone Europe, where I came to understand there were more tribes as equally troubled and troublesome as the Spanish.

Padre Calabaza, Father Pumpkin I called him, though not to his face, because he looked like a pile of assorted native squash in robes, informed me as to the history and hierarchy and regiment of Catholicism which, as I'm sure you know, unlike the other countless piles of rituals and beliefs which fill the world, is the one true form of religion on this earth.

"Why?" I asked him once in the confessional, because none of us boys were allowed to talk to anybody unless we were spoken to, with the exception of meals where we could whisper to the kid next to us as long as we acted absolutely subdued. That whole submission thing was something that drove me crazy. You always had to be throwing yourself on the ground saying you were nothing but a miserable, small speck of animal poop and submitting yourself to the Almighty who was the greatest, most powerful, and meanest chief of all known existence. Almighty as he was, he had to be reminded every waking moment that it was so, and by us, of all people, lousy ingrates. And you were supposed to want to get to heaven so you and the rest of his minions could throw yourselves on your faces in front of him full time.

"Who is this?" said Father Pumpkin, because I was in the confessional and he couldn't see me.

"Roberto," I said. If you recall, that was my Christian name. And that little question, "why?" cost me a meal. I had to go to Lunch Prison, as the boys called it; sit in the corner of the lunch hall with my head between my legs, a public spectacle for others who would risk heresy.

In general I was considered a smart kid. I learned my Latin and spouted my catechism with the best of them. But brains were a dangerous commodity around there. Intelligence could lead to questioning and arrogance and other evils too grievous to mention. Look at Lucifer, for example.

When I got out of Lunch Prison, Father Pumpkin escorted me into the bowels of the monastery, past walls of entombed bishops and rectors, down to a leaky dungeon with walls of chains and metal spikes, instruments of torture too gruesome to contemplate and too numerous too mention. Made Comanche torture look like a game of stick and hoop. Pumpkin knocked on a thick door and pushed me into a room that smelled like warm moss. Behind a desk sat a yellow haired priest with pale eyes and skin like translucent soup. Only half of his face worked.

"So this is the great questioner," he said, lifting the one eyebrow he could lift.

"Is this hell?" I asked.

He lurched forward with a bony finger. "You're the Indian boy."

"No, Father, I'm Mexican," I told him. "Full blood."

He looked at me closely, turning his good eye on me, then the bad one, then the good one again. "Among the Nahuatl possibly," he said to me. "Do you know who they are?"

I was just a boy, but watching him look at me convinced me that he wasn't the type I could easily lie to. There are those you disarm with lies and others that you try to imbalance with the truth. The truth is more dangerous but a person who can't be lied to is more dangerous from the start.

"I know of them," I said to him. I answered him in Comanche Nahuatl, which you might know as Aztec.

"I see," he said, settling the question of whether or not he understood it himself. "Their witches were clever men. They wore the True Faith like so many vestments, underneath seething in their own magic." He lifted his chin. "Come forward," he said and I stepped up cautiously to his desk. "You are hard to get a bead on."

That's because like any scared kid I was trying my damnedest to be what he wanted me to be. I'd have sprouted wings for that son of a gun if he'd let me out of there.

"Yes, my son, I believe in magic," he said. He put that bony finger of his right hand on my chin. "Don't you believe that the Almighty sustains us in every second? If He were to blink for an instant everything would be gone. All time, all history, gone. Isn't that miracle enough to contemplate with awe, without question?"

Well it was miracle enough to me that anybody could think such a thing up, let alone believe it, but I tried to look contemplative.

The blond priest sat back again. "When we first came here we had to torture the Nahuatl witches into confessing their heathen magic. They were reluctant, because to admit it meant their deaths. But we are not like the American Protestants who send their witches to the devil. If an Aztec witch accepted baptism, his confession helped us send him to heaven."

Seemed to me a quick formula of baptize and slaughter. Why the hell didn't they do it for everybody? But I didn't think it was my place to question what kind of confession you got out of somebody who was being tortured to death. Why bother telling the truth at all? In fact, they probably didn't. I just figured it was another one of those things the Spanish got backwards.

"As long as there are miracles, my child," he continued, "there will be those who doubt the nature of miracles. The Inquisition is as old as the Church herself and will survive till the day that all the living perish and all the dead return."

I already knew the dead could return. There were those among the Comanche who thought that's what white people were in the first place. Ghosts. We'd been sending our dead off to the west for thousands of years and now the Hunting Grounds of the Dead were all filled up and the dead were coming back from the east as white people; that's why they had no regard for living things. It sounded a little fetched but it made as much sense as anything this priest was telling me.

"What do you have to say?" he asked.

Given that I didn't understand half of what he was talking about, it was hard to answer. I guess I'd been sent to him to have my bones chilled and there was no doubt in my mind that he'd done it. I wanted to say I missed my mother.

"I long for my mother, the Church," I whispered.

He rocked forward again, peering at me. "If light was good, and dark evil, then evil would be easy to spot, would it not?"

"Yes, Father," I said.

"I see the light inside you, Roberto, but I do not see whose light it is. The light of magic or the light of miracle. The light of Satan or the light of God."

Now he stood. I could see he once was tall or had a body that could have been tall. I'm sure all of that drooping and crookedness meant something extremely holy about him, though as a Comanche, even if still a child, I was more inclined to read him for what he was, a man who spent too much time protected by celibacy and darkness. The man needed some fresh air. He needed to ride a horse.

"Well then," he said, his eyes piercing me now. I swear I felt as naked as glass. "Let us put you in God's light and see what we see."

You wouldn't think that asking "why?" in the confessional would cause such a commotion, but I guess the rest of those little Catholic pumpkins had the why squashed out of them long before they got sent up here to holy school. Most of them were second sons in their families, which meant that the family land and money was already earmarked for their older brothers and they'd been shipped out to do the next best thing, that is become powerful clerics whose job it would be to influence everybody's morality towards doing nothing that would change anything.

If Comanche society was one of communal anarchy where power and authority were kept absolutely separate, then this Mexican society was one in which nobody shared anything and power was consolidated and wielded every second in every way. Everybody was sustaining their own world the way the big white God was sustaining his. It was all work and no play. And where were the women in all of this? Part of that got answered during the Big Change, which is what happened soon after I left that meeting with the Crooked Inquisitor. Though I still spent breakfasts and dinners and nights and prayers in the dormitory with the other little pumpkins, I now had a new mentor from mid-morning till late afternoon, Sor María Juana de la Cruz. That's right, a nun. And a young one, too. She had a face as gentle as moonlight, little delicate hands like dove's wings. She moved quietly, but full of life, like a girl chasing her pony. Her full breasts, pushed down somehow to deny their presence, bulged at the sides of her robes like pillows. She taught me Spanish grammar, Latin, Greek, the New Testament, mathematics, the histories of Greece and Rome. She taught me how to write, and I was in love the moment she took my hand and traced the first alpha.

Now you'd think that in a society as caught up in sin and temptation as that one was, the last thing they'd permit was a troublesome boy on the edge of puberty fraternizing with a virgin. Crazier, that they'd let them spend time alone. And it would make no sense at all to let them out of your sight to walk the streets of the biggest city in the world. You had to figure what the result would be, but of course the opposite was expected despite being given every opportunity to disappoint them.

I figured it was all a part of my personal Inquisition, to find out, in some upside down Spanish way, what kind of light was shining inside me. The whole darn Catholic way of thinking was to place you in one Garden of Eden after another so you spent your whole life on the edge of Doom. But the Crooked Inquisitor had bewitched me. If I was evil, I'd do evil, whether or not I tried to be good.


Mexico City was a marvelous place. The remnants of the Aztecs were everywhere. What wasn't one of their ruins was built out of them and what was new was built by Aztec slaves, including giant churches, they called them basilicas, that made you feel puny. That, I suppose, once again, being the point. Instead of opening up to the Sky People the Spanish tried to bring the sky inside. And despite the joy they took in conquering and torturing Indians, by looking at their statuary they obviously took great pride in being tortured themselves.

I'll be the first to admit, I found the whole torturing Jesus thing kind of confusing, let alone going to church on Sunday and pretending to eat him. As a Comanche there were plenty of things we didn't eat, which included certain animals and all people, spirits, and ancestors. It was because we lived out in nature and had our heads on right. These city Indians like the Aztecs, they fed people to their gods and then ate the people and it was just a matter of one-upmanship on the part of the Spanish to eat the gods, too.

There had been Indians living in cities down here in Mexico before whites ever crawled out of their European caves. They even invented the wheel and didn't bother to use it. They made little toy carts for the kids to play with but never bothered to make a real one, which should say something about their attitude. Nine out of ten people in Mexico City were still Indian, and anything that got done in that town got done by Indians, including building all those basilicas. That was one of the first things Sor María Juana de la Cruz showed me. In every church there were angels with forked tongues, pillars with the Feathered Serpent, Quetzacoatl, wrapped around them, St. George dressed like the war god, Huitzilopochtli, fighting a devil who looked an awful lot like his brother, Mictiantecuhitli, the god of the dead.

Those Indians got conquered, tortured, and converted and in three hundred years they hadn't changed a bit. Back in the days before the Spanish came, the Aztecs had a temple on top of a mountain north of the city to the goddess Tonatzin. She was just another version of their great virgin mother goddess, Coatlicue, but these Aztecs, it seems, really had only about two or three deities when you got down to it and liked to give them different names for different functions. To each his own when it comes to gods and goddesses, that's what I say.

Anyway, the Spanish rolled in, conquered, tortured, and built a big basilica to a new virgin mother, the Virgin of Guadalupe, and put a statue of her right there where the statue of Tonatzin used to be. But nothing changed for the Aztecs. Not a thing. People still brought her their corn and babies and crawled around her picture weeping on their knees. She still cured the sick when she saw fit.

For the Aztecs, Coatlicue was a virgin and the mother of all the gods, including her own grandmother! You'd think that was an unbeatable postulation till you heard that the Catholic virgin who took her place, the Virgin of Guadalupe, the Virgin Mary, was the Mother of God but not a goddess! For the love of your mother, I was never around such a bunch of woman haters. How could you love your own mom, let alone your wife, with attitudes like that? The whole business was the product of cultures that spent too much time indoors.

"Why are you telling me this stuff?" I said to Sor María Juana. We were, of all places, at something call a zoo. Among other things those crazy Aztecs did was to collect plants and animals from all over their known world and keep them in captivity so they could go look at them in their spare time, when they weren't tearing the hearts out of living prisoners. Joy and wonder if the Spanish didn't have to do them one better and bring in plants and animals from every continent so you could wander around gawking at a lot of unhappy creatures of the Lord stuck in tiny cages. I saw my first elephant there.

"In India and Africa they use them for work and in battle," said Sor María Juana.

"They look too slow," I said.

"And you know something about battle?"

"More than you," I told her.

"And what do you have against knowledge?" she said. "I thought you were the Why Pumpkin."

"I was never one of those little pumpkins," I said. Boy, information sure flew around fast in that monastic world. "I've got every padre in Mexico City waiting for me to believe something nasty and pagan so they can flay me like an Aztec witch, and you're here filling me full of subversive thoughts."

Sor María Juana lifted an eyebrow and looked at the elephant. She tended to walk around with one delicate white hand, her right, folded inside her left one, and what she did just then was release them and fold her left inside her right. I'd been around these Catholics long enough to suspect Sor María Juana's job was as much to entrap me as educate me and I guess I'd shown her some cards I'd been hiding.

"Subvert," she said. "Since Eden, it's been a woman's job to subvert."

Well that was an interesting way to put it. A vendor, a mestizo, came by with some nuts and of course I got them for free because I was with a nun.

"A lot of the sisters aren't allowed to talk or go outside," I said.

"Cloistered ones," she said, not turning from the elephant.

I offered him a nut and he took it from me with his trunk, gentle as a bird.

"A little bit like these zoo animals,"I said.

"No," she said. "Cloistered nuns choose."

"'Oh, they do," I said to her.

"Yes," she said. She looked at me. "They do." Then she laughed. She had a giggle like, well, you'd want to say a sky spirit, a fairy to you European types, but it was more earthly, more womanly than that. It sounded like something that you'd like to carry home with you to sleep with."The elephant likes you," she said. "He recognizes something."

"What might that be?" I said.

"I don't know," she said. She giggled again. "What might it be?"

I imagine we had come to some kind of rapport, teasing each other with our secrets. Looking back, I'd say we were flirting had I known what it was then. She took my hand, she was still a little taller than me, and walked me through the zoo, pointing out the animals and flowers and I hid my arousal as well as I could. It wasn't like we were ever really any danger to each other. Indian boys are taught restraint as well as anybody.

Though Mexico City is pretty far south, it's high in the air and even in the summer is neither warm nor dry. One of its sporadic summer thunderstorms broke over us and we rushed under a gazebo where we interrupted a pair of mestizo teenagers groping at each other, a concession to the Indians, they could court in public if they did it out of sight. The Gachupines, Spanish born, and Creoles, the Mexican born Spanish pure bloods, did their courting in an open square. In a festive atmosphere, vendors sold tamales, fruit drinks, mangoes doused in hot chili pepper, a real treat if you've never had one, the smell of roast goat and the sound of cheerful guitar and horns wafting through the air. The girls, accompanied by chaperones, paraded on the inside while the boys circled outside in the opposite direction, everybody casting furtive glances as they pretended they were ignoring why they were there in the first place. Of course, as I've learned again and again, any society with that much invested in its chastity has got that much more invested in its sordidness.

The Indians were less formal and more direct, and in that way more innocent. These kids sneaked off to neck in public. Anybody sneaking off to neck in public isn't going to do much more than that. The circumstances tend to control the outcome. So it was bad luck for that pair. They might be allowed to kiss in public, but not while sharing a gazebo with a nun.

"So," I said as the cold rain came down, "are you stuck being a nun?"

"I am a sister to the Church," she said, staring out into the rain. She didn't turn to look at me at all. "I am married to Christ."

"Do you live in a dorm, like me?" I said.

"I have my own room where I live and pray. It has a bed and a bath as well." She folded her arms inside the sleeves of her robe. "When I'm not teaching you, I study at the University."

"A bath in your room?"

"And a servant." She turned to me. "My parents make it possible. I have given up much to serve Christ," she said. "Wealth. Horses. A future husband, and children." She paused. "I don't have to give up bathing." She looked into the rain again. "I am a poet and a musician. I recite for the Cardinal and dignitaries. I do not just teach the classics to promising little boys."

Well so much for her vows of poverty and humility. Not that it made me despise her. No, to see her hot like that, assertive, her cheeks flushing under her white habit, it made me love her all the more.

# 17

"I SOLD MY LAND," said my father, Hermano O'Donohughe. "I am a merchant now." He'd left dressed as a caballero, with spurs, boots and hat, and had returned dressed in silk breeches, a three-pointed French sailors hat, a silver watch and chain, Italian leather shoes. All of this, of course, he pointed out to me because at the time I didn't know an ostrich feather from creme brulee.

"When are we going back to Santa Fe?" I said to him.

"I am leaving for Spain with a shipment of gold, spices, tobacco, and when I return I will be twice as wealthy as when I left."

"What about our empire?"

"Gold will be my empire. My land was in the south. I don't think the Maya will ever be tamed and their land is almost unworkable except by them."

"So you sold it back to them?"

"How could I? They have no money."

"But it's their land."

"Look around you," said my father. "Is this Aztec land?"

"Yes," I said.

We'd taken his carriage to a small cafe in Coyoacán, a suburb south of the city. When Mexico City itself was Aztec, called Tenochtitlan then, it was an island in Lake Texcoco, connected by causeways to the shores. The Aztecs on this shore sold salt from the lake shore, as well as fruit and flowers to the Aztecs in Tenochtitlan. The town here was called Huitzilopochco, after the war god, Huitzilopochtli, which really meant left-handed hummingbird. That's a beautiful name for a god, isn't it? Those Aztecs were poetic and deep, as well as cruel.

The Spanish couldn't say Huitzilipochco. It sounded like Churubusco to them. So while they tore down the Left-Handed Hummingbird's pyramid and built their church, San Diego, and their convent, Santa María de Los Angeles, they kept the original name for the place, Churubusco, so to speak. The Spanish had long since filled up the lake, a European travel solution if you ever saw one, but the town of Coyoacán was still laden with the original fruit trees, calla lilies, and bougainvillea, all of it flowering in the dry of winter. The place smelled like paradise, and I've learned since then that the smell of paradise is a warning, among others, that foretells doom.

Of course, this was all stuff that Sor María Juana, hearing of this excursion with my father, told me the day before. She was an absolute storehouse of pre-Spanish history.

"I have enlarged your allowance at the school," said my father. "They say you are performing superbly under the tutelage of Sor Juana."

"Sor María Juana," I said.

We were having coffee, my first ever, and eating amazing, dark chocolate, the combination so powerful that along with the perfume of my father's cigar, the bright yellow of the cafe walls seemed to vibrate.

"I'm not cut out to be a Franciscan," I said to Hermano, my father.

He laughed. He had a thin little mustache now. I wondered what Many Powers would think of him and in that moment I missed her sorely.

My father put a finger to his lips. "A secret. They are Jesuits, really. The Franciscans would never risk giving anyone so much education."

The Jesuits, I knew from Sor María Juana, had been thrown out of America by the Pope years ago.

Hermano blew some smoke in the air. "They do the work of the Church, for the Church, behind her back."

By that point in the conversation I felt very much like a rich little mouse cornered by a benevolent cat.

"I want to go home," I said. I surprised him. I guess I even surprised myself.

"To Texas?" he exclaimed. "If you go back to Texas, you'd better learn English. That's what they are saying in Europe. *Tejas será norteamericana.*" Texas will be American."

The thought of me wanting to return to the Comanche, I guess, was completely beyond him.

"Don't you ever think about the People?" I said.

My father frowned heavily. "You are no soldier, Roberto. I don't think you will be much of a rancher or a merchant. And with your bloodline, some of which we keep secret, you will need your brains to survive. You are still a child. I have to think about your survival."

"Take me to Spain with you," I said.

"I do not have time to watch over you."

"You won't have to watch over me."

"Or the money to educate you in Spain."

Undoubtedly, he was sure I would never pass for a Spaniard in Spain, and that could prove to be a real embarrassment.

"What will happen here?" I asked him. "After I'm educated?"

"There is time," said my father.

"I don't think they really like me here," I said to him. "I think they suspect me."

"Of what?"

"Everything."

My father finished another small cigar and motioned for our bill. "Roberto," he said. "Gold is gold. Gold is gold in the north and in the south, in Spain, in Mexico, in Rome where the Pope abides. Everywhere," said my father, Hermano O'Donohughe, "gold is gold."

The year seeped into spring. My father went off to Spain, and if it weren't for Sor María Juana my life, as the Spanish say, would have been a veil of tears. Whatever foolish altruism or pride prompted Hermano-Many Wounds O'Donohughe to save the blood of his kin from the depths of heathen hell, it became clear that now that I'd been saved he didn't know what do with me. Throw some money at the problem. Gold is gold. That was what my father had become.

Sor María Juana continued my education under the supervision of Padre Pumpkin who reported to the Great Crooked Inquisitor, their interest in me still a sacred mystery to yours truly. Besides my official education, Sor María Juana continued my real one, without at any time admitting that that's what we were about.

Frequently, we walked to the center of Mexico City, in El Centro. Where the great temples of the Aztecs once stood, there were now government palaces that opened into a gigantic public square, the Zócalo, and a giant basilica. In the Zócalo the Indians still set out their crops and trade on blankets, the same as they'd done six hundred years previous, when the Aztecs first came, and thousands of years before that wherever else they lived. Sometimes Sor María Juana did the shopping for her convent, ordering corn and beans, even livestock, mostly pork.

The idea of eating domestic animals was still pretty new to me. It confounded sense to take the spirit of a fat, pacified creature. I guess it explained the reason there were a lot of fat, pacified individuals everywhere, and those that weren't were kind of ornery and frustrated. Some of these wealthier folks never even saw the animal they ate. It was just another example of how these people separated everything from everything else. I was beginning to think that white culture was just a bunch of killing and taking things apart, then putting them back together in odd combinations. Then you sat and thought about why everything was so strange.

Here at the center of Mexico lived the great new Emperor of all of Mexico, Emperor Iturbide. His empire included, I learned to my surprise, the very plains where I'd been born. That's right, the Mexican Empire, like New Spain before it, claimed to own land that they'd never even lived on. Not only that, the Americans claimed they owned it, too, without any regard for the people who'd been living there since the beginning of time, the Comanche, among others.

Down here in Mexico now there was a lot of unhappiness about the Americans who on the one hand were admired for their ideas about democracy and on the other hand feared as land grabbing Yankee bigots. And if there was one person who liked to talk about democracy the most, it was the Emperor Iturbide himself who was just being emperor until everything could sort itself out, not having enough land of his own, I guess, to be ready for democracy.

Iturbide claimed to be a Spanish pure blood, but it only took one look at him to see he was as half-bred as me. I saw him sometimes, passing by on his big gray gelding or in his carriage, surrounded by an army of mounted and booted troops, on his way back and forth from the palace here in the Zócalo to his castle in Chapultapec Park, the same place they kept the zoo. From the Aztecs to the Spanish to the Mexicans, that much hadn't changed.

Next to the Emperor Iturbide, more often than not, on a stallion as black as obsidian, rode the young and gallant General Antonio López de Santa Ana, a tall, Spanish pure blood if you ever saw one, with skin almost as white as his stallion was black. He was famous for helping the Spanish to brutally squelch a *norteamericana* rebellion in Texas back in 1813. In that one they killed everybody. Even the People heard about it. And in this recent Mexican revolution, just when things looked dark, he'd changed sides at the last minute and threw the victory to Iturbide, though there were some who claimed he changed sides after the victory had occurred. He was handsome and famous and haughty and smooth, gracious and brutal, cunning, dashing and brave. As he rode he looked out over the Zócalo with sympathy and disdain. Speaking as a Mexican, which I can do, he embodied everything we loved. We couldn't help but admire him.

It was on such a day in the Zócalo, after the Emperor and his general passed, horns blaring and thumping troops, the clatter of horse hooves echoing all around, that there came a hard, summer rain and then the sun suddenly spreading, the steam rising from the gray cobblestones of the great square—a Mexico City day if ever there was one—when Sor María Juana took me to see the great Aztec calendar. It had been dug up accidentally back in 1790 during the last renovation of the Cathedral. The Spanish had thought they'd destroyed everything, but somehow they'd missed this twenty ton circle of carved rock. They'd have destroyed it then, but by 1790 the climate had changed a little in Mexico City. The Indians, still as vehemently Aztec as they were now fervently Catholic, if that makes any sense, had grown unruly enough that destroying such a find as that calendar might have made them unhappy.

It always took a decade or two for the Spanish to decide what to do about anything, and by 1810, when they decided to bury the thing again, all of South America was coming apart and in Mexico an old priest named Hidalgo had organized the Indians into a farmer army that went into full revolt. The peasant Indians fought under the banner of the Virgin of Guadalupe, who may as well have been Coatlicue/Tonatzin, and the Spaniards fought under the flag of the Virgen de los Remedios, the same Virgin Mary Cortés used. As we say in the plains, the sun shines on everybody. It took ten years of bloody fighting, but that's how they ended up back where they started, with an emperor, only a Mexican Emperor instead of a Spanish one.

Anyway, they never did get the calendar re-buried and it ended up in the back of the church where the only people who were allowed to see it were the folks who would have no interest in it because they knew it for the absolutely

heathen thing it was. I got in there with Sor María Juana whose studies
in heathenism were tolerated because being a nun she was powerless to do
anything with the information.

It didn't take much looking at that thing to realize those Aztecs were crazy
geniuses. Using the path of the sun they could calculate every hour of every
day for stretches of fifty-two years, which to their thinking was a century. Back
home we used the moon cycle and couldn't keep one year straight from the
next, let alone count them. Some time or another during the twelve seasons we
always had an extra moon, there being thirteen moons in a year if you didn't
know that, and I wouldn't be surprised if you didn't because most people who
can read live in cities and most people in cities don't know a star from a firefly.
Like Many Powers had foretold, they thought the moon came up when the sun
went down.

Time was not our forte on the plains, but then again, it didn't have to be.
Time is important to farmers, and to the city folk who milk them the way the
farmers themselves milk goats and cows. The Aztecs had eighteen twenty day
months, named after the seasons like Drought Month, Falling Fruit Month,
Wind Month, which had to do with whether they had to sweep out the house
or gather a harvest or save water, a lot like us except we only counted twelve
and it had mostly to do with buffalo. And if we had an extra moon, well, they
had extra days, five of them at the end of the year called Nothing Days because
they didn't know what to do with them and so they all had to do absolutely
nothing on those days or tremendous bad luck would befall everybody, not just
the individual who transgressed. All of this they just kept track of with some
notches on the outside of the circle of that calendar.

But if that wasn't enough counting, they had another calendar, too, even
more sacred. At the center of that huge stone was a picture of their sun god,
a really big, ugly son-of-a-virgin. You could see why they had to feed him live
human hearts. He was surrounded by his four predecessors, each as ugly as
him, and other various serpent gods. That thing didn't just keep track of the
days, but had the whole history of the world on it, at least according to them.

Outside those serpents was a circle of thirteen numbers, which I figured
to be the moons but Sor María Juana said no, they were the Thirteen Skies.
Around them were twenty pictures, mostly of animal powers as I saw it. The
Aztecs rotated the big circle around the little one in opposite directions. The
first day was 1 Crocodile, the second was 2 Feathered Serpent or Wind God,

and so on till you got 260 named and numbered days with the feast of some god or goddess on each one. Combined with that first seasonal calendar, they pretty much had a unique day for everything and everybody in all the fifty-two years, a human life span by most reckoning, at the end of which the first day of both calendars matched up and they started over.

Every four years they somehow ended up with an extra day because their year was a quarter of a day short. The more precise you try to be, the more mistakes you make. Europeans handled it with a leap year every four years, but the Aztecs collected those days for fifty-two years and piled them all up at the end. Twelve of them. They were the Really Big Nothing Days, as dangerous and unlucky as any days ever.

The sun could go out, the whole world could end on those Really Big Nothing Days. It had happened before, four times according to the Aztecs. Doused by Rain, consumed in Fire, eaten by the Wind. The last time it happened real close by, which I'll tell you more about later. They couldn't go outside or light fires or wear clothes or bathe during those Really Big Nothing Days. Men and women had to separate because women turned into jaguars and ate their husbands, not that you could blame them, given their general treatment.

They could tell the future of the world by looking at the stars and consulting that calendar. Each individual inherited their name and their destiny based on the day they were born. Of course if you were born on one of the Really Big Nothing Days, you were about as good as poop on a deer hoof. Born on 1 Wind, you could rule the world. Word was that Cortés showed up on the Really Big Nothing Days and they knew he was coming. The Aztecs thought Cortés was Quetzacoatl and he may as well have been for all his destruction. And you'd have thought the Mexica wouldn't have fought him so hard, knowing that the world was over for certain anyways, but one thing I learned about the Mexicans, when they knew they were doomed they became the most hellish fighters on earth.

You could not be anything but bedazzled by Sor María Juana's knowledge of all this, let alone her interest. There we were in a cathedral big enough to house the Hopis; giant crucifixes, statues of Jesus and Mary in twenty different forms, every saint known to Spain sculpted or painted in or on some wall, and this nun is showing me the Aztec calendar. Of course one thing the Aztecs and Catholics had in common was they had a deity or feast day every time you turned around.

"You know," I said to Sor María Juana as we walked back out into the sun and buzz of the Zócalo, "I was raised without religion."

"I know," she said. "Now you have been saved."

"But the People did all kinds of holy stuff," I said, trying to keep things in her tongue. "Everything we did was already holy. You didn't have to believe anything."

She turned her beautiful cheek toward me and raised both eyebrows. She liked knowledge, you had to give her that.

"You mean everything they did was heathen," she said.

Well, heathen, holy, what's the difference? But I kept it to myself.

"Then why do you like all this old Aztec stuff so much?" I asked her.

"I love the people," she said. "It's part of them."

We walked silently back to my prison. I hated being thrown back in with all those little pumpkins. I just wanted to find a way to put my head down on Sor María Juana's breast.

"I don't want to go back in there," I said.

She nodded, and as she walked away I followed her down the street all the way to Saint Geronimo's a few blocks away, stopping at the outer gate.

"My prison," she said softly.

You could walk right in there through the first garden to a foyer where there was a huge metal door with a sliding window, that's as far as you'd get. But in that foyer was a big painting of another nun. Underneath was her name, Sor Juana Inéz de la Cruz.

"I walk in her path," said Sor María Juana.

"Who is she?"

"A famous nun who lived here. She could have been a countess, but she chose to marry Christ and become a poet. Everyone in all of New Spain and all the courts of Europe knew her work. Men threw themselves beneath her balcony, their hearts bleeding for love. She learned everything she could about the Mexica and spoke out for them. Finally she went to work among their diseased where she died of the plague."

"Do you want to die of the plague?" I said.

She smiled.

"Do you want me to throw myself under your balcony?"

"Draw some of your allowance and I will take you on a secret journey," said Sor María Juana. She put her fingers to my cheek and I felt it clear down to my bones. "Can you find your way back?"

I could. Though it would be the first time I was out in Mexico City alone. I thought of running right then. Taking off for El Norte and wherever fate would lead, but the warmth of Sor María Juana's touch on my cheek and her promise of a secret journey led me right back to little pumpkinland, a willing prisoner. Of course, she never told me that her namesake, Sor Juana Inéz de la Cruz was censored and quieted by the Inquisition and given a death sentence to go work with the poor and diseased. Like a lot of things, I had to find out the dark side on my own.

# 18

I DIDN'T KNOW HOW MANY pesos a secret journey would take,
but I'd been saving up my allowance for a long time while making plans for
my escape, which wasn't easy. The Church watches your money closer than it
watches its own, because soon enough it's going to be theirs. So I learned early
on to establish my reputation as a charitable being, something which came
natural to a Comanche seeing as it was our common habit to give everything
we owned away to each other for any excuse whatsoever. That kept the whole
private property thing really fluid. You gave something away and you'd end up
with it back in your lap a week later. There are those who have contended that
we practiced some form of communal behavior, but there was never anything
communal about us, we were just generous to a fault.

But here in my Christian phase, I guess Catholic would be more accurate,
I knew getting favors returned could be subtle and complex, like everything
else in the One True Church. Sometimes I gave every cent of my allowance
right back to Padre Pumpkin. Other times I gave it to the poor, though always
through a source where my generosity would be noted. I even bought candies
and treats for the other pumpkins, despite the fact that most of them were
richer than me and I didn't even like them. The rest I stashed, so when I drew
five pesos to give to Sor María Juana for her convent, Padre Pumpkin didn't
blink, and on top of the other fifty pesos I had squirreled secretly away, I had

enough dinero for quite a secret journey. A first lieutenant in the Mexican army didn't make fifty-five pesos in a month.

On the morning of our secret journey I had to leave right after prayers, before breakfast, before dawn. Sor María Juana was waiting there with a carriage and driver and we headed north on the newly dubbed Avenida Insurgentes right out of town. From there we followed a little path called the Pachuca Road. We clipped along pretty good, but it was well after sunrise when we arrived at one of the most amazing sights I'd ever seen, an ancient stone city, completely abandoned, with brick roads, temples carved with jaguars and dragons, pyramids so massive and tall they stretched into the sky. This place made even the Zócalo look puny.

Though we were high in the air, which you could tell from the cool, dry wind that swept through that dead city like a zephyr through a canyon, purple and green mountains swelled and rose all around us like a sea. That wind howled constantly. It moaned and whispered and bellowed and called. It moved things about, fluffing the grass, the trees, the big, spreading agave cactuses, like they were feathers. The land squirmed under our feet like a lizard, the dust blowing into the surrounding vegetation as if the earth was preening itself like a bird. For lack of a better way of putting it, everything in that dead city felt alive. It would take an idiot not to recognize that this was the city of the great God of the Wind, Quetzacoatl.

"This is Quetzacoatl's city," I said to Sor María Juana. Unlike her, I was prone to believe he was still there.

"More," she said as we began to walk. "It is the birthplace of the gods."

She went on to tell me that this city was so old that it had been abandoned a thousand years before the Aztecs found it. The sun god at the center of the Mexica calendar, she reminded me, was the fifth sun god in the history of time and the other four faces surrounding him were the first four. After Quetzacoatl ate the Fourth Sun and ended the world, the gods got together and, like any Indians, argued for a long time about what to do. The short of it is that two of them, one out of bravery and love, and the other out of pride for fear of being shown up, volunteered to throw themselves into a huge fire that was built at the top of the biggest pyramid. Those two crazy gods threw themselves into that god fire and burned up into the sky, creating the sun and the moon.

But neither of them, once they were up in the sky, would move. They just sat up there motionless. I guess they felt they'd done enough, just getting burned up for the sake of everybody else. So Quetzacoatl, that crafty devil, convinced the rest of the gods that if they sacrificed themselves to him, he'd blow the sun and moon into motion. Of course, being a son-of-a-bitch, he killed them all and didn't bother to blow the sun and moon into motion until much later, when he felt like it. Then everybody got reborn and the world started over under the Fifth Sun, Tonatiuh, known as Nahui Oilin, the Movement Sun, but from that day on it took blood sacrifice to keep him moving. Guess he got spoiled.

"That's a better story than Adam and Eve," I said.

"But Adam and Eve is true," said Sor María Juana.

"So what sun are we under now?"

"The natural sun of the One, True God, created on the very first day of the world."

"The Sixth Sun, created the day after Cortés destroyed Tenochtitlan," I said.

"You're funny," she said. "It's a good thing I understand your sense of humor." Bless God, whoever it is, that I had a subversive female for my Catholic mentor.

"My People have a spirit person like Quetzacoatl," I said to Sor María Juana.

"Your people?"

"We call him Coyote."

"Coyote is a manifestation of Quetzacoatl," she said.

"No kidding," I said.

"There are many tales of him among the Maya. But for Catholics, like you and I," she smiled, "Coyote is Satan."

"Coyote isn't that bad," I said. "Just mischievous in a big way."

"A very big way," she said. "We call it mortal sin. And as you have learned, it takes only one and a completely virtuous life becomes damned and ruined."

We were walking into the center of the city, on La Avenida de los Muertos. According to the Aztecs, some of their Way Back People found this place all set up for them by the gods two thousand years ago and they rolled in and set up shop. Lived like kings, so to speak, as long as they were willing to sacrifice a few thousand of their own kind every year to keep the sun moving. They cut their hearts out while they were still alive, right atop that huge Pyramid to the Sun, then rolled them down the steps and buried them here on either side of the street, had big trenches built into the pyramid to accommodate the flow of blood. If you could believe Sor María Juana, they considered it a great privilege to get sliced up. It was such a privilege in fact that these city Indians built cities modeled on this one all over Mexico and fought wars with the other cities so they could get captives to sacrifice. This went on for twenty centuries until the Spanish came along and straightened them out.

"In the end," said Sor María Juana, "they, like us, really believed in only one God. But they were overwhelmed by ignorance and found His manifestations everywhere and deified them. Your People," she said, "despite all their spirit beings, probably have one great God, no?"

Well, it was true. Even the heathen Comanche believed in a single, mysterious, unfigureable source of everything, the Great Everywhere Mystery. But it was a long way from there to the Holy Trinity and Jesus on the cross.

We walked to the top of that Pyramid of the Sun. You felt you could see all the way to Texas from up there. Down La Avenida de los Muertos, at the end of the city, stood a pyramid almost as big as this one, the Pyramid of the Moon, surrounded by temples, courts, and colonnades, the walls and floors painted red, yellow, green, blue. Some of the walls held murals of eagles and jaguars, and processions of captured enemies being led to the sacrifice. The unpainted walls of these buildings were made of red, volcanic stone, the mortar between studded with shining obsidian.

At the other end of the city a huge ball court was carved out, with stone hoops high up on the walls. These Indians played a ball game where the teams tried to hit a ball through those hoops with their thighs and shoulders. Of course the winners or losers or everybody got sacrificed when it was done. And next to that court was another huge temple, the head of Quetzacoatl protruding from every crevice, his body winding up and down. On the winter solstice the sun struck the temple at dawn and made it look as if the shadow of Quetzacoatl was crawling up the steps. That was a damn lot of work for a couple of minutes of one day a year.

I have to admit, I was astounded. Who could possibly have built this stuff two thousand years ago? If it wasn't gods, then it must have been the First People. I expressed that to Sor María Juana.

"There are similar things in Egypt," she said, "which are even older."

"Is that near here?"

"In Africa, like where the elephants are from."

"Well see, the gods are everywhere."

Sor María Juana laughed. "You mean God is everywhere," she said.

She spread her arms out. I'd never seen her do anything like it before.

I have no joy, I have no gladness.
The earth does not fill me.
I have suffered sorrows in the world,
The earth has only been lent to us,
Tomorrow, or the day after,
The Giver of Life will beckon us to His home.

She turned to me. "That is an Aztec poem, Roberto. And the people who lived here, in Teotihuacan, a thousand years before the Aztecs, wrote such poems. And the people before them. And the people of the future, too, will write them."

The wind kicked up again and I felt a cold chill as clouds swept over the high valley. On top of that pyramid, on top of the world, the shadows of huge thunderheads flew against the mountains and the red stone temples. Up there, it really felt like the wind could eat the sun.

Sor María Juana felt me shivering and we sat down together, staring out under the wind swept clouds of Teotihuacan. She held me and brought my head to her breast.

"All things pass," she whispered.

I couldn't have been more in love with her. And I couldn't have been more confused about what to do about it, so I just nuzzled into her breast. It was the happiest moment of my young life. But there was a noise behind us and Sor María Juana jumped up.

It was a testament to the level of my distraction that I didn't know where he'd come from, but there, as big as life, so to speak, standing behind us on the top of the Pyramid of the Sun, was General Santa Ana. He wore a bright blue military coat, lined in red, blinding white leggings tucked into black boots that shined like the night.

He lifted his voice. "Nothing but the flowers of sorrow are left in Mexico," he sang. "As warriors and wise men have perished, so must we, for we are but mortal."

"We wander here and there in our poverty," said Sor María Juana. "Where once we knew beauty and valor, now we see bloodshed and pain. We are crushed under our ruins. Have you grown weary of your servants?" Sor María Juana said softly.

And General Santa Ana responded. They whispered and sang together. "Are you angry with your servants, oh Giver of Life?"

Santa Ana removed his cap and bowed. "Good sister," he said, "I was drawn by your poetry."

He nodded, lowering his eyes like a boy. He was the self-proclaimed Napoleon of America and it would be ludicrous for him to deny his greatness. Amid my jealousy and awe, Sor María Juana made my introduction, and as he shook my hand I saw in his dark eyes something which evaded magnificence. I couldn't put my finger on it, but you felt in his touch and his smile that he could be all things to all people while at the same time being true to you.

His entourage came up behind him and he spoke to me. "You will forgive me if I borrow your mentor, briefly, to discuss Aztec poetry and the One True Church." He turned to the soldiers behind him. "Captain de la Peña, take Roberto and introduce him to Cielo de Noche," he said.

It was a wonderful morning for me. Captain de la Peña took me to the Pyramid of the Moon and the Jaguar Temple. From a vendor he bought me peeled mango, skewered and dipped in hot chilies, a real Mexican delicacy, juicy, sweet and hot, and he took me over to the horses to visit Santa Ana's black stallion, Cielo de Noche, Sky at Night. De la Peña unhobbled him and I took his halter and lunged him quickly into a small circle around me. Contrary to what you might think, most stallions are quite docile and willing to please as long as you keep their noses from a ready mare.

"I can see you come from a wealthy family that owns many good horses," said de la Peña.

"Oh yes," I said, using the Castilian *th* sound, as would a European Spaniard, instead of the Mexican *s*. "At home I have a beautiful young mare."

"A boy and a young, hot mare are an unusual, but beautiful match. Where is your home?"

"Now? Tejas. We own millions of acres."

"Béjar?" he said.

"Yes," I said. "Near Béjar." As a Comanche I new the territory well. Béjar was still pretty Spanish then, Creole anyway, what was left of it. There was a mission their called San Antonio, or, at times, Alamo, for the cottonwood forest nearby. "My father is now in Spain," I said.

"You are a Saldaña?"

I recognized the name. One of the last, huge Spanish ranchería, southwest of Béjar. We'd raided it for horses, but the Saldañas were well armed and respectable defenders; it was easier to ransack Béjar. "From my mother," I said.

"Ah," said Captain de la Peña, "he should return home. The *norteamericanas* are close, in San Felipe de Austin and Goliad-La Bahia. They keep slaves and don't worship the Church. Another fight is inevitable."

I liked Captain José Enrique de la Peña, whose name meant grief. He had a chiseled, sun-worked face and big, hard hands, hard, piercing eyes, but a gentleness in his heart. He'd lost his own family in the last uprising, when the first Texas cessationists, called filibusters, took Béjar in 1813, on the heels of Hidalgo's revolution in the south. Though the Texans claimed to have shot their Spanish prisoners by a misinterpreted order, their first rush through the city murdered anything in front of them. When the Spanish arrived under General Arrendondo, Santa Ana, then only nineteen, was with him. They captured a thousand Texans, shot them, skinned them, and hung their carrion by their heels from the branches of the cottonwoods. The skinning was an Aztec touch, though the Aztec would have skinned them alive.

News of this brutality and counter-brutality swept through the plains. Even we Comanche, known for our resolve on the battlefield, had never encountered such massive devastation, and we simply didn't believe it until we began our own raids into Béjar soon after the Spanish army left. Until recently, with the arrival of more Americans, Béjar was practically a Comanche vassal. We just showed up and extracted what we pleased.

"Nothing is accomplished by brutality," whispered de la Peña, "not even revenge."

I had to give it to him, there was something blessed in a sorrow that deep. It was an attitude that made the Mexicans dear to me, even years later. They were ruthless, but deep. And it made the depth of their kindness miraculous.

I released the line on Cielo de Noche, turned my back and walked away from the stallion who followed me like a pup, nudging my ear with his soft nose when I stopped.

"So you are a horse mystic," said de la Peña.

"No," I said. "I just know them."

"You must know of the Indians then, in Tejas, who live with horses, eating and sleeping with them. There are some, they say, who are born on horseback, who live and die on the backs of their herds, people whose feet in all their lives never touch the ground."

I looked back at de la Peña, whose dark eyes glistened under his lowered brow before he broke into a small grin, a grin I returned.

"So, would you like to get me in trouble with the great general?" he said, offering me a leg up.

I took it, and took hold of that black stallion's mane. I raced bareback down the cobblestone Avenida de los Muertos on the back of Cielo de Noche. On the stallion of the great General Antonio López de Santa Ana, I ran under the Temple of the Sun and the Temple of the Moon.

19

AS WITH A LOT OF GREAT MEN, you couldn't be guaranteed whether a rash act would draw Santa Ana's joy or wrath. I imagine that drawn by the thunder of Cielo de Noche's hooves on the cobblestone he was waiting for me at the horses when I returned. I was apprehensive till I read the look on de la Peña, which had more mirth in it than sorrow, if you could paint one over the other, which you had to in his case.

"You are a lucky child," Santa Ana said, offering me his arm, but pulling me down solidly from the horse's back. "But one must be a bit foolish to be brave." He turned to de la Peña. "You see how well I have trained this animal," he said.

"Yes," de la Peña said, his face now stoic.

"May you ride at my side when Mexico rules the hemisphere," Santa Ana said to me. He put his hand in my hair and gripped it hard, the line between his affection and anger indiscernible, but I can see now, looking back, that if it weren't for Sor María Juana I might have ended up hanging upside down and skinned.

"You, servant of God, my breast is thine," Santa Ana said to Sor María Juana, bowing, without for a second relinquishing my scalp. "To all eternity, divine Mistress, I'll do your bidding still."

I found those lines a few years later in the Harvard Library, somewhere in the middle of *Don Quixote*. If you can picture that whole thing, that Santa

Ana had read Cervantes and was willing to quote Quixote, the noble buffoon, well, he was either a man with great distance from himself or some kind of fool, and one moment to the next he was one or the other or both. That kind of sums up Santa Ana in a lot of ways, not that it was the end of things between me and him. Far from it.

Santa Ana sent an escort home with our carriage. Sor María Juana had a glow in her cheeks I'd never seen before.

"It was kind of our lucky day," I said to her. "I had a lot of fun."

"But what did you learn?" she said.

"Did you get to be like Sor Juana Inéz de la Cruz today?" I said.

"The poor cannot help themselves, Roberto," she said to me, taking my hand. "What we give them, in mercy, is like the angel St. Augustine met on the beach who tried to drain the sea with a leaky spoon."

"You'd think an angel would know better," I said.

"It was a lesson for the saint," she said," not for the angel."

"And what did he learn?" I said.

"That a saint inhabits neither heaven nor earth. Can you imagine, Roberto," she said to me, "what good Santa Ana could do for the people of Mexico?"

"Well," I said, "not really."

"I would martyr myself to show him the way," she whispered.

Looking back, I can see it was in Sor María Juana's nature to turn everything into a crusade. It made things easier. At the time, I simply found her lovely and mysterious, so I faked a yawn and placed my head on her lap. She ran her fingers through my hair and I felt her heart beating in the softness of her belly. There is a place between heaven and earth, I thought, and young and naive as I was, I knew I was close to it. I lay in her lap dreaming she was dreaming of me. All of which made me hatch an insane plan to spend more time with Sor María Juana, a way in which I could be with her in ways that only the blessed could, a way in which I could see all of her all of the time.

# 20

THERE IS NO CATHOLIC who can be bribed unless you convince them as to the virtue of the service they're rendering and pay them well. It took only three such virtuous acts and one minor act of deception that night to put me inside the walls of Saint Geronimo's and face to face with Sor María Juana's maid servant. For starters, five pesos each to my hall monitor and monastery guard so they'd stay asleep.

Once outside, I spent a little time softening my features and bringing my hair down around my cheeks. I was still young, and Comanche to boot, without a stitch of hair on my body or face. And much can be done with posture and movements which are humble and delicate to convince someone who is not looking to be fooled. I wore my cassock and pulled its hood closely around my head.

Outside Saint Geronimo's, five pesos rewarded a virtuous steward for seeing how important it was for me to contact my big sister, a novitiate, with a personal message from her loving mother. In the servant's quarters, among the Indian girls, conditions were more relaxed, and Sor María Juana's servant, Celia, was delighted to lend me her dress and shoes to take the night off with double pay.

I tucked my jaw, widened my cheeks, and placed her scarf over my head. In this way I brought Sor María Juana the towels for her evening bath, and her tortillas and tea.

"Where is Celia?" she said when she opened her door.

"I'm taking her place tonight," I whispered.

She was dressed in a simple, white robe which touched the floor and she wore a light veil over her hair which, it turned out, was shoulder length and straight. Her room, which I've later found to be like the rooms of many white women, was mostly bath and bed, though more so. A small desk and chair sat near the foot of her feather bed, a reading chair with candle lamp near that, and a huge, deep, ornately tiled bathtub below floor level, a descent of three steps down from the clay tiled floor. There was a cabinet with drawers on which sat a wash bowl, a mirror, and some small, colored bottles. Near the tub, a shade to dress behind, hand painted with scenes of angels; a large armoire, and next to that, a small, wooden chest. There were two windows, one near the desk which looked out into the courtyard, chapel, and garden, and the other, opposite, with a small balcony which opened to a cobblestone alley.

"I'll have tea now," she said, and I broke the crisp tortillas, adding honey, and poured her tea as she sat to read, her face delicately silhouetted under the soft lamp light. I watched the movement of her breasts as she breathed, the minute quiver of her nostrils as she brought in and sent out the spiritual air.

"Are you going to draw the tub?" she said.

I stood dumbly.

"Do you know how?"

"Oh, yes," I said, moving to the tile pit on the other side of the room. I'd had a bath or two since I'd arrived, but the water for our tiny tub was heated tepidly over an open fire and added to the tub bucket by bucket.

"Don't be proud," she said, giggling in that musical way of hers that sent my skin into bumps. "Just pull that valve. A hot spring feeds it. And you'll just pull the other knob to drain it."

I pulled the valve at the top of the tub and the hot water poured in, steaming. It smelled oddly of sulfur, like hot springs do, though I'd always thought Catholics had associated the smell of sulfur with the devil.

When the tub filled I pushed the valve closed and Sor María Juana rose from her chair. She stepped between me and the tub, turning her back to me as she wriggled her feet from her slippers, then unbuttoned her robes. She pulled her garment from her shoulders and allowed it to slip down her white arms, catching it at her wrists where I plucked it away.

Back with the Comanche, I'd often spied on the girls when they bathed together at a stream. But here, alone with the sacred white nun, her skin translucent in the flickering candle light, I thought I might be overcome by the softness; her dark hair falling to her shoulders, her shoulders falling off to her waist, the roundness of her hips and the soft bulges below her armpits where her breasts fell softly.

She walked into the tub. Immersed. I beheld my triumph, the naked Sor María Juana as she soaped her neck and arms. If Christ Himself had invited me into His tabernacle, I couldn't have felt more bestowed than I did by the soft sound of her hands slipping over her skin and the cascading water that blessedly fell from her body and back into the tub.

"What is your name?" Sor María Juana asked me quietly.

"Xocotzin," I said. It was the name for the last phase of the waning crescent moon, a common Aztec name for a youngest daughter. This she would know.

"Your Christian name."

"Adela."

"Santa Adela," she whispered, "from the French, Saint Adelaide, the wife of King Lothair of Italy till his death, and then the second wife of Otto the Great, Emperor of the Holy Roman Empire who died in 973." Sor María Juana almost sang this as she washed. "She was the victim of court politics until she became a great and generous hearted nun and founded a convent in Alsace. Saint Odilo called her a marvel of beauty and goodness," she chanted. Her voice lifted into the air, dropping softly against the stone walls, lighter than velvet, huskier than silk. "Santa Adela, little one, pray for me tonight."

"Yes, Sister," I said.

She lifted her soap and cloth to me, smiling. "My back," she said, and bent toward me.

I gently soaped and rinsed her neck, her shoulders and back, stopping at the water line where the tiny crack of her white buttocks emerged. I almost fainted, but Sor María Juana immersed herself again, pulled the drain valve and stood. I draped dry towels over her as she walked from the tub and took her robe behind the painted screens.

"I'll go now," I said. I figured I had a lifetime of memories already, if not a dangerous addiction.

"Get my gown and habit from the closet," she said, "and then stay. I'll need one more thing."

I got her clothes for her and handed them behind the screen, and it was then that I heard the strumming of a guitar outside the balcony. I went to the window and peered out to where three men began singing. They sang about their swelling, painful hearts, and how they would die without Sor María Juana's prayers if not her love.

"Three?" I said to Sor María Juana as she came up behind me. I guessed that if you weren't going to make love to them, it didn't matter how many suitors you permitted, but I guessed wrong.

"They represent only one," she said, stepping onto her little porch. They threw her roses. She threw them coins. "Now silence," she said to them. "Tell him, now he may come."

She turned back to the room. "Go to the door and let him in, then go," she whispered. "I need your silence, too," and she gave me a peso. "This tryst, unholy or holy, will save Mexico."

She lifted a rug beside her bed that revealed a trap door which led to a stairwell beneath the alley. There, waiting, his arms full with calla lilies and wine, stood the great General Santa Ana.

It goes without saying that my disappointment was monumental, though before I left Sor María Juana's room, Santa Ana gave me enough pesos to break even for the night. And despite my world shattering chagrin, I couldn't pull myself away from the keyhole from where I saw the eventual President of Mexico's very own white butt. Needless to say, it wasn't motionless. And Sor María Juana must have had some Aztec in her, because she went to the sacrifice with indescribable enthusiasm.

So the fireworks in there were almost as good as the fireworks outside, where the liberals of Mexico had temporarily taken things into their own hands and begun their revolution against Iturbide. The streets of Mexico City were full of guns and blood and everyone on both sides of the revolt was looking for Santa Ana to lead them. But they couldn't find him. And they weren't going to look for him in a convent, either, where he waited until he heard which side was going to win, in this case, the liberals. In the morning, he slipped out and headed for his army at Vera Cruz where he declared allegiance to the new Mexican Republic.

I took all this as an indication that it was time for me to leave Mexico. Undoubtedly, my father, Hermano, would wait in Spain until the air cleared and he could return on the winning side. And his instincts had been remarkably accurate. He'd liquidated his fortune in land for a fortune in gold, and in

Mexico, where land was changing hands faster than sweat, it was a lot easier to hide gold than acres.

But for me, the commotion in the streets seemed to cry a real dissatisfaction with the current relationship of power, wealth, and religion. Being young, and in Mexico for the first time, I thought it would be only be a matter of hours before the poor, Aztec population reclaimed all their gold from the churches and didn't rest till every priest, soldier, and Creole was strung up like a trussed turkey.

The best time to show you have nothing is when there's everything to lose. I rushed back to the monastery and gathered up my grubbiest old leather leggings, discarded my shoes for some sandals and ripped up my shirt while the rest of that place slept like a mausoleum under a lightning storm. Well, they were rich. Maybe they didn't understand a crisis. The regular guards sure did. They were nowhere.

I gathered up my pesos and riddled the commissary for tortillas; hid the pesos in a pouch under my armpit and put the tortillas in my pack. I figured if I had to I could walk to the outskirts of the city and all the way to Texas.

I moved quickly down the hallways and out into the garden. Outside the walls occasional gunfire rang out, shouts, and the movement of troops signaled by the thump of feet and the clatter of hooves and wagon wheels. The worst of it though, and if you haven't heard it, well, it's the most frightening thing, the sour crying of the Mexican military trumpets, a blaring combination of Teutonic and Aztec cacophony that's enough to make you beg for death. It convinced me I was witnessing the fall of everything.

Relieved to let my features fall back into their Indian own, I bid farewell to El Ciudad de Mexico. I pulled down my hat and stepped through the gate, only to find a pale figure waiting for me there, my old friend, that white angel of death, the Great Crooked Inquisitor.

He offered a bony finger in my direction.

"Disappointed?" he said.

How could anybody ask you something so vague and absurd in a circumstance like that and be correct? Admittedly, he possessed a certain genius of perception, if not foreknowledge.

"In God?" he said.

"No," I said to him. "God has never disappointed me."

He grinned slightly, scratching his chin. "No," he said, "I'll bet not."

I don't know why I was frightened by him. I could have whisked by him, or pushed by him, or passed through him like a ghost.

"I'm sure I haven't disappointed you," he said, almost straightening up for a moment. "Maybe your mentor, Sor María Juana?"

I could never tell with the Inquisitor whether he knew everything or just acted like he knew everything good enough to get you to confess even if you were sinless.

"She is like all of Mexico," he whispered, "pure of soul, but her body soiled by her own blood."

"That's why I'm going back to Tejas," I said.

"The Church, too, is a woman," he said to me, raising his bone white hands, turning them. They shined like ivory in the torch light. "But her ministers are men." He cocked an eyebrow. "Do not despise Sor María Juana. There is no deed purer than a good intention."

If he was trying to tell me Sor María was bloody and he was bloodless, I believed him. If you ran him through with a lance he'd probably bleed ether or something worse.

"I need a horse," I said.

He motioned toward the stables. "Take two," he said. "Satan himself doomed half the dominion of creation by his own free will, yet within God's inevitable plan." He stepped aside. "The mark of the Church is on you, diablito, little devil, little coyote. You cannot leave Her now, even in Tejas, even in hell."

At another time I'll tell you about the hostile Indians of Sonora and Chihuahua, whose lands you must pass through on the long trip to El Norte, but I don't want to die of old age while I'm trying to write down the stories I lived through. After a long and perilous ride, I reached the land of the Honey Eaters. I returned home. Like any good Comanche, I went first to my horse, Fireblood, who was so happy to see me she tried to bite me and poop on me and kick me. No doubt about it, that mare loved me. Then I went to my mother's lodge. Many Powers barely looked up from a tattered copy of the King James New Testament.

"I'm glad you're back," she said. "It's time to learn English."

21

MY MOTHER GOT THAT Bible from a Presbyterian missionary from Tennessee. He'd rolled into camp looking for his wife who'd been carried off by the Liver Eater Comanche during a raid on Nacogdoches. Knowing that his wife was probably a lot happier with them than she ever was with him, the HorseSleepers listened to him every night for a month, nobody understanding a word. They fattened him up on buffalo and sold him to the Karankawa who ate him. We, ourselves, do not eat Presbyterians. But Many Powers kept his Bible.

That was a good deal for us, given that we didn't even own him. Seeing as I had the New Testament practically memorized in Spanish after spending more than a year with the Jesuits, between the two of us, me and Many Powers learned English pretty good. Many Powers didn't give much of a hoot for Latin or ancient Greek, because nobody spoke them. I tried to explain that they were power and medicine languages for the whites. How when the Catholic priests spoke Latin they turned bread and wine into the body and blood of their God, sort of. She asked me if I ever saw it happen and I said, sure, lots of times. I even ate it.

"You ate the white God," she said. "The big medicine."

"It doesn't look or taste any different," I said. "And nothing changes except how you choose to feel. You have to have faith."

"Ah," she said. "Faith." She'd heard of faith. "When whites believe in crazy ideas."

"Ideas mean a lot to white folk," I said.

"Tell me," she said. "Your father had too many. They made him brood and act crazy."

"That's what I mean," I said. "They're a broody, crazy race." I didn't even want to try to explain about sin or guilt.

Ancient Greek was the power language, I explained. Whites, from what I could gather from the Spanish, liked to keep things separate, like medicine and power for example. They kept their medicine over in religion and spoke Latin about it and kept their power over in science and spoke Greek about it. Though for the Spaniards in general, if not those Jesuits, power and medicine were often big enemies.

Of course this conversation occurred before I got a good Protestant education at Harvard, though my views haven't changed much.

"Many Wounds never explained this," said my mother.

"He couldn't," I said. "For him it was just the natural way. They spend a lot of time in buildings and for them being in those buildings is like being in some separate place from the world. They stay inside those buildings and have a lot of ideas and religion about the world that they hide from and want no part of. Then something natural happens to them anyways, like an earthquake or bad storm or a disease or something and they get all upset and resentful and want to kill everything. They're good at it, too. They make stuff that can kill like you wouldn't believe."

"I told you about the buildings," said my mother. Though I could see Many Powers had her doubts, seeing as I was young and impressionable; but Many Wounds had told her enough over the years about cities and all, so she knew she had to take me seriously.

"Many Wounds loved you," I said, not really knowing. "He's just too white and crazy." Had he been half Indian like some of the Mexicans, he might have had a chance, but being pure Spanish he didn't have a prayer. Now, I could see it.

"It doesn't matter now," Many Powers said. "He had some Coyote in him or you would not exist."

"Maybe," I said. "You want to learn to write?"

"You bet," she said in English.

My mother spent some time in bitterness after the departure of me and Many Wounds, and for a time went back to her girlhood habit of riding out with

raiding parties. Being a widowed shaman, she didn't have to be a virgin. That's
where her liaisons with Always Hits began, and now his lodge and horse corral
were pitched right there next to Many Powers' tipi. When I wasn't doing power
and medicine with Many Powers, I was over at Always Hits training FireBlood
who needed all the training she could get. If that horse didn't want to go
somewhere, she'd jump into the air and turn around, coming down heading in
the opposite direction at full speed.

"What's your problem?" said Always Hits.

"What's my problem?" I cried at him.

"That's a skill. She's very athletic," he said. "Don't keep her from doing a
wonderful thing. Just teach her to do it when you want her to."

That was an important thing to learn about horses. You never teach them a
damn thing. You only get them to do what they want to do anyway when you
want them to do it.

In general, the HorseSleepers were happy enough to have me back, though
as the half-breed son of a female shaman, I was a bit of an anomaly even for the
Comanche. But no one could deny that I had a knowledge of things that were
uncommon to most of my peers. And though I wasn't the best young brave with
a war club or the lance or the bow and arrow, I had a mare who could run like
a falling star and, well, I was smart, even if a little too smart to be brave. But as
Many Powers said to me, "Just because you are not like other men does not mean
you are not a man."

Within a year, Little Owl sent me out again to find another animal power for
my manhood, and Coyote came to me on the first cold night, just before the
dawn, a half-dead rabbit in his jaws. He placed the rodent at my feet.

"Would you kill my protector?" I said to him.

"Would you have her die?" he said. Why did the world have to be so enigmatic?

As snow fell, I took the small animal in my arms and she came to life. She
sprang from my arms and ran across the snow where Coyote was upon her again
quickly, grabbing her neck and breaking it with a shake. He tore the animal
to shreds and laid the pieces in front of me as the sun broke over the distant
hills. When the rays of the morning sun struck the rabbit, her pieces came back
together and she ran into the sky on the first beams of sunlight.

"She will live below the sky warrior's feet," said Coyote.

"Chased by dogs," I said.

"Forever alive," he said. "Some say First Rabbit created the world."

"Some say it was Coyote," I said.

"Only by mistake. Only for fun. Anyway, you are stuck with me now," he said and laughed.

Within another year I took my first buffalo, which wasn't easy, because old FireBlood was the kind of horse who thought she was smarter than you, which might have been true enough from a horse perspective, but not from mine. That horse lived in the moment, and moment to moment it was a new battle to decide who was in charge. For instance, being right handed, I liked to come in on a buffalo's right shoulder off FireBlood's left lead. She preferred the buffalo's left shoulder on her left lead, leaning into the animal while leading with her outside leg. That would've been fine if I wanted to hug a buffalo, but if you want to put a lance through its heart you have to have some distance and leverage. But once I learned to twist away from the animal's head and put my weight into FireBlood's lead leg, I could put an arrow right through a buffalo's wind pipe, no easy trick for a weakling with a bad aim. Soon enough I had half the clan running down buffalo off the opposite side on the wrong lead. There's nothing worse than a smart horse, though you never will learn a damn thing from a dumb one.

The longer I was away from the civilized world of Mexico City, the more it became a dream. And the more I returned to the natural world of human beings, bestowed as I now was with Coyote's guidance, the less I called up any illusions or tricks. The last thing you want to do with your power is use it. Many Powers told me that if you always went around presenting a mask, it was only a matter of time before you lost yourself behind it. So until I proved otherwise, I as still Rabbit to all the HorseSleepers.

Even brave young warriors like us didn't spend all of our time hunting buffalo and elk or organizing raiding parties. In fact there was a whole cadre of us adolescents who didn't have a stitch of coup. We spent time hunting small game and hopping and roping ponies and watching the girls bathe. Some days we hit stones with a stick and ran back and forth between goals. One day somebody left a buffalo bladder out in the sun and the damn thing got rubbery and bouncy and we spent a few days running around with it and kicking it and tackling each other.

Later, remembering the ball courts down in Mexico, I put one of our hoops from the hoop and stick game up in a tree and we threw the buffalo bladder through that. Of course we didn't have any teams or scores. Like everything else we did, everybody just went in and out of the game as they pleased, playing it for themselves, and left with an opinion of how they did. If everybody thought they won, well, so much the better.

It was a time when the river of change seemed to have flowed to an eddy. Now there was talk of a time when no whites existed in the world and how it might happen again. If the Spanish had been on the edge of these Great Plains a hundred years before we arrived, well ten years ago they'd crushed the Americans and now, ten years after that, they were gone too. The Mexicans showed no real appetite for Texas or fighting. We were the lords of all we could see.

Of course we'd heard about the huge, white strongholds in the east where the sun rose, but cities came and went. Indians had built them a thousand years ago or more, up and down the Mississippi River on one side of us and over toward Santa Fe on the other, Tenochtitlan, Babylon, Athens, Rome. Cities come and cities go. They rotted or got conquered or both. But there were never any cities where we lived and there were never going to be any.

All the big white tribes of Europe had been over here and where were they now? Mexico would just be Indian again, simply by interbreeding if nothing else, and the Yankee settlements just east of us, hell, they were easier to harvest than prickly pear. Texas was hell and we were the demons who ran it. We did as we pleased.

But among us, only Many Powers saw it ending. Maybe it was something Hermano-Many Wounds told her, though I'd been right down there in the heart of the Mexican Empire and met the greatest general in the world, Santa Ana himself, and I didn't really see what we had to fear. I told my mother. "He's not coming up here. There's no cities and no nuns."

"Americans," she said. She'd heard how they'd run roughshod on the Creek, Cherokee and Choctaw. And now, white Rangers were annihilating the Karankawa and subduing the Caddo. But those Indians were generally pacifists and farmers, if occasionally cannibals. A bunch of scruffy, musket loading Texans were no match for mounted and fully armed Comanche warriors and if they were, hell, we'd run away.

"You're a boy," she said, "and boys are almost as foolish as men."

"Well, I'm about to be a man," I said, foolish enough to assert it. I glanced over at Always Hits who knew that Turkey Feathers and Wind Sister had planned our raiding party on the Caddo to initiate a lot of the young bucks like me. But Always Hits was wearing the smell that Many Powers gave him the morning he delivered FireBlood.

"I hear your horse calling to you," he said without emotion.

"You will be a man," Many Powers said to me. "Unfortunately there is very little anyone can do about it." She lit some sweet grass and watched the smoke rise straight up to the smoke hole. "It always used to lead us," she said. "Now it goes to the spirits and waits."

"For what?" I said.

Many Powers lit some bitter grass which failed to rise, but sat sourly among us in the air. She whisked it with her hands. "What more is there to say?" she said.

"I am certain I hear his horse calling for him," said Always Hits.

"There is only one thing worse than a man who always wants to make love to you," said Many Powers.

"A man who does not want to make love to you," said Always Hits.

Well, I thought I heard my horse calling me. The next night, Turkey Feathers, Fat Otter, Wind Sister, White's Horse, Doe Skin, Twin Cub and all the others of us danced for our Caddo raid. The raid where we would take our first coup and become warriors. The rest of it you know.

22

THE RAID WAS a disaster, but we'd had recovered our dead. The ride back to camp was too long and hard to bring back the bodies, so we put them to rest by dropping them down a steep, narrow ravine where no human or animal could get down to them. Then we covered them with rocks to keep off the vultures and ravens.

Two days later we found our band camped near the Colorado River and as we'd expected the other members of our divided raiding party had already carried the news of our raid to the village.

It was a glorious and sad thing to die in battle, the best way to die, particularly in victory, which is how we chose to construe the events. Turkey Feather's father, Dark Eagle, was a powerful individual, probably our biggest war chief, and Turkey Feathers was his first son. Three other families, as well, had lost children: White's Horse, Doe Skin, and Twin Cub, on a raid that the women in the band were against from the start. Now a sort of bemused little Caddo womping had turned into an armed conflict of vengeful proportions.

When only a few weeks ago we felt invulnerable, now it seemed like we had horrible enemies in every direction. The Utes, once our brothers, had joined up with the Navaho and were pressing down on the Yamparika, the Root Eater Comanche, in the northwest. From the northeast, the Pawnee, armed with French guns, had cut swathe through Kiowa hunting grounds and were raiding our herds. A young Cochise had the Apache stirred up in the southwest and Texans were kicking ass and taking slaves in the old Spanish colonies to the east.

Dark Eagle, deep in mourning, gave a horse to every family in the band, including three to me, one for each scalp. He gave away buffalo robes and weapons. He took down his tipi and scattered the ashes of his fire in every direction, six in all, including above and below. With three other families in mourning and a dozen others honoring the first coup of their warriors, everything in the tribe that wasn't tied to your favorite horse changed hands several times. Consequently, I gave away everything I owned but FireBlood, including that fine set of Chiricahua bow and arrows I got from Cochise when I was traveling with my father. I gave them to Twin Cub's father, Teaches Horses to Swim. I gave McKenzie's muzzle loader to Dark Eagle and the Bowie knife to Walks Crooked, Doe Skin's mom.

I still came out ahead with a half-dozen ponies, several Cheyenne blankets, buffalo robes, skins for my own, new lodge. I got a buffalo lance from Always Hits and a new bow and arrows from Fat Otter's dad, the singer, White Calf. Wind Sister gave me her war club in return for Henry Wax Karnes Jr.'s musket, and Little Owl, now an old man himself, gave me his grandfather's spirit chaser war shield from which he'd hung strips of pelt and teeth from a coyote. Teaches Horses to Swim gave Cochise's bow and arrow to Fat Otter who gave it back to me.

Women related to the dead scarred their forearms and cut off their hair. Wind Sister vowed she wouldn't marry until she had the scalp of Turkey Feather's killer. That would most likely be Henry Wax Karnes, himself, I said to her, Henry Wax Karnes who undoubtedly had made the same vow about the scalp of yours truly.

"I will take him with his son's rifle," she said.

We danced hard and long all night, despite being tired from our long ride. And as the stars circled and the sliver moon rose, the story of my medicine grew.

Near dawn I walked from the fire and sat. Across from me, one of Fat Otter's sisters danced. Her hair, thick and unbraided, fell over her shoulders. She had just run behind the pony each girl was given when she became a woman, and now she danced in the soft, yellow hide of a buffalo calf, the first dress of her womanhood. Myself, I'd just buried our raiding party's war chief, saved lives, taken lives and scalp, and returned with coup. I was a warrior now whether I liked it or not.

Since I'd returned from the raid, besides receiving gifts I had been given the great honor of being left absolutely alone unless I chose to draw someone to me by contacting them with my eyes. I guess I'd been watching that girl, but to be honest, if I made eye contact, I'd have to say it was at best inadvertent. She came over to me and sat down anyway.

"You will need someone to build and care for your lodge," she said.

I looked at her now up close, the fire crackling at us in the gray dawn. To be honest, I wasn't that attracted. Curious maybe. She seemed to have big, petite features.

And I couldn't really tell if she was fat or skinny. She seemed robust and delicate and had a way of looking at you meekly with her unusual nose pointed down with the tenacity of a badger. Her eyes, peering over the bridge of that nose, were as soft as a doe's and as piercing as an eagle's. Under the hoarse singing of the chanters and the drums and whistles of the dancers, her voice sounded as soft as a powerful river in the distance.

"I think I hear my horse calling for me," I said, standing up.

"Oh," she said, "one of those."

"One of those what?"

"A boy who only loves his horse."

"A man," I said. "A warrior."

She giggled at me. A thrilling sound, so soft and condescending it made my nipples hard. That giggle made Sor María Juana's trill sound like a roosting bird's. I guess I am just a victim of female laughter.

She pointed to the east ahead of the splaying light of dawn where the morning star flashed out like the blue stones the Zuni worship. She turned from me. She walked away and then turned slightly, speaking to me over her shoulder. "That is me," she said.

Most Comanche men don't take wives until well into their thirties. If you couldn't live that long you probably couldn't produce worthy offspring anyway. At that point one tended to take a younger wife because, well, they're younger, or as Many Powers said, a great warrior is barely a match for an innocent girl.

Unlike some other plains tribes, we didn't have warrior societies serviced by women-men, berdaches to some. The Cheyenne, who had a club or category for everything, called them heemaneh, helpers of the Dog Soldiers. Back in old Europe I guess they'd be squires. Nonetheless, we Comanche had our share of women-men, but our warriors didn't use them as helpers. And not being wordy people, we just never gave the activity a name. So sometimes, among us, young women became warrior helpers until the warrior or the girl moved on.

Not even the Cheyenne had a name for a warrior princess like Wind Sister. We ourselves just tended to let them be what they were. I'll say this here and I won't elaborate, but Wind Sister had never gone anywhere without Doe Skin, and whatever her business with Turkey Feathers, she mourned Doe Skin's death equally and coveted an equal vengeance for it.

A young man could always take things into his own hands. I don't want to be more specific, but you can have sex with yourself. That's what sweat lodges were for, among many other things. But you can't do that for twenty years and remain sane. That's another reason some of the other plains tribes had Contraries, crazy warriors who did everything backwards and lived to die fighting. That's what celibacy will turn you into. Anyways, that's what it does to an Indian. And that's why Contraries stop being so contrary when they marry. In fact, they're notorious for marrying dominating widows, being no match for innocent girls, I suppose.

But most of us were just regular people and had to solve things in regular ways. We didn't go in much for adultery, as whites called it; it just made for trouble. But we practiced sex before pairing and especially among young people it was as common as daylight. Older girls tended to matriculate younger boys into the world of sex by sneaking into their tipis. That's how they kept warm until they chose a warrior and then his family went through the charade of asking her family for a marriage. Us young bachelor stallions were just practice for them, but for our part we could use all the practice we could get. If you were a real sad case, you tried to place yourself conveniently in locations where the girl you'd taken a fondness to often passed by, preferably someplace private. If you were lucky she bothered to notice you.

I'm kind of going through all of this because I had to explain it around then to a Frenchman who came wandering into the tribe around this time. I know it might seem odd, but if a Comanche happened to find you wandering around the plains he might be as liable to hug you as skewer you, though you'd have a lot better chance if you were friendly and offered him something to eat. As a people, Comanche men loved eating almost as much as we loved riding and fighting. But if you happened to wander into our camp, hell, we'd treat you like a brother. Smoke with you, feed you, give you presents. Don't ask me why, we were big on hospitality. Though if you stayed too long you might get traded for something because as much as Comanche men liked gambling, the women liked trading, and we liked pleasing them. So you might get adopted and traded for a tanned buffalo coat or a shiny sea shell before you could blink. If you had a fast horse and a happy wife, you were one satisfied Comanche.

Now one day, completely by accident, I happened to be looking for a cottonwood switch to whack old FireBlood with so I could get her to cooperate without having to speak Latin, and I guess I wandered near the path the girls used to go down to the stream to bathe, because I looked up and there was Morning Star, eying me like I'd placed myself there for her to find me. She had a way of staring sideways over that expressive nose of hers that made you think she was looking over it, as well as looking right at you, with both eyes, which, of course, was impossible.

"Looking for me?" she said.

According to her, I responded, "All my life," though I could hardly have meant it, not having had much of a life till then.

She stepped from the path and into the brush and the next thing I knew, I kissed her on the lips. She immediately lowered her forehead gently to my chin and clutched at my chest with her nails, just enough for me to feel them. I had never felt anything so demure and wild at the same time. Then she stepped back, running her hands down my arms until my fingertips rested in her palms.

Back in the direction of the lodges, I heard the commotion of whinnying horses and barking dogs, and then shouting. She tilted her right brow at me and smiled before I ran back toward camp.

# 23

IT WAS THE ARRIVAL of the famous French scientist Alexis de Tocqueville. He came riding in with a couple of mules, one packed with coffee and wine skins and the other with pens, ink and paper, our dogs yapping at the feet of his tired horse. Of all the white tribes we dealt with, the French always seemed the easiest to get along with, willing to trade what they had for what we had and then leave us alone. They'd been an easy source for guns and ammunition in times gone by, figuring, I guess, that the havoc the Indians wreaked on the Spanish and English was all the better for them. But then the British ran them out of the north and the Americans bought them out of the south.

That's when the Creeks and the Choctaw and Cherokee found out the difference between the French and the Yankees. But we still ran into French trappers and traders out of New Orleans now and then, as well as these science types.

As I've said before, we were friendly enough to anybody who wandered into camp. Indians in general are great hosts, though among the Comanche you had as good a chance of getting ignored as you did killed. We didn't really have anybody we sent out to greet people.

Tocqueville kind of caught us in the breach between mourning and revenge. He sat there in the middle of camp, announcing in French that he wanted to speak to the chief, except we didn't have a chief. And how many of us did he think spoke French? He tried signing, as well, but nobody would look at him.

Morning Star poked me from behind. "I bet you speak that white tongue," she said.

"*Un peu*," said I, "a little," which struck Morning Star as pretty funny.

"Well," she said, "be a man a little."

That was kind of a joke, but you'd have to be a Comanche to understand it. It's another thing that whites never understood about us. We liked to kid around all the time, often with a straight face.

It was a chance to practice my French, if nothing else.

I gathered up FireBlood and threw on enough of my war equipment to look *formidable*, as the French might say, then rode over to the Frenchman. Fireblood was in one of her disagreeable moods, of which she had many, so we kind of danced around him sideways and he had to rotate his head to keep track of us. We probably looked pretty warlike and fiery, but really it was just my lack of control. FireBlood's ears were going haywire to boot, because she'd never seen or in particular smelled a Frenchman before; they kind of smell like a dead flower. She had one ear straight down sideways and the other rotating, indicating she thought he might be some cross between a Pawnee Contrary and a she-bear in heat.

I said, "*Bon matin*," and Tocqueville took off in French without a blink, explaining his whole scientific enterprise, some of which I understood— disinterested study and all that—though I hadn't been to Harvard yet and didn't understand a lot of the subtleties.

Tocqueville was studying America and currently gathering artifacts and recording Indian cultures throughout the northern continent before we were all wiped out. Thoughtful of him.

"*Dum vivimus vivamus*," I said to him, which is Latin for "While we live, let us live."

"*Monstre sacre!*" said Tocqueville. "Latin!"

"Do you speak it?" I said in French.

"Some," he said. "Very little."

"Well everybody here speaks it, but they probably won't do it in front of you."

"And French as well?"

"Only on the chief's birthday and she's not here right now. We speak Spanish at weddings, English at funerals."

"Your leader is a woman?"

"*Dux femina facti*," I said. "*Cherche la femme.* Woman always leads, *ne c'est pas?*" It was a bit of a misquote in each case, but you know what happens in translation, especially out in the middle of nowhere.

"This is remarkable!" said Alexis de Tocqueville. "I must stay here and study you."

I've always said that there's nothing more gullible than a scientist, especially if he thinks he's discovered something. Everything he sees will prove to himself he's right.

"*Cui bono*," I said. "What's in it for us?"

"Coffee? Tobacco? Wine? The perpetuation of your culture for posterity?"

"'French wine?" I said. I knew a little about it from my picnics with Sor María Juana. Catholics are wine drinkers. And those Spanish padres felt you should be working with the best ingredients possible if you were going to change it into the blood of Christ.

"But of course," he said.

"Bordeaux?"

"Burgundy."

"We prefer a Bordeaux," I said. "But not too young."

"But surely," stuttered Tocqueville.

I raised my hand to silence him and turned FireBlood to walk away.

"*Sacre bleu!* All right," he said. "I have a little Bordeaux."

I whistled and a pack of adolescents, who now shadowed me everywhere in my new warrior status, showed up and carted his food mule to my lodge.

"But monsieur," he said.

"Monsieur Coyote. *Et toi?*"

He introduced himself. "But Monsieur Coyote," he said, almost crying. "My wine!"

"It's like money in the bank," I said. "We'll pay you back double in all the dog you can eat. Now don't walk anywhere. Always ride. And sleep with your horse or somebody will take it."

I had some of the young girls and a few of the boys who liked practicing housekeeping set up a little tipi for him, not too far from mine, just big enough for him and his horse. Then I spent the day giving everybody in the band a phrase or two in English, Spanish, French, Latin, or ancient Greek—whatever else they said to him could be in sign language or Comanche—just something they could spout at Tocqueville when he came around. It was a day's labor, but important for him to learn our culture.

# 24

SOME INDIAN TRIBES got rubbed out by whites in a blink. Others, near the end of their wars, started talking story to them and letting them write it down, so there'd be something left. Everybody, individuals and tribes alike, had a lot invested in how that came across and you'd have to be a member of that particular tribe to know where the fibs lay in that kind of storytelling. Others, like us, kept their mouths shut or told outright lies. As Many Powers said, all victories and defeats are temporary.

It was early in The Moon of the First Cold Wind, but the first cold wind of the month whipped up that evening. Snow fell from the gray dusk and coated the ground, the lodges casting blue shadows under the occasional moonlight. It was a great night to be a Comanche.

I rode FireBlood up to the crest where the other young warriors were riding naked and letting the first snow melt on their hot chests. Not that we liked snow, but like everybody else, we liked the first snowfall. Especially since in some years we didn't get any snow at all, particularly when we kept winter camp at the south edge of the plains. Up here on the plateau, things were less predictable. Thick Robes had suggested we were in for a harsh winter, based on the thickness of the buffalo hides and the fur on our ponies. But contrary to what people have come to believe in that regard, animals were as fallible in predicting the weather as anybody. Sometimes they even had something at stake in lying to you. If you don't think there's such a thing as a dishonest animal you're a fool.

We had quite a time up there, on the crest between summer and winter, boyhood and manhood, youth and death, sorrow and revenge, all of that going unsaid, of course. There was a big meeting coming up about what to do about the Caddos and the Rangers and though there wasn't a coward among us, that blanket of snow covered some blood, so to speak. We tended not to fight in the winter. It put things off.

I remember pulling up FireBlood in that circle of fury, young bucks taking coup on each other like a game of tag, sweating underneath the snow, the steam pouring off my pony and seething from her nose as her heart pounded beneath me. I peered down that hill at a semi-circle of elders who stood wrapped in Cheyenne blankets outside Dark Eagle's lodge, the smoke from their pipes rising up into the snowflakes. The established warriors were riding off to the sweat lodge, the girls throwing snowballs and the women making fires. The smell of roasting buffalo was enough to make your gums hurt. Alexis de Tocqueville, wrapped in his smelly French wool, sat outside his little tipi on the back of his tired horse, his cold, scientific eye scrutinizing us savages. Talks Peace's youngest son, Sad Little Dog, rode by and yelled at him, *"Aut vitam aut culpam!"* which in Latin means, "You just behave yourself!" though the kid didn't know that.

I took a thump on the back of the neck and turned to see Fat Otter ride by and then pull up, the darkness coming down now as fast as the snow.

"You're not invisible," he said.

"No," I said, rubbing the back of my neck. "Just in awe." He'd given me a headache. "All Comanches are gray in the dark," I told him.

He took another swing at me, but FireBlood, a better warrior than me, simply sidestepped his blow.

"Haa!" he said. "I swung at a ghost!"

Well, neither honesty nor wisdom ever pay.

"There will be a war council," he panted, his round body both perched and planted onto the back of Two Sides, his stout paint.

FireBlood turned her butt to the two of them and launched a stream of mucous urine. As I stood in the stirrups, Fat Otter struggled with Two Sides who, though gelded, could still go rigid and mount a hot mare. Mares seldom come into season in the winter, unless provoked by stallions. I didn't think

Fireblood would come in season again until spring, but it seemed she had one more in her. I pushed FireBlood forward as she rumbled a come-on at Fat Otter's pony. My horse just liked to make trouble.

"She wants to make me jealous of a gelding," I said.

"It doesn't matter who loves who once you are on their backs," said Fat Otter, which is something Comanches often said to each other when one of them professed affection for his horse. It meant a lot of things you couldn't understand if you weren't a horse person and understood all of them immediately, but it usually had to do with making your horse obey you when it was underneath you, when, in fact, a horse often has a lot of ideas and desires of its own. If you've never been in love with your horse then it's hard to explain.

"You're turning into Turkey Feathers?" I said.

"Shouldn't someone? Besides, I am not the one who changes from one thing to another, you are."

I took out my knife and held it on my wrist, a sign I was willing to mix blood with him. "Would you be the battle brother of a Coyote?" I said.

"I will more likely be your brother-in-law first."

"I am not interested in Morning Star," I said.

"What does that have to do with it?" said Fat Otter. We drew blood there, astride our horses, as the snow came down around us and the darkness blackened. Fat Otter turned Two Sides and rode off and I took FireBlood down into camp.

I don't know why I ended up where I did. I guess I was just feeling warm and brotherly toward Fat Otter and, I don't know, it was just on my way, but I stopped outside White Calf's lodges for a moment. White Calf had a big family and couldn't keep them all in one tipi. The warm smell of buffalo wafted through the snowflakes and the next thing I knew I was standing at a lodge door when a hand came out and pulled me in.

Morning Star pulled me down on top of her and placed me between her legs. Half-way through I wasn't even sure I liked it, but before we were done I thought it was okay. I sat up and looked around. "What happened?" I said.

Morning Star got up and came back with two cups of wine.

"Where did you get this? What are we doing?" I said to her.

"Didn't you say you preferred Bordeaux?"

"Where is everybody?"

"I find it a strange taste, myself," said Morning Star.

"You don't speak French," I said to her.

"Your mother does."

"My mother?"

"I speak the language of women. Many Powers speaks French. Do you think the Frenchman is the only one going around like a blind fool? Look to yourself. Anyway, we gave him back some of his wine. He is an idiot, but not a complete idiot like some."

"Like me?"

"Do not get moody," said Morning Star, taking my wine and sitting herself down, face to face, on my lap. "I barely like you and will not live with a man who makes love and gets in a mood."

"Well, I barely like you," I said.

"Uhmmm hmm," said Morning Star. She placed her naked breasts on my chest, placed me inside her softness and held me by the hair. "Then it will be difficult to seduce me," she said.

Truer words have never been spoken. So there are things you don't learn in the sweat lodge.

# 25

WE ALL MET THE NEXT MORNING, the world covered with snow. Anybody who wanted to come to these things could, because we didn't have any rules. We didn't come to any conclusions. Nobody voted. Everybody did what they wanted when we were done.

It started at Dark Eagle's because it was his idea, but too many people came so we couldn't fit in his lodge. We moved outside and built a fire and since we had a fire it seemed a waste not to cook something since we had a lot of buffalo meat, and it would be senseless not to do a bunch of smoking since we had a lot of Tocqueville's tobacco. There are two ways to deal with abundance and I needn't point out how we dealt with it.

Before any of that, I ran into Tocqueville on the way to my lodge in the morning because I'd spent the night with Morning Star.

"Are you going to marry that girl?" he said.

"*Valenti non fit injuria,*" I said, which in Latin means, To a willing person no harm is done.

"What language will you speak at the pow-wow?"

"*La nuestra,*" I said in Spanish. Our own.

"I suppose I cannot come?" he muttered.

I wasn't going to tell him he could if he hadn't figured that out for himself. I tied up FireBlood and rode off on another horse. I'm a moody individual, if you can't tell, and Morning Star had kept my moodiness in check all night.

When I got there I sat down next to Many Powers who sat to the right of Always Hits.

"How was the Bordeaux?" she asked without looking at me

"To be honest, Mother," I said, "French wines finish a little light at the back of the palate. I got used to heavier, Spanish wines in Mexico."

"I did not care for it myself," she said. "It contains a lethargic spirit, bad for love and war as well."

Comanche, in general, unlike a lot of Indians, weren't that big on coffee or whiskey. We were already completely wild and didn't need it to loosen us up.

"White people have to make themselves half asleep before they can do anything," I said. "Relax, fight, make love, pray."

"Nonetheless, you were pleased that a woman went through so much trouble for you. Men are easy. If you think you proved something last night, that's all you proved."

Always Hits leaned over and spoke to me over Many Powers' breasts.

"The Burgundy worked well for me," he said.

My mother's chin barely moved in his direction. The corner of her lip broke in the slightest smile. "Men are good for fighting," she said, her chin moved slightly toward me, "and mating."

Well, besides horses and hunting, what the hell else was there? Eating. That was it. But though the Comanche didn't have a word for it, Many Powers was a philosopher. Born a white man she'd have ruled the world. I told her that once and she said, "Born a white man, I would have been married to a woman like me."

Being simple, it took me most of my life to figure that out, but I guess she meant what she always meant, that women have all the significant ideas and men just ignore the best of them and steal the rest. If she were a white man, she wouldn't be Many Powers, a Comanche shaman, she'd be a white man, the same as any of them.

Hits and she grinned when she said it.

It looked like everybody was there for this meeting. Dark Eagle passed his pipe and the sun rose higher in the sky before the pipe made its way back. He wore his buckskin and eagle feathers, and held his war lance. He stood and talked about a lot of stuff: how good the sun was, even on this cold day; how lucky we were be Comanche, free on the plains like the wind, the buffalo, the horse; what a lucky man he was to have his wife and family, and his son who died honorably in battle. He was glad everybody came to talk, because he was considering what form his revenge should take, when, and against whom. For now, that's what he had to say.

Talks Peace talked peace, of course. That was his job. "It is winter now," he said. "We lost young warriors, but we took many lives, as well. These Texans are not like the Wichita or the Apache, or even the Spanish or Mexicans. We will not quiet them with a harsh blow. Let's listen to the Earth and wait."

That's when Wind Sister spoke out. "Last night the ghost of Turkey Feathers came to me as a snake and lay on my belly. Now I am with child. The Moon of Flowers will be too late for me to ride and avenge Turkey Feathers and his son will be born in a world without balance."

Now if you think she believed that a snake who was really Turkey Feathers had impregnated her, or that any of us believed it either, than you're as silly as Alexis de Tocqueville, who I saw sneaking around at the edge of the circle, not knowing that nobody cared whether he was there or not. Though probably that snake really did come to Wind Sister in a dream and, for us, dreams were as important as anything else. If you don't pay attention to your own dreams, then what do you pay attention to? What everybody knew now was that she'd likely slept with Turkey and put a curse on the Caddo raid. She let the band know that without admitting to it. Now her child had a father, whether Turkey Feathers did it when he was alive or later as a snake or an otter or a ghost. It didn't matter, among the HorseSleepers virgin birth was as common as cacti. But to have that baby come forth while his father's murderer was still stalking the earth would be outright shameful.

I knew everybody was going to want me to talk, because I was the hero of the raid and in my family Always Hits was better known as a horseman and a lover than a warrior. Many Powers always found battle irrelevant. Lucky for me, people hardly understood my point when I spoke anyway. Not that it mattered, the way that Wind Sister had put us all in front of a spear.

The parents of White's Horse, who had no other male children, as well as Doe Skin's parents and two older brothers, got up and stood behind Dark Eagle. Wind Sister stood.

"It's senseless to punish the Caddos," said Thick Robes from where she sat next to Talks Peace.

"Brother," said Fat Otter to me. "How do you kill Texans?"

You just knock them on the head like anybody else, I wanted to say. It isn't how they die, but how they kill. "They are cruel and relentless," I said.

Always Hits spoke. "Do they die like cowards then, if they kill like cowards?"

"They're all individuals," I started to say, but Many Powers stopped me with a glance before I went off on nonsense, true as it might be.

"It is difficult with the Rangers," said Dark Eagle, "in that you cannot find them. They wait for us to strike, then gather quickly and follow. They pursue us when we scatter."

"Then we'll send a small raiding party," said Wind Sister. "Let them pursue us into a waiting war party." She was a born strategist and it was too bad she'd soon be making babies instead of war.

"That will work once," said Many Powers.

"Then let it work once then," said Fat Otter's father, White Calf. He stood.

"In Mexico they say a great war is coming against the Yankees. They do not mention us," I said.

I waited, hoping somebody would conclude that we should let the Texans and Mexicans fight it out, but nobody did.

"You've taken Karnes' son and given me his rifle which I will give to my son," Wind Sister said to me. "You don't have to come."

"Oh, he's got more sons and more rifles, too, I'm sure," I said. I stood up.

"Talks Peace," said Dark Eagle. "Let the Earth, our mother, speak. When the snow melts I will ride."

There was a lot of hooting and log pounding after that, whistling and dancing, but no rifle fire. We may have been anarchists, but we were also a disciplined, warrior society, like the Spartans, in fact. Anyway, we never wasted a shot. Unlike arrows, you can't go retrieve musket balls very easily and we didn't have the wherewithal to make our own.

White Calf broke out in song:

When the snow melts
We will take the hair of Texans
They will know who we are
The People, Lords of the Plains


It may seem awful literal to you, but he meant it. He sang it over and over and everyone started joining in. I looked across the way where Morning Star stood behind White Calf and Fat Otter and the rest of the family. She gave me that look a woman will give you. You idiot, it said.

I shot her my hardest, stoic, warrior glance. It said, Of course I'm going. I'm going to fight. I guess we were in love.

In two days the snow melted and Dark Eagle and the other war chiefs began to get ready, though Dark Eagle himself would be the absolute authority during the raid. He'd proven himself plenty of times. Each of us gathered our ponies, our weapons, and our medicine bags. We stocked up on buffalo jerky. Everywhere there was the great, beautiful silence around the sounds of getting ready: the nickering of the horses and the shuffling of their hooves, the stretching of leather and clatter of gathered arrows, the click of arrowhead sliding against arrowhead as you placed them in your quiver. And around it all, the silence of the women.

If you read anything about Indians nowadays, you'd think we operated like a beehive. But every woman who sent a man off to battle, or went off to fight in it herself, had her own opinion about it, filled with various mixtures of love, loyalty, ferocity, hate, and despair. A joyous heart for every heart broken. And every warrior who went off had his reasons and opinions, too. My mother, Many Powers, who'd rode into battle, irrelevant as she found it, never said a word to me before I went off.

My new lover, Morning Star, on the other hand, said, "I would like a big, Texan knife."

"It's not a shopping trip," I said.

"A Bowie knife."

"I'm too young to marry," I said sternly.

"Everything is a shopping trip," said Morning Star. "You will never be a good mate if you fail to understand that."

"I'll see what I can do," I said.

She clutched me by the chest in that way of hers that just made me crazy. "If I liked you more I would ask for a rifle."

It was a good thing we didn't like each other much or we'd have been miserable with gifts. So I left my new, difficult lover and my troublesome, wise mother and got on my clever, irritable mare. Alexis de Tocqueville was waiting outside his little tent.

"Are you going into battle, Monsieur Coyote?" he asked.

"The dead will follow the dead," I said to him in Comanche.

"*Je ne comprends pas,*" said Tocqueville.

*"Amor gignit amorem. Mors ianua vitae,"* I said, which in Latin kind of means that love begets love, but death begets it all. "Every so often, in the fall, all the young men leave their bands and travel to other bands and live with other women. It's a big deal that's got to do with death and love and the passing of things," I said. *"Capiche?"*

"You are a very strange man," he said. "I never know what to believe."

"Don't believe anything," I said.

"Everyone here utters a phrase to me, in Latin, French, but always the same. They never really wish to speak."

"It's because you're an outsider," I told him. "But if you want to join the tribe, you'll have to eat a raw skunk's butt. Every warrior and woman has to do it eventually or we pack them off to the Apaches." I gathered up my ponies.

"I will think about this while you are away," he said.

With that I rode over and found Always Hits and the two of us joined the party as it formed at the edge of the camp. Dark Eagle rode forward and we followed him. We were striking at the center of white Texas. San Felipe de Austin.

26

SINCE THE LAST TIME we'd traveled toward Austin, there were more
settlements, more ranches, more farms, and as we moved east, it wasn't easy to
travel undetected amid all that settling. And though we didn't believe in land
ownership, we'd always pretty much regarded the territory west of Austin as
our range. Two days out we camped at the Flint Rock Waterfalls west of San
Felipe. Dark Eagle and a number of the older men were clearly disturbed by all
this incursion.

It was said that Stephen F. Austin, and Sam Houston, too, were friendly toward
Indians in general, and Mexicans as well. In fact, despite being a Yankee, Austin
had become a Mexican citizen. White Calf reminded everybody of that as we met
in council that night.

"He is not my friend," said Fat Otter to his father. "He is not our friend."

"He does not need us. He has enough friends," said White Calf.

"He has too many friends," said Dark Eagle. Meaning a man with that many
alliances couldn't be trusted.

We were about to plan our raid when Wind Sister and a dozen others who'd
broken off from the party earlier in the day, rode hot into camp with about twenty
new horses, two white children, a boy and a girl, a half dozen scalps, and a dead
HorseSleeper, Wet Badger, strapped into his saddle.

Wind Sister, who could still ride, but not lead, pulled up her sweating stallion and raised a long scalp. From the looks of it, it was a woman's. "It has begun," Wind Sister said.

Apparently a little horse stealing episode had turned into a full scale misunderstanding. A Comanche can steal a horse right out from under your nose if he chooses, just to humiliate you. Other times we want you to know we're doing it, just to humiliate you. If you're a half decent human being, you'll accept it or try to steal your horses back. There doesn't have to be any fighting involved. But these Texans, when you tried to steal their livestock, they tried to kill you and that tended to produce hard feelings. It happened all the time and we pretty much saw it as a refusal on their part to learn our ways.

In this case, nobody minded too much that we'd been discovered. Getting discovered had been part of Sister's mission in the first place. There was nothing like a little horse stealing in the area to get Texan ears up for Comanche and that's what we wanted. But I guess one of the ranch women had been up late and heard the horses stirring. Minutes later the men came out firing, which might have been okay had they not killed Badger. People wonder why they got slaughtered by Indians and got their ranches burned down. Well, that's how. Ourselves, we tended not to kill women unless they were toting muskets. As to the slaughter of children, we tended to take them captive. All the stories I heard about smashing babies against trees were made up by whites. I mean who the hell would smash a baby against a tree? Though as things went on, Comanche raids got more brutal. But war is brutal and we didn't invent it.

Wind Sister dismounted.

"There were no survivors," said Dark Eagle.

She said, "No."

Dark Eagle was calculating how long it would take for word to get out. Probably a day or two at the most. But more, we hadn't planned on any violence against anybody but warriors. This revenge raid was against the Rangers, not against the populace in general. Now things were going to get bloody. You could see it in the eyes of the braves who'd returned from the skirmish, and it was infectious.

"The plan is unchanged," said Dark Eagle. He spoke to everybody, but he looked at Sister. "But you should not ride to Austin with blood in your eyes and on your hands." What he meant was, despite this disaster, we weren't heading into San Felipe de Austin to do battle, but to draw out the Rangers. The ranch killings were an aberration, an accident, and it was too bad, but we hadn't intended it and we'd go on as before. As a group, we were formally disassociated from the incident and to our minds it was over.

"Coyote," he said to me, "you will lead them in."

Once honor is bestowed upon you, there's no escaping it. Put another way, among the Comanche a half-breed has to prove himself a million times. It's how a coward like me becomes a famous killer. Before the HorseSleepers were done with me, I'd be so deep into the legend of their atrocities that I wouldn't be accepted anywhere in the world but among them. Always Hits put his hand on the back of my neck. Fat Otter hugged me so hard he wept. Like it or not, I would be a war chief.

# 27

I TOOK MY RAIDING PARTY out in the morning, a dozen of us, including Fat Otter. We had already prayed over our medicine and painted ourselves and our war ponies, and because the ride was short we carried no supplies and brought no extra horses. Still, I held up the attack on the outskirts of the city. As much as Dark Eagle wanted last night's raid wiped from our memory, now that the unfortunate event had occurred I thought we should use it to our advantage. Besides, this was my raiding party and I was its war chief.

"You're all going to wait here," I said. "Maybe overnight. I'm going into town to see what's going on."

"The others are waiting, brother," said Fat Otter.

"We'll send a runner back when we go in."

"Are you going to make yourself invisible?"

"Kind of."

Fat Otter had taken to wearing the floppy, wide brimmed hat he'd acquired when he and Sister showed up at Ghost Mountain after my encounter with Erastus Smith, Old John McKenzie, and Henry Wax Karnes Jr. That hat had dropped off Erastus as he ran away and Fat Otter had picked it up and added a few feathers. I made him lend me that hat. Unlike a lot of the other braves, I always wore the plainest buckskins, and with my hair tucked up under that hat, and carrying a knife and musket, I figured I could maybe pass for some kind of white guy. I wiped off my war paint, of course, and threw a lot of dust on my face, caked it on some with saliva. I'd wait till I'd left the others before I actually tried to change my features.

"Everybody wait here," I said.

"Return with my hat," said Fat Otter"

"If I'm not back by noon tomorrow," I said to Otter, "then you come and get it. But keep your eyes out and your ponies ready to run. If I'm lucky you might not have to ride into Austin at all."

Indians are excellent at waiting and the Comanche are the best of Indians. They'd just sit there like bobcats waiting for a mouse. I knew it. I threw some blankets over FireBlood's saddle, so just the stirrups showed. Most whites thought we rode bareback, so just the sight of the stirrups would be enough to throw them off. I wiped off her paint and took out her war braid. I put my knife at my hip and cradled the rifle in front of me on my forearm. "Now don't be an idiot," I said to FireBlood, and we walked into Austin.

I called on Coyote on the way in. I concentrated on my father's features. Called forth my white half. I prayed to all things above me and below me, in front of me and behind me, to my right and to my left; to the four-leggeds and to the two-leggeds, the water people, the air people. Coyote walked out onto the plain, and behind him I saw Doe Skin. The skin on the back of my hands began to turn pale and I became longer and more rigid. From Doe Skin I became aware that I would have to let a little death inside of me to become a white man.

Being Comanche, I might have been a bit irreligious, but I was no cynic. I thanked Coyote and Doe Skin both. By the time I reached the edge of Austin I was pretty confident. Given all I'd been through, I guessed I knew more about being white than half the whites themselves.

# 28

IT WAS JUST MY LUCK that the first person I encountered was old Erastus Smith. I was wearing his hat and just over the hill I had John McKenzie's and Henry Wax Karnes Jr.'s scalps on my war lance. But I couldn't avoid him. San Felipe de Austin wasn't much back then. In fact it was more or less a kind of hacienda with a couple hundred people who serviced the ranch settlements around it, most of them in what used to be Caddoan Indian land east of there between the Colorado River and the River Brazos. Everybody there was supposed to be Catholic, because it was Mexico, but there weren't ten Mexicans in the town, no church, and but one priest who traveled among San Felipe and the other Texan settlements: San Antonio de Béjar, Washington-on-the Brazos, González, Goliad-La Bahia, Nacogdoches, etc., trying to find a real Catholic.

Most the population was white and male, and if any religion at all, then Protestant Methodist, so they drew the morality line at being drunk in public. It being okay to drink in private, they had a lot of saloons. Stephen F. Austin himself had a big house there that his daddy built, a kind of governor's mansion, but there wasn't a town square around it like in the Spanish or Mexican towns. Like most American towns, as I was to learn, Austin was not a community as much as a hotbed of financial interests. So I rode up to the first saloon and there at the door of the place sat Erastus. I could see his dim intelligence flickering with recognition. Had he been an animal, and not a man with his pride and the legend of his self in the way, I'd have been dead the minute my smell went under his nose. One bit of knowledge that saved me a hundred times was that just like almost any man who got on a horse thought he could ride one, so too, any man who had a thought, thought he was a thinker. It didn't take much for most men to impress themselves.

"You're a stranger," said Erastus, getting up from his chair in front of the saloon.

"Not to me I'm not," I said. As I've said before, my habit of not making any sense was deeper than my desire to communicate, and that seemed to be the case whether I was cavorting with Quanah Parker, Henry James, or Erastus Smith. Lucky for me, nobody seemed to take it personally.

"But you look familiar," Erastus said.

"Well, I told you I was," I said.

He scratched the back of his head with one hand and put his hand on his pistol with the other. "That's a nice rifle," he said.

"Yes, it is," I said. "I got it in Béjar."

"You mean San Antonio."

"I meant San Antonio," I said. Mexicans called it Béjar. Yankees, San Antonio.

"You Spanish?" said Erastus. "Mexican?"

Most Yankees got Mexicans and Spanish mixed up.

"You speak any Spanish?" said I.

"A little."

"I'm not Spanish."

"French?"

"Maybe."

"Maybe?"

"You know any Italians?" I asked him.

"'What's an Italian?" said Erastus.

"I'm Italian. I'm Roberto Donatelli,"

"Donna is a funny name for a man. You're lucky it's your second name, I guess, and not your first name," he said. He was eyeing his hat now. "That hat looks familiar."

"This style is real popular in Rome," I said. "In the Senate. Aren't you Erastus Deaf Smith, the famous scout?"

He perked up at that. I was studying his new wide brimmed hat and I could see it wasn't nearly as nice as his old one; a lot stiffer and no feathers.

"You and Henry Wax Karnes are famous all the way to Europe," I said.

"That so?" said Erastus Smith. "How would you know?"

"I'm an Italian. Italy is in Europe."

"Not in New York City?" said Deaf Smith.

"No, it's been in Europe for a long time," I said.

"And how long is that?"

"Day one," I said.

He scratched his chin. I had his mind running, but it wasn't the kind of mind that got much exercise. It was tiring quickly and every time it stopped for a rest his eyes wandered back to my hat, or his hat, depending on how you wanted to look at it.

"You having a little problem establishing civilization around here?" I asked.

"What do you mean?"

"The native people," I said. "What do you call them? Indians?"

"Red devils," he said. "Injuns. But we killed them all east of here. Now we're heading west. One direction at a time. You can't kill everybody all at once in all directions."

I nodded seriously when he said that and repeated it softly to myself, but loud enough for him to hear, because I could see he had imparted to me what he regarded as some important wisdom.

"I don't know too much about Injuns," I said, "but I came in from the northwest and saw a bunch of them camped out."

"How many?"

"Ten or twelve. They had spears and arrows."

"Horses?"

"Sure."

"Where?"

"Upriver."

Smith scrutinized me, but at least he wasn't thinking about his hat now.

"What were they doing?"

"Painting themselves and their horses," I said.

"What's going on with your damn horse?" said Erastus Smith,

I hadn't looked, but FireBlood's ears were spinning like there were two hundred white people around us and she was right. I grabbed an ear and told her, "Stop being an idiot!" in Comanche.

"What are you talking?" said Erastus.

"Italian," I said. "She's just a little crazy."

"She's not the only one, I'd say." He hesitated and a flicker of recognition came over his eyes and passed. It was hard to read, but maybe he thought he knew something.

"Come down off that horse and have a drink with me, Mr. Italian Donna," Erastus Deaf Smith said.

"Roberto," I said. I tied FireBlood to the hitching post and suggested she behave. Smith took a gander at her reins.

"Bought them in Santa Fe," I said as we entered the saloon.

"What were you doing there?"

"Shopping," I said. "We Italians like to shop."

Erastus Smith stopped at the bar where he picked up a bottle of whiskey and led me to a door on which he knocked two times, very deliberately. In a moment the door opened and smoke poured out. It took a second or two for the air to clear before I made out four men sitting at a table, smoking cigars and gambling with cards, poker, I figured. Many Wounds had taught the HorseSleepers a version of it, played with drafts, not cards. A fifth man with huge, mutton sideburns stood behind the card players. He wasn't wearing a uniform, but he had a military air about him in that he stood too rigidly and wore a sword. I figured I was in some Texas power place. In my experience with whites, whether Mexican Catholic or Yankee Methodist, when there was whiskey and no women, then plans were being hatched for conquering the world.

# 29

LEAVE IT TO TEXANS to bring you into their lodge and offer you neither drink, food, nor smoke. The youngest of them, who'd opened the door for us, sat back down and they went back to their game. The standing soldier peered at me through the smoke. Military types had a way of measuring you in the first moments, and if you were unlucky enough you gave your life trying to disprove the misimpression.

In a minute, the youngest and thinnest of them threw in his cards and cursed. He was nervous and wiry. "Throwing away thirty-five hundred acres, Colonel Travis," said the man next to him, who was broad and dark and carried a Bowie knife on each hip.

"Colonel Travis is a patriot, Bowie, not a Filibuster," said the big red-headed fellow across from him, and he when laughed, he kind of roared. He wore a fringe jacket over a silk shirt and a Cherokee head band. That pretty much put it together for me that he was Sam Houston. Filibusters, I remembered from my stay in Mexico City, were the Texans who led the last revolt up here, the ones my old friend General Santa Ana skinned and hung upside down in the cottonwood trees, every last one of them. Since then, Stephen F. Austin, who I figured was the well-dressed man who sat opposite Travis, did his best to disassociate from those types, who had risen again in the lapse of power that had occurred up *norte* since the demise of the Spanish. The Filibusters were, for the most part, identified with Yankee land grabbing and Austin was trying to pass himself off as a loyal Mexican citizen.

Austin had white, delicate hands, with fingernails shinier than the Great Inquisitor's. When the bet came to him, he doubled the pot, which I now noticed wasn't money, but slips of paper on which they wrote down acres of land.

"First you occupy it legally, then you hold on to it," said Austin softly. "No grabbing involved." He turned his head slightly to the left. "You're sweating, Colonel Bowie," he said.

Houston let out another giant laugh. "Ha-haa!" He poured himself some whiskey. Drank it. He turned to Deaf Smith and nodded at me. "Is this my opium delivery?" he said.

The military type behind him grunted and Houston laughed again. I didn't learn till later that he was Zachary Taylor, soon to be a general in the army of the United States and, if you know your history, quite a factor in the war against Mexico some years later. I guess he was just having a vacation, because he sure wasn't in U.S. territory.

I'll be the first to admit that it's the easiest thing in the world to put things together from the back end, after they've already played out, but according to everything I've ever heard since, this group was never together in one place, not this early in the game, let alone in cahoots. Nonetheless, you had to like old Sam Houston, who the Cherokee called Big Drunk, because you could read his pretensions like a smoke signal. It was disarming, which might explain why he was still such close friends with the Cherokee as well as General Andrew Jackson who kicked their butts off their land.

"Who would want this God-forsaken place," said Taylor, and Houston laughed again as Bowie cashed out.

"The Comanche, for starters," said Smith. "This fellow says he spotted a giant war party of them up river."

Travis jumped to his feet and Bowie's hands went instinctively to his blades as he pushed his chair back and licked his lips. Houston grinned and Austin's face remained unchanged.

"Smith," said Austin quietly, "in public, remember, you're supposed to be deaf."

Smith stammered and said, "He don't know that. He's from Italy, New York."

"Ha-haa! My ass!" said Houston and slapped his own forehead. He looked right at me and laughed and I couldn't help but grin a little.

Austin stroked his clean shaven chin and Travis breathed on me. "He's a beautiful boy," said Austin. It's hard to describe how he said it, but at the time it made me uncomfortable, if you know what I mean.

Needless to say it made Sam Houston laugh so hard he was holding his belly. "Oh, Governor!" he said.

My knees started to quake under the oppression of young Travis' whiskey and cigar breath.

"Let the boy breathe, Travis," said Stephen F. Austin. "Colonel Bowie, hands on the table. Major Houston," but he couldn't finish. Houston's eyes were wide and lips tight with mirth. "Major Houston," Austin said with the slightest edge to his voice. He looked at me and Smith.

"You don't need Indian trouble now," said Taylor from behind him.

"No," said Austin, "we do not." He spoke to Smith. "How many?"

"Two, maybe three hundred," said Smith.

That almost knocked me off my feet. Maybe I'd underestimated Smith and he was the greatest scout in the West.

"Is that true?" Austin said to me.

"Give or take several hundred," I whispered.

Sam Houston laughed so hard he put his head down on the table.

Bowie, who was sitting back now, dark and calm, sipped his whiskey casually, as if to imitate Austin's confidence and caution. "Why don't you send your Cherokee friends after them, Sam?" said Bowie.

Houston lifted his head and straightened up like you'd put a stick up him. He peered at Bowie. "Because it would be senseless cowardice," he said. "I would not exploit my friendship with the Cherokee to have them slaughtered on the open plains by the Comanche, if, indeed, those Indians are hostile and Comanche."

"What the hell else would they be?" said Deaf Smith.

"Wandering Caddo or Karankawa, Wichita, Apache, even Cherokee," said Houston.

Smith breathed heavily at him. "This is revenge for Peach Creek," he said.

I must have shown recognition on my face, because Austin was inspecting me. For the moment news of yesterday's mishap hadn't yet reached town.

"Then this is Henry Wax Karnes's business," said Jim Bowie.

"You know he's in Tennessee," said Smith.

"That's why I said it," said Bowie.

Well that was bad news for us, because Karnes was mostly who we'd come to kill. I needed to get back on the plains and tell the People that this whole battle wasn't worth the effort. Unfortunately there was a knock on the door just then and the bartender delivered the news of Wind Sister's raid.

Sam Houston dropped his hands at his sides and began to weep. Huge tears rolled down his red cheeks. "The chickens have come home to roost," he sobbed.

"I thought you killed them all at Peach Creek," Travis said to Smith.

"Tribes of them wiped out," sobbed Houston. "The wanton massacre of Rousseau's *bon savage!*"

"*Mais oui,*" I whispered and Houston looked up, madness in his eyes.

Travis now paced back and forth from me, walking to the back of the smoky room, only to reappear, emerging from the smoke, then disappear again like some kind of wraith.

"We killed a few hundred," said Deaf Smith. "And their chief. But the rotten son-of-a-bitch who murdered Karnes' son got away."

Bowie unsheathed one of his knives. "The Coyote," he said.

"Coyote," said Travis, appearing from out of the smoke.

"The changeling," wept Houston. "The creator!" he wailed. "The Trickster!" he cried to the air.

"That's right," said Deaf Smith. "I had him by his scalp and he vanished out of my hands."

That place felt more and more like a lodge full of over-smoked shamans. And news sure traveled fast on the plains. I hadn't even recalled introducing myself to Smith at Peach Creek.

"Let's all calm down," said Stephen Austin softly.

Meanwhile, I furrowed my brow and rubbed my chin thoughtfully. "Coyote," I said.

"Young man," Austin said to me, "are you an Indian?"

"No, sir," I said. "Italian"

"Italian?"

"*Italiano. E pluribus unum.*"

In an instant Travis appeared out of the smoke and pushed me up against the wall. "That's not Italian," he said. "It's Latin."

"I'm an ancient Italian," I said.

Sam Houston lifted his head from his hands. "Ha-haa!" he laughed. "Another lost tribe!"

Travis's breath alone was enough to execute me. "You're a damn spy," he spit at me.

"For whom?" I said.

"Ha-haa!" roared Houston. "He's right!"

"For the Comanche," said Bowie calmly.

Sam Houston shook and held his hands over his face. "A Comanche spy," he said. I couldn't tell now if he was laughing or crying.

Austin raised his hands for quiet again. "Well, if he is, he's a damn clever one. Regardless, this hand has been ruined." He threw his cards down with a flick, overhand, not under.

Zachary Taylor stepped up to the table, placing the fingers of his left hand on its edge. "What would it take," he said to Smith, "to surprise them and rub them out?"

Houston shook his head. "You haven't got a clue, General." He began to weep softly now. "I'm depressed," he said.

Smith rubbed his chin. He had a classic Texan dilemma. It was easy enough to sit behind a wall with your long rifle and calculate that the ten Indians in front of you were really a hundred. But if you actually had to prepare an attack based on that kind of tomfoolery it got more complicated, especially when *egos*, that's Roman for big selfs, got involved, because Texans always wanted to be outnumbered in their minds yet maintain a clear numerical advantage. For the Texans to make war on us with any honor we had to be twice as brutal and half as smart, clever as a fox and dumber than dirt, ignorant, superstitious, cowardly, dangerous, wily; the most superior inferior foe they'd ever encountered.

"Thirty men," said Smith.

"Thirty," said Austin. He was too smart to not know something wasn't quite right.

"Elixir," whispered Sam Houston, who stood up. He was an enormous man. Big face, big red features. His eyes narrowed at me before he strode out of the room.

"Take the men out tonight," Austin said to Smith. "If possible, just scare the Indians off." He didn't look at me or Travis who once again had gently gripped my throat. He looked at Bowie. "We'll hold onto the Italian until the situation clears up."

So I got my first visit to jail. I wouldn't want to live there, but it was all right for a spell. All you had to do was sit and wait. Travis took great pleasure in putting me in the jail cell. In that way he was like old Turkey Feathers. He liked being in charge of somebody and any excuse would do.

"I'm a lawyer," he said to me for no apparent reason.

"Well good, it looks like I might need one."

"So don't try anymore phony Italian."

"*Mea culpa*," I said.

He gave me a good shove and put the iron door between us.

"Whoever you are," said Travis, "you'll need to choose a side. Mexico or Texas. There's no room for Europe here."

"You know," I said to him, "us ancient Italians got that conquering thing out of our systems a long time ago."

"Maybe you're just crazy," said Travis.

Sometimes it's better to be crazy than lucky. Survival is a hairline kind of thing and nothing will ever change that. Among the good news on my side of the bars was that Deaf Smith got all full of fervor and forgot about his hat, or my hat, or Fat Otter's hat. But I figured I'd done my job. If Deaf Smith listened to orders, Fat Otter and the gang would take off on sight. If the Rangers didn't follow them, that would be that. No trap. No fight. No Henry Wax Karnes. I'd be out in the morning. Unfortunately, things seldom go as planned.

# 30

THE SUN CROSSED the back window of the cell before FireBlood showed up and put her nose up to the bars. It wasn't that big of a town, so I knew she could have found me earlier. She had ears good enough to recognize my breathing through a wall, smell and sight that could pick me out of a crowd like a lost buffalo calf looking for its mother.

"All right. Good girl," I said. I petted her nose and she nickered with her lips and nibbled my fingers like I should feed her something, though I had nothing to feed her.

Till now I have tried to refrain from talking endlessly about my horse, something a human, man or woman, Indian or white, is prone to do because you spend so much time in intimacy with them, that is riding right on their backs when you're not cleaning their fur or braiding their mane or cleaning their noses or their eyes, washing out fly sores and trimming their damn feet, all of which they managed somehow to do on their own before they met us. A horse is a damn scaredy-cat and a big baby, too, and when you get them out of the herd you've got to do everything for them, that's the price of you becoming the big horse in their lives, which is how they see it, being horses, which they will always be and nothing will change it. Treat your horse like a human being and you're in for a hard time. You can barely treat a human being like a human being, but that's another story.

I had reached a level of rapport with FireBlood, much as Always Hits had taught me, by exploiting her talented foibles. For one, though she did not like to behave, she did like to be rewarded, and because she wasn't the most affectionate of beasts I often rewarded her with food. Now people will tell you that you can't use food to train a horse because a horse will just eat whatever is around it, but that's not always true. They have their preferences, like anybody. So unfortunately I had reached a compromise with FireBlood whereupon if she did something I asked, I gave her a snack, a dried bean cake soaked in honey, and she'd become astute enough to guarantee the snack was available before she conceded anything. I guess the French would call it a social contract.

Any riding Indian will carry a rawhide rope on his saddle, just like anybody. If FireBlood would turn sideways for me, on the rope side, which she was perfectly capable of doing, I'd tie that rope around one of the bars and maybe get lucky. I petted her nose again. "Come on, sweetheart, turn for me," I said.

She put her ears forward, then back. There were snacks in a parfleche right under the blanket, but I couldn't reach them, or the rope, if she didn't turn.

"FireBlood," I whispered.

She lifted her head to peer inside the cell, but she didn't see any snacks in there. She backed up and showed me her teeth.

"You asshole! Come over here!" I said.

She planted her feet, kind of defiantly, as if getting ready to rear up. She lifted up about two inches, plopped down, then lowered her head demurely.

"This is not a damn seduction, you idiot."

I could see that she didn't care for that tone of voice. One thing you learn quick with horses, if something doesn't work you try something else. I reached in my pocket as if I had something for her. "Come," I said.

She tilted her head to see if I really had anything in my hand. She didn't budge.

"Damn you," I said. "If I don't get out of here, what are you going to do?"

That was what white folk would call a rhetorical question. Generally doesn't work with horses.

FireBlood turned her butt to me, lifted her tail, and let out a big fart. In some contexts that could be construed as affection, but in this one that would have been a stretch.

"If I get out of here I'm going to eat you," I said. Well, anybody knows you don't get anywhere by getting mad at a horse, and that's just where I got.

Just then I heard a key in the cell door. A young woman stood there, dressed in a Mexican skirt and blouse, but her thick hair and rounded features indicated she was Coahulitecan, who were a loose group of desert tribes south of the Rio Bravo, or Rio Grande, depending on your disposition, Mexican or Yankee.

"Señor Austin invites you to luncheon," she said.

That meant a great big lunch. Mexicans liked to get up late and have a little juice, then put in a few hours of labor well into the heat of the day before breaking in mid-afternoon for a huge meal. You got drunk and went to sleep, then went to work again in the cool of evening if there was any light left. Most Yankees hated it and found it lazy, but to my mind, Mexicans worked harder than anybody when they worked and played harder when they played. Most of them being Indian, like me, they didn't even have a word for job.

I looked at that girl and that open cell door.

"What would Socrates do in this situation?" I said.

"He'd have lunch," she said.

"You've heard of Socrates?"

"No, but there is an armed guard at the door who will take us to Señor Austin."

I sat down. A Comanche rarely passes up an opportunity to eat, but when we eat, we just eat, we don't do business and I figured Señor Austin wasn't inviting me out just to be cordial.

"Are you a friend of Señor Austin's?" I said.

"Are you an ancient Italian?"

You'd think, being raised by Many Powers, I'd have known better than to condescend to a woman, but I guess with half of me coming from Spain it just came natural.

"I am, in fact, a friend of Señor Houston's," she said.

Sometimes conversation is like stacking sticks with your eyes closed.

"And Señor Austin does not have a woman friend."

She giggled a little and you know what a female giggle does to me. "You are a cute boy," she said.

I'd worked hard on this disguise, but cute wasn't part of it. Women just liked me. Hell, everybody liked me.

"I'll go," I said, "but you have to promise to stay and have a talk with me when I get back."

"You're coming back?"

"I can assure you," I said. "I'll be back."

So she and the guard accompanied me down the street to Stephen F. Austin's hacienda. Had the situation been more dire I wouldn't have delayed my escape on account of a single armed guard who I figured I could handle, but ironically enough, this had become an information gathering interlude. As a Coyote I was driven by curiosity even to my own demise. Austin knew this on some level or another because he dismissed the guard at the door.

"Señor Donatelli," said Austin, which I guess he translated from what Deaf Smith had gathered.

"Close enough, Señor," I said. Don't think I was a bit intimidated. To my mind, I was Comanche royalty, though there never was such a thing, and as you'll recall, in Mexico I'd rubbed shoulders with God's earthly crew and seen the naked butt end of the most powerful general on two continents. Lunch with a Yankee *Tejano cacique*, a Texas chieftain, meant nothing to me but my life.

The help brought out huge tureens of cold soup and plates of tortillas and fish. They were black people, with skin like obsidian and thick, curly, black hair. I'd heard of them before, but this was the first time I'd seen them. They were from Africa and I wanted to ask them about elephants, but I didn't think it was the time or place.

"I wish I'd have known I was coming to lunch," I said, "I'd have dressed better."

"*Esta viernes*," said Austin in Spanish, meaning it's Friday. For Catholics, a fish day. "I assume you are Catholic, like the rest of us."

Well I was as Catholic as he was, but as a Comanche I didn't care much for fish, though I'd eaten enough of it in the same situation down in El Ciudad de Mexico.

"I know friends of the Pope," I said. "But to be honest, I'm a Lutheran."

"In Italy?" he said.

"Plenty," I said. "Up north." I later found this lie to be true. "In fact we don't even speak Italian up there. *Nous parlons française.*"

"*Vraiment?*" said Austin, flicking his napkin out. "Really?"

"*En vérité,*" I said. Indeed.

"Well," said Austin, motioning me toward the fish with an upturned palm, "though by law we are all Catholic here in Texas, we are yet permitted to speak English."

"I've always found it to be a perfectly adequate language," I said.

"Most adequate," he said. "And the language of this continent."

One of the black servants dished me out a bowl of cold, white soup. It had green particles floating in it.

"Leeks, sir," the black man said.

"The French are practically gone," I said to Austin, "but there's still plenty of Mexicans on this continent. And Indians."

"I feel sorry for the Indians," said Austin.

"Your sympathy will likely go unappreciated," I said.

He lifted an eyebrow. "They belong to an era which no longer exists. And Mexicans are filthy and unproductive. A mixed breed."

I hesitated to tell him that the Mexican Indians had built the biggest cities in the world and the breed they mixed with was pure, white Spaniard. Off the top of your head you might think it a good pairing. Aside from that, Austin was technically Mexican, as were all his cohorts. Of course, he was under the misimpression that Cortés had conquered the Aztecs with a couple dozen men. What I told him was all the stuff Sor María Juana had taught me about the Mexica, and how Cortés had to gather a huge Spanish army and artillery, build a navy, and get thousands of Indian allies to conquer a Tenochtitlan that had already been ravaged by the plague, and even then the siege took weeks.

"You seem to know a lot about it," he said.

"Didn't Aristotle say learning was the highest pleasure?" I said.

"I wouldn't know," said Austin.

But in fact, he would. Everybody I ran into in San Felipe de Austin was a lawyer or a colonel or both. We went on like this for quite some time over our cold leek soup and catfish tacos before we settled down to port wine and coffee. I took a cigar, as well. Leave it to a white man to put the smoking at the end. The black servant lit us up.

"This has been quite enjoyable," said Austin. "It's refreshing to encounter an educated man out here."

"A lot of ruffians," I said.

Austin blew smoke, then said, "Yes."

"Jail is not so very enjoyable for me," I said to him.

"No," he said, "I imagine not."

"Have you spent much time there?"

"In fact," he grinned, "I have."

I didn't know he'd just got back from a diplomatic trip to Mexico City where he'd been visiting my old friend Santa Ana, trying to patch things up. He'd sent a letter back to Texas, I guess, saying some rather candid and uncomplimentary things about the Mexicans and his intentions for Texas. Of course, Santa Ana read all of Austin's correspondence, so he threw him in the Mexican hooskow. Word is the treatment there is not the best. All of this Stephen F. Austin told me there at lunch. He was pretty resentful about the whole thing, but the fact is, Santa Ana could have had him flayed if he'd wanted. Austin got off light and lucky and he wasn't supposed to come back resentful, but respectful of how magnanimous Santa Ana had been. Texians, as I learned they called themselves, were not Tejanos. Santa Ana didn't understand that. And Mexicans were not Yankees. Austin, for all his accommodations toward Mexico, didn't have a clue. I wondered what he'd have done had the situation been reversed.

"Señor Donatelli, there is often not much evidence to go on out here on the frontier," Austin said to me. "A man is only as good as his word."

"That doesn't leave many good men," I said.

"No," he chuckled, "it doesn't. But you are a bit mysterious and I wonder why you have brought us any word at all."

When I didn't fall into the trap of explaining myself he lifted his eyebrows, smiled a little, and nodded. He wasn't that difficult to delight. He had a certain delicate way about him. I wouldn't really call it feminine, I'd call it precise or effete.

"You're a sophisticated young man," he said. "A European. Here on the frontier it's often difficult to find," he paused, "worthy companionship."

"You mean a horse isn't the answer to everything," I said.

"Only very few things," he said. He let his cigar go out in the ash tray and sipped his port. "My power here among these hooligans is limited," said Austin. "Men like yourself often become victims when ruffians seek a justice which is greater than themselves but as narrow as loyalty. Individual rights can be ignored. I fear for you." He sipped his port again, allowing that to sink in. "Since we have no cathedral of our own here in San Felipe, nowhere to go for asylum, you would not be offended if I offered you," he paused again and looked away, I dare say it was a bit demure, "the sanctuary of my affection," Austin said.

I'd sure hate to be a woman in a civilized place, though it was tough enough on men. Even the One True Church never gave you anything for free, let alone Stephen F. Austin. I sipped my port and put my cigar down, too. I was always a bit apprehensive when it came to choosing the form of my torture.

# 31

I TOLD GOVERNOR AUSTIN, which is what everybody called him long before he governed anything, that I was neither inclined nor disinclined to take his offer because I had, like Socrates, a higher commitment to the state of Law, even if, like Socrates, I might enjoy an occasional foray with pleasure and beauty, be it male or female. But whether just or unjust in my individual case, whether played out fairly or unfairly, a human being had an obligation to abide within the codes of civilized order, even more essential in a land teetering on the frontier of uncivilized disorder. Every individual was therefore an example *par excellence.*

*"Exempla sunt idioso,"* said Stephen F. Austin, which in Latin meant literally that examples are odious, but in this case was just a subtle reminder for me to avoid being explicit. He had his reputation. Nonetheless, said I, in the morning I would be exonerated by the facts of the field and his honor would be left uncompromised by them, as well.

Austin's eyes narrowed and that armed guard showed up faster than you could swallow your words.

"That you would guard my honor, sir," he said. "Allow me to guard yours."

That was the first of that kind of phony, Southern gentleman talk I'd heard out of him. Texans, or Texians I guess, could pour that syrupy language over you like you were just so many pancakes, as if using the word 'sir' brought them some degree of integrity. I don't even know why I turned him down. I probably had fewer inhibitions than he did and I'd already done a dozen more scurrilous things. But giving a powerful man what he wants will gain you nothing but another opportunity to give him what he wants. Anyway, I had a full belly and my friend was waiting for me when I got back to jail.

"Now what?" I said to her. We spoke in Spanish.

"He'll probably kill you," she said.

"You sure?"

"You think you're the first?" She put her hands in the pockets of her skirt and giggled.

"You seem pretty amused," I said to her.

"We all like to think we are the first," she said. "Special. Especially men."

"He'd have me killed anyways."

"Yes," she laughed. "Maybe. Life is unfortunate."

"That's an interesting way of putting it," I said.

"But it is true that you are a spy or you wouldn't be here."

"And it's true that you are a spy or you wouldn't be here," I said.

She laughed and laughed and then sat down. "All men here are holding secrets from each other and trying to get everything. They are all . . . pirates. That is the word. Pirates for the land."

"And you're not," I said to her.

"I am a woman," she said. "And so by a few minor capitulations I am saved from the pain of glory and death."

"While you're young," I said.

"When I am old I'll have nothing they want. It will be easier."

Sometimes I think the whole history of Texas was a series of underestimations. Every race thought themselves superior to every other. Every individual thought the person in front of them was some kind of idiot. For most men, women didn't exist. For most whites, Indians were a different species. For the Yankees, Mexicans were animals.

"I am Luz," she said. "My band and my family were killed by Lipan Apache because they found their horses among us, old horses we'd found wandering after Mexican caballeros rubbed out a band of Karankawa. The Lipan sold me to the Tanima for horses."

"The Liver Eater Comanche," I said.

"Yes, that's why I know something about your face," said Luz. "Though I have never seen an Italian."

"The Comanche are not bad to their women," I said.

"No worse than others," she said. "How can you let the buffalo run free, but own your women?"

"We eat buffalo," I said.

"Texas is a land of men who have left women," Luz said to me. "Travis cannot function like a man. I know this because whores talk to each other. So in Alabama, when his wife took a lover, he murdered him and left her for dead. Bowie is a smuggler and slave trader. He has made a fortune selling the Africans like meat, by the pound. He married into Creole land, stolen from my people, the Coahuiltecan, then abandoned his family to the cholera and inherited everything. Señor Houston left a wife in Tennessee. Even I don't know why."

I guess she figured I knew enough about Austin on my own.

"Do you have a mother?" Luz asked."It amazes me that all men have mothers. How can something that comes from a woman turn into a man?"

"Feel free to speak your mind," I said.

"You see? You are in jail and yet you think you can condescend to me," Luz said.

"I guess you don't get to say this kind of stuff to Señor Houston," I said.

"In fact, that is one difference about him. He lets me say what I please. And when he listens, he often learns something."

"I'll bet that's true," I said. "You'd get along with my mother. She says the world is upside down and women should be running everything."

"If it were that simple," said Luz.

"It's just one of the things she says," I said to Luz.

This girl was like a sharp stone sticking up into the sky, a thing of beauty and hard loneliness, with a mind like a bird of prey. She got up again and came to the bars of my cell. I walked toward her, but not close enough where she'd think I'd try to touch her. I didn't want her flying away. She looked at me, a hard, Indian look, eyes narrowed. It's hard to explain.

"Do your people have whores?" she said to me.

"I really don't believe in them."

"You are not an Italian, whatever it is," she said.

"No."

"I will tell Señor Houston what to think about you."

It wasn't too much later that Major Houston himself, soon to be General Houston, came in. Huge, red-haired man, ruddy, he looked like he'd been laughing or crying or some combination. He took out a Cherokee greeting pipe and loaded it.

"You'll smoke, of course," he said.

I took it and smoked. It was not tobacco in there, or jimson weed or anything else I could recognize. I later learned Houston was an opium addict and I guess that's what that was. I suddenly felt like my body was a rock and my mind a bird inside it. Houston smoked, too.

"An interrogation device," he said, and laughed, "Haa!" in that big laugh of his. "So you're an Italian spying for the Comanche."

"No, I'm a Comanche spying for the Italians," I told him.

"'Ha-haa! That's good. That's good. Sad in a way." He got a little teary-eyed. "But good."

He passed the pipe again. My body got heavier and my mind got birdier.

"That Luz is something else, isn't she?" he said.

"You should marry her."

"Ah," said Houston, "I'm an old man." And he began to cry a little.

"I'm sorry," I said.

"Oh, it's funny, too," he said, a tight smile breaking underneath his weeping cheeks. "I've ruined enough wives." He wiped his cheek with his sleeve, then he took a deep breath and straightened up. "Forgive me," he said, "I'm not always like this. Just most of the time! Haa!"

He reached through the bars with a huge paw, remarkably quick, and patted my shoulder hard enough to knock me backward. "Ha!" said Houston. "That was my horseman's nudge. A man that spends time on the ground has got straighter legs and won't rock like you did." He smoked some more. "Remember that the next time you take up a disguise."

"Who else would know that?" I said.

"You never know," said Houston. "I talk a lot."

Oddly enough, unlike me, the more opium he smoked, the steadier he became.

"So you're just here to get to know me?" I said.

"Hell no!" boomed Houston. He crossed his arms in front of him and pulled out two huge flintlock pistols from under his coat. "I'm here because we've got Coyote O'Donohughe in jail right here in San Felipe de Austin and nobody even knows!"

# 32

"THOUGHT YOU'D BE older," said Sam Houston. "With a reputation like yours."

Needless to say, I didn't feel much like talking. Not that it ever stopped me.

"Oh, you're going to give me the quiet act," said Houston.

"What have I done?"

"Scalped Henry Wax Karnes Jr., among others. Led numerous nefarious raids against innocent settlers."

"I never led a raid in my life."

"Peach Creek. Cold blooded murder of Texas Rangers."

"What's murder?" I said. "What's a Texas Ranger?"

"You know, you put a Cherokee in a situation like this, he'll talk your ear off," Houston said.

"Your friends," I said. "Not mine."

"How do you think I knew who you were? You want news to travel, you tell an Indian. How do you people communicate so quickly? Your saddle is Comanche," he said. "I met your horse. Only a Comanche can train a horse like that. For Christ's sake, you're wearing Deaf Smith's hat! That dummie!" He roared with laughter, holding his sides. Then, suddenly, he lowered his pistols and began to weep. "The Cherokee. Those poor people. At least I got them to move out here. They had to walk the whole way, but some of them

162

made it. Better than Agamemnon did for Troy. We massacred the Creek. If I could only have died then, like Achilles, young, glorious." He opened his shirt and bared his arrow wounds, a knife wound, a bullet hole scar. "The Choctaw. The Chickasaw. We rubbed them out!"

"You will not rub us out," I said.

"Oh, we will, boy," said Houston. He began to cry now, dropping his guns. He sat down on the floor and put his face in his hands. "God help us, we will."

It's always been a mystery to me what a white man will ask God's help to do.

"We're killers," cried Houston. "It's true. But you don't use the land like we do. We need it. Without Texas, what will we do with our slaves? Did Stephen ask you to sleep with him? Don't answer that, I know the answer. I could have been President of the United States! I was Governor of Tennessee! I was betrayed by a bitch! A whore! And now I'm out here, banished like the Cherokee, taking orders from that little prick Austin! Oh, my God!" cried Sam Houston. He reloaded his pipe and smoked and that seemed to calm him down. He pulled out the cell keys and opened the door. "Get out of here," he said.

"I murdered Texas Rangers," I said, which was not a smart thing to say, though it was manly.

"I invented the Texas Rangers!" cried Houston. "Get out!"

Given he could change his mind in two seconds and fill me with lead balls, I headed for the door. The only person outside, standing in the shadow of the building, was Luz. I stood dumbly in front of her for a moment.

"He is not crazy," she said. "I explained to him. You are worth more to him alive."

I circled the jailhouse and found FireBlood, peeved and snackless, but I didn't give her time to think about things. You give a horse time to think, she'll decide not to do something every time. I hopped on her back and turned to hightail, but there, blocking my way, was none other than James Bowie, knives glittering in the sun.

"I never trust Houston," he said.

"Really," I said. "I think he likes you."

He flipped the knife in his right hand from handle to blade tip and cocked his arm to throw it, but this was the kind moment all of FireBlood's bad behavior had been trained for. She jumped straight up and turned in the air, planted her two back hooves in Bowie's chest and came down at full speed.

He must have said something really nasty to her while the two of them were out there waiting for me. Bowie never recovered from FireBlood's blast in the chest. There are lots of stories about how he got hurt before it all ended for him, but the truth is he was kicked by my Comanche pony, FireBlood. I say this *sin dolo malo*, without malice, because before it was all over, me and Jim Bowie were fast friends.

In seconds, I was riding out of that snake pit called San Felipe de Austin and into the plains. If I was lucky I could catch Fat Otter and the others before Erastus Deaf Smith found them. It might prevent a lot of unnecessary bad feelings, if not a massacre

# 33

THE FIRST PERSON I ran into out there was Deaf Smith, riding in the opposite direction toward San Felipe all by himself. He always had a tremendous reputation for being the first one into battle. He also had a rather less legendary habit of being the first one out. Call it instinct.

"Don't bother," he said to me after he pulled up. "It's too late. There's a thousand Comanche out there and they're coming this way!"

He didn't even wait for me. He kicked his poor, foaming beast and galloped toward the colony.

It didn't take much to follow the trail and see what had happened. Deaf Smith and his gang ran into Fat Otter and the boys who, of course, were out numbered and according to plan hightailed it west. Seizing the advantage of having triple the numbers and disobeying Austin's orders, Smith went after them. A few miles later I found a score and a half of Texas Rangers, stripped, scalped, and lying dead among their horses and mules which they'd shot or slit the throats of to use for cover. Once again, a total waste of good animals. It made no sense to kill perfectly good horse flesh just because you were doomed. By that time, though, they'd run up on Dark Eagle's war party and really were outnumbered and had probably shot off their muskets during the chase, so they faced about three dozen arrows a man from mounted Comanches before they got more than one or two shots off. Needless to say, it didn't last long or take much and you won't read about it anywhere because it was an ignoble defeat.

I caught up to Dark Eagle and the rest of them, moving pretty fast toward home, in the opposite direction of San Felipe de Austin. So contrary to everything I attempted to prevent, I was the great hero of the battle for having lured those Rangers into the trap without risking a single Comanche life.

"Everyone should give you a scalp," said Fat Otter. "You have earned a coup from each of us. Everyone knows how the Coyote, my brother, walked defenseless among the enemy and, invisible, whispered to them like an ill wind. Like a Firebird, he flew among them inflaming their hearts. Then flying before them, his war cry filling the sky like thunder, he led them into our trap and their doom."

"Puberty has not been good for your sense of reality, Fat Otter," I said. "I spent the night in the calaboose."

"Maybe your body did," he said.

"You weren't even there!"

"The facts speak for themselves, brother," said Fat Otter. He gave me a Bowie knife he'd recently acquired in the medley. You might think I mean melee, but I don't. Texians used medley went they meant melee.

"I think you will need this for someone who is waiting for you," Fat Otter said of the knife. And he didn't mean Henry Wax Karnes, either. He meant his own sister, Morning Star.

Just ahead White Calf broke into song:

Coyote walked among the whites
Coyote betwitched the whites
Coyote led them to us
They laid down their weapons
And gave us their hair
Coyote, the Trickster, lives among us
No one can kill us
We are the greatest warriors of the plain

"Will you stop that nonsense!" I yelled,

Everybody was whooping and loping and having a general good time. You never saw such a happy bunch of Comanches as after a good massacre.

Dark Eagle road up beside me. "Today you brought us good fortune," he said.

"I brought you disastrous fortune," I said.

"Do not think so far ahead," said Dark Eagle.

"We didn't even get Henry Wax Karnes," I said to Dark Eagle. "He's back in Tennessee."

"We will have our day with him, too," said Dark Eagle, and rode off.

Everybody started riding up to me and giving me stuff: coonskin caps, scalps, pistols.

"Stop giving me stuff!" I shouted at them.

That got a big laugh and Always Hits brought over a pony to load my booty on.

"This is crazy," I said to him.

"What is greater? To walk among the enemy in their own camp and lead them to slaughter, or to face them on the battlefield when they are already as defenseless as buffalo calves?"

"I don't want this reputation," I said to him. "It's just going to get me killed."

"Choose instead that the sun will not set tonight," he said.

All that was left for me now was to try to come to peace with Wind Sister, who I saw riding quietly beyond the hoopla.

"I tried to stop it, Sister," I said to her. "When I saw Karnes wasn't there."

"Dark Eagle has already forgotten Turkey Feathers," she said. She looked at me for a moment, then looked down again. I'd forgotten how big and strong she was, and how much I'd been in love with her before so much happened. All that thick, black hair flowing down over her white buckskins. She had high cheeks and thin, pretty lips, smooth copper skin.

"He hasn't forgotten him," I said.

"I don't want to live in his lodge."

Well that didn't give her a whole lot of choices. Carrying Turkey's child, she was pretty much in Dark Eagle's family now.

"Dark Eagle is a good man," I said. "A good provider and powerful."

"You have no idea what it is like to be a woman," she said.

"No," I said, "I don't." Though unbeknownst to me, I would one day have the opportunity. For the time being, it wasn't a conversation I wished to indulge in, I'd just end up being told off. "But I like women," I said.

"I believe you do," she said quietly.

We rode on together for a while at the back of that herd of celebrating Comanche. There's no solace for a brooding woman. That's a famous Comanche saying. But the way most men dealt with it was to just leave them alone till they came around.

"Maybe it's all for the best," I said.

"Nothing is ever all for the best," said Wind Sister.

I've probably forgotten to mention what a pessimistic bunch we were. Indians weren't happy people in general. Happy isn't really what you'd call us. And Comanche were probably some of the most negative of anybody. I just rode with her there in the wake of everything, back to the high plains.

As it flies across the plains, the dust and noise of a few a dozen warriors and their ponies can be seen and heard from a great distance, especially if you're listening for them. If you're in camp, the horses hear it from miles away, long before even the dogs. Then the women send the girls and boys out on their ponies, several of whom go rushing back to camp once they spot you. When the rest of them make contact, they can tell right away how things have gone, and the war chief will let them know if there's anybody who will have to mourn. Then the fastest of them heads back and the dancing and singing and cooking has begun before you arrive. It's not a place where you'd want to be a dog if there's no buffalo meat around. There's a famous Comanche saying about that as well.

When I rode in my herd of boys took FireBlood. Tocqueville was outside his little tipi, but I didn't stop for him, I went right in my lodge for Morning Star who I knew wouldn't be out dancing with everybody else. No, that wasn't her style. And she couldn't have cared less about that Bowie knife. I never even got a word out until after she pulled me to the ground and she had me inside her.

"Now talk to me," she said.

"I can't," I said. "I'm preoccupied."

"I think I hear your horse calling you," she whispered and giggled both.

"You do not hear my horse calling."

"I think you've grown larger than before you left."

"Maybe you're smaller."

"No, you are larger," she said. She pushed me back with her palms until I was almost sitting up. "There," she said, "that's better for me. It hits the good spot." She bit her bottom lip. "Do you want a child?"

"No," I said. "I'll get out."

Now I'm sure you're absolutely unaware of this, but as a Comanche warrior one of the things we savages practiced was, for lack of a better word, restraint. A Comanche warrior comes when he chooses. It's one of the many things you teach yourself in the sweat lodge. But if worse comes to worse you just retreat. It doesn't take a genius.

We spent a lot of time in the sweat lodge talking about women. I'm sure women do the same. But after a million moons, so to speak, we haven't passed on any significant information to each other or figured anything out. For all my restraint practice, nobody ever told me a girl like Morning Star would have muscles inside of her. Suddenly she was dancing around my member like a warm river and when I tried to get out she'd grabbed me like a fist. She held me and laughed and laughed. She'd gone far beyond giggling. That girl could trill.

"It is a beautiful knife," she said.

"Why didn't somebody tell me about that!" I said later to Always Hits.

"Because the HorseSleepers need babies," said Always Hits. "Young men would never decide to have babies on their own."

"It's a conspiracy!"

"Maybe. Maybe the world is a great conspiracy. In that regard, your mare is due if you wish to keep the line."

"If I'm supposed to be such a powerful individual," I said to him, "how come nobody cares what I think?"

"Do you hear my horse calling to me?" said Always Hits. "I think that is him."

My mother, Many Powers, said to me, "Do not become like a man who mistakes the great forces of the world for the things which make the world. Look at the stars. Do you think the people of the stars care about us?"

"There are no people on the stars," I said.

"Why not? There are people here."

"We are not star people."

"How do you know what we look like to them?" She burnt sweet grass and its smoke fled upward to the smoke hole of her lodge. "How do you know when a storm is coming?" she asked me.

"The wind comes up and there is a smell of rain," I said.

"How big will the storm be?"

"The big ones come from the north," I said. "In the Moons of Ice Grass, Hiding Buffalo, Snow."

"What can you do about it?"

"Go in my lodge."

"If you have no shelter?"

"Turn your back, like a horse," I said.

"Okay," she said, "now let's have something to eat."

"Mother, I am too famous for no reason," I said to Many Powers. "I wish to have a reputation as ordinary as my self."

"*Mala suerte*," said my mother. In Spanish, bad luck. "But I just talked about that."

"I didn't entrap the Texans. I tried to prevent the raid."

"*C'est la guerre*," said my mother.

"Mother."

"We have already spoken of all of this."

"We have?"

"While you can, make babies, hunt buffalo, enjoy love and a warm fire. Concentrate. If you cannot smell the storm in the air, then soon you will."

"And where will I hide?"

"Coyote," my mother said, "you will run until you find another storm. Now let's eat."

# 34

ALEXIS DE TOCQUEVILLE didn't eat a raw skunk butt, but he thought he did. We gave him a peyote button which, if you'd never seen one, nor a severed skunk butt, you might mistake one for the other and besides, the peyote probably tastes worse. We danced around, blew on some whistles and hit some drums. I gave everybody a little something to rattle off in Latin or ancient Greek. Then we made him take off all of his clothes and gave him the peyote skunk butt.

"It is a very big skunk butt," he said.

"*C'est votre choix, monsieur,*" I said to him. "I've seen bigger. But we're not going to stand around here chanting all night while you make up your mind. You eat the skunk butt or you don't."

He ate it all right. As I've said, if you've ever tasted peyote, you'd probably prefer skunk butt. We danced him around until the peyote took hold, then I led him out to the bluff.

"I feel quite strange," said Alexis de Tocqueville.

"I bet," I said.

"And what now do I do?"

"You do nothing," I said. "I'll see you later."

"*Mais Monsieur Coyote, je suis immobile.*"

"That's good," I said, "because it's worse if you wander around."

"Worse?"

"Enjoy the stars," I said. "I'm going to get some sleep."

And I left him there. Hell, for the sake of the civilized world, it was the least I could do.

# 35

THE SKUNK BUTT THING pretty much ended Alexis de Tocqueville's fascination with the Comanche, Lords of the Language Arts. Years later, at Harvard, I saw he published a book about the United States and there was nary a word about us Indian linguists or Indians in general. He was interested in government, it seemed, and, to be truthful, that's one thing we never had much of, and thank the Everywhere Mystery for that. Though I'd heard rumors that he'd tried to publish some of the findings he'd accumulated during his more western sojourns in a final volume. His academic peers found it too absurd and fantastic to believe; thought he'd eaten one skunk butt too many, I guess.

Soon after Tocqueville rode out, minus most of his tobacco and wine, Wind Sister did, too. After she left, the women said Sister had been taking a potion of cotton root bark, known to instigate miscarriage. She held to her word. She wouldn't let Turkey Feather's son enter a world stalked by his father's murderer, nor live with the child's grandfather who had failed to avenge him. That was a hard one for Dark Eagle to swallow, despite our successful raid, and he'd been doing a lot of hard swallowing in recent days. To the rest of us, well, we figured he'd done his best. He'd gone right out, attacked under the Last Dry Moon of autumn, before the Moon of the Wounds, the Moon of Winter, and the Scars of Spring, and though we took only one casualty, wounds and scars were exactly what we ended up with. Talks Peace had been right about that. Sometimes there's no failure like success.

So while I set myself the task of someday finding Wind Sister and returning her to the HorseSleepers, Sister headed east, toward Henry Wax Karnes and Tennessee, while Henry Wax Karnes set his sights on scalping me. Foolishly, I suppose, I felt responsible for the mess, and when I didn't I found that I had a new nemesis right there among the HorseSleepers to remind me. Talks Peace's son, Sad Little Dog, was coming of age and, of course, unlike his father, he was an absolute little son-of-a-bitch, no offense to Many Robes. Though I guess Talk's Peace, in his younger days, was known as Makes War on Everybody. More often than not, peace chiefs came from warriors who were real bloodthirsty in their day. It all makes more sense than you want to think about. Now his son, on the verge of adulthood, was on the war path with everyone. There's nothing worse than an anti-authoritarian type among a bunch of anarchists. So he latched on to the most obvious object of tribal adoration, yours truly, and hated me the most.

If I saw him, I said, "Hello."

"I hate you, you weasel fart," he said. "You are the cause of all our problems!"

"What problems?"

"All of them! Some day I will kill you!"

I spoke to his dad about it, you know, me being a father-to-be and all, and Talks Peace said, "Don't worry. He's young. Everything will be all right if he doesn't kill you."

It made me think that maybe we could have used a few institutions around there after all, something like Dog Soldiers or Contraries, something to funnel all that hot blood.

Where was the life of the simple savage? If Rousseau had spent a month with the HorseSleepers instead of Alexis de Tocqueville doing it, we'd have changed the course of Western European thinking, if he could have got it in print. If you believed Many Powers, all the important ideas ever held by the human race never saw the light of day. Just the bad ideas surfaced. That explained the whole mess. Of course, she believed that all those buried good ideas were thought up by women, as well as the few decent ones that managed to slip out, which were stolen from women by men. She had a new book that Alexis de Tocqueville left to her called *A History of the World* or, in French, *Une Histoire du Monde.*

"What's history? said Always Hits.

It was a cold late autumn night, but I had a nice fire and a pot of buffalo stew. Hits and Many Powers, me and Morning Star, shared a big, rolled tobacco stick and a skin of French burgundy.

"It's stories about your ancestors," I said, "only white folks write it down." I pointed at the printed words in the book. "Writing," I said.

"Are they true stories, like ours?" he said.

"No, they make it up. They tell good stories about their tribe and bad stories about everybody else they can think of. That's why it's called the history of the world."

"Are we in there?" asked Morning Star,

"Not yet," I said.

"It's not the story of this world," said Many Powers. "It's some other world."

"Europe," I said.

"This writing stuff down is really a waste of time," said Always Hits.

"When they aren't doing stuff like that, they're killing people by the thousands, or enslaving them, so you have to see it as benign in comparison," I said. "That goes for science and philosophy and the other stuff they do as well."

"Science," said Morning Star. "Like Alexis."

"Sort of," I said.

"Have you heard of this Hammurabi?" Many Powers asked me.

"I learned about him down in Mexico," I said. "He was the ruler of an ancient white tribe and the first person to write down white people laws."

"Why would you do that?" said Always Hits, which made Morning Star laugh.

"So they don't have to remember them," laughed Morning Star.

"That's right," I said."Nobody listens to them, except kind of after the fact. But if you're in power you can drag them out and use them against your enemies."

"They get inside power?" said Hits.

"That's right," I said. "Whites don't have their own power, they have to find it and get in it, like you get in your lodge. They can't keep anything inside themselves, so they have to write stuff down and build stuff, like places to learn or to talk to their ancestors or their God. They only have one God, maybe two, they're very poor in that way. And they can't keep that stuff in their hearts so they have to go to those places to get it and do it. That's why things like writing and the wheel are so important to them. So anybody can trade for the power, or buy it with money."

"Guns," said Always Hits.

"If you don't feed your dog," said Morning Star, using a Comanche saying, "it will find its own food." She meant that it all fed back into white folks' basic destructive tendencies in the end.

"That is exactly why Hammurabi could not have come up with the idea to write down laws," said Many Powers. "It goes against everything we know about what men think about. You know that his wife gave him the idea. She probably told him one hundred times before he heard her, and the rest, the important things, like how to make peace and food and keep the numbers of their people down without war, he ignored. And men will always ignore."

That was my mother's theory of the world's problems, the Mrs. Hammurabi Theory, and nothing in the history or future of the world, ours or that other one, was ever going to contradict it. But for the time being, it was a good winter for smoking and talking, which we Comanche did a lot of. It had always amazed me when Tocqueville was around, how surprised he was that we sat around and talked and gossiped, worried about our kids and bitched about our lovers and war chiefs, told stories or talked about ideas and wondered about the world, had fears and doubts. He seemed to think that if you didn't have buttons on your coat you were missing the part of your soul that had thoughts.

"So," I said to Morning Star, after one of those sessions, "what do you think of it?"

"It's fun enough," she said. "It's something to do. I don't mind setting up the tipi, skinning hides, working with beads. I like to talk with the women about babies. I like to hold their babies and think about our baby. How she will be sweet and smart, like me, and wily like you."

"A girl," I said.

"Thick Robes says so, as does Little Owl. She could tell by my heart beat and he by the way warm ashes lay on my belly."

"Whites would call that hocus-pocus, I said. "Silly magic."

"They live outside their own bodies," she said. "Yes? Anyway, the big thoughts are okay by me. I don't mind them. But they're like the hot air in a buffalo bladder left in the sun. After a while it will explode and be flat and rotten. And the air stinks and leaves its odor." She shrugged.

"We play a lot of fine games with those buffalo bladders while they're full," I said.

"That is exactly my point," said Morning Star. She gave me that look over her nose. "Is it too difficult for you to understand?" And she laughed that giggle of hers that wrapped itself around my heart.

And as much as I loved to wrap myself around her, I loved having her turn my world upside down with her talk. Looking back, I think Many Powers was right about a lot of things. Had Morning Star been the son of a wealthy white European, why she might have been Keats or Mozart or Hegel. I met enough white men before I got old who believed that a man made his own life, but most of them who believed it started out with a whole lot of life already given to them, and money, and needless to say they weren't Indians or women.

As we settled into the early winter, I spent the warmer days down at the stream with Morning Star, bathing her, combing her thick, black hair over her broad, little shoulders, waiting for her belly to grow. We lay down next to each other, naked on the warm rocks in that late autumn sun. On the days of the first Northers, we often sat outside the lodge next to our fire. She lay back into my lap as we sat under a buffalo robe and we watched the snowflakes cover us, or melt sizzling in the air as they came down over the flames. I thought about where I'd been and feared where I was going to go. I wanted Many Powers to be right about how to live. I wanted to hunt buffalo and have babies and live with Morning Star. I wanted Many Powers to be wrong about me always running away from trouble into more trouble. As I looked forward to a long, cold winter of settling into domestic bliss, that's all I wanted. No surprise then that a Chiricahua Apache rode into camp one day, looking for me and carrying a message.

# 36

HE SAT PRETTY STRAIGHT on his pony, looking plenty suspicious. Already the Apache had picked up a lot of white dressing habits: colorful cloth head bands, floppy hats with feathers, pants instead of loose open-sided leggings; when they could they gave up their knee high moccasins for boots. These western Chiricahua let their hair fall straight down, unlike the eastern Apache who still liked to shave half their heads. This one carried a Mexican army musket, an old British Brown Bess with the eagle and snake motif of Mexico stamped on the lock-plate above the trigger. The piece took fifteen different steps to get a shot off and I could see the load and fire instructions carved in Spanish onto the wooden stock.

I came out and we looked at each other quietly for a while. When most people saw me they were surprised I was so ordinary looking. They always figured that with all the power I had to change shapes, I'd assume a more impressive visage. Needless to say, though I'd become somewhat of a master of disguise, Sam Houston's recognition of me aside, my ability to actually change myself into something else was as of yet quite mythical. Besides, as Many Powers warned me, if you spend all of your time being things other than yourself, then you're not yourself anymore. All that aside, there's not a thing in the world wrong with being unassuming, it can keep you out of trouble.

The Apache spoke to me in sign language. "I am Benito Corredor, the Road

Runner," he said. "I am sent to Coyote O'Donohughe by his great Apache brother, Cochise."

A lot of those Apache had double names now, half Spanish and half Apache, having been dealing with the Spanish for three centuries, not that I should talk. He didn't have to say it wasn't his choice to be there, either. And as much as I tended to complain about my growing fame, there were moments when this kind of notoriety fed me.

"I am Coyote O'Donohughe," I said. "Come on, let's eat."

We smoked and ate some prairie dog. You had to be careful with the Apache, because they were easy to insult. They'd eat a lizard, but not a turkey, eat a horse or a mule but, like us, avoided fish. They smoked, but not tobacco, and though they moved in with their wife's family, they weren't allowed to look at their mother-in-law. They weren't as bad as the Cheyenne, but you can see what happens, even to Indians, when you start having a lot of rules. Everything you do becomes a parody of something else you're doing, if you know what I mean.

After the prairie dog, Morning Star brought in the buffalo meat and mescal cakes. Mescal was considered a real treat by the Apache, and over there in the desert they didn't get to eat much buffalo, a point of contention since we ran them out of the buffalo plains. He saw coming in that I had a lot of horses, too, and my war staff lined with scalps, my lodge full of whites' weapons. I'd tried to give that stuff away after the raid on San Felipe, but as a matter of principle among the HorseSleepers, I got more back than I could possibly unload.

When we were done eating Benito put down his bowl and burped. I lit some white sage for him. Apaches are crazy about white sage. Benito smiled. "So where does the horse sleep?" he signed.

We all laughed and I got up and walked to the Apache bow and arrow that Cochise had given me on my first trip through Chiricahua territory.

"I was there," he said. "You've done well for a Kiowa among the Comanche."

We laughed again and I took down a Pennsylvania long rifle from the side of the lodge and gave it to him. "Then you will understand this gift." We both knew he'd end up with Cochise's old gun after he delivered that rifle to him, so it was kind of a gift to him, too, but I added a pistol. "For you," I said. I could have given him another rifle—we had more fire arms than we had balls to put in them—but there has to be a hierarchy to your gifts. He understood that, too, and thanked me, saying my generosity was greater than my reputation, etc. We both had to thank each other and compliment each other, as well as Cochise and Morning Star, and we had to smoke some more, so it all took quite some time. This was not the kind of thing an Indian hurried up about.

But finally he told me why he'd come. They'd spotted an army of Mexican soldiers coming over the Rio Bravo at Piedras Negras.

"What's new about that?" I said.

"There are many more than usual."

"Eventually we'd steal your smoke signals and figure that out for ourselves," I told him, and he took it as I meant it and smiled. "Besides, it's the business of our war chiefs."

"No," he said, "it's your business. Your father is with them."

"My father?"

"Hermano O'Donohughe. Your people called him Many Wounds."

"It doesn't matter," I signed. "We don't care about him anymore."

"It matters," he said. "The army heads for Béjar, but he has broken off from them and heads here. He has strange animals with him. It is always a sign of change."

Well strange animals were certainly a sign of change. An Apache inference was never far from its premise.

"If you wish, Cochise will dispose of him," Benito said.

I told Benito to thank Cochise, but that wasn't necessary, though I guess my father's pecuniary reputation had penetrated even the Apache and his return was, indeed, a threatening sign. Worse than missionaries were surveyors and merchants. Their arrival usually meant that white folk were planning on staying, if they hadn't squatted themselves down somewhere behind your back already.

Surveyors were less a threat at first, because everybody hated them and nobody argued about wiping them out. But merchants had things people wanted and a lot of Indians liked that they came around. You could kill them and take their stuff, but then they couldn't come back and others were less likely to come your way again. Besides that, they tended to be defenseless and it was harder to build a rationale for massacring them, even if you were simple savages, *comme nous*. Their presence was insidious because some Indians dealt with them as individuals instead of the harbingers of doom they really were. In that way, a man like Cochise had a lot of foresight, and the favor, stated in Apache, was not that he'd take Hermano out, but that on my word he'd leave him alone. Once again, without him even knowing it, I would save my father's worthless butt.

"Well," I said to Morning Star after Benito Road Runner had left, "we better go see Many Powers."

"Don't bother," she said to me. "The birds have already told her."

# 37

I EXPECTED QUITE A RUCKUS when my father, Hermano Many Wounds O'Donohughe returned to the HorseSleepers, not so much that any of us were excited as that his entourage included a remuda of horses, a dozen black African slaves, two Jumano Indian scouts, six camels, and a new wife who was accompanied by a female retainer. And there wasn't anybody in that bunch who wasn't at his beck and call either, though I later witnessed that he made a rather insincere show, on occasion, of toadying to his new wife. Our scouts spotted them two days off and smoke signaled in, then sent a rider. We knew everything about them before they arrived, except that his wife was an Italian, which was something a little outside a Comanche scout's discernment; not that Hermano wouldn't expect us to know everything ahead of time, if he remembered anything at all. I wondered how Many Powers would deal with this advent, but she was the first one out of her lodge that day. And Always Hits rode out with her as we went to greet them, so to speak, long before they reached the outskirts of our camp.

I had to hurry to catch up because FireBlood was moving like a slow turd. I'd interrupted her breakfast, which she always hated, though she hated it worse to be left behind. She loved me to ride her and loved to give me trouble about it. And that horse must have kept time on something like the Aztec calendar because everyday she had something new to be trouble about. That day was spook-at-a-prairie-dog day, which was a brand new fear as far as I could discern and an absurd one, too, because how could you live and graze out on the plains and be afraid of prairie dogs? Nonetheless, every prairie dog that my war horse spied created a wave of terrified consternation which caused her, every twenty or so paces, to jump and run away, first one direction and then another, running sideways at incredible speeds as we proceeded on out to meet my father's caravan.

Once I got out there it didn't get much better. The two parties stopped in front of each other at a polite distance while me and FireBlood proceeded to run between them sideways. My horse bucked, jumped up and turned around, then ran sideways the other way. It was quite a show. But as the Texians say, when your horse rears up, just take off your hat and wave. The next time FireBlood pranced sideways between them all, I just put my arms out straight like Jesus. "Hello! Hello!" I yelled. Nothing like comic relief in a tense moment, though it did not do much for Comanche dignity.

"It is the Spaniard in him!" yelled my mother.

"How-how!" said Hermano O'Donohughe. Of course no Indian ever said How-how. Who knew where the hell he picked it up. He looked back knowingly at his traveling household, removed his plumed hat, and bowed.

That was it. Nobody seemed to care about anything except the camels, which I'd seen before, in the zoo down in Mexico City. No big moments. No showdowns. Many Powers had a lodge built for Hermano on the other side of the camp, farthest from the bathing stream and closest to the area where everybody went off to poop. Hermano accepted it graciously and put up his own tents: one for his office, one for him and Francesca Maria Donatelli, his wife.

The Africans took the tipi and by the second night the Jumanos were in there, too. We sat around singing songs and telling stories with those guys, most of whom spoke some Spanish and French, as well as English and Dutch. One of the Africans, a big, articulate fellow named Jericho, said that technically none of them were slaves at the moment. When Hermano left Genoa, Italy, he bought a boat of slaves from the Dutch coming out of Gibraltar and sold most of them to the Spanish in Cuba. But when he returned to Mexico he discovered that the Mexicans, in spite of other faults, had outlawed slavery. Of course, Hermano had known that, but like most everybody else, believed the Americans and Europeans that the Mexicans had outlawed slavery just to spite the Anglo-Texans, and really weren't serious about it. But, in fact, as often as not, they were. So Hermano put a gun to his slaves' heads and promised to pay them someday.

"Why don't you just take off?" I said, pouring Jericho and his friends a little Medoc.

"For now," said Jericho, "this is the best job in town. Besides," he grinned, "all around us are the bloodthirsty and hostile Indians."

But now Hermano was headed for Louisiana where, in a marketing maneuver that James Bowie and his brothers had turned into standard procedure, he was going to turn these men in as run-away slaves, collect the bounty, then buy them back for less than half the reward. Then he'd sell them in New Orleans for another profit on top of that. New Orleans wasn't a bad situation for an African if they could stay in town and hook up with a French household, but out on the cotton plantations it was hell. Back in Africa, before they got appropriated by the Dutch, most of these fellows lived a lot like we did only without the horses.

"Did you ever see an elephant?" I said.

"A sea of them," said Jericho. "And cats, lions, as big as your war pony."

He had some great stories about animals in Africa, but I'm not going to go into it. This here is my history of Texas, not *Une Histoire du Monde*.

When I talked to Hermano about the slave thing, he portrayed himself as an honest businessman, simply living within his moral milieu. Now Bowie on the other hand, said Hermano, went over the line. He'd buy his slaves worn out and half-dead from the Laffite brothers on Galveston Island, where the Laffites kept their famous Maison Rouge. Back then Galveston was a pirate island from which those French Laffites raided Spanish and Mexican shipping. Bowie put in his slave order and had Laffite deliver them on the shore of Texas. Then the Bowies marched them straight to New Orleans, all in a matter of days.

"*Con Dios!*" I said to my father. "I'm glad you'd never stoop so low."

"This is what I like about America," said Hermano O'Donohughe. "You can make money without giving anybody anything."

"Pain and misery aside," I said.

"Don't be a fool, Roberto."

"Coyote," I said. "My name is Coyote."

"Pain and misery are inevitable."

"Around some people."

"Sometimes, my son, one must inflict to avoid."

I had him and Francesca over to my tipi for buffalo steak, mesquite beans and mescal bread, a dessert of peeled prickly pear cactus fruit. Of course, like

Indians, we smoked first. Hermano and Francesca brought their own flatware. Afterward I poured Bordeaux.

"I couldn't get my hands on any Tuscan chianti," I said to Hermano. "My importer is French."

Morning Star kept a watchful eye on her step-mother-in-law who avoided conversation by pretending that she only spoke Italian. Hermano said they'd met and married in Florence.

"You should go to Italy, Roberto. It is the crown of Europe."

"Coyote," I said. "My name is Coyote."

"We have heard there was an Italian, a Donatelli, in fact, traveling through San Felipe," said Hermano.

"That was me," I said.

"You are not Italian at all," said my father.

"Neither are you."

My father paused. "Was it not the HorseSleepers?" he said, referring, of course, to the raid.

"*Voulez vous du porto?*" Would you like a bit of port wine? I asked Francesca Donatelli in French. "I rolled some tobacco sticks, as well," I said to Hermano.

"I have Italian cigarettes," he said. In America, even among whites, nobody'd yet seen a cigarette.

Morning Star stood up. "You are both so impressive," she said in Comanche which, thank the Great Everywhere Mystery, was all she spoke, though it didn't keep her from missing much. "I think I hear my horse calling."

"All right," I said, and she left, leaving me and Hermano to impress Francesca.

"I don't know why it took me so long to discover that you had returned here," my father said.

"You didn't have to come."

"You are still my son."

"And who is Many Powers?" I said.

He looked at me straight. "Your mother."

Now Francesca stood. She thanked me, in Italian, and called her retainer who came in immediately and accompanied her out.

"She hears her camel calling," I said.

"Do not make light," said my father. "We have a fine life. And you have a miserable one."

"I have the best life possible," I said.

"If you are lucky enough to live very long."

"I have everything."

"You have nothing. No wealth. No security. Not even a shirt."

"I have a shirt," I said.

"An animal skin."

"I have the freedom to move, to hunt, to ride as far as I can see. My wife is young and smart. I have a place among my People."

"You have no money, no land."

"All of the land is ours."

"Then it will all soon be taken away!" said my father.

It seemed we had a fundamental disagreement. I tried to light some sweet grass that Many Powers had given me, but it wouldn't even take.

"The Sun knows me like a brother," I said to Hermano O'Donohughe. "The Moon is my sister and the Wind is the voice of my mother, the Earth."

"Enough," said my father. "I know all about this talk. Remember? I have chosen my life as well."

I took that as tacit acknowledgement that I'd chosen mine. I took a brand from the fire and lit his cigarette and then my tobacco stick and we smoked our separate fires.

"General Cós has crossed the Rio Bravo to occupy Béjar," my father said to me.

"I'm delighted for him," I said. "And for the people of Béjar."

He ignored me. "Santa Ana has repudiated the Republic."

"I'm shocked," I said.

"For once your cynicism is not misplaced. He has backed the last six revolutions, each time refusing power only to consolidate his own."

"Maybe it's the best thing for Mexico," I said, recalling Sor María Juana's devotion to Santa Ana and figuring it couldn't be absolutely misplaced. She did have a head on her shoulders, even if it was listening to some other part of her body. In the realm of human interaction there was nothing new there.

There was a way in which you could regard Santa Ana as immoral and unscrupulous, capable of first allying himself with, and then betraying, anybody, Royalists, Federalists, Republicans, Creoles, Mestizos, Indians, Gachupines, you name it; he'd side with anyone in his quest to rule the roost. On the other hand, you could argue that he'd been cast into the fires of powerful ambition and just lacked a political philosophy beyond his own survival. I think there's a philosopher, an Italian one in fact, who wrote about stuff like that.

"So the Constitution of 1824 has been defenestrated, so to speak," I said.

"Anyway, you are a well-spoken Comanche," my father said. "Yes, it is out the window, as is Santa Ana's pretense of following it, and the Tejan pretense of championing him."

"That's a lot of pretense out the window," I said.

"And usually what follows is war."

"May the Great Everywhere Mystery bless them all," I said.

"Don't be a fool, Roberto."

"Coyote," I said.

"When it is over, the People will be wiped off the face of the earth."

"So what are you doing with Cós?" I asked him. "I thought you were betting on the English speaking tribes."

"You see where I'm headed. I left Cós."

"What's the matter with Europe?" I got some more port.

Hermano eyed it for a moment before accepting more. As you've probably heard, Indians are not good drunks and I guess I was Indian enough to keep my father on guard.

"In Europe everything is based on blood. I am a Spaniard in Italy, a Creole in Spain. In America, only money counts."

"As long as you're a white man," I said.

"I shall be a rich, white man," said my father, Hermano-Many Wounds O'Donohughue. He sipped. "And you are my son."

"I thought we were done with that rhetoric," I said to him.

"Your education is a wasted pity," he said. "The coming war in Tejas would be comedic if it were not real. Santa Ana can muster so few troops he conscripts starving Maya. He has an army of barefooted farmer Indians. The only person who will come north is his brother-in-law, Cós, whose army of two hundred wears the only military uniforms left in Mexico. The Texans have more commander-in-chiefs than soldiers. Anyone who is not a colonel is a general. The rest are governors of Texas. The Mexican army has no leaders. The Texan army no followers. Cós agreed to cross the Rio Bravo only if he were sent to occupy the Alamo in San Antonio de Béjar, a place which is both worthless and indefensible and so, of course, in this war, it has become an outpost in the most strategic of cities, a gateway to the nothing on either side that no one should want.

Cós is gambling that if he occupies Béjar, such a show of force over so little will convince the Texans that Mexico means business. They will leave him alone. The war, in proper Mexican fashion, will end by entropy."

"He doesn't understand the Yankees," I said.

"No."

Well, as different as we were from the Mexicans, the Mexicans were different from the Texans. It would be like wolves and rabbits trying to sit down and talk peace. But my father was right. The Texans were liable to shoot each other to death before they ever saw an enemy.

"Come with me to Louisiana," said my father.

"I like our chances right here," I said.

My father stood up. "*Buena suerte,* Roberto." he said. "You have no chance here."

"My name is Coyote," I said. "*Buenas noches.*"

After he left I went straight to my mother's.

"Be quick," she said to me. "Hits is coming over."

"Have you talked to Many Wounds?"

"You don't have to be an Apache to honor the names of the dead," she said. When I didn't say anything she spelled it out.

"Many Wounds was a great marksman with the long rifle. A great gambler. A poor rider. A brave enough warrior. A pleasing lover. How was he as a father?" she said.

"Not so good. Always Hits is a better father."

"I loved Many Wounds," said my mother, "but he no longer exists. Towards Hermano O'Donohughe I have no feelings. *C'est la vie.*"

That's when we were interrupted by Always Hits. "Your horse," he said to me.

"I hear her," I said.

Back in my lodge I had one miffed squaw.

"Do not expect me to be a slave like your father's wife," said Morning Star.

"I didn't see her lift a finger," I said.

"A slave of the heart. To have no mind or feelings but your husband's."

"I'm sure she has thoughts and feelings," I said.

"But she does not own them."

"Unlike you," I said, going to her.

"Don't try to fool me," said Morning Star. "The colt follows the stallion. You want a white wife. A useless softness who does nothing." She turned away from me.

"A lot of those white, farm women work real hard," I said.

"That is the other kind of slave."

"What did I do wrong?" I said.

"Shall I come to the conclusion that you will eventually come to? You were born."

"You'd make a good Christian with an attitude like that," I said.

"And you will never make love again with an attitude like that."

"I'm sorry," I said.

"I don't want to live with a man who can leave my world for the *monde*, the world that doesn't know about this one."

I went to her again. "This is my only world," I said. "The world where you are and the world where I am in love with you."

She wept. I had never really seen her cry before. "When you go away, I won't follow you."

"I will never leave," I said.

"You will leave and I will not follow you," she said.

"I love you," I said. "I will never leave this land. I will never leave the HorseSleepers. I will never leave you."

"I will not follow you," Morning Star cried.

I held her and said, "I will never leave."


My father left the next day, minus eleven of his black slaves who decided to become Comanche. Nobody was going to stop them, either, even with me explaining to them that it wasn't an easy road.

"Easier than trying to become a white man," said Jericho.

I had to admit, those were pretty exclusive, if reprehensible, ranks. Though mysteriously, it was Jericho who decided to follow Hermano to Louisiana. My father was a practical man. Now he needed Jericho more than ever and he agreed to give Jericho his freedom if Jericho promised not to leave him.

"You're not free if you've promised not to leave," I said to Jericho.

"I have no intention of becoming a wild Indian," Jericho said.

"Jericho will leave you in a second," I said to my father.

"For what?" said Hermano O'Donohughe.

"I have no love for buffalo meat, nor horses. When we reach New Orleans, Monsieur O'Donohughe has promised me an exquisite filet mignon."

"Fat chance," I said.

Jericho grinned. My father bowed his good-bye to the unassembled HorseSleepers with a sweep of his plumed chapeau.

"It's the hair," Morning Star said to me after the caravan had left and our new African Comanches went out for a bow and arrow lesson with Fat Otter and Always Hits. "They want to grow out their hair."

"I don't think you understand men," I said.

"I don't think you understand anything," said Morning Star. She came to me. "And I don't really like you," she said.

"I understand that."

"We are very different."

"Thank the Great Everywhere Mystery," I said.

"If I could choose not to love you, I would."

"I choose to love you."

"For now, you do. Another difference," she said before kissing me. She pulled me down to the floor of the lodge.

"I love you forever," I said.

"To believe that," said Morning Star, "I would be a fool."

Nonetheless, that's the way I spent the Moon of the Shortest Day and the Moon after that, the No Buffalo Moon, too, making love to Morning Star, enigmatic as the preliminaries might always have been. Those were the longest, most beautiful two months of my life, with their long, dark nights and short, blustery days.

We Comanche spent a lot of time in our tipis and in the sweat lodge in the cold months because it's difficult to hunt on horseback in the winter. For one, the buffalo go into hiding. I don't know where they go. Maybe they go stand in the forest and eat bark, but over the centuries it just became a kind of holy thing to leave them alone during the cold, short days. Besides, horseback riding is more difficult in the winter time. When the ground isn't wet and sloppy it's covered with snow, and if you think it's hard to spot a prairie dog hole at a full gallop, try it on a snow covered field. We just had too much regard for our horses to be out there breaking their legs for them.

Winter was the time we spent training our horses to respond more and more quickly to subtle commands. You'll hear stories that a Comanche could capture and break a wild mustang in two hours, and that's true. But that doesn't mean that you can do much more on them other than stop and go. You can't even use them to pull a travois. They're too full of themselves for that. Travois pulling takes an older, calmer animal. And some horses you train more than others, depending on their temperament and your needs. But your war pony has got to respond to subtle foot commands if you're going to charge into battle or into a herd of buffalo while manipulating a lance or lariat or bow and arrow or even a rifle.

A horse has got to feel your relaxation and confidence right through your butt. And you can't be whipping him and spurring him all the time or he just gets dull. You can train fear out of an animal, but you can also make it afraid of you and you don't want to ride a thousand pounds of something that's afraid of you because he'll try to run out from underneath you.

It doesn't take anything to teach a horse not to be afraid of gunfire. All they have to do is be exposed to it enough times without ill consequence. But how do you make them behave once they aren't afraid anymore? I've seen plenty of cavalry horses that weren't afraid of guns, and they'd budge, too, if you spurred them, but they got so dull to having their ribs pounded that a tribe of Comanche couldn't make them run away. I've witnessed hundreds of American cavalrymen who pounded on the sides of their horses while we ran them down. If the animal takes no joy in running, which is their natural impulse, and no has no fear, how are you going to make him go? That's why you've never seen a Comanche wearing spurs.

Horses don't think things out ahead of time very often. Planning is not their strength. They're flighty and stubborn and clever and lazy. But they're not unwilling to please if they like you. You train a horse with affection and steadiness, patience and reward. You make obedience easy and disobedience an inconvenience. When you're done, you won't even have to touch that horse with your foot; you just shift your weight and she'll give. That animal will be so aware of your body that she'll do whatever you ask almost before you've thought it, so you better watch what you're thinking.

So you don't just train the horse, you train the rider, you train you. It's a mutual thing and if you don't understand that every time you get on your horse you have as much to learn as you do to teach, then you're an impediment to yourself as well as your animal. Each part of your body has to operate absolutely independently from every other part, and so does the horse's, and you have to do all of it together, in complete cooperation and coordination.

Anyway, we did that kind of training in the winter months when we were living on jerky and stale bread and things were slow. Without the details, which no Comanche is ever going to give you, that's what Always Hits, one of the greatest horse trainers in the history of the world you never heard of, taught me. You won't find it in Xenophon, who wrote the ancient Greek horse training manual, either. The Comanche didn't write it down. In fact, it barely gets said. It's so secret it gets passed on by the sense of touch.

It was near the end of that month whites call January. I'd gone out with Fat Otter to hunt antelope, though Sad Little Dog had followed us, unwanted though he was, and he walked behind us and kept up his insults the whole time.

"You are not brave," he said to me. "You don't shoot well. You don't ride well. You are dominated by your horse, your mother, and your wife. Your reputation is false and will only bring doom upon the HorseSleepers."

It would have been easier to refute him had any of it been false. I'd have called him a Harpie if he could have understood what it meant. Finally Fat Otter turned around and hit him on the head with his quiver and that quieted him long enough for us to bag a few rabbits. It was cold and starting to get dark, so we turned back toward camp, looking forward to some rabbit stew and a nice, hot sweat bath, *sans* Sad Little Dog, though I'd probably have to buy him off with a rabbit. Unfortunately, when we got back, we found the third visitor of the season waiting at the winter camp of the HorseSleepers. A Cherokee brave, he came in from the northeast. Three messengers, bad news and bad luck, that's what we say. His ponies were tired and you could see they weren't much to speak of to begin with. Like the Apache brave who'd come at the beginning of the winter, he was hungry and generally put out by his assignment. He signed peace and, as always, contrary to our reputation, we welcomed him. He had a big message. It was a big deal. And, of course, he was looking for me.

# 38

THE CHEROKEE HAD been around white Anglos a lot longer than most of us plains types, so unlike the Apache they'd already had a reform movement in terms of wearing white clothes and the rest. The Cherokee were an adaptable bunch in general and you could find that admirable or you could find that despicable depending on how you liked to find things. Word was that they were so good at mimicking white living, to the point of running huge plantations and owning black slaves—hell, they even built churches and became Methodists, wore dresses and pants and shoes and coats—that the Anglos ran them out. They were better white bigots than the whites themselves. And they got wealthy at it, too. Not that hiding in the woods would have saved them. The Seminole, Creek, Choctaw, and Chickasaw, among others, all tried that and the Anglos came in and chopped down the trees and killed everybody. My old friend Sam Houston could point to his scars and tell you which of those tribes helped him earn them. Over where the sun rises, beyond the great forest, if you couldn't live in water up to your waist you weren't going to get to keep your land.

But the Cherokee tried the conformity and peace thing, so even under the terms of white morality it was harder to find reasons to slaughter them. Nonetheless, the Yankees decided to slaughter them anyways until Houston, whose life they'd saved on several occasions, convinced Big Chief Andrew Jackson to just throw them off their land in the middle of winter and make them walk without food for a thousand miles to the Oklahoma Territory where a bunch of Wichita and Kiowa and Osage already lived. Of course a couple of decades of living like whites suited them real well for the walk. Half of them died getting there and half of the rest died when they got there because their crops failed that summer when it didn't rain. The ones that lived brought all kinds of new diseases with them, so everybody was real delighted to have them around.

So you can understand why in terms of copying the whites the Cherokee had come full circle. You couldn't find a stitch of white anything on a Cherokee. As Indians went, they were reactionaries, ultra-conservatives. A lot of them, like this messenger, even shaved his head and just grew a short crop down the middle, like in the old days, because long hair was a real nuisance in the woods. They dropped the farming and started riding horses and fighting with the Wichita over buffalo. Word was, though, that when Houston left his wife and governorship back in Tennessee, he hid out with the Cherokee again. For better or worse, they liked him and to be honest, I did too.

I rode out with Fat Otter and greeted the Cherokee where he waited on the eastern edge of the camp. His name was Flat Top and I invited him into my lodge for something to smoke and eat. He declined, signing that he'd first give his message, which was for everybody, as well as me, and then we could decide if we still wished to feed him. From the start it sounded like it was going to be great news.

"You're not going to get to talk at everybody," I said in English. I figured, being Cherokee, he'd speak some English.

"We no longer speak that tongue," he signed.

I guess I should have figured that, too. "Well, you can listen to it," I said. Sign language was universal in the plains, but it had its limitations of expression. "The People don't assemble to listen to each other," I said to him. "They're not going to gather around to listen to you."

Usually Indians are more polite, but he'd already cut right to the business by refusing to smoke and eat.

"Call them anyways," Flat Top said.

Otter puffed out his chest and prodded his paint pony, then began riding around Flat Top in a tight circle. It was threatening stuff, you know, like the preliminaries to a cock fight, but though the Cherokee pony shied, Flat Top himself remained stoic. He gathered his tired horse and ignored Otter pretty good. But the point had been made. Fat Otter was simply pointing out that there'd been a breach of etiquette.

But with Indians this could go on forever. A brave like this one wasn't going to apologize. We'd just end up with a dead Cherokee and be sitting around in the sweat lodge speculating as to what the message might have been, which is good sport for the winter months but there are obvious disadvantages if the message turns out to be important. That aside, killing a messenger before he gives you his message is the kind of thing the women never let you live down. I think there's a parallel among white folks, but even they wait to kill him after he gives the message.

So I gave out a loud yip-yip, etc., letting the band know what they'd already chosen to ignore, that this Cherokee was here with a message. Some kids showed up, and a half-dozen of our new African Comanches. This kind of thing was new for them; I guess they were curious. And Flat top, seeing this was as good as he was going to get—I guess he'd pictured himself lecturing to a thousand Comanche warriors stretched over the plains—gathered himself and began signing and uttering.

More or less, he said this: The reputation of Coyote O'Donohughe extended all over the plains in the four sacred directions, from the south land of the Apache to the north land of the Cree, from the rising sun to the setting sun. Coyote has led a thousand raids against white settlements. His staff is thick with white scalps. It is said, disguised as the wind or an eagle, he rides with every war party. But now the Texians are very angered and Chief Austin has decided that thousands of Rangers must ride against Coyote's People and destroy all of them. He, Flat Top, has been sent by Coyote's friend, the great Texian Chief, The Raven, Big Drunk Houston, to warn the HorseSleepers. But if Coyote will leave the HorseSleepers and give Houston his word that he will not lead any raids against the Texians, Big Drunk will convince the Rangers not to attack.

Well, Otter was right. We should have killed him before he gave his message. And all of this only confirmed for me that being a living legend was just the last step before becoming a dead one. Of course, all of those so-called raids just amounted to the telling and re-telling of the two raids I'd actually been, well, for lack of a better word, involved in. As it got passed from person to person, band to band, tribe to tribe, the story changed so much that by the time it came around again it sounded like I was some combination of Achilles and Arjuna (Sor María taught me about those fellows and I learned more about them at Harvard); a completely different thing, though there were enough similarities to mark it all as a peculiarly Coyote story. On the other side were the Texian stories: if thirty Texians went out to kill ten Comanche, they'd say that they fought a hundred of them, then it was only a matter of time before I'd led a thousand Comanches in a hundred attacks against ten Texians and managed to murder three of them.

But you had to figure that the threat against us was real enough. White men, in general, were big on symbolic gestures, and not having a clue about what the consequences of rubbing out the HorseSleepers would be, Austin undoubtedly felt that a strike like that would put the Comanche thing away long enough for him to get on with his revolution against Mexico. Besides, Texians loved to kill Indians. For them it was more fun than shooting buffalo. If Austin was having trouble conscripting volunteers for his Mexico war, he could gather up a bunch of madmen to slaughter Indians and once he had them together, hell, just turn them south.

But Houston knew a couple things. For one, we preferred to stay out of the whole mess from the start, and for another, we weren't a bunch of mud-hut squatting farmers like the Indians Austin had cleaned out northeast of the Sabine. Getting me out of the picture would save a lot of lives, Comanche, and Texian as well, and it would simply confirm what we'd have chosen to do anyways, that is, stay out of it, because if the Comanche wanted to fight, then getting rid of one war chief wasn't going to stop them. Besides, I wasn't even a war chief and more, after San Felipe, everybody but Wind Sister figured everything was even with the Texians. But as I said, white men were big on symbolic gestures and Sam Houston knew that if I said I'd leave I'd keep my word, as long as I didn't have to commit to how long.

"Austin will not make war on your people, but you will be pursued," Flat Top said, because Houston knew if he asked me to turn myself in, then there would be a war. He knew his Indians, or if he didn't, Luz did. And if I left, Texian and Comanche alike would get to slip nobly out the back flap of the lodge, willing to fight but not having to, leaving everybody off the hook. On his side, keeping me alive left him a big wild card out on the plains. And avoiding a war with us kept another Texian Commander-in-Chief, besides himself, from consolidating an army and a successful military campaign. White Texas was a viper pit.

"Okay," I said to Flat Top. "Let's eat now."

We went over to Fat Otter's and stewed up the rabbits because I was afraid to face Morning Star. I wasn't going to take it to council after Flat Top left, either, because I didn't want anybody getting the idea to fight or run. It was one thing to lure a white militia into a trap, which they weren't going to fall for every time, another to face them in pitched battle. And if we ran away we were liable to come back next year and find a city where our hunting grounds used to be.

Many Powers took it philosophically, as you might expect. *"C'est la guerre,"* she said.

"Don't over-react, Mother."

"Do not worry so much about Morning Star," she said. She came to me. "Men are replaceable."

"I'll come back."

"Nonetheless, I will get pregnant again while there is time."

Well, that was hardly sending me out with my shield and telling me to come back with it or on it, but she didn't create this world of war and loss, she was born into it. Her next son would be full Comanche and born in rage. But it was a much different kind of rage that I had to face that night with Morning Star.

"All the signs have said you would leave," she said.

"But not the signs in my heart," I said.

"A man's heart does not know how to love a woman."

"Come with me," I said. "I can disguise us."

"I cannot be your white wife. I will not be your Indian whore."

"Men have always gone to battle," I said. "That wouldn't change no matter who you married."

"Unless I married you and you changed."

"Men don't change," I said.

"No," she said. "Women change. And the world has changed. This is no longer about taking coup and winning ponies. It's big war with whites, and death everywhere. The whites have changed everything, but Comanche men have not changed and so they will die."

"We've changed," I said. "We can make death with them."

"That is the wrong change."

"But this time I am leaving because I can keep war away from the HorseSleepers. I haven't chosen to be the one around whom the circle of the world turns. But I am a great Coyote and it has happened to me."

"The world will spin with you or without you, Coyote," whispered my wife, Morning Star. "I will not sympathize with the man who leaves me."

That's why I didn't talk to Dark Eagle or Talks Peace or White Calf or even Always Hits about any of this; I would have just been resented. In that way, Sad Little Dog was a chip that never fell far from the buffalo. You couldn't do a good deed for a Comanche warrior, not if it came in the shape of diplomacy. They fought or they didn't and that's all they understood. But a Coyote was a trickster, not a warrior, a natural creator of dishevelment whose intentions always proved irrelevant to the good or bad outcome of his acts. As his occasional embodiment, my people didn't have to like me, but they had to accept me, and women had to accept us men and let the chips, so to speak, fall where they may.

Morning Star might not have sympathized with me, but she loved me and I loved her. Our night was not filled with tears, but with passion. Or, as she put it, she'd already cried in this future a hundred times. I awoke beside her heat, before dawn, and we prepared my ponies, gathered up my guns, parfleche bag, food, white clothes. Above the first red hues of the rising sun, Morning Star's namesake scattered her steady light into the deep, blue eastern sky. She rode with me to the edge of the village where beyond stretched the rivers and forests and plateaus, once the hunting grounds of the Caddos and Apache and now the cotton fields and war fields of Texas.

I touched Morning Star's face and kissed her.

"I love you," I said.

"I love you, Coyote," said my love. "I will wait here with our child."

"I love you," I said again.

It wasn't Morning Star who cried now, it was me. My heart ached. I knew, inside, I was not at all brave. If the Rangers were scouring the plains for Coyote, well then I'd head for the most unlikely place in the world to look. I'd sit among the whites in their heart of nothing, between the wastelands that nobody in their right mind would fight over. I was headed for the safest place in the world. Béjar. San Antonio. The Alamo.

Part Two

# 39

I HEADED ACROSS the plains for east Texas and the Alamo, the worst of winter behind me and the worst of spring ahead. The sun still crossed the southern sky in a low, winter arc, but by now in the Month of Winter Grass, February to some, you could feel the sun warm your face as you rode in the mid-afternoon. In the southern plains, the buffalo herds would begin to stir, and it would be a good time to hunt them, before they shed their thick, winter fur.

I'd taken my war mare, FireBlood, and a pack mule carrying jerky and mescal bread, mescal bean and acorn meal cakes, two skins of Alexis de Tocqueville's French wine, a blanket, and a suit of white man's clothes: a cotton, button down shirt, leather trousers, a belt. My friend, brother, and brother-in-law, Fat Otter, had offered me a pair of boots he'd gleaned during our raid on San Felipe de Austin, but as of yet I couldn't abide the confinement of boots. I settled for calf high moccasins. Enough frontiersmen wore those in lieu of boots, which were often hard to get once you were out here in the middle of nowhere. Of course, I abandoned my bow and arrows and other Comanche weaponry, carrying a Bowie knife, a big flintlock horse pistol, and a percussion cap Pennsylvania long rifle. I cut my hair and wore a floppy hat that my mother, Many Powers, picked up the last time we traded in Santa Fe.

I could never figure out why she'd traded for that thing. She never wore it. She never wore anything made by whites. But the day I left she pulled it out and said, "You see?" My mother, who taught me shape shifting as well as the art of disguise, thought more about it than I did, besides having a knack for thinking about the future, something we Comanche men seldom did.

Morning Star, on the other hand, gave me no material object to aid my adventure, nor to remember her by. On the buffalo bedding of our lodge on the night before I left, she touched me and placed me inside her with a miraculous, passionate delicacy that made me ache, repeating over and over with each different caress of that long, body heat night, "Remember this. And remember this." That was her way. There'd be no solace for my aching love but a speedy return.

I still carried my parfleche, which I could always pass off as war booty, and in there I carried my medicine: tobacco, white sage, Jimson weed, war paint, a dry peyote button, as well as my animal powers, the claws and teeth of a coyote, and the hind foot of a jackrabbit. I was headed for what I figured to be the safest place in Texas. The Alamo. Santa Ana's brother-in-law, General Martin Perfecto de Cós, had taken two hundred of the only uniformed soldiers in Mexico up to San Antonio de Béjar in December, figuring a show of great force over a monument both worthless and indefensible, in the middle of a bunch of land nobody really wanted, would chagrin the disunited Texians and keep them pinned down on their River Brazos settlements, if not send them back east of the Sabine River where they belonged. That's the kind of place I wanted to be. A place nobody wanted. And all the better that it was close to home and Mexican.

It was just a few years back, after the last failed Texian revolution, that we Comanche practically owned San Antonio. Stabled horses there, rolled through whenever we wanted and took what we pleased. But we didn't want the darn place either. I didn't want to be away from the HorseSleepers and Morning Star any longer than I had to, and having been raised Comanche most of my life and Mexican the rest, I generally preferred Mexicans to Anglos. For one, most of them were at least half Indian.

As I rode left of the arcing sun, southeast, toward Béjar, a rider came directly out of the east at a steady gallop. A rider coming directly out of the east brings death. You can bet against that, of course, but there's no reason not to be cautious. I took FireBlood from a trot down to a slow walk and cocked my weapon. This rider came west in a black whirlwind and it didn't take me long to realize that this was no normal horseman, but some kind of devil or ghost.

That rider came on like a tornado, but I stood my ground. I prayed north, south, up, down, west, and east; thanked the four-leggeds and the two-leggeds, and then I waited as the whirlwind came around me, circling. I looked at FireBlood's ears for some indication who this was, but her ears were straight up and plain scared, though she wasn't going to run anywhere because that thing had us surrounded. I reached in my parfleche for my power, but that s when I heard my name coming from the whirlwind.

"Coyote!" it said.

I recognized the voice. The wind died down as if Earth Mother had sucked the tornado into herself in a single breath. There, where once the tornado raged, sat Doe Skin on her favorite pinto, Three Skies. She still carried the scar on her neck where her head had been separated from her shoulders, and though she was a small, pretty girl, her hair and nails had continued to grow in death. Her long nails folded around her pony's reins and her war staff. Her hair, which always had streaks of red, ran long and loose to her knees.

"Doe Skin," I said. "Sister."

"If you call the dead your sister," said Doe Skin, "you are brave."

"Just foolish," I said.

"You must be foolish to be brave," she said. "The dead need your memories. That is the air we inhabit."

"Your parents think of you everyday, though they do not speak your name. Wind Sister has left the HorseSleepers to avenge you."

"You honor me, Coyote," she said. "But you have already avenged my death."

She meant that I'd taken the scalp of her killer, Henry Wax Karnes Jr. But Doe Skin was always extremely close to Wind Sister and died before I could ever figure out what she felt about Sister's liaison with Turkey Feathers. Given the circumstances, I just wanted to keep things positive.

"Are the Plains of the Dead so full that you are ready to come back as a white?" I said. That's what some of us believed, that when we died our souls went west, but when the land of the dead filled up with Indians, they d start to return to life, out of the east, as white people.

"It will never be so full," she said without cracking a smile.

Well okay, the dead don't have to banter. Death is dark. I guess if the dead started grinning at you it would be even more disconcerting than all the glowering they tend to do. "And are the Plains of the Living so mad that Comanches must dress as whites?"

With Comanche this kind of preliminary talking can go on for hours if you let it and nothing original will ever get said. We're a people who take great comfort in saying the same stuff over and over. Things had settled down so now FireBlood started to get nervous. She sniffed at Three Skies, but she'd never encountered a ghost horse before which, of course, didn't have a smell. Soon enough, she'd disregard it if she couldn't pick a fight and decide I was standing around in the open plains shooting my mouth off at absolutely nothing. More, she didn't have a lot of tolerance for that kind of thing. I'd trained her for battle, but I'd never thought to train her for mystical encounters.

"I've got life saving business in Béjar," I said to Doe Skin.

"You will not save your life or anyone's life in Béjar."

"I will if I have to," I said.

Doe Skin sighed in a chilling whistle that moved the grass and moaned in the mesquite bean and cottonwood trees. The east wind, I remembered, is the breath of the dead. "I am not wandering. I am a messenger. The concerns of the living are not our concerns. But you have promised to bring us back, if only for a short time."

To be honest, I didn't really remember making precisely that deal. I had called upon the Ancestors to help me during that tense situation with Old John Taylor and Henry Wax Karnes Jr., and I did abuse Doe Skin's head a little bit in my various deceptions, but I hadn't agreed to anything that I knew of. It's just the nature of being a Coyote to get in over your head before you even know what you're getting into at all.

"Tell my parents I am not wandering, Coyote," said Doe Skin. "But the dead are moving to make room for more dead." The wind began to pick up in a whirl around Three Skies' feet and soon Doe Skin disappeared in that tornado of wind that rushed west and then evaporated into the sky. Later I heard there were a lot of tornadoes that day, white people, of course, attributing them to the weather. But any Indian could tell you that the dead were heading west and soon there'd be plenty dead in the east to replace them.

I reined FireBlood and started southeast again for San Antonio. My delay with Doe Skin took a lot longer than it felt and I arrived at the outskirts of the colony with the fall of dusk. There wasn't a soul in the Alamo. The streets of the city were lit and the air filled with the sound of trumpets and guitars. Texians, and a few Tejanos, too, danced in the streets. I didn't know where Cós was, but it looked like the Texians had taken back the town. I should have hightailed it for somewhere else right then, except something made me curious. There at the edge of town, tethered and guarded by two men, stood Cielo de Noche, the battle stallion of General Antonio López de Santa Ana.

# 40

ON THE EDGE OF TOWN, on Calle de la Soledad, bordering the river, sat a ranchería that James Bowie inherited from the Governor of Coahuila and Tejas. Bowie married the governor's daughter, Ursula Veramendi, in 1831, white calendar. So he automatically became a Mexican citizen. There was a lot of talk about when and where he abandoned his family, but one thing for certain, he was gone by the time the cholera killed them all in 1834. He immediately inherited a ton of money and 750,000 acres of Mexican Tejas. He can't help it if he's lucky.

One story had it that his grief was so deep when he lost his family, his wife and kids, he fell into drunkenness. Then the Veramendi family tried to write him out of his inheritance and he had to sue them to get it, but the way Mexican bureaucracy worked it might have taken years. More depression and drunkenness over that. So he was through trying to do it from the inside, so to speak, and turned to running slaves.

I tethered FireBlood at the gate of the palace, though the party had spilled out onto the streets of San Antonio de Béjar; a lot of Texians gone crazy on corn whiskey, so there weren't too many Tejanos out in public. It was the kind of situation where the poor had to protect their daughters.

At the door of the hacienda, checking weapons, was Erastus Deaf Smith. The last time I'd seen him I was heading back to the HorseSleepers and he was turning tail.

"Donatelli!" said Smith.

"That's my mother's name," I said to him. "It's a European thing. Now, like an American, I'm using my father's name, O'Donohughe." One thing about deception, there's no lie better than the truth.

"Like that injun?" said Deaf Smith.

"What injun?" I said.

"Son," said Smith, "I don't think you have the savvy to survive in this country."

"What's going on here?" I asked him. From the doorway I could see things were a little more civilized, as Texians go, inside the palace. Anglos in various tattered uniforms drank whiskey from glasses. Some Tejana women wore colorful, Mexican dresses, and the few Anglo women wore gowns. There was music and dancing.

"Where have you been?" shouted Smith. "Austin declared war on Mexico in September. We took González Town. Fannin's holding Goliad. We fought Cós here for three weeks in December before trapping him in the Alamo and running him out. Me and Mike Fink and Henry Wax Karnes took this town house by house, a crowbar in one hand and a musket in the other. Hell, I got wounded right on the roof of Bowie's ranch here when we took it back." He bared his shoulder and showed me the wound. "Colonel Milam took a bullet in the head right where we stand. Of course, he's dead. But Cós signed for the Constitution of 1824 and promised that the Mexicans would never cross the Rio Grande. It's over. We own Texas!"

That Constitution of 1824 was the Republican Constitution the Mexican liberals created after they threw out Emperor Iturbide. Of course, none of the last dozen dictators had listened to it let alone Santa Ana. But needless to say, old Deaf Smith's summary was a bit confusing. Even if Stephen F. Austin had only declared allegiance to the Mexican Republican Constitution as an excuse to revolt, it didn't mean they were free of Mexico if Cós signed for the 1824 Constitution. It didn't mean anything. Hell, Cós didn't have authority to sign for anything anyway.

"So that s why Santa Ana is here," I said. "To sign the peace."

"Santa Ana? What're you crazy? He's hiding down in Mexico. You'll never see his chicken butt up here in Texas. We already destroyed the whole Mexican army."

Well, to be honest, I'd seen Santa Ana's butt, both naked and clothed, and had some idea about where he'd put it and where he wouldn't. But it was obvious to me that Smith wasn't the man to discuss this with.

"Where's Karnes?" I said.

"You mean Colonel Karnes."

"Yes, Colonel Karnes."

"He left with Colonel Neill for Washington-on-the-Brazos when Bowie showed up to blow up the Alamo. They're going to form a national government over there."

"But he didn't blow it up," I said. "It's right over there."

"Hell, we might need it. But we blew some holes in it celebrating."

"Why would you need it now? And why would you blow holes in something you might need?"

"You Europeans don't understand anything," said Deaf Smith. "There's still plenty of hostiles west of here. Comanche, in particular. I'm leaving tomorrow to join Houston up in Cherokee territory. We're going to be a nation; we'll need an army and a commander-in-chief, and forts."

That didn't explain the holes, but it explained something, I guess.

"Colonel Smith," I said.

"I'm not a military man," said Deaf Smith. "I'm a scout."

"Erastus."

"That'll do."

"You forgot something?"

"What's that?" he said.

"You're deaf."

"Shit," said Deaf Smith. "You knew that already."

I moved inside to try and locate Bowie, but I didn't see him. Who I did see off in a corner of the hall, surrounded by a bevy of matrons and maids, Texian and Tejana alike, was none other than the President of Mexico, the great General San Antonio López de Santa Ana. He had on his white military riding pants and high, black boots, but he wore a civilian shirt, ruffled at the neck and wrists. On the other side of the hall, I spotted Colonel William Travis, decked out in a new military uniform. If anything, it looked French.

I wandered over to the ladies' table where there was a bowl of punch that didn't have tequila or whiskey in it. Though my time in Mexico City and my interlude with Alexis de Tocqueville had given me a penchant for wine, we Comanche tended to avoid hard liquor. I scooped out a cup of punch and walked casually over to the circle surrounding General Santa Ana. After a while he looked up and spotted me, then casually looked away. He was a notorious womanizer, but he had the kind of charm, and romantic style that just seemed to make women all the more interested, though right now these women were teasing him about being nervous as he waited for his betrothed to appear. By this point I assumed they weren't aware who he really was, because I happened to know that Santa Ana was currently married.

He looked up again and I nodded and smiled. This time he held my eye for a moment before looking away. The band played some lively Mexican music and men asked women to dance, which winnowed the crowd around Santa Ana a little. As I listened, I had to admit, that the Mexican trumpet was as joyous as the military trumpet was terrifying. Santa Ana lifted his glass to his female entourage, caught my eye again, and excused himself. He sauntered over to me.

"My friend," he said to me. "Let me say, before you utter a word, that you are a dead man."

"When I rode Cielo de Noche down La Avenida de los Muertes, you said I would ride with you when you conquered the hemisphere."

"A metaphor of hope, only," he said.

"The stallion looks good for his age," I said to him.

"Roberto," said Santa Ana. My Mexican name. "I remember now. But I'm sorry to say it changes nothing."

"Why don't you just roll into town and round everybody up? You could end everything right here," I said.

"There is rain in the air, Roberto. No one wants to fight in the rain," he said. "Besides, I am getting married!"

"You're already married."

"You are boring me, Roberto," said Santa Ana. "Go and enjoy your last few hours of life."

"I think you've misread my sympathies, great General," I said to him.

He laughed hard. "Your sympathy is irrelevant, my friend. Unless you enlisted in our great army. But in no time I would have you executed for a lack of incompetence."

"That's funny," I said.

"I can be delightful," said Santa Ana. "Now go away. I await my betrothed."

Well, if that's the way he wanted it, fine. It's too bad I liked him so much. He was funny, in a cruel sort of way. I glanced around the room for Bowie, though he seemed nowhere in his own house. But I happened to spot Travis standing stiff and austere on the other side of the room. Like Santa Ana, he was taller than me, especially with the lifts he wore in his boots.

"Colonel Travis," I said.

He gazed at me down his nose. "Donatelli," he said. "If we didn't need manpower I would have you shot."

I sure was a popular man around there in the wanting me dead department, even with the wrong identity.

"Donatelli is my mother's name," I said. "I'm using my father s name now, like an American. O'Donohughe."

"Like the Indian."

"What Indian?" I said. "Who's in charge here? I have some important information."

"Unfortunately Bowie was elected Commander of the Alamo by his own men today. Because he lets them get drunk. This party started after we ousted Cós. It continued until Crockett showed up and then they celebrated that. Now they're celebrating Bowie's election. Like Bowie, these men have been drunk for two months. When he's not sick, he's drunk. And right now he's drunk."

That wasn't the first time I heard of Crockett. He had a reputation for helping Andrew Jackson and Sam Houston slaughter the Creeks.

"I thought he was supposed to blow up the Alamo," I said.

"Houston sent him to blow up the Alamo," said Travis. "Houston sent me to blow up the Alamo. Houston told Neill to blow up the Alamo."

"Well?"

"Houston is hiding out with the Cherokee," said Travis. "He has an army of zero men."

"You saying he's a coward?" I said.

"Let us just say he is intimidated by bravery and intelligence."

"Yours in particular," I said to him.

"Mine in particular," said Travis.

I guess he felt angry enough about everything to be forthright, though he was pretty much regularly that way. "Anybody run against Bowie?" I said.

Travis looked at me so hard his lip almost curled.

"Sorry," I said. "That's a pretty nice uniform. Did you get it in New Orleans?"

"Yes,"said Travis. "It's Irish. But the best I could do, for now. I bought it from and Irishman, in fact, named Herman O'Donohughe. Very reputable."

"O'Donohughe," I said. "Like the Indian."

"What Indian?" said Travis. "You aren't related to Herman O'Donohughe?"

"No," I said. Though Herman O'Donohughe was certainly likely to be my father, Hermano. And I'd hate to find out what Travis paid for that French uniform, but I bet it was a lot more than my father paid for it, if he paid for it at all.

"There is a rumor," Travis said. He had a way of talking straight into the air without looking at you, as if he were addressing the immortals. "There is a rumor that Santa Ana will not honor Cós's agreement."

"No kidding," I said.

"That he is forming an army of ten thousand of Mexico's best in Mexico City and will march on Texas in the spring."

"Colonel Travis," I said. "I don't know how many men he brought with him, but Santa Ana is already here."

"That's madness," said Travis. "We have scouts everywhere."

"Maybe they all got drunk."

"How close do you think he is?"

"He's in this room, damn it!" I said. "He's right over there!" I pointed across the room.

Santa Ana, seeing me, laughed and waved at Travis, who nodded regally.

"Mr. O'Donohughe," said Travis, "that is the brother-in-law of Antonio Menchaca. He is betrothed to the adopted daughter of Doña Santos Ximenes. It is a Tejano thing and not our concern."

"I thought all Texians were Tejanos," I said.

"Please," Travis sneered.

"Well where's Menchaca?" I said.

"He left," said Travis. "Almost all of the Tejanos have packed up and gone."

"You don't wonder why?"

"Mexicans are not fighters."

"Who the hell are they running from?"

"Us?" he said.

That made more sense than anything else he'd said, and I'd have given up on that glorious blockhead if Santa Ana, who had his whole army a buffalo's breath from San Antonio de Béjar, hadn't given me only a few hours to live.

"Colonel Travis," I said, "Sir. You can end this whole war right now by walking over there and arresting the President of Mexico. Texas will be yours and the Comanche's."

"Texas is already ours," Travis said. "We may have to fight to keep it, but there is plenty of time." He looked down at me, finally. "Mr. O'Donohughe, examine the absurdity of what you are saying."

"Have you ever seen Santa Ana?" I said.

Travis pulled out a small hand pistol and leveled it at my head. "If you have ever seen him, then you are a traitor and a Mexican spy whom I will execute this very second."

The last time he saw me he accused me of being a Comanche spy. Now I was a Mexican spy. It seemed every time I tried to do somebody some good, they assumed the opposite. While most people, who said one thing and meant another, were taken at face value, I told the plain truth and ended up hung out in the sun like a buffalo skin. That says something about human acumen, but nothing I can fathom. Maybe the truth is always just too absurd. Or like my Mother, Many Powers, always said, the world is upside down and you don't fix it by standing on your head.

The band had apparently taken a break during our conversation, because the music kicked up again and people began to shout and dance. William Travis lowered his pistol, I decided to try one more time.

"Colonel Travis," I said. "Take him into custody like you did to me when I showed up in San Felipe de Austin."

"It is his wedding night," said Travis. He caught the eye of a Texian belle who came toward him and put out her hand. He bowed to her and then turned to me. "Santa Ana could not march troops here, sir. We're having the worst winter in history. Horrible snow storms deep into Mexico. When it hasn't snowed, it has rained. There were twisters today and tonight you can already hear the thunder of another storm."

"You sure it isn't cannon fire?"

"Don't be a dishonorable fool," Travis said and turned back to the woman.

"Where's Bowie?" I said.

Travis turned his head toward the floor where I saw a boot toe sticking out from under the table cloth of the liquor table. I went over there and found James Bowie in a stupor under the table. I shook him.

"Colonel Bowie," I said. "Wake up! Santa Ana is here!"

Bowie raised his head, startled. He was a big man, not as big as Houston, but an inch taller than Travis and a good deal broader and older, as well.

"Santa Ana!" screamed Bowie. "Hurry up! Surrender!" Then his eyes focused on me and he suddenly relaxed. "Oh, Donatelli," he said. "You son-of-a-bitch. If I could get up, I'd kill you."

Good thing I came in disguise. Who knows what feelings people would have had about me if they knew who I really was.

"Donatelli is my mother s name," I said. "I'm using my father's name now, like an American. O'Donohughe."

"Like the Indain," said Bowie.

"Indain?"

"An Indain by any other name is still an Indain," James Bowie said.

"Colonel Bowie," I said, "Antonio Menchaca's brother-in-law is really Santa Ana."

"Antonio Menchaca's brother-in-law is Enrique de la Peña."

"Captain José Enrique de la Peña is on Santa Ana's staff!" I yelled at Bowie. I knew. I'd met him down in Teotihuacan when he let me ride Santa Ana's stallion.

"You're thinking of Lieutenant Colonel José Enrique de la Peña," said Bowie.

"No, you re thinking of Lieutenant Colonel José Enrique de la Peña and he's not Lieutenant Colonel José Enrique de la Peña, he's Santa Ana!"

"You're making me dizzy," said Bowie. "You know, I haven't felt well since the day your damn horse kicked me in the chest. If I could get up I'd slice off your cojones."

He reached vaguely for his big Bowie knife, but gave up.

"It was an accident," I said.

"My ass," said Bowie.

"You're not going to arrest Santa Ana?"

"Arrest Antonio Menchaca's brother-in-law, Enrique de la Peña, on the night of his engagement? What're you crazy? We're having a party!"

Well I wasn't going to wander through that labyrinth again. The next time through the bull might come out and eat me.

"You can end the war with Mexico right now by arresting Santa Ana," I said.

"Right," said Bowie. "Just show me where he is."

"He's right across the room!"

"If I have to go through that again I'm going to puke," said Bowie.

"Then we should all get our asses in the Alamo, because the Mexicans are here!" I said to him.

Bowie lay back down on the floor and spoke to the air. "The Alamo is indefensible," he said.

"Then blow it up and get out."

"We can't blow it up."

"Why not?"

"Because Houston said to blow it up. Who the hell is Houston, telling me what to do."

"The Commander-in-Chief?"

"Nice try," said Bowie. "I should kill you, you little son-of-a-bitch," he said, but instead he passed out.

Just then there was a lot of commotion and I poked my head out from underneath the table to see Santa Ana's betrothed, Lucia Ximenes, the adopted daughter of the wealthy Tejana, Doña Santos Ximenes, slowly making her way down the long, balustrade of the stairway. She was a small, delicate, round-faced, Indian girl, a dark intelligence in her black eyes. She was a beautiful young woman and I recognized her immediately as Coahuiltecan, a confederation of tribes from the Mexican north, close to rubbed out now by the Lipan Apache and Mexican vaqueros. She was assertive, yet circumspect as she moved down the stairs in her full length, satin gown, bare shoulders covered by a colorful, Mexican, silk scarf. She was deeply confident and a little shy. She waved across the hall to Santa Ana, who grinned and waved. She was smiling. She was Sam Houston's mistress, Luz!

# 41

THERE WAS A HELL OF A LOT of courting and dancing and flower throwing, kissing and bowing and curtsying, shouting and toasting and more dancing before things settled down enough for Santa Ana to release Luz to dance with other men. We Comanche did not partake in much organized dance, though Sor María Juana had taken me through a step or two down in la Ciudad. I watched the feet real close. It looked like if you could count to three or four you could do most anything, and if you moved your hand the woman did something for you. I waited for a waltz because I wanted to move slowly and stay in talking distance. And I didn't want to dance anything where you had to give up your partner, like one of those Texian wheel dances.

When I queued up for my turn, the President of Mexico said to me, "My friend, I like you so much. You have cojones and I will enjoy taking them."

"I like you, too," I said. Hell, what did I have to lose besides my cojones? My head, maybe. I took Luz's hand and walked her to the dance floor, one, two, three, one, two, three.

"Coyote," she said, being one of the ones who knew.

"That's right, I said. "The Indian O'Donohughe." I felt I knew her well enough, Indain to Indain, as Bowie might say, to get right to the point. "I suppose you're the only one here who realizes you're about to marry Santa Ana."

"Not the only one," said Luz, dipping as I raised my hand. We spun and she threw El Presidente a kiss, which he returned to her offering me his most gracious and friendly grin. "Some Tejanos know," said Luz. "The ones who are leaving tomorrow."

We stepped back and bowed to each other, then came together again, one, two, three. In another context it might have been kind of fun.

"I guess you're not worried about hurting General Houston's feelings," I said to Luz.

"Houston arranged to have Bowie bring me here and have Doña Ximenes adopt me. Given that Colonel Bowie was supposed to blow up the Alamo and evacuate, this should have been the safest place in the world."

Wouldn't you know it, an act of love. "It would still be safe if Santa Ana would just take it now, or Travis and Bowie arrested him," I said.

"Men," said Luz. "You are so unfigureable."

We stepped into a line to waltz hip to hip around the room.

"You're not worried about the lives of those Texians?" I asked her.

"Or my own life?" she said. "And the lives of those Mexican soldier-boys? Their poor wives and children? The lives of these Tejanos who must leave their homes? Should they fight for the white Texians who hate them? Mexicans pillage, Coyote, Texians pillage and rape."

I had to hand it to her. Luz was probably the smartest person in San Antonio de Béjar, but she'd been on the bottom too long to have much sympathy for anybody.

We turned to each other again.

"Santa Ana's already married," I said.

"Name a Texian who is not. Where are their wives?"

"He'll discard you."

"Like Houston?" she said.

The music stopped. I took her hand and walked her back to General Antonio López de Santa Ana, President of Mexico.

"You dance divinely, Señorita Ximenes," I said to Luz as I gave her hand to the general. "Put a good word in for me."

"*Buena suerte*, Coyote," said Luz.

Overhearing, Santa Ana raised a single eyebrow, then laughed. "I like you so much," he said to me. "You are far too clever to live."

I bowed to them and decided to find a safer place to sit out the war, maybe Santa Fe. There were some wonderful hot springs up in the Blood Mountains, a good place to sit and watch the snow melt while it sizzled into the hot, sulfur water. I could do some gambling, maybe get some nice turquoise for Morning Star, some bear claws for Many Powers. Sit this whole thing out. Even padres and Pueblo Indians would be better than the madness of white Texas.

I turned for the door, and to my relief, approaching us was William Travis with two armed men. He bowed to Santa Ana. "Señor de la Peña, if you will excuse me," he said. "But I must interrupt."

It looked like something I said had finally penetrated and Travis was going to take a precaution that made sense. Then those two brutes took me into custody and threw my butt in jail.

# 42

I GOT TO WATCH from the door as Santa Ana's coach appeared and Señor Enrique de la Peña and Señorita Lucia Ximenes, known to a few of us present a General Antonio López de Santa Ana, President of Mexico, and Luz, mistress of Sam Houston, departed, Santa Ana's war stallion, Cielo de Noche, tethered behind.

The next day, from my jail cell in Colonel Travis' military office at the corner of the town's Civil Square, I watched out the grated back window as the Tejanos continued to gather up their belongings into wagons and two-wheeled carts, preparing to evacuate San Antonio, now a ghost town of homeless Anglo drunks. Santa Ana was right about the weather. It was raining like hell. Texians who couldn't find an abandoned *jacale*, one of the stick and mud huts the Tejano peasants eked out their lives in when they weren't being run out of them, slept under broken wagons or on door stoops. At least the rain had ended the party.

Outside my room Colonel Travis, one of the few Anglos in San Antonio de Béjar without a hangover, sat in his office with his feet up on a desk, contemplating the future of Texas.

"*Bella horrida bella,*" I said at him. War, horrid war. I figured he wouldn't know it was a quote from Virgil, but he was a lawyer and recognized a little Latin the last time he put me in jail. Besides, as much as he hated Roberto O'Donohughe, as Coyote O'Donohughe I didn't have a prayer. There's nothing like throwing around a little Latin to keep the Indian haters off your heels.

His back was to me and he spoke without turning. "Bowie took ill last night," Travis said. *Manus e nubibus,* a lucky break. *Muftis utile bellum.* Meaning a lot of people profit from war, and I guess he meant himself. "All of Texas will rally here. The Louisiana Grays are only the first to join me. Men from González will join me, too. Fannin will have to come up and reinforce me from Goliad. The volunteers from Kentucky and Tennessee will rally around Crockett. God and Freedom for Texas!"

Travis might have been an idiot, but he wasn't a stupid idiot. Of course, as my mother always said, smart idiots were the worst kind. He sure liked to use the word *me* a lot.

"They all better hurry up," I yelled to the back of Travis' head.

"Don't be a fool. We have months."

Later that day, two Tejanos, in an apparent act of heroism, sympathy, and foolishness beyond comprehension, rode back into town and begged to see Travis when they found out that Bowie was indisposed. They said they were sent by Antonio Menchaca, de la Peña's purported brother-in-law, if you remember, who I figure was trying to come out a winner on both sides of this invasion, or reoccupation if you were taking Santa Ana's side. Of course they never gained the privilege of Travis' visage, but a hungover pioneer named John William "El Colorado" Smith, known as Redhead, who'd declared himself Mayor of San Antonio last night during Bowie's party and seemed to have run unopposed, wandered into the office later in the day to convey the message that the Tejanos spotted the Mexican army, including cavalry and artillery, southwest of Béjar.

"What do you think?" Travis said to Redhead.

The Mayor burped. He was soaked and wet and still pretty bleary-eyed from his hangover. "You can't trust them. They're Mexicans," said Redhead.

And Travis said, "That's what I think, too."

"What's not to trust?" I shouted in through the tiny, barred window in my door.

"This is the second time in ten days they've come in with that rumor," said Colonel William Travis. "Menchaca started it before he left town ten days ago. And where are the Mexicans?"

"They want us to run away so they can have the town back," said

Redhead Smith.

"No sense taking any precautions," I suggested.

Travis hesitated a moment, then stood. "You might be right. Round up any of the remaining Tejanos, including those messengers, and place them in custody," he said to Redhead.

"What're you crazy?" I yelled.

Travis whirled and threw himself at my cell door, pulling it open and grabbing me by the neck. He turned to Redhead. "Find a pair of eyes on somebody who's not drunk and bring him here!"

"Doc Sutherland," said Redhead.

"Bring him!" said Travis.

So in a little while the four of us, Colonel William Travis, Mayor Redhead, Doctor Sutherland, and myself, Travis' hand still grasped firmly at the back of my collar, were traipsing across town in the rain to the San Fernando Church. We climbed the frail, wooden belfry tower to scan the flat plains, across the black horizon to the slopes called the Alazan Heights, looking south and west for the Mexican Army. The hard rain had stopped, but the sky was brooding and dark and there was still a constant drizzle.

"See anything?" said Travis.

"Hell," said Redhead.

"Sutherland?"

Sutherland, a little gray haired man in a bowler, squinted. He put his glasses on. "No," said.

"What about that?" I said, pointing at the hills. "See that line at the top of the slope?"

Travis looked out at that black landscape. "Trees," he said.

"Trees!" I said. I turned to the church plaza and began ringing the bell. "The Mexicans are here!" I yelled. "The enemy is in view!"

Travis hit me so hard with the back of his hand that my own bells rang as sleepy Texians started to drag themselves out from under wagons and off of door stoops and ran to the tower. There was some shouting and a woman screamed.

"False alarm!" Travis yelled down to the Texians gathering below.

Several of those drunkards tried to crawl up there with us and a couple of them made it. They peered out.

"Nothing," one of them said.

"Traitorous fool," Travis said to me. "Causing panic. There are women and children here." And he proceeded to throw me off the tower.

It was a good fall, probably the height of three men, but I was still young and soft back then and landed on my butt in a cushion of mud. Travis had already scrambled down and grabbed me before I could get up.

"You have any patrols out?" I gasped at him.

He grabbed me.

"Just a precaution," I whispered.

"Maybe I better ride out and see," said Sutherland quietly. A reasonable man. "I'll take Redhead."

"All right," said Travis. "Take a horse."

I don't know what else he expected Sutherland to ride out on, but I figured he was trying to make it sound like an order and that he'd thought it up. While still looking at the doctor he threw me one handed into the hands of a couple of his huntsmen.

"Put him back in his cell," Travis said. Then he bellowed out to the crowd. "There are no Mexicans! I'm telling you all that there are no Mexicans!" He turned to me with his straight and moral gaze. "And there will be no Mexicans until I say there are Mexicans."

"You don't doubt the existence of Mexicans," I said to him as softly as I could, "if I can make a point of logic. You just don't think that they're here right now."

"I'll have you shot in the morning," Travis said.

# 43

THERE'S NO ROOM for philosophers in Sparta, as the Greeks used to say. Among the Comanche we say, you are too smart to be a warrior. That, unfortunately, was me. One thing for certain, Colonel William Travis, unlike Santa Ana, had very little sense of humor. And if I was waiting for Sutherland to save my foolish, truthful hide, I was in big trouble because those Texians were so unprepared they didn't even have any horses nearby. They didn't even have any hobbled. At least they'd turned the herd out to pasture east of town where there weren't any Comanche to ride away with them. Who knows where my own faithful steed had wandered, probably off with the rest of those knuckleheaded beasts. I'd be lucky if she didn't come back pregnant with the foal of one of those chubby, worthless, Tennessee nags.

By the time Doc Sutherland gathered up a couple ponies and prepared to head west toward the slopes, it was near dawn. The rain had stopped. I just hoped those Mexican troops were careless enough to build fires. He and Redhead rode west on the Laredo Branch, a miserable little path that passed for a tributary of the old Spanish Camino Real, which was another miserable little path, just a little bigger. To be honest, with all their penchant for progress, I hadn't yet seen a road built by white folk that could match the streets built by the Mexican Indians two thousand years previous. Down in Mexico City they were still using them. Sutherland and Redhead rode for the Alazan Heights, only about a mile and a half away.

The dawn broke red and sunny and Colonel Travis awoke early, but he couldn't roust up enough hooligans to form a firing squad. He came to my cell door and said, "The execution is changed to high noon. God and Texas."

"*Vita brevis*," said I. Life is short. In Comanche, Let the dead follow the dead, but that's something you'd only say to another Comanche.

"For you, shorter every minute," said Travis.

"For everybody," I said.

He scowled and was about to speak when we heard horses and shouting outside. In not too long Sutherland came in, his right leg dragging, his left arm over the shoulder of a pioneer who wore a cap that made him look like a duck. I later learned he was Davy Crockett. Sutherland was gray with pain where he wasn't white with fear.

"The Mexicans," he gasped. "Artillery. Cavalry. At least fifteen hundred infantry. They're upon us."

"Impossible," mumbled Travis, but he collected himself. Comes a point when your opinions are irrelevant. He straightened, breathed in, stuck out his chin. "The Mexicans are here!" he said. "God and Freedom for Texas!"

# 44

BEING LOCKED UP at the time I wasn't really privy to the actual
event, but it's well known that Doc Sutherland and Redhead ran into about
a hundred-fifty Mexican cavalry the moment they hit the Alazan Hills. They
spotted the rest of the infantry and artillery as the cavalry spotted them. And
they probably would have been left totally alone had they just tipped their
hats and rode on by, but the dummies turned tail. Had those Mexican cavalry
officers been pure Indian instead of high mestizo, they'd have probably just
shrugged, but I suppose they had enough white in them to chase somebody
who was running away.

Sutherland's horse went down in the mud and landed on that right leg. He
said his horse got knocked unconscious and he couldn't get his leg out till the
animal woke up. I guess those Mexican cavalrymen were really hot on his tail,
given that his horse had time to take a nap, but you never questioned a Texian
about a story concerning his own bravery. Anyway, I liked Sutherland well
enough. In general he was a discreet and sensible being, and self-sacrificing to
boot, not that I'd call that a virtue in most cases.

Needless to say, Travis released me from prison to fight for Texas. He opened
the door of my cell and grabbed me by the throat and said, "On your honor, I
will free you if you'll fight for Texas and God."

"*Aut vincere aut mori*," I gasped back at him. No sense being disagreeable in a situation like that.

"Victory or death," said William B. Travis. "I like that, O'Donohughe."

We rushed outside now, Sutherland limping badly. It was one of those bright, clear days where the slightest sound could either delight you or hurt your ears. In the distance came the drums and horns of a Mexican military band, a cacophony like nothing on this earth; the dreadful and unrhythmic blast of two score bugles all playing the same wretched song out of tune and out of time, those drums pounding behind.

We ran to the tower, but you didn't even have to climb up it to see the line of cavalry winding like a parading snake down into the plain, the coats of the horses shining in the sun, heads bent taut and feet prancing in that Mexican style, somehow almost in step with that horrible band. The cavalrymen raised their sabers so the breadth of the blades reflected the light like a hundred flying stars in the daylight. Behind them the black line of the infantry and the shouts of men pulling cannon.

"Across the river!" shouted Travis. "To the Alamo!"

Texians broke in a thousand directions, everybody running which-way and that. We didn't have a prayer. Despite all the warnings, we didn't have a bushel of corn or a strip of beef. The horses were out foraging. The defenders were drunk. Despite taking all the time in the world, Santa Ana could still walk into San Antonio and take everything without firing a shot.

Travis turned to me. "Bring the horses to the fort," he said.

That fool had given me my ticket to freedom. But it takes a dishonest man to make a fool into a fool. Maybe he knew that. Maybe that's why he could lead everybody into one disaster after another. I'd given him my word. And despite what you might have heard, a Coyote, a Comanche, keeps his word. He just tries to interpret the word he's given as ambiguously as he can. Besides, though I was a coward, I wasn't a total coward. As Many Powers once said to me, "A man who is not a total coward is more dangerous than a man who is not totally brave."

As the Mexican Army began to surround San Antonio de Béjar, I ran out to gather the horses for the Alamo.

# 45

IN THAT FLAT PASTURE east of town I found the herd, as well as my own loyal, true, steed FireBlood. She was halfway happy to see me. She walked away from a gelding who'd been swishing flies away from her face with his tail and came toward me a few paces. Then she turned, raised her tail, and offered me a big fart. She faced me again, put her ears back and showed me her teeth, then glided forward and gave me a kiss. I loved that horse. She was brilliant and fast, even now in her teens, but she was not an easy read.

I gave her some sweet grass I'd gathered on the run and slipped her mecate over her nose. Then I mounted her bareback and rounded up the rest of the animals, an easy task because FireBlood was a lead mare and had already taken charge of that sexless bunch of slugs those Texians called horses. But as I gathered up those beasts, I reconsidered my loyalties and figured things might work out fine. By the time I got back to the Alamo, Santa Ana would have marched into town and gathered everybody up and the whole thing would be over. I'd disguise myself as a Tejano and sneak off to Santa Fe where I'd contemplate the mysteries of the Anglo fiasco from my private sweat lodge.

But if Santa Ana was cat-like in his speed and savvy, then he was no different than a bobcat once he'd cornered his prey. He slapped a paw down on either side of those Texians and watched them run back and forth in between. His army circled San Antonio with such absolute lethargy you could have gathered up a thousand cold rattlesnakes and herded them out of San Antonio de Béjar, which is what a good portion of those brave Texians did, minus the snakes. They ran. They headed out, north, where Santa Ana left a corridor open for anyone who wanted to run. Then he slowly marched into town.

Two hours after I got the horses into the Alamo, Mexican cavalry officers walked the streets of San Antonio helping the last of the Tejanos and Texians alike pack up their wagons and carts to head wherever, the Alamo included if they wanted. Contrary to what you might think, the Mexican reoccupation of San Antonio de Béjar wasn't the least bit hostile. The Mexican soldiers, there were a couple hundred with uniforms, were gracious people who didn't want to be there. But as far as they were concerned, they were still in Mexico and anybody who hadn't declared themselves a rebel was a Mexican citizen, pure and simple, as easy as you could make the Sign of the Cross and say *Buenas dias.*

Texian insurgents woke from their stupors and wandered into the streets and ran into Mexican officers.

"Where's the Alamo?" they shouted.

They got pointed down Portero Street, toward the river. If they got lost, a friendly soldier was there to show them over the foot bridge to the Alamo. Nonetheless, seeing as it was so casual and friendly, it was hard to take this battle very seriously, especially when upon my unopposed return to the fort I found Bowie in the middle of the plaza lying on his back and directing traffic. A young Tejana propped up his head and two more stood at his side. Davy Crockett and a slew of Tennessee volunteers as well as an Anglo girl who I later learned to be Susannah Dickinson, fifteen year old wife of the artillery captain, Almeron Dickinson, stood around him. Susannah was a black-haired, blue-eyed little thing with a jaw set like an iron trap and an infant, a baby girl, in her arms.

"How much food?" said Bowie from his perch on the earth.

"A day's worth of corn and beef," said Susannah Dickinson.

"Guns?"

"Everybody has one,"she said.

"Almeron said we have forty-five cannons," said Bowie.

"Only a dozen of them are put together," Susannah said.

"How many Mexicans?"

"Between one thousand and six thousand, depending on who you ask," she said.

"I'm asking you," said Bowie.

"Call it a thousand with more coming," said Susannah Dickinson. "And there's a hole in the north wall as wide as two long wagons."

"You got any liquor?" Bowie said to Crockett.

"Sure do," said Davy. "Pennsylvania Red Whiskey."

"The best," gasped Bowie.

"Let's surrender," said Davy Crockett.

"Agreed," Bowie said.

Except that inside his new war office, I found Colonel William B. Travis at a wooden table, scratching out a letter to Colonel Fannin down in Goliad.

"I'll have you edit this O'Donohughe. You're an educated man."

I'd have never given him that much credit. His butt was tighter than his self was big.

"We have removed our men to the Alamo," it said. "We have four hundred men, who are determined never to retreat!"

"Better make that a hundred forty men who want to surrender," I said. It was easy enough for me to read upside down, but he spoke out loud as he wrote, as well.

"I suppose it would make us sound more desperate," said Colonel Travis.

"It would be more accurate."

"Facing ten thousand Mexican regulars," he scratched. "We have but little provisions, but enough to serve us till you and your men arrive. We deem it unnecessary to repeat to a brave officer, who knows his duty, that we call on him for assistance."

"I'd lower the number of Mexicans if you expect Fannin to show up," I said.

Travis sneered. "God and Freedom for Texas!" he scrawled.

"Victory or death," I suggested.

"Yes!" said Travis. And he signed, "Victory or Death!"

It was hard to know what was going on or who was doing what around there. Unlike a Comanche band where no one was in charge of anything and absolutely nobody had any authority, at the Alamo everybody was in charge of everything and absolutely everybody had authority. But just then the most fortunate or unfortunate event occurred. Just as the Mexicans raised two flags of Mexico, one over the San Fernando church tower and another over Bowie's own mansion on Soledad Street, Santa Ana's new headquarters, the last round of Texas volunteers raided the mud and stick *jacales* outside the Alamo and showed up with a hundred bushels of corn and forty head of lowing beeves.

"A sign from God!" shouted Travis, and ordered Almeron Dickinson to fire our biggest cannon, the eighteen pounder, at the town. Kaboom!

"Jesus Christ!" shouted Bowie from his power spot at the center of the plaza.

"Almeron, are you crazy?" Susannah Dickinson yelled up to her husband.

That cannon shot smashed up half of Bowie's mansion and would have assassinated Santa Ana on the spot had he not been out in the streets philandering with every young Tejana who passed by. As it was, Travis didn't even believe Santa Ana had yet arrived with the army in front of us. But it sure infuriated Bowie to find out his house was blown up. He got off the ground and had Travis by the throat as the Mexican military band launched into the Degüello, the Song of Slaughter, and the red flag of "no mercy" was raised up on the San Fernando bell tower. Like it or not—friends and enemies alike—we were in for a battle now.

# 46

TOO LATE AS IT WAS, none of that stopped Bowie from trying to surrender. In fact we tried to surrender a lot during the whole episode, and the Mexicans tried to let us surrender. One of those times, later in the siege, I was even sent to do the surrendering. But there was always some basic, cultural misunderstanding, if I can be so bold to say so, that kept that simple act from taking place. Mexicans tended to say one thing and mean another, but the Texians always took what the Mexicans said at face value. Then the Texians would respond with some sincere offer they planned to renege on which the Mexicans interpreted as saying one thing but meaning another, only not the thing the Texians meant. Having been there, that's as simple as I can put it.

After the Mexicans responded to our cannon shot with a few grenades of their own, Bowie sent one of our many colonels, Green Jameson, with a letter of capitulation, over to Santa Ana under a white flag of truce. Of course Bowie, one of the few Texians who understood the Mexicans a little, apologized for the cannon shot, but said the cannon was fired after the Mexicans raised their red flag and before we'd received their message that they wanted to parley. Santa Ana had never sent a message that he wanted to parley, but Bowie couldn't let them think we were both apologizing and surrendering on our own accord. God and Texas!

Now as I heard later from the great General Santa Ana himself, under the most intimate of circumstances, he wasn't going to parley with some buckskinned hooligan who called himself a colonel, but he was gracious enough to send down a colonel of his own, José Batres, to tell Bowie to stick his capitulation up his ass. God and Liberty for All Loyal Mexicans!

But while Jameson was there, Travis sent his own messenger, Albert Martin, to talk to Santa Ana and the great general sent Colonel Almonte, who spoke English, down to talk to him. At that point Santa Ana put all of his officers on alert to be ready to receive each of us when we all emptied out of the Alamo, one by one arriving with our own terms of surrender, which he figured would happen before the night was over. Victory or Death!

And while Colonel William B. Travis was busy surrendering, he was also writing heroic letters begging for supplies and reinforcements and sending them out of the Alamo as fast as he could scribble, and just as fast the Mexicans were capturing the messengers. Santa Ana read the letters, gave them back to the messengers and sent them on their way. Let the reinforcements come. General Cós, who'd returned with Santa Ana, had already tried holding the Alamo and Santa Ana knew it was indefensible. As he saw it, the more the merrier.

I saw the note that Colonel Don José Batres addressed to Bowie, because I was in Travis' office with Bowie, Crockett, Travis, Jameson, and Martin when the messengers got back. I'd written the communiqué to Santa Ana for Bowie in Spanish and now I was in there because I was the only person in the Alamo who could speak, read, and write it. The note said: "As the Aide-de-Camp of his Excellency, the President of the Republic, I reply to you, according to the order of his Excellency, that the Mexican army cannot come to terms under any conditions with rebellious foreigners to whom there is no other recourse left, if they wish to save their lives, than to place themselves immediately at the disposal of the Supreme Government from whom alone they may expect clemency after some considerations are taken up. God and Liberty!"

"Said 'clemency' in there," said Davy Crockett.

"What did he say about me?" said Travis.

"What about the red flag?" said Bowie.

"No mention," Jameson said.

"Son-of-a-dog, calling us rebellious foreigners," said Travis.

"How many of you are citizens of Mexico?" I said. Everybody kind of looked around for a little bit.

"Bowie is," said Jameson.

"Catholics?" I ventured. "Spanish speakers?"

"What the hell are you trying to get at?" Travis growled at me.

Bowie coughed hard, bending over. He looked worse by the minute, but he glanced at me and held my eye.

"I like that word clemency a lot," Crockett said.

It's probably as good a time as any to mention that he never wore that notorious coon skin cap and he didn't wear buckskins, but riding pants and boots, and a worn waistcoat over a white, button shirt. The hat he did wear had a visor that made him look like a duck, because he walked a little duck footed and he had a protruding butt.

"What do we choose to disregard," Bowie coughed, "the flag or the clemency?"

Travis said, "What kind of clemency was given during the last . . ." but he stopped short.

"Rebellion?" I offered.

Travis turned to Bowie. "I'm going to kill this kid," he said to him.

Bowie barely looked at him. "We need him," he said. "We need everybody. So stop sending bloody messengers out every two minutes!"

"From what I recall," said Davy Crockett, "those prisoners in 1813 were taken in open battle."

"And flayed alive and mutilated," Travis said.

"In terms of surrender," said Crockett, "the earlier the better. The longer we hold out, the more of them we kill. The more of them we kill, the more resentment." Crockett was affable and intelligent. I don't know how many bears he killed before he was three, but you could be damn sure a bear would never kill him because he'd be long gone at the sight of it.

"I agree with Colonel Crockett," I said.

"Who the hell are you to agree or disagree with anything?" said Travis.

"If we surrender they probably won't kill all of us," Bowie said. He sat down and bent over again. When he straightened up he continued. "They might take a couple of the top dogs back down to Mexico City."

"Me," said Travis. "I'll never let them take me."

"They could execute the officers and free the enlisted men, or the opposite," Bowie said.

"There are only officers here, from what I've seen," I said.

"I'm a private," said Davy Crockett.

"You're a colonel!" said Travis. He pounded on the wooden table. "We fight," he said. "We fight, we fight, we fight!"

"I think he wants to fight," Crockett whispered in my ear.

Finally, Jameson spoke again. "They seemed reasonable, hospitable men," he said softly. "They served tea."

"Tea!" screamed Travis. "What about my negotiations?" He turned to Albert Martin.

Martin had tried to stay out of this and wished he could have. He also had the unfortunate Yankee habit of avoiding the easy lie, even to his own demise. Then again, maybe he was just itching for a fight. Some men are. "They'd never heard of you, sir," he said. "But Almonte said that by the wording of your message you seemed a silly, pompous man, bent on your own demise and the demise of your compatriots."

"Damn every one of them if those aren't the words of war!" screamed Travis.

"Fine," said Crockett, "now you have your war. So how do we surrender? I never surrendered before."

Bowie tried to speak, but he began coughing. He bent over and held his chest, hacking up phlegm. Then he fell from the chair and lay motionless on the floor.

Jameson went to him and Bowie whispered up to him. "Laudanum," he said.

From then on we were all in the hands of Colonel William B. Travis. God and Texas. Victory or Death.

## 47

THAT NIGHT WHEN TRAVIS sent a letter off to Houston, he got all the events reversed. As I came to learn, Americans were always suspicious of education and unlike me most of them were proudly self-educated or educated poorly and proud of that. But for all his faults and bone-headedness, Travis comprehended that he stood at a crossroads in history and he wanted all his letters to be spelled correctly and be grammatically correct. That's how I became the secretary of the Alamo high command, which included editing Travis myriad epistles and communicating his commands to that drunken invalid commander, James Bowie. I kept a list of all the volunteers at the Alamo, as well, and rest assured I had the foresight to make sure it was a list that did not contain the name Coyote O'Donohughe or, for that matter, any other name that could be ascribed to my personage.

Travis wrote to Houston that he opened fire at the Mexicans with the eighteen pounder after they'd refused our negotiations and sent up their red flag of "no mercy," whereupon the Mexican artillery proceeded to bombard us relentlessly throughout the night.

"You don't think you're stretching the truth a little?" I said to him.

"No one is motivated by truth," said Colonel Travis.

I took the letter over to Bowie's sick room on the south end of the fort where two of Bowie's Tejana cousins-in-law and an Indian healer, Andrea Ramírez

Villanueva, waited on him.

"You want to know what Travis wrote to Houston?" I said.

"Fuck, no," said Bowie.

And so our defense of the Alamo began in earnest.

The Mexicans had but two cannons half the size of our eighteen pounder, though each of those weighed as much as four horses, so the rest of their artillery consisted of a slew of five pound pieces that were light enough to drag from Zacatecas, where Santa Ana had just settled another rebellion and conscripted the prisoners. Mostly Aztecs, or Mexica, they were given the choice between soldiering and the firing squad, which meant the difference between slow death and fast death for most of them. Those Indians joined the Maya recruits that Santa Ana had gathered up before he left Mexico City and that pretty much constituted the Mexican infantry. Years later I saw pencil drawings of our battle, Mexican and American alike, and they all showed the Mexican army belted, bayoneted, and shining like the army of Napoleon, but in truth most of those boys were running around bare foot in what looked like two-piece, white pajamas. The lucky ones wore sombreros.

Not that they weren't tough. They'd marched from Mexico City through the Sonora desert in the dead of winter through sleet and rain and even snow, and they did it in a few weeks. Something else to be said for Santa Ana; anybody who knows a lick about the history of warfare knows that the forced march is one of the greatest strategies of battle, from Alexander the Great, to Caesar, to Robert E. Lee, to Quanah Parker; you spring upon your enemy long before they expect it and you've more than half the battle won. Santa Ana's march to the San Antonio de Béjar was nothing less than that.

Mexican ground soldiers, the Texians called them ground hogs, an odd pun given who was really hogging ground around there, carried thirty-year-old British, Brown Bess flintlock muskets that threw a big .75 ball but took a mountain of powder to set them off. Antiques. The pan under the firing hammer to those things was so exposed that you couldn't protect the powder from getting wet in the rain. Worse than that, they took a half-hour to fire and reload and the Mexican gunpowder was so lousy that if you didn't blow yourself up trying to shoot your gun, you still had to fire the damn thing from your hip to keep from blowing your face off. Even so, you had to count to five after you pulled the trigger of one of those old hand cannons to see if your gun fired at all. Hell, the Texians captured a ton of that powder from

Cós when they took the Alamo in December and couldn't use the damn stuff, so stored it next to the chapel. Travis planned to blow the whole thing if we lost the walls, a kind of mass suicide, as if we weren't already planning one.

Now during the night the seven score some colonels and captains of the Alamo who weren't planning war with Travis in his office were all gathered up at Bowie's and decided to mutiny. Myself, I was overjoyed when they showed up before dawn and refused to work or fight till I learned that the strike wasn't about surrendering but about getting their daily food rations which, as negotiations broke down, amounted to rum and whiskey.

Of course Travis stood fast. He said he was willing to fight Santa Ana on his own if he had to, and as the dawn stretched out over the plains around the Alamo, perking the dew on the scrub oaks and pecan trees and cottonwoods, Travis ordered Jameson to raise our flag, the flag of Mexico, it turned out, with the numerals 1824 under the cactus and eagle. Responding to that affront, the Mexicans set up their two nine pounders just across the river and in minutes knocked out three of our cannons, including our eighteen pounder, and lobbed a few grenades inside the walls.

They could have walked right in through that breach in the north wall if they chose, but after that bombardment, fifteen year old Susannah Dickinson, infant baby swaddled in her arms, strode out of the chapel and lit into those "worthless recalcitrants" as she called them, and as the first Mexican infantry came timidly across the river to hide in the *jacales*, little Susannah Dickinson gathered up a dozen of those volunteers and set them at work on moving earth and building a breastwork across the northern breach. With Crockett leading the way, the rest of those boys ran to the walls. When the Mexicans came out of the shacks and into the open, about a hundred yards away, those Anglos opened up with their Pennsylvania longs, as well as with grape shot from the remaining cannons, and that line of Mexicans dropped.

Those percussion cap long rifles did us a dozen disservices before all was said and done. They needed clean, pure powder and you had to keep the ammunition, that is the balls, oiled, as well as the barrel chamber. You couldn't leave them sitting around loaded and ready or they got all fouled, so you had to fire them off every hour or so whether there was anybody to fire at or not. They were of no advantage in close fighting, particularly because they couldn't carry a bayonet, unlike the Brown Bess and, as I came to learn, a bayoneted rifle was a hell of a weapon when it came down to hand to hand combat and we didn't have any. We had to face them with rifle butts and Bowie knives.

But when it came to picking off enemy combatants like so many field squirrels, the long rifle couldn't be matched. More Mexican boys dropped in those first minutes on the mesquite fields outside the Alamo than we had bodies inside the whole bulwark.

I was on the wall with Crockett after the first volley when the Mexicans turned and ran, and after the second, after everybody reloaded and we plastered the backs of the ones that were left as they ran away with their wounded. That was a new one for me, shooting at running wounded, but as I quickly learned, this was not a situation which cultivated ennoblement. For the moment, I thanked the Great Everywhere Mystery that I was such a lousy shot. I had yet to really straighten out my loyalties, though I could see that I was getting more and more implicated every second.

"Now the resentment starts," said Crockett.

Next to him stood a huge, bearded man, bigger than a black bear. "You kill 'em one at a time," he said.

"Ah, Henry," said Davy Crockett. "We die but once."

That's when I realized that Crockett had come from Tennessee and that a certain Henry Wax Karnes had earlier headed there to fight Indians. There he stood, a big bear of a man who looked like his son, a son whose scalp I owned; a man who lived to murder me as slowly and painfully as possible, and a man who I was pledged to murder and scalp to avenge Turkey and Wind Sister. Ain't life funny.

"Let's get out there and burn those damn shacks," I said.

"You're right," said Davy, and we rushed down the ladder to the plaza to get our horses where Susannah Dickinson was yelling, "Almeron, get somebody out there to burn those God-forsaken shacks! And somebody start reaming out this well before they seal off the aqueduct!" That being the stream that brought water into the Alamo.

Travis stood outside his office, his eyes darting. He yelled, "Give them hell, boys!" as me and Davy and Henry Wax Karnes saddled up, lit torches, and galloped out the south gate. Torching those shacks out in the open field on horseback, I felt at home, and as we rode among the fleeing Mexican troops, I couldn't help but club a few of them on the back of the head as they ran. One of them recognized a Comanche coup when he felt it and turned, astonished, yelling to me in Aztec Nahuatl, "Brother, join us! Do not die with the Anglos!"

"*Omnia mores aegat*," I muttered, which pretty much meant that in the field of death, in the end it didn't matter who you died for.

I spun FireBlood back into the flaming shacks as the air exploded with artillery fire. As Susannah Dickinson predicted, a dozen Mexican soldiers ran to dig up the moat that surrounded our fortification, to cut off our water flow, while another half-dozen more, dragging a small cannon, tried to secure a footbridge.

I ran for the dozen digging up our water trench, beside me, Henry Wax Karnes. If I'd had my bow and arrows I could have taken out eight of them before they lifted their guns. As it was, I was lucky that half of them were digging and none of them had mounted bayonets. The six with flintlocks fired off at my approach, but as usual, two of them misfired and two of them fell down from the kick of their weapons. One of them just plain missed and the other took down Henry Wax Karnes. That's what you get for being so big.

I rode into the shovelers and bowled them over. When Crockett rode down on them, too, they scattered as a volley from the Alamo cut down three of the artillerymen dragging the cannon to the footbridge.

A loud chorus of whoops sang out of the Alamo and behind the din I heard Susannah Dickinson yell, "Almeron, tell them to fire!"

"Fire!" yelled Almeron Dickinson and a roar blew from the Alamo walls like thunder. On the other side of the river, bodies flew. The Mexicans at the footbridge fell and the rest of the retreating shovelers went down. Crockett and I rode over to the abandoned five pounder, but it had been knocked out and we already had twenty cannons in the fortification that we couldn't put back together.

Now came another advance from the Mexican lines.

"Time to go," said Crockett.

"Karnes is down," I said.

"They'll take him. We have to go."

But I turned FireBlood around and headed toward the Mexican line. Karnes was kneeling one arm up, Indian style, when I swept over to him and he grabbed my extended arm and leapt onto my horse behind me as if he were as light as a bird.

"Where'd you learn that?" I said.

"Where'd you learn it?" said Karnes.

And we left it at that.

As we turned for the fort, I heard the crack of distant rifle fire and then musket balls whizzing by us like bees.

"Those sound like Bakers," said Crockett, which I later learned were new long distance rifles carried by mestizo marksman. A man like Crockett could tell the make of a musket by the crack of the discharge and the whiz of the ball.

Behind us, as we hightailed it through the gates, the Mexicans advanced again and the shacks of poor Tejanos burned. Cheers roared from our walls. As we dismounted, Susannah Dickinson, directing a well digging party, hit fresh water at the center of the plaza. Susannah Dickinson grabbed Karnes, threw his arm over her shoulder and led him toward the mission where the women stayed, our first hospital patient.

Beyond the walls, the lookouts spotted the Mexican cavalry riding to cut off the roads to Goliad and González and the Mexican troops tightened their circle, surrounding us now on the east, south, and west. A barrage of cannon fire splattered our walls and exploded into the plaza. Half-way between the gates, one of the grenades exploded and I turned to see the first casualty of the Alamo. My horse. FireBlood.

# 48

THERE'S AN OLD COMANCHE word for horse, a word we no longer use but which we hear as children in our night time stories. God Dog. We believe the Animals were the First People, and that all animals and humans as they exist now came from them. Now, in this late age, the First People, the Animal People, no longer walk among us, but come to us in the snow, in the night, in the moon, in the wind, and yet bring us their power. But the horse was not among the First People. A man or a woman can gain the power of any animal but the horse. The horse came into the plains on its own and befriended us and made us the most powerful people on earth. The horse has its own medicine. Its own spirits, good and evil. Its own Land of the Dead.

The Great Everywhere Mystery brought the horse and let us learn to think like the horse, which finally made human beings equal to the other animals who were all, as we said, one step closer than us to the earth and sky. The horse made the buffalo our life and minion.

I loved FireBlood more than anything in the world, next to my wife and my mother. But not knowing how long Santa Ana's siege would last, or when we would receive reinforcements, I knew that any animal lost inside the Alamo walls would have to be eaten. As a Comanche, I did not eat the flesh of my enemies, nor the flesh of our helper, the horse, unless the Earth Mother turned her shoulder and left nothing else. To draw your strength from a living thing, animal or plant, is to take their medicine inside you. The First People did not have to live this way, living on rain and dew that tasted like honey. But the First Coyote tricked the Two Leggeds into tasting the Earth, and when they ate their first worms the cycle began.

Everyday, transformation upon transformation, the creatures of the Earth and Sun devour each other, become each other, to live, and that's how First Coyote invented Death. It's also why People don't usually want to become Coyotes.

On the other side of poor FireBlood, who gave her life for God and Freedom and Texas, stood little Susannah Dickinson, baby under her breast, her cold, blue eyes staring at me through the first, warm exhalations of heat above my animal's death.

"We'll need her skin for the interior breastworks," she said.

When I said nothing she spoke again.

"The bones can be ground for wound paste," she said. "The rest we can eat."

"I only want her liver and her heart," I said.

"To eat?"

"To bury."

Now it was Susannah Dickinson who got quiet. She wasn't a Comanche. She couldn't know. Her eyes narrowed under the slanting light of late winter sun. Among Indians it wasn't so uncommon to find a girl her age with all the authority and intelligence of womanhood, but whites tended to keep their girls as helpless and senseless as possible, and if they couldn't, they'd pack them off to a convent. Of course, these Yankee Protestants were a different breed than the Spanish I'd known down in Mexico, but they were still white.

We were the only ones out there in the middle of that plaza, everyone else taking cover from the Mexican bombardment against our walls. But I knew how to create total privacy in public, or silence in a din, and I prayed for it and got it. I removed FireBlood's headstall and reins and pulled off her saddle. I kissed her forehead. In Comanche, I began my song:

My horse, I thank you for all you have given me.
My horse, I thank the Great Everywhere Mystery for your life.
My horse, I will never again utter your name.
My horse, go, run now in the sky and make the thunder.

I kept singing as I went to my knees and opened FireBlood's stomach. I didn't care what Susannah Dickinson saw or thought now; I drew out my hunting knife and opened my horse's stomach, extracted her liver and reached up under her chest for her heart. My arms full with her insides and my body covered with her blood, I sang till the sun blinked and FireBlood's heat left her and came to me, ready to follow.

When I stopped, Susannah Dickinson said, "You ride like a demon. I'll tell Almeron to give you the pick of the remuda."

"I'll need it now." I said.

She nodded and I turned for the corrals.

"What are you?" Susannah Dickinson said to my back. "What are you?"

# 49

I PUT FIREBLOOD'S heart and liver in a sack, then picked out a red
sorrel beast that looked young and strong, proud gelded and still full of
trouble. I saddled him and rode out the south gate, circled the fort to the
north where the Mexicans had yet to surround us, then flanked their lines and
headed into the west plains, the land of the People, the horse, the buffalo, and
buried FireBlood there under the high, blowing grass. I could feel a Norther
coming in, the first blue, wet air at my back as I faced the sun and sang my
horse's song for the last time.

I could leave now, I guessed. I'd already seen more boys drop in a minute
than I'd witnessed in my whole youth on the plains, and we Comanche saw
ourselves as warriors. But there comes a time when a man or a woman steps
into their fate and has to play their role in the *Histoire du Monde*. And though
the Comanche wanted no part of the *Histoire du Monde*, the *Histoire du Monde*
was coming toward us whether we liked it or not. Travis was right about me. I
was a spy. But not the kind of spy he suspected. I was a spy in the house of war.
As Doe Skin had reminded me, my time would come, the dead would return
at my beckoning and the world would change.

I couldn't go home, as much as my heart ached for the love of Morning Star,
who carried our child. It could cost them all their lives and, besides, I'd given
my word. Among Indians, your word still meant something, probably because

we didn't write them down. As Many Powers had said to me before I left, if I ran to Santa Fe the war would just come and get me. Better off in the middle.

When I jumped on the back of that big sorrel, I could see the ghost of FireBlood facing the wind, ears back, teeth bared, as nasty in the horse Afterworld as she'd ever been in life.

"Run in the sky now," I whispered. "Make the thunder."

And I headed back for the Alamo.

# 50

James Bowie looked about as gray as you could be and not be dead. He sucked laudanum while Villanueva moved an egg up and down his hot skin. She had so many smelly candles lit around his bed he looked like a shrine.

"Guess if you die we won't have to change anything," I said to him. "It already looks like a funeral in here."

"I've been deader than this," he said. He offered me a drink, but I turned him down. "Crockett says you're an Indain," Bowie rasped.

"Crockett's a sissy," I said. I'd been hanging around these pioneer types long enough to know how to talk to them.

Bowie coughed and laughed. "He's a perceptive sissy," said Bowie.

"There's a Norther coming in," I said to him. "It'll bring snow. The northern roads are still open. We could all walk out of here during the blizzard."

"Crockett doesn't know horse Indains, but he's seen plenty of that Indain snake oil in the woods," Bowie said.

"What does it matter?" I said. "I'm fighting with you."

"That's what I told Travis,' said Bowie. "But he thinks you're a spy"

"A spy for whom?"

"For somebody." Bowie coughed again, then lay quiet as Villanueva passed the egg over his forehead. "What's it saying?" he said to her.

"That you're sick," she said.

"I know that," said Bowie.

"Then thank Jesus the egg doesn't contradict you." She sang something over him in a language I didn't understand, but I recognized. It was the language of women. She looked at me for a moment. Bowie drank laudanum. Outside, the darkness had fallen and the bombardment stopped, but the first gusts of a Blue Norther moaned against the walls.

"I hate that damn sound," Bowie said.

"You never hear it out on the open plains," I said to him. "Only when you live behind walls."

Bowie raised himself up and lifted his chin. The shadows made by the candles flickered over him. "Where's my god-damn knife?" he said.

The snow came that night. The wind blew for two days. We had to sneak out of the fort in the dark to gather wood scraps from the remains of the *jacales* to make fires. In the morning, when we huddled on the makeshift ramparts, we'd find that the Mexicans had inched a little closer. They'd fire their guns and we'd fire back, though it became real apparent that we wouldn't be able to keep it up for long or we'd run out of powder.

When the cold wind stopped, the rain came in from the south. And when it wasn't raining the Mexican military band fractured the night with the Degüello, that horrible horn music and pounding, only to stop and yell and begin firing their guns, faking frontal attacks. Sometimes us inmates would get miffed and start firing off toward the campfires until Susannah made Almeron Dickinson go around and stop the waste of ammunition.

"Tell Susannah a shot or two won't matter," I told him. I was up on the southern earthworks, near the chapel, with Davy Crockett who was a good man to pass the time with in conversation.

"If they don't fire off every once in awhile the powder will just go bad in the guns," said Davy. "And it's good for morale."

"That's right." said Captain Almeron Dickinson. "I forgot. I'll tell her."

"He's a good man," said Crockett, "but he don't belong in a battle."

"Unlike his wife," I said.

"But like me," said Crockett.

"That's not your reputation."

"I like open land," Crockett said to me. "I fought the Creeks because, well, I was there and I had to pick a side. I lost my family in that war, if not to the

Creeks, then to somebody who pretended they were. I'm no friend of Andy Jackson's, but the Creeks weren't my friends either."

"You could have got out," I said. "Run away."

"That's why I'm here. Running away. Like you. I can spot a run-away in a second. Anyway, now we're both here."

That was something I wasn't going to talk about.

"I'd just as well better march out and die in the open air," said Davy Crockett. "I don't like to be hemmed up."

I couldn't have agreed more. What I'd have given to jump on a horse with two score arrows, wreak havoc and head for the hills. Hypothetically, anyway, because I was still foolishly telling myself that regardless of the circumstances my sympathies lay with the Mexicans.

Crockett pulled out a whiskey flask, unscrewed the lid and sipped at the open lip. He offered the thing to me and, as I've said, I'm not a drinker, but circumstances overruled. I could barely taste anything through the burn.

"Not a drinker," he said.

"Did you really grin down a bear when you were only three?" I said to Davy.

"Was your mother impregnated by a snake and now you can change yourself into any living thing?"

"You're confusing me with Horus or Huiztilopochtli," I said.

"Maybe," said Crockett, "if I knew who they were."

"Would a Comanche?"

"One who could fly in the wind and speak every language in the world."

"You don t believe any of that," I said.

"So that answers the bear question," said Davy Crockett.

I took a bigger hit on that crazy water before I gave him back the flask. "So this is the kind of shenanigans that gets you elected to the U.S. Congress," I said.

"No," said Crockett. "It's the kind of shenanigans that gets you un-elected from the U.S. Congress."

Well there's nothing like facing imminent death next to somebody to build an acquaintanceship. Getting to know these Yankee Anglos, you couldn't help but like some things about them.

"Who'd believe," said Davy, "that Jim Bowie, William Travis, Davy Crockett, and Coyote O'Donohughe would end up in the same little Texas mission facing Santa Ana."

Well he could throw in Mike Fink and Henry Wax Karnes too and it wouldn't change anything.

Just then a volley of cannon fire exploded from the Mexican lines against our walls. The dust cleared and we heard Susannah Dickinson yelling out, "Hold! Hold! Load! Now fire!"

"Fire!"yelled Almeron Dickinson.

And we released a barrage. We all cheered. What the hell.

"You forgot to include Susannah Dickinson in that list," I said to Crockett.

Davy didn't look at me. He just peered out over the breastwork. "Well," he said, "I got Indian enemies and I got Indian friends."

And may the Great Everywhere Mystery bless the distinction.

During those tortuous nights, unable to sleep, Travis scribbled off letters to Houston, to the two other self-fashioned Commanders-in-Chief, Grant and Johnson, one to Fannin in Goliad, another to the volunteers in González, one to the men of San Felipe de Austin and San Patricio, and one more to the Texian congress at Washington-on-the-Brazos. For God and freedom! For Texas! He begged for men and supplies, Victory or Death! But as the week wore on, it became more and more apparent we'd been hung out to dry, by Travis and Bowie, if not Houston and the rest. We were out there floating in an ocean of mesquite without a damn friend.

Travis began to walk the ramparts where we all ate and slept, waiting for our allies to come; waiting for the Mexicans to charge. He sent out another round of messengers, ones we couldn't afford to lose. He walked those walls gazing, one hand to his forehead, the other pointing his sword at the Mexican lines. "I will have you, Santa Ana!" he yelled. "I will have you yet!"

The Mexican sharpshooters unleashed with their Bakers, but they never managed to hit him. He was too crazy.

When I wasn't correcting his letters, I watched on the south breastworks near the chapel with Crockett and the Tennessee volunteers, except for Henry Wax Karnes, thank the Mystery, who was still laid up in the mission.

Travis walked the walls, screaming at the Mexicans.

"I wish they'd damn hit him and we could surrender," said Crockett. "Or just take the field against them. Americans fight in the open field. They don't sit in church yards waiting to be attacked. I don't like to be hemmed up." It was something he said again and again.

"Surrender on your own," I said.

"What're you crazy? You surrender on your own."

"Santa Ana wants me dead," I said.

"And not the rest of us?" said Crockett.

"Me in particular."

"From what I hear everybody wants you dead."

Well that was nice to hear. A grenade shook the wall beneath us. "Fuckers!" somebody cursed.

"Why'd you tell Bowie about me?" I said to him.

"Because, Mr. O'Donohughe," Crockett said to me, "you're a suspicious character. Besides, nobody gives a shit anymore."

"Not Henry Wax Karnes?"

"Maybe Karnes," said Davy Crockett.

Being a fool, I went to see him. He'd been hit in the chest. Missed his heart, but cracked some ribs and took out a lung. He pushed himself up when I came in. Two of the women rushed over, but he waved them away with his big knife. He breathed heavily and badly.

"You know who I am," I said to him.

"You saved my life," he said.

"In battle," I said. "You kill the ones in front of you and save the ones next to you."

"And my son was in front of you." He had that knife out. He could have put it in my throat already if he wanted.

"He was a warrior."

Karnes propped himself up a little higher.

"You know," I said, "you spend half your life trying to kill somebody and end up fighting next to them and trying to save them. It makes you wonder why you do anything."

"If we get out of this alive, I'll kill you," he said.

Well, he wasn't a philosophical man.

"When they start coming, I want you to help me out of here. Prop me up against the wall and give me some weaponry."

"You have my word," I said.

"If each of us can kill five of them."

"The rest of them will only outnumber us ten to one," I said.

"What the hell are you doing here?" said Henry Wax Karnes.

"I thought it was the safest place to hide," I said.

By the end of the week we were close to despair when things began to turn around. El Colorado Smith came through the Mexican lines from González where the men of the town were preparing to come to our relief. Bonham rode in from Goliad where Fannin had launched a rescue mission and was heading for the Alamo with cannons, supplies, and four hundred men. From the southwest, Frank Johnson from San Patricio was heading for Matamoros with a prairie full of men, guns, and horses. They were going to storm Matamoros, load up with supplies and join Grant, who'd been marauding south Texas behind Santa Ana's lines. Soon they'd head for the Alamo. Any day now the Texian congress was going to declare independence and Houston would be here with the Army of Texas.

That same day the weather broke. The sun poured over the prairie and when the dusk fell we drowned out the Mexican Degüello with Davy Crockett's fiddle, while a Scotsman, John McGregor, blew on his frightening bagpipe. I thought those Mexican horns were horrible till I heard that bagpipe. It sounded like a thousand dying frogs. But we were dancing and singing in the Alamo. I imagine, five hundred yards away, behind the Mexican lines, they were scratching their heads. Because they didn't know what we knew. Now I just had to figure out how to convince Crockett, among others, not to expose me when this was over. All we had to do now was hold out a few more days because the Alamo was about to be saved.

# 51

TRAVIS WAS GLOATING. He paced his office, chest out, a new spring in his damnable step.

"Mr. O'Donohughe," he said to me, "you're going to regret having not been a citizen of free Texas."

"Colonel Travis," I said "unlike you or anybody else in this fort, I was born here."

"Not in Italy?" said Colonel William Buck Travis. "Not Ireland?"

"There's nothing like the folly of doomed men," Bowie said when I reported to him. Anymore, when he wasn't shivering, he was sweating so hard you could hear the water dropping from him onto the sheets.

"I don't think you understand," I said to him. "Travis was right. Texas is rallying."

"Killing cleanly," muttered Bowie to me, "and in a way which gives you artistic pleasure and pride has always been one of my greatest enjoyments."

I glanced at Villanueva, who now attended Bowie so constantly that she kept her clothes in a cabinet in the room. His sisters-in-law sat in the corner working rosary beads. Bowie lay with his big knife across his stomach and a crucifix on his chest. He held a loaded flintlock pistol in each hand.

"He shall fight his way," Villanueva said to me, "even across the last River of Breath."

Bowie turned his head, his eyes on my face but not seeing it.

"There is a feeling of rebellion against death which comes from its administering," he said. He spoke almost out of his voice, as if he were translating his thoughts from Spanish. "To rebel against Death. To give Death. In that moment, you are God." He turned to Villanueva, his eyes focusing. "It's why we men so much enjoy killing," Bowie whispered. He turned back to me. "In the moment of death, you and your victim are one. You share the one certainty."

He turned away again, his eyes drifting. "In cafes," he said, "all men are brave."

But around the rest of the Alamo, spirits were high. Susannah had Almeron repair our eighteen pound cannon and Travis ordered Almeron to fire three times a day, at dawn, noon, and dusk, so the reinforcements would know where to find us, and so they'd know that the Alamo still stood, undefeated. He broke out rum and whiskey and ordered the slaughtering of two beeves. With no letters to edit for the first time in days, I walked the grounds, bantering with Crockett, checking in on Bowie, and thinking about my wife, Morning Star, wintering with the HorseSleepers, carrying our child. When I returned to them, Always Hits could train a new mare for me.

Along with running the artillery and fortifications, Susannah Dickinson, with a certain disdain, organized the hospital and ran the kitchen. Since our day out in the plaza over FireBlood, she gave me a pretty wide berth. But between Bowie's illness and Travis' notoriously high self regard for himself, by himself, when most people had information or questions for either one of them, they came to me. Further, I had, by circumstance, become one of Crockett's sidekicks, and more, Travis' suspicions of me, since he'd never done anything about them, were translated by the constituency as fear. The contortions I'd pulled to bury my horse's innards only added to my power. I had, once again despite myself, become a powerful, dangerous and legendary man, though less powerful than Travis, less dangerous than Bowie, less legendary than Crockett, if a little weirder than all of them.

I was cutting swathe down to the chapel, to fetch some whiskey to mix with Bowie's opium, when the first of our promises came storming through the south gate. Colorado Smith had ridden out that day toward González, met two score of volunteers on the plains, and guided them through the Mexican lines. It was dead silent out there on the Mexican front as those boys rode in to our whooping and gunfire, grapeshot scattering from the Alamo walls in all directions. At the door of the chapel, Susannah Dickinson, her tight eyes and grim face growing tighter and grimmer, met me, whiskey already in hand.

"They'll wake my baby," she said.

"*Gracias*," I said, taking the bottle.

"Don't speak that slop around me," said Susannah Dickinson.

"Well then, thank you on behalf of Colonel Bowie," I said.

She looked out. "Fools," she said. "You see any extra ammunition kegs among those volunteers? Any cannon? Any food?"

"We need the bodies," I said to her.

"I see forty more mouths to feed and forty more guns to fill." She turned to me. "When Travis sends out his next messenger, tell him we don't want anybody who hasn't got food or ammunition."

"I shall," I said.

"I have a family to save here," she said.

"We all have them to save."

"But not here. Tell Bowie that whiskey never cured anything. Tell him to get rid of that Voodoo witch."

"I'll try to state it more diplomatically," I said. Why bother telling her that Voodoo wasn't Mexican?

She grabbed my arm as I turned to leave and looked into my eyes. Inside, her child began to wail. "I hate Mexicans," she said.


"So why don t you turn yourself into a bird and fly away?" Villanueva said to me when I returned with the wiskey.

"Because I'd shoot him out of the sky!" yelled Bowie. "I should have shot you the moment I saw you," he said to me, then laughed.

"You're feeling better," I said.

"Fuck, no," Bowie said.

I told Travis what Susannah Dickinson said about ammunition and food supplies.

"All right," he said and added it to the letter he was finishing for Bonham who he was sending out again, this time to guide Fannin from Goliad, and Grant and Johnson from the southwest, God and Freedom for Texas! Victory or Death!

We celebrated those boys from González and our optimism didn't flag, day or night. Our cannons boomed and in response not a peep came from the Mexican lines, no cannon fire, not a shot, not a grenade, not a note of the

Degüello. The days warmed. Almeron Dickinson boomed the eighteen pounder toward the red flag of no quarter. The Alamo stood defiant and strong and ready to be reinforced as Santa Ana, Travis figured, planned one of his famous, night time escapes, skulking back to the Rio Grande and beyond to far away Mexico City where he'd claim victory from his retreat. That's what he told me and Bowie and Crockett when we met in Bowie's room in the late afternoon.

"We should surrender now during a moment of strength," said Davy Crockett.

"Are you crazy?" said Travis.

Crockett pulled his duck cap down on his forehead. "No," he said.

Bowie sucked laudanum and pulled himself up in his soaked bed, the sweat falling from his scalp and around his face in huge drops. "What's San Patricio got?" he rasped. "Another forty, poorly equipped. Grant and Johnson are horse stealers, not generals. Houston told us to blow this place up. He hates us. He ain't coming. Fannin's a coward. If they all show up we're outnumbered five to one, fortified or open field."

"One of us is worth ten of them," Travis said.

"No sense trying to prove that," said Crockett.

"Then why the hell are you all here!" Travis yelled. He stood erect, hand on his sword.

"I didn't think Santa Ana would be fool enough to come north, Buck," Bowie said to the air. "And now I'm too fuckin' sick to leave."

Crockett just pulled that duck hat down lower over his face.

"Mr. Crockett," Travis said.

Crockett took a breath. "Just passing through, Mr. Travis."

"It's Colonel Travis!" said Travis. He turned, furious. Saw me. "What in God's name are you doing here?"

"You requested my presence?" I said.

He narrowed his eyes and looked down at me, which he could do even to a man taller than him. "Two counsels for surrender," he said. "Mr. O'Donohughe, off the record, your opinion."

"Santa Ana said he'd kill me if he saw me again," I said.

"Again?" said Travis.

"You were there, Colonel Travis, but I don't want to get into it. For the sake of these two hundred some men, I'd surrender."

Travis turned again and began to pace. Bowie had drifted off by now. He blew a breath into the air. He said, "Fuck."

Crockett ducked his head.

"There are only two problems with all of your plans," said Travis, spinning on his heels. For the life of me, there wasn't a person in the world he reminded me of more at that moment than Santa Ana himself. "One, our opponents are cowardly. But more importantly, we are on the verge of victory!"

He might have been crazy, but that's probably why he was in charge. A minute later, a knock came on the door and Villanueva opened it at Travis' nod.

Almeron Dickinson came in and saluted. "There is a Mexican at the gate," he said, "with a white flag."

Travis's head spun, looking for all of our eyes. Maybe he knew more about Santa Ana than the rest of us. When a madman meets a madman, you just get more madness, it doesn't cancel out. Me and Crockett followed him out of there.

"Tell him to wait there, outside the gate," Travis said to Almeron.

Travis strode back to his office and turned to me and Crockett at the door. "Santa Ana's scouts must have informed him of our reinforcements," he said. Then he went inside to prepare the terms of Santa Ana's surrender.

# 52

AFTER AN HOUR or so passed, Travis opened his door. "Mr. O'Donohughe," he said and I followed him inside. He turned. "You will negotiate for us."

"A spy?" I said.

"When I asked for terms, who did they send?"

"You sent Albert Martin and he spoke to Colonel Almonte," I said.

"I was ignored!" said Buck Travis.

"You could ignore him right back," I said.

"You speak Spanish," said Travis, ignoring me.

I found it interesting that no matter where I spent my time, among the Comanche, Mexicans, or Anglos, whoever was in charge of things eventually came to disregard my opinions without blinking, then put me in the middle of a mess.

"So I'm your insult," I said to him.

"Don't take this personally, Mr. O'Donohughe," said Colonel Travis. "History is bigger than you."

"What's our position?" I said.

"They will cede Texas to me as far as the Rio Grande. Santa Ana will sign the peace. They may all go free, leaving the cannons and ammunition." He stopped. "I want this settled quickly, Mr. O'Donohughe."

"Before all the other generals and presidents of Texas get here," I said.

Travis looked me straight in the eyes. I dare say, in that moment he looked downright authoritative. "Your honesty only hides lies more deep," he said to me. He turned away again. "I'll have the Mexican messenger brought to the munitions storage. Take some whiskey."

Crockett was still waiting for me outside where I informed him of my enterprise. He fingered the visor of his duck cap with both hands. "How big of a chunk of Texas you going to bargain for, Ambassador O'Donohughe?" he said.

"Colonel Crockett," I replied, "my People already own all of Texas."

Crockett put his hand on my shoulder as we walked. "Well," he said, "one war at a time."

He walked me to the chapel where I got a bottle of whiskey and two glasses from Susannah Dickinson, then I went to the munitions room to treat with the envoy of the President of Mexico.

# 53

THE MAN WHO ENTERED the munitions room as representative of General Santa Ana was the real, bonafide Lieutenant Colonel José Enrique de la Peña. He squinted at me as his eyes adjusted to the dim candle light and I poured us glasses of whiskey. He took the glass as I offered him a powder keg to sit on.

"Mexican powder," he said in Spanish.

"It's not very good," I responded in English.

"The infantry muskets do not need good powder, if any. They do their best work with the bayonet." He sat down and lifted his whiskey to eye level. "We joked in camp," he continued in Spanish, in apparent disregard of whether or not I would even understand, "that there would be no wine here."

"*Ni español*," I said to him. "The President could have sent Almonte who speaks English."

It was then that he recognized me. If you'll recall, when I was a boy, duly extracted from the Comanche by my father, Hermano-Many Wounds O'Donohughe, when he sought to return to his life as a Spanish Mexican in Mexico City, I spent a cozy afternoon with my mentor, Sor María Juana, at the ancient pyramid city of Teotihuacan. I didn't know, at the time, that she'd planned a romantic liaison with Santa Ana, but while those two recited Aztec poetry to each other amid the ruins, de la Peña showed me the sights and, once he understood I was a horseman, took a little resentment out on Santa Ana by letting me ride the general's war stallion, Cielo de Noche, down the Avenue of the Dead. As I stood in front of de la Peña there in the Alamo, I recalled his face on that windy day in the city of the Wind God, Quetzacoatl, his eyes dark with sympathy and wisdom, a sad smile under his mustache that occasionally hid his mirth. It was the quality of his face that made me love Mexicans and Mexico.

"Roberto," he whispered. He stood. "War is terrible."

"Only for mothers and foot soldiers," I said.

"And friends," said Enrique de la Peña. He took off his hat and sat down again. We touched glasses. Outside, the air suddenly lit up with fiddle, banjo, and fife as the Alamo defenders began singing.

Ol' Santie Annie
We'll spank him on his fanny
Send him home to Nanny
And Texas will be free!

"The line between a fool and a brave man," he said. "Santa Ana, of course, has brought his nanny."

"And his mistress."

"And his mistress, as well."

"And his new wife?"

"Do you mean my new wife?" he smiled.

"She was Houston's mistress," I said.

"All the better," said de la Peña. "All the better." He listened again to the tune. I knew his English was not good, but he probably knew it better than most Texians knew Spanish. "I generally do not dispute with jingles," he said to me. "But Santa Ana *is home* in Texas."

"As am I. Do you want to talk about freedom, too?" I said.

"Surely not," he said. "Anyway, the message I am bringing was not important enough to send Almonte. In fact, the President is unaware I have come."

Of course, de la Peña thought I was the son of a wealthy San Antonio land owner, not the half-breed son of a Spanish Creole merchant. He undoubtedly figured my family had something to gain by siding with the *norteamericanas*. The implicit Texian alliance with the United States, as well, was always perfectly clear to the Mexicans.

"I'm only here because Santa Ana has promised to kill me," I said.

"It is a risk we all must face," de la Peña said. He shrugged. "Better a condemned ally than a doomed enemy."

If you didn't understand the Mexican temperament, you might find that statement absurd, but the idea of sacrifice, self or otherwise, was bundled up deep inside Mexican self-esteem.

"My love for Mexico, Roberto, is greater than my love of self, and greater than my fear of Santa Ana," Lieutenant Colonel José Enrique de la Peña said. "He may be mad, but he has done the impossible many times. Defeated the Spanish at Tampico. And raised an army of ill-fit, poor men to march here, across the winter desert. It has been cruel, and though I approve of few of his techniques, no one else could have done it. If we do not stop the United States now, we will lose the continent to the North Americans."

"What about General Urrea?" I said.

"Urrea is an infinitely better soldier, but in the end, no statesman," he said.

"What about the Republic? Democracy?"

"Is that what you and the Anglos are bringing to Texas?" said de la Peña. "Not slavery?" He sipped at his whiskey. "I wish I could save you, Roberto," he said to me.

"So you're not here to surrender," I said.

That made him chuckle, but with his sad eyes, and his mouth squeezed around the burning whiskey, he produced the oddest expression, as if each part of his face held a different emotion.

"What does your reconnaissance tell you?" he asked.

"That the North Americans are rallying and reinforcements are coming from everywhere. We will soon have you at bay here, and surrounded on the plains."

"Like Vercingetorix did to Caesar," said de la Peña.

"Vercingetorix lost," I said.

"Exactly," de la Peña said.

He drank again and spoke to me most seriously. "All of Colonel Travis's correspondence, by various means, has been intercepted," he said. "José Urrea cut down Commander Johnson's troops outside San Patricio. They are all dead but for the brave Johnson himself, who fled. Urrea met the combined forces of Dr. James Grant and Richard Morris near Agua Dulce. Those who were not killed were executed. Dr. Grant was captured, his feet tied to the hind legs of a mustang and his hands tied to the tail. When the horse was set free it kicked him to death. It matters little. The three commands did not total a hundred fifty men. Houston is on the Brazos without an army. Fannin has retreated back to Goliad where he will soon be surrounded by Urrea. The reinforcements from González are the last you will see."

I suppose that information only struck me as depressing because it rang so true. This whole Alamo thing was just plain stupid from day one.

"I'm glad the great President has his nanny with him," I said to de la Peña.

"Surrender at our discretion," said the Lieutenant Colonel.

"To be executed?"

"Here you will surely die," he said without malice. "While Urrea rushes to victory after victory in the south with a third the men, Santa Ana sits here in siege in front of ten score men who defend a pile of ruins. Your deaths in battle mean more to him everyday. Surrender. You have nothing to lose."

It became pretty clear to me right then that his mission wasn't purely humanitarian. Our surrender would help foil Santa Ana and undermine his power. He'd have to execute us or take us prisoner, the first a disgrace and the second a burden. De la Peña, though loyal enough as a soldier, was a Republican. For all the heroism and bluster going on behind these Alamo walls, what it all amounted to was that how we chose to die might alter the future of somebody who temporarily ruled Mexico.

"These Protestant types have never banged their heads in front of a statue," I said to him. "They'd rather die standing up."

De la Peña stood and shook my hand.

"Cielo de Noche must be getting pretty old," I said.

"This will be his last campaign," said my friend.

"I lost my horse here, under your first bombardment," I told him.

"Ah, your mare," he said. "You spoke of her. I remember."

We stood for a moment in silence. The singing and dancing had stopped outside, as though the length of our discussion had been a bad omen.

"*Suerte*, my friend," I said to de la Peña. "I shall see you in battle."

"*Con Dios*, Roberto," said de la Peña.

# 54

TRAVIS DIDN'T TAKE the information well. He tromped around. He stormed. He thought it was all lies.

"He's a spy!" he yelled at me. "You're a spy!"

"I told him we'd fight them," I said.

He turned to me, his face ashen, trembling. "Texas shall rally," he whispered. "Reinforcements will come."

"I think the attack is coming soon," I said.

He walked away from me, his chin up. He paused as if listening for something from the sky. Then rifle fire exploded outside, and shouting. The gates opened and Bonham rode through to the cheers of the men. From Travis's door we watched Bonham dismount and walk quickly through the crowd of men who patted his back and fired off rifles.

"You see?" Travis said to me.

Bonham entered and shut the door. He saluted clumsily and stood in front of Travis, lingering in that quiet moment between hope and despair.

"Grant and Morris, Johnson, hundreds of others have been slaughtered by Urrea," he said to Travis.

"Fannin?" Travis said.

"He sends his regrets," said Bonham.

"Regrets?" Travis hissed, but it wasn't the hiss of an attacking rattler. I'd say more like the hiss of something cornered.

"Any word from the Brazos?" asked Bonham, meaning Sam Houston. But when Travis didn't answer, Bonham turned to me.

"Houston doesn't have an army," I said.

Bonham began working his lips with his teeth. His body seemed to sag now that he realized that he'd just ridden day and night, rushing to his grave.

Travis stood straight. For the first time in our acquaintance his eyes met mine dead on, then Bonham's. "Tell Almeron to fire the cannon as usual," Colonel William Buck Travis said. "Break out the last of the whiskey tonight. Assemble the men at dawn."

# 55

AT DAWN THE NEXT DAY the garrison of the Alamo lined up in the plaza single file. I'd gone to Bowie the night before and he'd insisted on being there as well, so before sunrise me and Crockett went to his room and carried him out on his cot, even though he wasn't yet awake. Then I went and got Karnes, too, who limped out, an arm over my shoulder, his huge chest heaving with fight, but his body shuddered. I leaned him against the mission wall.

As the red sun came up over the eastern rampart, Travis emerged from his office in his French military uniform and stood before us. Bowie lay at the center of the line with me and Crockett on either side, Crockett's Tennessee volunteers spread to his right. Then came Bonham and his Alabama Red Rovers, the González volunteers beyond them, and to my left the New Orleans Greys and the handful of Tejanos who'd stayed with the fortification. At the end of the line stood Almeron Dickinson who held Susannah's hand as she stood mightily behind his shoulder, baby in arms.

The Tejana women and girls stood outside the chapel door. Villanueva and Bowie's sisters-in-law watched from outside the door of his room. I'd been too busy to think about why most of those women were still there, but I suppose any number of them had romantic attachments at this point, with dreams of their own haciendas and brown-haired, blue-eyed kids with velvet bronze skin, running loose and herding up cows. It didn't matter that these boys hated

Mexicans. The women made good wives. That you could both love and despise your wife at the same time was one of the things I never quite understood about these Anglo types, though that a woman could love someone who both loved and hated her was something I was soon to learn.

A good half of this bunch were kids even younger than me, and nobody but myself born in the Texas territory that they were about to give their lives for. Travis had a slave there, Tim. I'd rarely seen him. He worked in the makeshift stable. But now he stood behind Travis as he addressed the assembled garrison.

"My brave companions," Travis began. "I must come to the point. Our fate is sealed. Within a very few days—perhaps a very few hours—we must all be in eternity. This is our destiny, and we cannot avoid it. This is our certain doom."

Travis paused and looked up and down the line at this bunch of ill-fed, barely clothed vagabonds he'd thought to make the core of his Texas army.

"I have deceived you long by the promise of help. But I crave your pardon. In deceiving you, I also deceived myself, having been first deceived by others." He swallowed hard. There wasn't anybody there who wasn't swallowing hard. "Fannin and Houston, in fact almost all of Texas but for a few hundred men who attempted our rescue and were cut down by the Mexicans, have failed us. We are surrounded by thousands and we have no hope of reinforcement. I give you your right to surrender or attempt escape, though surely, if you do, you will be slain within ten minutes of leaving these walls. But it is your own choice and anyone who wishes is free to go."

He stopped again. For a man who often looked down on everybody, he showed a tremendous talent for looking all two hundred of us in the eyes. He drew his sword.

"At any rate," he breathed out heavily, "it is my preference to stay. And I will stay if I am the only one. I will stay if I am to remain alone and fight. And not just fight, but kill and kill and kill!"

I don't know if he was expecting a huge cheer, but he didn't get one. We stood there silently as he put his sword to the ground. He strode down toward Almeron Dickinson and scratched a line in the dirt as long as that line of men.

"All who stay with me," he yelled, "cross the line!"

There was a young boy there named Tapley Holland who leaped across, then everybody else. Even the sick and wounded straggled over that line to Travis. Before I could think twice about it, the only people on the opposite side from Travis were me, Crockett, Bowie, and a Frenchman named Louis Moses Rose who'd fought with Napoleon over in Russia. Bowie, who sometime during that speech had come awake, looked up at Rose and said, "You seem unwilling to die with us, Rose."

"*C'est vrai, certainement,*" said Rose, reverting to his French. I guess he figured Bowie and a few others would understand him, like myself; but not anybody else.

Now Davy Crockett was the only one in the fort with enough status to speak up and not be called a coward, not, as I learned in the time I'd spent with him, that he'd care. He lifted the visor on his duck cap and shifted his rifle, Old Betsy, across his chest. "Colonel Travis," he said, staring over at the two hundred men who'd gathered around Travis. "I am as afraid to lose my life as any man, and as willing to give it in the right cause. But if we sue for peace now, only on the condition that our lives be spared, we could live to fight Santa Ana on another day and defeat him. But if we make our stand here, then we shall surely all die."

Travis let the silence fall, as if he were permitting the silence of the men under him, who of course wouldn't speak for Travis or up to Davy, speak for itself.

"I think we have already answered that question," he said quietly to Crockett.

Crockett put the butt of his musket in the dirt and tucked his cap down again on his forehead. He turned to Rose. "You may as well conclude to die with us, Mr. Rose," he said, "than die out there alone."

"You're going to fuckin' die anyways," said Bowie. "Now will some of you boys carry me over there before Travis thinks he's in charge? You may have to carry Mr. Crockett as well."

That got a chuckle from everybody, even Crockett, and two pioneers jumped over and helped me and Davy carry Bowie over the line. That's how I volunteered to die at the Alamo.

Louis Moses Rose, on the other hand, stood firm. "I have already survived one massacre too many," he said, and the whole garrison stood and watched as he went and gathered up his dirty clothes and walked to the northern breastwork. He turned, saluted, and dropped down into the early daylight. I guess everybody was expecting to hear the explosion of Mexican guns as Rose was blown to smithereens, but the silence bespoke every doubt in the Alamo about the decision we'd just made.

"It's dawn," spoke out Susannah Dickinson, her shrill voice like heat lightning. "Almeron, fire the cannon!"

Almeron hesitated until Travis nodded to him, then he took his crew and mounted the wall. They stoked the big eighteen pounder and fired it off toward the Mexican lines. Everybody cheered behind that boom and headed back to their positions on the walls. Villanueva walked over to Bowie and gathered up four men to carry him to his sick room. Crockett turned sullenly, his shoulders sagging, and I went to join him, but Travis called to me. I followed him inside his office where he laid his sword on his desk. He spoke without turning around. "Mr. O'Donohughe," he said. "Go to Santa Ana and negotiate our surrender."

# 56

NOW THERE WAS A CERTAIN beautiful young Tejana named
Trinidad Saucedo, an orphan girl still in her teens, under the care of the
matron, Doña Petra. Petra ran the kitchen under Susannah Dickinson and
kept the young Texians clear of Trinidad with an iron spoon. Like half the
women there, she was related to Bowie as some sort of cousin-in-law or other
and had stayed at the Alamo out of loyalty to him. But I knew from talking
to Villanueva that Petra grew increasingly worried about Trinidad Saucedo's
safety, let alone her virginity, as things deteriorated.

Though it was easy enough for the Tejanos to come and go from the Alamo
if they chose, to do so would put them under the suspicion of spying, and Doña
Petra, not being a woman of means, knew of no one left in San Antonio de
Béjar who she could trust to look after the orphan's interests. Petra herself was
loathe to leave Bowie in his time of need. That was her dilemma. My dilemma
was to somehow surrender the Alamo to Santa Ana before he killed me.

I went to Villanueva who stood over the sweating Bowie, the room filled
with smoke from the recent firing of his flintlock pistols and the ceiling above
him splattered with bullet holes. People later attributed those holes to Mexican
rifle fire, or Bowie's madness, but as I've said before, you couldn't sit around
very long, even indoors, with a loaded musket gun of any variety or the powder
would foul. You had to fire the damn thing off and reload it, and clean it, too,

which Villanueva did for him now. Bowie's sisters-in-law never trusted me and always hustled away when I entered, which was just as well. I stood with Villanueva on opposite side of the dying Bowie.

Seeing how weak he was lying there, it was amazing that he'd gathered himself for the reveille on the plaza only an hour before. Villanueva kept the light down low now, to protect Bowie's feverish eyes, which gave the whole place a tomb-like aura, like you'd been buried alive with one of those Aztec kings.

"Señora Villanueva," I said softly. "You know who I am."

"Of course," she said.

"Say it," I said.

"I shall not say the name of the Trickster," she said.

"O'Donohughe," whispered Bowie. "Is death beautiful? How beautiful is death. It is dark, like my mistress."

"How beautiful death is," I whispered back to him, and he smiled a hard smile. I'll tell you, it was hard not to like these Texians for that hardness.

"I will try to save the Alamo," I said to Villanueva.

"Why should you?" she said.

"I cannot guarantee it. Tell Doña Petra that I can save Trinidad Saucedo, but she must give me her name."

"Jesus Christo," she said, bowing her head and making the sign of the cross. "The soul of an innocent girl."

"Not her soul," I said. "I'm not the Devil. Just her body and her name."

"Is Death the body of a woman?" said Bowie.

"My body is the tomb from which all life springs," Villanueva whispered in Nahuatl. It was a quote from Coatlicue, the Mother of all the Mexica gods. There was a lot of communication going on in there, despite the fact that none of us were really speaking to each other.

"I will come for Trinidad at dusk," I said.

In the mean time, there was a lot of work to be done. In the ten some days I'd now spent at the Alamo, I'd slowly relaxed my disguise, allowing my features to fall back into my own, something that went unnoticed by my compatriots in the Alamo, partly because they'd grown familiar with me and partly because they had other concerns. For the next half-day I'd need great power. Walking into the shadows of the north wall of the chapel, I changed myself into a raven and flew into the city of San Antonio.

# 57

IN TOWN I RESUMED my form and in the streets inquired as to who was the wealthiest family still left in the colony. I was told there was a ranch owned by a widow named Doña María Francesca de los Reyes. She was related to General Manuel Fernandez Castrillion, who had come on the campaign with Santa Ana. I purchased a horse and rode the short distance from San Antonio to the Los Reyes Ranchería, north of the settlement where I met with Doña María Francesca.

She was suspicious enough, especially when she heard I was a refugee from the Alamo. She'd spent years bringing the hacienda back from the decay it fell into under the direction of her husband, and now faced being run off her land, if not by the occupying Mexicans, who planned on divvying up Tejas among the victorious officers and establishing military colonies, that is if Santa Ana didn't burn everything to the ground to create a buffer zone between Mexico and the United States, then by the fleeing Texian rebels who sought to denude the land in order to deprive the occupying forces.

She had a small, but prolific farm there: cattle and pigs, chickens, corn already planted in the fields, along with gardens of sweet and Irish potatoes, squash, and beans. Unlike the big Anglo ranches, she didn't own slaves or grow cotton.

Though a ranch owner, Doña María Francesca dressed in work clothes, a simple blouse and long skirt with an apron. When I came she had me brought to her in the kitchen where she worked making bread.

"Is there no one in this war interested in nurturing the land?" she said to me.

"I'm afraid this war seems to be about killing as many people as possible," I said.

She wiped her hands with a towel. "So why don't you run away?"

"I'm going to save as many people as I can, one by one if I have to," I said, though that was as much news to me as it was to her. It's the nature of a Coyote to find himself in situations, not create them, and to take on impossible tasks which, no matter how well intentioned, produce more problems than they solve. So I accepted what I said to her as the truth.

Doña María Francesca tilted a brow toward me. She was not a handsome woman at first sight, a little on the round side and neither young nor tall, but her carriage and intelligence made her attractive.

"And you . . . O'Donohughe?" she said.

It was then that I noticed, below her crucifix on the far wall, and next to a painting of the Virgin of Guadalupe, a Comanche Promise Blade. It's a complex thing to explain to a white person. The Promise Blade was a stone knife you gave to somebody you slept with to show how committed you were to them, even though neither of you really had any intention of marrying. That's why it was a knife and not, you know, a ring or something like that. Doña María Francesca caught me looking at that Promise Blade and we really didn't have to discuss our implicit connection. My father was one darn romantic son of Spain.

"Hermano is my father," I said.

"Hermano is not a name," she said. "I see it in your height and build, and your feathery mustache, but you look nothing like your reputation."

"The orphan girl isn't well," I said to her. "I think it's sleeping fever. But she will recover." I said this because to take someone's form drains them so completely that they have to sleep while you steal them.

"A spell," she said.

"I'll leave a letter with her, so that when my father passes through, he'll compensate you for her care."

Doña María Francesca went back to kneading her bread. "Just bring the girl," she said. "Bring more if you can."

"One will be difficult enough," I said.

With Villanueva I met Doña Petra and Trinidad Saucedo in the shadow of the chapel wall. Stout Doña Petra was suspicious enough of me, if for nothing else than my official liaisons with Susannah Dickinson. She felt Susannah Dickinson was great at running a fort, but lousy at running a kitchen. Blinded by all of her own concerns, like most everybody else around there, she never bothered to look to see who I was, but Trinidad, not a day older than Susannah Dickinson, though a lifetime deeper and more innocent, shrank from me when we approached. Her hair fell thick and black in waves from her shoulders. Her eyes were black like eternity and her skin, smooth and olive-brown. I could go on, but her beauty was indescribable, beyond approach or possession.

"Do you know who I am?" I said.

"Yes," said Saucedo.

"Doña María Francesca de los Reyes will take her," I said to Petra. Even as I stood there I had to be building the power that would transform me, something anyone could feel if they were sensitive enough. Villanueva made the Sign of the Cross as Petra hugged the girl. "There is little time," I said.

58

HAD I BROUGHT A PISTOL I might have ended Santa Ana's life then and there, though in the end it wouldn't have changed anything for the Texians. Besides, I hadn't come to murder Santa Ana anyways, but save the lives of those foolish Anglos I'd started to regard as human beings in the last eleven days. There wasn't an iota of security to be found in Santa Ana's palace headquarters. Officers lounged and servants moved about with drinks and food, hardly an atmosphere of siege or battle, though I'd never been part of a big European style army, so I didn't know how they went about it all.

I walked cautiously enough, but it seemed my beauty was the simple explanation for my presence; just another beautiful girl in Santa Ana's *harén*. To the left of a stairway, inside a room with an open door, the generals of the Mexican army argued with Santa Ana about the campaign. I could identify them quickly enough as they addressed each other. Besides Santa Ana himself, Generals Sesma, Romero, Filisolo, Almonte, and Castrillion, and a group of lesser officers including de la Peña who I heard finishing his contribution.

"The enemy is surrounded and cannot be reinforced," he said. "What few who would make it through our lines will be trapped with the others. An army larger than our own does not exist in Tejas, but any such force that is organized and brought here can be met and defeated in the open. The Tejanos are citizens and allies. Leave a small force here. The Alamo has no importance either politically or militarily. Advance to the capital. We can take Tejas almost without blood."

Of course, being absolutely right, he would undoubtedly be ignored.

"Without blood," Santa Ana said softly. "Should we not make a wasteland of Tejas, as a buffer between us and the North?"

"This is not a civil war," said Filisolo. "Nor a war of one nation against another. The Anglo settlers and farmers are not our enemies. Those who have taken up arms here are outsiders who have never grown a single seed. Our enemies are bandits and thieves who are seeking to murder Mexico, their benefactor. Let us destroy the rebels and nurture the farmers."

"They are slave owners, as well," said Santa Ana.

Almonte, Castrillion, and Romero, in order, discouraged an immediate attack. If they simply waited, the Alamo garrison would starve and be taken without losing a single Mexican life. If Santa Ana really wanted a military victory, then he should wait for that as well. Within the week, General Gaona would arrive with more troops and larger cannons, big enough to blow down the Alamo walls and leave the rebels helpless.

"The issue is the prisoners," said Filisola. "They deserve execution."

"Executing prisoners is the one thing that could unite the North against us," de la Peña said.

"I could march to the capital if I chose," said Santa Ana, meditatively. "While I sit here, Urrea rides to the south of us, gaining glory with fewer men."

"We can neither feed nor clothe our own men," Filisola said.

"The question," Santa Ana said softly, "is not one of life or death, but whether or not the Jaguar Sun will rise if it has not eaten. Our soldiers are men of the earth. Where is victory without blood?"

Well, Santa Ana might have been motivated by the pettiest desires for glory, but his reasons were of the highest order. You might have thought him mad, but his argument was that his soldiers, mostly from Aztec and Maya lineage, were men who believed that blood sacrifice was the only way to appease God and perpetuate life. It would be criminal on his part to drag them all this way without a dangerous battle. It seemed we'd come full circle. I would meet Santa Ana again over the religion of the Aztecs and the body of a virgin.

I stepped into the room. "This is our Sun in which we live now, great generals," I said. "But without blood, even the Divine Sun will fall into the fire, and there will be hunger and we shall perish."

Those generals were deadly quiet as I walked into that room. Surrounded by that avenue of manly pomp and power I felt like the damn Queen of Spain. But Santa Ana, recognizing the Aztec Poem of the Fifth Sun, stood. "Out of the hurricane from which the World is torn, amid the violent winds and clouds, the tranquil moon wends her way in space," he said to me. It was the Poem of the Second Sky. How could you know that much poetry and be so damn cruel? "Who is this oracle?" he said to me.

"I come to beg you for the lives in the Alamo," I said.

"But you have said the opposite," said Santa Ana. He looked around at the room of men. "Who among you could have put it so simply?" he said to his generals. "And who would have thought Travis to be so cunning?" He put out his hand to me. "You will have my decision," he said to the generals, "by tomorrow, noon."

# 59

I WAS ALONE WITH General Antonio López de Santa Ana, President of the Republic of Mexico and Commander of the Army. I had not come forward and taken his hand when he offered it, so he walked from behind his command table and stood ten feet in front of me. He said nothing, but in the deadly quiet I could hear the air flow in and out of his nostrils. At that distance he didn't have to look down at me, nor I up at him, yet I could feel the exhilaration of his desire, as if now, because he was in my presence, the world had suddenly come alive for him, and everything, from the texture of the carpet to the color of the walls, the movement of his own hand in the air, were all breathable and miraculous because of me.

A woman servant entered the room with an armful of wildflowers, sweet grass blossoms, bluebonnet, and lupine, and gave them to me. Their sweet smell reminded me that on the Plains it was now the Moon of New Grass. Comanche braves were riding out to gather ponies to train and ride into the spring buffalo herds. Trapped in the Alamo, I'd forgotten. And now, in the body of a girl before the President of Mexico, I began to forget my manhood, began to forget everything but the eyes of the Emperor, as blue-black as the sky behind the Path of Stars.

"Had I known there was such beauty here," said Santa Ana, "I would have dedicated my life to civilizing Tejas at the moment of my birth."

"They say you plan to burn from the Rio Bravo to the Brazos and make Tejas a wasteland," I said.

"Many things are said," responded Santa Ana. "But words will not burn Tejas." He turned his head as if to stare at his own shoulder, first his left, and then his right, then looked up and away before settling down upon me again. "Can they ignite a heart?" He offered me an indiscernible grin, so self-effacing you knew only a man of tremendous confidence and power could afford to display it. "In this night, in this crevice of peace, calm and dark amid the plains of horrible war," he paused again. "Whatever tomorrow will bring, tonight let us talk and eat, and we shall see who is really to be saved, and who is really doomed."

There was a part of me that still found Santa Ana a little corny, in a dangerous kind of way, even if he could paraphrase Homer. But that was the old part. The new part of me was a sixteen year old girl in front of the most powerful man on the continent.

He came and kissed my hand and walked me to his dining room and we ate and drank wine. We never did talk about the Alamo. He talked about the beauty of women in general and my beauty in particular. I won't bore you with the details, but I was drunk and flattered. When we finished eating he rose from his chair and went and locked the door to the room, then came to me, and went down on a knee. He kissed my wrist, my arm. He put his hand on my chin and kissed my lips. To try to put it simply, I felt the desire racing through him, and marveled at his gentleness as he led me to a low platform full of pillows. When he began moving those pillows around I noticed there was plenty of room for the two of us on that thing.

"I shall make you the queen of Mexico," Santa Ana said, taking me down.

"You are already married, your Excellency," I whispered. Suddenly, I was feeling my first surge of ambivalence.

He stroked my hair. "It's true," he said. "Several times. But I am true to all of them. To you I will be as the moon is married to the earth."

I guess you just had to figure out where you were on the earth, and where the moon was shining. Not that it mattered to me. I wanted him. But I had to reconnoiter for a moment to decide whether or not giving him my body there and then was going to help my cause. I was still Coyote enough to remember that you never gained anything by giving a powerful man exactly what he wanted. I put my hand on his cheek. "Save the Alamo," I whispered.

His eyes widened and he laughed. "You are the most intriguing girl." He sat and pulled me up to him. I guess the amazing thing was that he didn't just lie to me and bull ahead. There were a hundred ways in which Santa Ana could have slept with me that night to no consequence for himself, but each time he maintained his honor. "So the crevice of peace has closed," he said. I took the pun stoically. "You will see that Mexicans are honorable." He touched my cheek. "But the lives of men are not so valuable. Your love is more valuable."

"Then let them surrender," I said. "Spare them."

"Little one," he said. "For the sake of all Mexico, no one can survive. The dawn after next will be their last."

"Spare the women."

"If you are among them," he said. He smiled and arranged some pillows so he could sit back. He closed his eyes and in a minute he was asleep.

Well, if Santa Ana could have taken my virginity at his whim, so too, I could have taken his life. When I left that room, given what everyone thought I'd done, and what I'd become, the next mistress of General Santa Ana, I was as safe as a snake in a mouse hole. I hadn't been a girl for six hours and already I'd practically slept my way to the top of the heap. As I walked down the stairs, Mexican officers got to their feet and took off their hats. A part of me wanted to go back there and wake Santa Ana and do whatever a woman does in that situation. Another part of me knew I'd failed, and that even if I were to become his lover, I'd end up like the others, cast aside. I didn't need much more confirmation of that than the sight of Luz at the bottom of the stairs

She was a comely young woman. I could admire that, even though I'd lost a kind of appreciation of her beauty I'd once had. She lowered a scarf from her thick, black hair and held it at her shoulders. "I wanted to see for myself," she said.

I stopped in front of her and said, "I came only to plead for the Alamo."

Then her face tilted in recognition. She placed her hands on the nape of my neck and moved my hair back behind my shoulders. "Coyote!" she gasped.

Involuntarily, tears came to my eyes. "You are uncompromised," I said, and began to cry, as much from confusion as anything else.

"For now," she said. "It doesn't matter. Tomorrow I leave for his palace in San Luis Potosí. I have his child."

She held me and we cried together. "How can the world be both so magical and so dire?" she said.

"It's only going to get worse," I said to her. "I'm going back."

"Do not be a woman, Coyote," Luz said to me. "Women suffer. Proud women are humiliated."

"To fight," I said.

She held my head and kissed me. "*Con Dios*," she whispered. "We shall meet again, if you live."

Of course, I passed up another opportunity right there to hightail it out of the area, but I still had my obligations, to Travis and Bowie and Crockett, if not to Doe Skin and others. But before I headed back to the Alamo, I walked out of the siege headquarters and into the lines of the Mexican soldiers where those young Indian boys sat frying tortillas in pork fat over open fires and wishing they were home. None of those boys knew I'd come from the bed chamber of Santa Ana, but among them I was as safe as an angel. Whatever stories you might have heard later about the army Santa Ana brought to Texas, except for the officers and cavalry most of these men were barely clothed; dressed in loose, white pants and long, buttonless shirts. More of them wore sombreros than military caps, and those that didn't have hemp sandals were shoeless. Around their necks they wore their power on necklaces made of string: fur and animal teeth, small wood carvings of the Virgin of Guadalupe and Tonatzin. They offered me food and mescal and we talked about their wives and kids, their farmland and dogs. Near dawn, as I walked back to the gap between the Mexican lines and the Alamo, I passed one of the last sentinels.

"Do you have a husband there, in the Alamo, Señora?" he said.

"Only a mother who has adopted me," I said to him. "Is your wife with you?"

"Some of the officers, only, have brought their wives. I have children. Four. All girls. In Chiapas. You and your mother should leave, Señorita."

"There are sick men there," I said.

"There are sick men here. But bullets do not make choices between the sick and well. I fear many will die."

"Are you afraid?" I said.

He took off his coat and put it on my shoulders. "You must be cold, little one," he said. He watched his own cold breath in the pre-dawn air. "I am afraid," he said. "But we fight best when we are afraid. Out there, there is nowhere to hide. Who will run across that field of death? Scale the walls in the face of gunfire? Courage is not a shield."

I took his coat from my shoulders and returned it to him. "I shall pray for you," I said.

"God loves the prayers of a child," said the sentinel.

After I took off the clothes of Trinidad Saucedo and returned to my form, I went to Travis with Santa Ana's refusal to treaty. He was at his desk writing a letter to his son when I came in. He stood, attempting to bring up anger, but his fists opened slowly and the color drained from his face. Gray with death, he let his arms drop and he sat. He put his face in his hands and wept.

# 60

"COME HERE, YOU little fucker," said Bowie. "I want to put a hole in you before the Mexicans do."

I didn't think he'd fire at me, but he did. Good thing he was too weak to hold the pistol steady.

"Shit," he said. "I'll probably be dead before they get here."

It looked like the prospect of inevitable death, one way or the other, had lifted his spirits.

"I came to say good-bye," I told him. "Though you're a no-good, criminal slaver."

"Thank you," said Bowie. "You little bastard."

"I'm taking that rhetorically," I said.

"You wouldn't know a damn rhetorical statement if it shot you," he said. He raised the other pistol, but he was too weak to hold it up. He breathed deeply and began sweating.

"When the attack gets under way," I said to Villanueva and Bowie's sisters-in-law, "I'll come for you."

"I want them all here!" yelled Bowie. "I want them buried alive with me in my tomb!"

"There'll be plenty enough death, Pharaoh," I said.

"There will hardly be enough death to go around!" yelled Bowie.

I walked up to his bed and touched him on his shoulder. "You're one strange son-of-a-bitch," I said. "Good luck."

"The feeling's mutual," said Bowie. "Now get out of here. Crockett will need a shoulder to cry on."

Bowie was right about that. Crockett and the Tennessee volunteers manned the most vulnerable position in the Alamo, the rammed earth breastworks on the south of the plaza, right of the chapel and left of Bowie's room and the main gate. Like the rammed earth that breached the gap in the north wall, the position that Travis had claimed for himself, there was no real way to protect yourself once you stood atop it. The rest of the walls had ramparts built up behind them so the gunners could stand behind the top of the wall to fight. Susannah Dickinson had arranged our dozen or so artillery so we had a battery of two cannons at each corner of the fort, cross firing in front of the walls, as well as one cannon placed about halfway in-between each of those. There was one on top the hospital pointing east across the chapel courtyard, one at the corner of the cattle pen, two big twelve pounders atop the chapel. All of these were loaded with grapeshot, to take out as many bodies as possible in a firing. Inside, Susannah had used cow and horse skins to barricade each barracks doorway, in case the Mexicans broke through and we were reduced to fighting room to room. The skins were framed on two sides and filled with dirt in the middle, with holes to put rifle barrels through. There were about a hundred and fifty of us healthy enough to fight.

Crockett was surely chagrined when I told him of my visit with Santa Ana, minus my transformation, of course.

"You just damn surrender," he said. "You don't ask for permission!" He pushed back his duck cap. "How many of them are there?"

"Thousands," I said. "More coming."

"Shit," said Crockett. "You know, everybody's got to get stuff up their butt in a situation like this. Don't be proud. Save your life and just damn surrender. Sure, Santie Annie says he's going to give no quarter. He's got to say that to humble us. But you have to be brave enough to surrender in the face of that. He's not going to shoot all of us."

"He's kind of amoral," I said, "in an honorable sort of way."

"Did you just offer an opinion?" said Davy.

"Maybe."

"Let's just walk out and fight them," he said. "Let's get on our horses and ride through 'em. Let's face them out in the open like Americans."

"They think they're Americans, too," I said.

"Why do you always miss the point?" said Davy Crockett. "We are about to die!"

Given the truth of that, I paid my last visit to Susannah Dickinson. Whatever her strident dispositions, I've always been an admirer of strong women, be they red, be they white, be they whatever.

"I came to say good-bye," I said to her.

"Why did you save Trinidad Saucedo?" she asked me.

"My reasons were self-serving," I said, because if I told her the truth she'd disregard it anyway.

"You are an untrustworthy individual," Susannah Dickinson said to me.

"That's probably true," I said. "But I'm a good-hearted untrustworthy individual."

"Your heart will be as good as your rifle and your knife," she responded.

"You might live through this," I said to her.

"Life won't be worth living if I do."

"It may not be up to you," I said to her.

"That," she said to me, "is nothing new."

There, in the hospital, a good thirty white men had joined Henry Wax Karnes and lay sick and wounded. The Mexican women moved among them, wiping the sweat from their brows, offering them the last of the whiskey. They spoke back and forth to each other, the women in broken English and the men in broken Spanish. Karnes held my eye and I nodded to him.

"These Mexicans pray to the same God you do," I said to Susannah Dickinson.

"They think they do," she said. She lifted her baby to her shoulder and it cried.

I spent the day at the wall, and as the night came down and Crockett and his men fell asleep for the first time in twelve days, I walked among the men of the fort. A pall dropped on the Alamo and a full moon lay golden in the east, then rose white as bones into the sky, laying pale light down on the plaza. Everyone slept, as if the fort had exhaled and everybody inside lie waiting to breathe in. Outside the walls, beyond the trench, even the sentries slept under the pale shadows of the moon. Everyone slept in the peaceful night. You had to be awake to hear the drums and bugles, to hear the shouts, to hear the clatter of war across the plains.

# 61

AFTER THIRTEEN DAYS of lying awake waiting for them to attack,
the Mexican army caught us at dawn, asleep. Waves of those Mexican boys,
barefoot, dressed in their simple, white pajamas and wearing stiff little military
caps or sombreros came running through the mesquite. They fired their old
flintlocks from their hips. At first they hit nothing but each other and they
fell under their own fire. Still others fell as whistling Mexican cannon balls
shattered among them, short of our walls. It was hard to imagine that they
wanted to kill us.

When the first of them got within fifty yards we opened with our first salvo of
musket fire and grapeshot, cutting down hundreds. Then our next volley fired off
and the Mexican charge wavered and fell back, until a new line, led by shouting
officers on horseback, drove them forward again into our guns. We'd been
trained by Susannah and Almeron to shoot and reload in alternating groups, but
that ended after the first two re-loadings. The Mexican soldiers, caught in the
open field between the strafing of our gunfire and their own exploding artillery,
some of them seeing battle like this for the first time, began to duck and fall
down among the mesquite bushes. It gave them no cover at all and left them
motionless and easier to hit, which we did. If we saw a man drop, wounded or
not, we shot him before he was prodded forward by an officer to charge us again.
Then we shot the officer.

It was hard not to hit somebody when you fired into that mass of humanity. In later years I heard a lot of stories. How we beat off charge after charge. How the Mexicans fell back, regrouped, charged, retreated, charged and retreated again. That it went on for days. In truth, there was never a single retreat. Within a few minutes there were hundreds of Mexican soldiers crunched under our walls where it was almost impossible to stand up and shoot down at them with our long rifles without exposing ourselves completely to the fire of those still coming in.

We didn't know what to do. Nobody'd ever seen anything like this before. Crockett yelled out not to fire at them at all, that they couldn't hurt us down there, but barely anybody could hear him. But then they began to throw up ladders that we tried to push away, though there were so many bodies holding them up it was almost impossible. We could see the visage of our enemies now, their reddened faces grimacing under the shower of blood and lead, their grunts and cries beneath us, the plaintive voices of men about to die, trying to kill us so as to keep from dying. With Crockett I moved above the barracks stockade where we managed to yank a ladder up out of their hands and pull it over the wall. That only worked once. But as they came to the top of the wall, they were ill prepared to do much. Their flintlocks were fired out and they couldn't wield their bayonets while hanging on to the ladders. We knifed them as they came over. I took my first Mexican boy by hand, as a Comanche would, turning the blade sideways so it slipped through his ribs and plunged into his heart. You killed a warrior quickly. You didn't leave him to die, holding his guts in his hands.

Of all the crazy things I thought then, I thought of a long poem Sor María Juana made me read as a boy back in Mexico City. It was about that prince in India, Arjuna, who didn't want to fight a war against his own brothers. The driver of his war wagon, who turned out to be one of his gods, told him it didn't matter. As the Mexican soldiers began abandoning their ladders, and crawling against our walls over the bodies of their own dead, I remembered what the god said. The soul was bigger than the self. People lived many lives. Kill your brother if you must.

Time was quick and endless, with those Mexican boys coming in waves, piling up underneath our walls. The shouting and groans faded. The roar of muskets and cannons disappeared. Raised an Indian, I'd never seen this kind of frightful carnage. Though in the midst of it, I fought without excitement. It all seemed dreadful and senseless and ordinary.

For the longest time it seemed like we had them right where we wanted them. The bodies piled up below us, the ladders fell. As they crawled up over the bodies of their own wounded and dead, to the height of our guns, we shot them down. It felt like we'd just hold them there forever. Then, right before us, the Mexicans infantry beneath our wall began to get up and run back. "Christ!" yelled Crockett. "We held them!" He looked like he was about to cry. To both the west and east, the charge fell away as well, as the whole thrust of the attack began to bunch up at the north wall. A cheer went up, even over our curses and the screaming of the enemy, as Travis gathered up men and rushed to the top of the northern earthworks. "Come on, men!" yelled Buck Travis. "Give them hell!"

A lot of our boys ran from the eastern and western bulwarks to the northern wall while Almeron tried to get our cannons pointed in that odd direction, because that was the narrowest part of the fort. It seemed crazy for them to put their whole attack there, where we could concentrate our fire. Now another wave of Mexican infantry came across the plains. We fired at them and dozens fell, the men beneath our walls groaning as their own artillery fire fell among them. I swear, we'd barely lost a man by that point, but outside the fort, the bodies of Mexicans piled up like something from the *Inferno*.

The final wave of white clad Mexican infantry came through the mesquite and we began to cut them down while others of us on the walls took Bowie knives to the men who crawled up the earthworks or over each other's bodies to the top. For the first time, Texians began to drop from Mexican gunfire and hand to hand fighting. It was the point of the battle that always comes, when everything is on the brink and the slightest thing, one way or the other, can turn the tide. In another moment we might have turned them back. On the other side of it, we were seconds away from being overrun.

From behind the Mexican lines the Degüello sounded out. For a moment, it was as if everything had gone quiet. The battle paused beneath the cacophony of Mexican horns. Then a round of cannon fire erupted from across the river and underneath it waves and waves of Mexican infantry and cavalry, greater even than the numbers beneath us, came across the plain. A huge cheer went up underneath our walls. Shouts for our blood. It felt like days had gone by since the battle started, but the sun had barely moved in the sky. Now everybody knew that this battle was done.

It's difficult to express that moment of despair. Travis raised his sword high in his left hand. His right hand went up, too, but didn't get farther than the side of his head. From where I stood, across the plaza, it was hard to see, but it looked like the barrel of that gun tipped inward, toward his temple, as it discharged. Whatever took him, whether Mexican bullet or his own hand, he fell over the wall into the mass of bodies below.

To the right of me and Crockett, the Mexicans came again against the south wall. They climbed the bodies of their own dead under the unmanned bulwarks on the other side of the barracks. At about the same time, Mexican soldiers began pouring over the northern breach. There was nothing to do now but fall back into the fort, but at the southwest corner, Mexican infantry had taken the big eighteen pounder and turned it in on the courtyard where we were falling back, blasting our own grapeshot at us as we ran for the barricaded interior.

I left Crockett then, convinced I'd seen him for the last time, and rushed down from the earthworks to the chapel. I gathered up two pistols and two muskets and headed into the hospital for Henry Wax Karnes.

"I told you at the beginning, you little bastard," said Karnes.

"Shut up," I said. I grabbed him and put his arm over my shoulder, dragged him out and put him up against the wall where he slouched, guns out.

"We'll finish this in hell," said Karnes.

The women from the hospital had already gathered inside, bringing what few wounded they were capable of carrying. As the Tejanas began to drop to their knees and pray Susannah Dickinson stood defiantly in the center of the room, her child on her shoulder. She ran to one of the Mexican girls and gave her the child. "Get me a gun!" she yelled to me.

But just then Almeron Dickinson raced into the chapel, his eyes scanning the room blindly, coming from the bright morning and into the darkness. We could hear the shouts of the Mexicans now through the open door. Finally he spotted Susannah and ran to her, sliding to her feet on his knees and flinging his head to her breast. He gave her something, I couldn't tell what. "They are upon us," he said. "They're inside the walls. It's the end."

"Fight them, Almeron," said Susannah Dickinson.

"I love you," he said. He got up with his rifle. "Save our child."

"Kill as many as you can," said Susannah.

Dickinson ran out through the open door and it was the last I saw of him till the bitter end. Looking around, I saw that Villanueva and Bowie's cousins had not yet made it to the chapel, so I ran for the door as well. Outside the

Mexicans had poured over the walls and now brought our own cannon to bear on the barricaded doorways of the soldiers' quarters, blasting them open, then flooding in with bayonets. Out of one room a white flag emerged, but as the Mexicans held up their guns the door opened and a barrage of rifle fire cut them down. The enraged Mexican soldiers charged in for the slaughter. Men screamed for mercy, for death, for revenge. The plaza was so full of death you couldn't run without stepping on a corpse or slipping in blood.

In Bowie's room, Villanueva stood at the door. His cousins knelt at his bed, weeping as he lay there, knife on his chest, guns loaded, dead. That was the metaphor of the Alamo. Travis committed suicide and Bowie died before he could fire a shot.

"Get to the chapel!" I yelled. But nobody moved. "When they break in here they won't look around!"

Bowie's sisters-in-law didn't look up, but continued praying over Bowie. Villanueva lifted a hand and turned it nonchalantly to the ceiling. "Save yourself, Coyote," she said softly. I might have, but there wasn't time. The first cannon shot burst though the door and the Mexicans poured in. Running for Bowie with their bayonets thrust forward, they rushed the bed which collapsed under the crush of men. From under the pile, Bowie's body was lifted on the spears of their guns and they threw him into the air. When his broken corpse fell to the floor, they fell upon him again, giving him a thousand deaths.

I froze as the first of them turned toward me. The room quieted as I pushed the women behind me and went to one knee, raising my rifle to my shoulder as I faced that sea of blades. I'll tell you for sure, it takes nothing to face certain death. It's the uncertainty that's hard. Outside the door of Bowie's tomb, the air raged with an infinity of gunfire, the eternal blood cry of those who had lost their brothers and friends, the moans of the dying, the cold breath of the dead.

"*Venga*," I said to those Mexican boys. "*Venga, mis hermanos.*" Come, my brothers. I tried to hold my voice, but it seemed to raise an octave as I spoke. "*Viva Mexico!*" I said. "*Viva la muerte!*" as the first of them lowered their bayonets and began their charge.

# 62

*"ALTO! ALTO!"* someone cried from the doorway. "Do not molest the women!" The sentinel who I'd met during my night in the Mexican camp ran from the doorway and put his body between me and the bayonets. He turned to me. "Little one," he said, "there is no need to give your life. The battle is over. Women and children are always spared."

Suddenly, I could barely hold the musket I was about to fire. My fingers appeared slight, my hair hung down thickly over my shoulders and my clothes languished on my body like oversized blankets. I dropped the gun and felt my breasts. I had changed back into Trinidad Saucedo.

They led us to the chapel to wait out the end of the battle, though as they led us, it was easy to see that no Texian was left standing. All that remained was the war upon the already dead, and the young Mexican, Indian boys, tortured by the months of the campaign, the starvation and cold during the weeks of siege, raged among the bodies of their own dead and took out their vengeance on the Texian corpses. They fired their guns till the lifeless bodies jumped like puppets, smashing the heads of the cadavers with the butts of their rifles until the brains of the dead Texians poured onto the Alamo dust. Lifting the corpses to their feet on the tips of bayonets, they stabbed them into a rigid and liquid dance. They put grenades in the mouths of the dead and blew open their heads.

Then, just before I entered the chapel door, I saw General Castrillion leading six bedraggled prisoners from the south wall. Five wore buckskins, but one wore a waistcoat and a distinctive cap with a duck bill visor. Davy Crockett finally got his chance to surrender.

Needless to say, the women in the chapel, particularly Doña Petra, regarded me skeptically. Whatever had I done? Returning to the Alamo to fight in men's clothes. Foolish child. But I figured that derision was the best the world had to offer me at that point and took it silently. Neither Villanueva nor Bowie's cousins spoke to me, for good damn reason. I'd transformed and they knew it. It's not the kind of thing you can talk about.

In another hour things died down and we women were paraded out through the bodies of the dead as the officers began to separate the corpses, laying the Mexican bodies in a row with their feet to the east, but beginning to throw the bodies of the Texians into two large piles. I saw Almeron Dickinson lying outside the chapel. His body was mutilated, though I recognized him by his coat. Susannah didn't look at him, but walked forward, her child at her shoulder. We crossed the mote that surrounded the Alamo, and then crossed the San Antonio River, both red with blood and clogged with swollen corpses; an avenue of the dead led to the headquarters of Santa Ana, the President of Mexico. But worse were the moans and cries of the wounded who the Mexicans began to gather in makeshift tents outside the town. The smell of the corpses and the wailing from the hospital tents made me almost too weak to walk. In his haste to surprise the Texians, then wait outside the Alamo like a bobcat outside a squirrel hole, Santa Ana had brought no doctors on the campaign.

Santa Ana, dressed in his field uniform, a simple black coat over dark pants, a white shirt and high boots, had his chair set up on the north side of the town plaza where he brought us forward to prepare to interview us one by one. But before that, General Castrillion stepped forward. Castrillion was an old man and exhausted by the battle. His voice cracked as he brought forth his prisoners who huddled together as if they might protect themselves, like horses, with each other's bodies. "Great Santa Ana, the august," said Castrillion. "Merciful General, I deliver up to you six brave prisoners of war."

Santa Ana cocked his head inquisitively as Crockett now stepped forward. He addressed Santa Ana immediately, introducing himself before anybody could speak. He was quite a talker, and spun out a tale about how he and his boys were just passing through Texas and happened to get swept up in Travis' misguided whirlwind. Had he known there was a revolution against Mexico going on in Texas, he would have avoided the area completely. As it was, afraid the Mexicans would take revenge upon any Anglo they found, he and his men took refuge in the Alamo, but had argued for surrender from the start and in the ensuing encounter had refused to take up arms.

Well, there's nothing like being on the losing side to make the injustices of war crystal clear. The fact was, Crockett did argue for surrender from the start. In fact he argued for it at the end. Hell, he even surrendered. Though he'd killed his share of Mexicans. But I had, too. I just had a better lie.

As I gazed at Crockett, I couldn't help but think that the white man's world was sorely confused. Under their ideas of truth, and what I later learned to be called "objectivity," they committed the cruelest of personal acts. As I've said before, it came from dividing things up that never should have been divided up in the first place. For us Indians, stars, rocks, animals, spirits, gods, people, living and dead, it was all personal. If we're going to torture you to death, you should take it personally, because it's meant that way. In fact, it's a compliment. Though it's one thing to think that it's an honor for somebody to have his heart torn out while it's still beating and another to have your own heart torn out.

Anyway, Santa Ana didn't speak a lick of English and Almonte, who did, wasn't in the plaza. I saw de la Peña, but he was back in the crowd. So Santa Ana didn't understand a word Crockett said. The great general kind of looked away and did his imitation of Henry IV in the Becket situation. He spoke to the air. "Did I say we should take prisoners?" he asked.

And with that a horde of the lesser officers fell upon Davy Crockett and the other prisoners. I'd like to say it was quick and merciful, but rather it was horrible. Castrillion wept as those Texians had their digits taken off one by one, then their hands and feet. I'll stop, because it didn't end there. Some officers vomited as they watched. Others turned away. But Crockett and his volunteers, once the slaughter started, took it wordlessly. Without a sound. They died like brave men, as honorably as anyone who'd ever been massacred.

They gathered the parts of those Tennessee volunteers in blankets and carried them back to the Alamo, then covered the blood in front of Santa Ana with dust. Then Santa Ana, with the help of the now present General Almonte, began his interviews with us noncombatants, bringing us forward one by one, starting with Joe, Travis' slave. He asked why you were there and what you did for the Texian cause. If you had a child he volunteered to adopt it. One woman took him up on it and Santa Ana adopted the boy. He gave everybody two silver pesos and a blanket and sent them off in a wagon with two horses in the care of Joe. That included Susannah Dickinson who, limping forward with a bullet wound in her calf and carrying her baby on her shoulder, made a long speech at Santa Ana, in English, of course, saying how proud she was of the men in the Alamo, especially her husband, Almeron, and how she wished she could have fought and died instead of enduring this humiliation. She said she'd like to kill Santa Ana and hoped somebody soon would.

Almonte translated a little of the defiance, but for the most part said that she'd thanked Santa Ana for his mercy to the women. Not that the president would have harmed her. In fact he offered to adopt Angeline, Susannah's baby girl, and raise her as his own. He was already starting to feel somewhat ambivalent about the Crockett thing. I could tell, because twice he stopped in the middle of his interviews and asked no one in particular, "Did I demand a slaughter?" Nonetheless, Susannah Dickinson and the rest were to be the couriers of his wrath, sent out to let the Anglos know what was in store for them if they didn't get the hell out of Tejas. He decided to send his own servant, Ben, along with them with a long proclamation which first said that all rebels would be prosecuted according to law, and next that all people in Tejas, no matter what their country of origin, should return to their homes and go on with their lives under the protection of the Mexican government. For all the terror wreaked by Santa Ana, he held that position from the beginning to the end. If you admitted to Catholicism and didn't own slaves, and weren't hell bent on seceding from Mexico, then you were left alone.

Before Santa Ana dealt with me, a young Mexican officer, his name was Francisco Esparza, came forward and said that he had a relative, Gregorio Esparza, in the Alamo. He asked if he could find him and have him buried in the Catholic cemetery with the Mexican dead. Gregorio's wife came forward then with her four little kids all hanging on her and crying. Santa Ana asked her if her husband fought for the rebels in the Alamo and she said he did. Then he asked her if she knew that her brother-in-law, Francisco, fought for Mexico. She said she knew that, too. Then he asked her if she wanted him to adopt her kids and she turned him down. So Santa Ana gave her two pesos and a blanket for each kid and granted Francisco the right to find and bury his brother in Campo Santo, the Catholic cemetery. Then he ordered the bodies of the Texians to be burned en masse without ceremony or blessing. Finally, he turned to me. "Little one," he said. "Mixtli."

That was a complicated allusion to an old Aztec legend about a young virgin who fell in love with a poor boy named Popoca. But she was already being courted by a rich man named Axooxco. Popoca went off to battle to prove his bravery and win a place as an eagle warrior, in order to supplant Axooxco's claims on Mixtli, the girl. So Axooxco, being your typical evil guy, figured he'd trick Mixtli into marrying him by having word sent to her that Popoca had been killed in battle. But instead of marrying Axooxco, Mixtli killed herself, only to have Popoca return and find her dead. Popoca mourned endlessly. And on the verge of suicide himself, the gods took pity on the lovers and turned them into volcanoes. You can see them some eighteen thousand feet above the Valley of Anahuac in old Mexico, where the cities of Puebla and Cholula are now. Mixtli is called Ixtaccihuatl, La Mujer Dormida or The Sleeping Woman. And stooping next to her is Popocatepetl, Popoco. If you go there you'll see them. They're unmistakable. Anyway, everywhere I've been somebody's got some story like that.

Of course, it was just like Santa Ana to think of himself as Popoca and not Axooxco. "Had I lost you in the Alamo, I would have mourned you forever," he said. He snapped his fingers. "Find this girl some clothes."

Standing in front of the Napoleon of the West, I didn't give two thoughts about abandoning Susannah Dickinson and the others to their wagon ride across east Texas. I wouldn't be safe as Coyote O'Donohughe or Trinidad Saucedo among those fleeing rebels. No, the choice was clear. For the time being I'd become the traveling companion of General Antonio López de Santa Ana, Commander-in-Chief and President of all Mexico, which at the time still included Texas. He might have been crazy, but hell, I might have been crazy. How long could I hold him off? Or keep his interest for that matter? A thousand nights? A thousand nights and one? Women have been in worse positions. For now, I was the concubine of the most powerful man on the continents of the Americas.

# 63

THE BODIES OF THE Texian rebels were still burning in two huge piles outside the Alamo when the news of the massacre at Goliad reached us. Contrary to later stories I heard from Anglo Yankees, which pretty much said that Fannin had been overwhelmed by Urrea much like Santa Ana had taken the Alamo, we knew differently. Urrea had sent word to Santa Ana when he reached Bahia de Goliad that he was almost out of ammunition, and that his 250 Maya infantrymen were exhausted and outnumbered. He feared Fannin would just march out and take him apart. So he sent his messenger to Santa Ana requesting permission to withdraw. That wasn't the kind of things Mexicans could decide very quickly and before Santa Ana even brought his generals together to discuss the matter, not that he'd listen to them anyway, Fannin had finally obeyed Houston's orders and on a drizzly morning abandoned the impregnable fort.

Whatever Fannin's other skills—obviously timing wasn't one of them—he could not cross a river, and immediately got his army bogged down outside Goliad on a tributary of the San Antonio. It started to rain like hell as Fannin eventually got his army across and headed for the forest around Coleto Creek. That's where Urrea accidentally ran into him.

Still outnumbered and without ammunition, Urrea feared that Fannin might turn and attack him so he began an engagement in order to disguise his retreat. But Urrea's army, as good as they'd been about moving forward, had a hard time getting themselves moving backward. Oddly enough, retreats are harder to organize than attacks. But before they could get packed up to leave, Fannin surrendered to an army he both outgunned and out-manned.

The rest of it you know. Urrea liked and respected Fannin, and though he was under orders to accept nothing but unconditional surrender, he promised he'd do what he could to save the lives of Fannin and his men. That's when Santa Ana relieved him of command.

I was with the great general that night he'd relieved Urrea and the lives at Goliad lay at Santa Ana's feet. We sat together on a small hill that overlooked the two huge piles of burning corpses outside the Alamo. The stench of bloating bodies had yet to be purged from the river, and the smoke that rose from burning the rotting flesh of my Texian compatriots made the air almost unbreathable, like the air in your throat after you'd puked.

Santa Ana gazed up. "Look at this metaphor, my Mixtli. The blaze of the funeral pyre obliterates the stars." He gazed at the fires again. "It is not without fear that I bring myself to speak, for to describe the bottom of the universe is no enterprise to undertake in sport. Beyond all others misbegotten . . . better they had been sheep and goats!"

That was a quote, more or less, from the beginning of the thirty-second canto of Dante's *Inferno*, if my memory served me correctly. It was something all of us little trouble-makers had to read in monastery school in Mexico City.

Santa Ana put his arm around me and drew me to him.

"Popoca," I whispered to him. "It's said that those who betray their country will be frozen in ice." I didn't want to contradict him too blatantly, but if you're going to burn two hundred corpses and quote Dante, you should get it right. Canto thirty-two, as I recalled, was the Ninth Circle out of Ten in the *Inferno*, and the farther down you go in Dante's hell, the colder it gets.

"The heart of an innocent and the mind of a witch," said Santa Ana, kissing my forehead. "I'm quoting a great Italian poet who dreamed of hell. The traitorous were trapped in ice while their bodies burned," he said.

So much for educating people in order to humanize them. It was something I'd have to remember to bring up with my mother, if I ever saw her again.

"Mixtli, come," said Santa Ana, lifting me. "There are other fires to burn."

Well it was a relief to get the hell out of there so to speak. We strolled through the quiet, Mexican camp. There was really very little celebration. As a people, I found that the Mexicans worked hard and played hard. They could fight ferociously and in their way took tremendous pleasure in blood. But they didn't rejoice in victory. Their souls were far too sympathetic.

There was a certain military type who now stood guard in intervals throughout the compound—I couldn't put a finger on their tribal origin, but they tended to be tall, thin yet muscular, with grim, heart-shaped faces—and these soldiers were as stoic and brutal as any I'd ever seen. But the rest of the army was in a kind of mournful peace. Officers and men mixed casually, many of them wandering to the wagons of the women who followed the army and camped on its fringe. Santa Ana, dressed in a simple shirt and riding pants, walked among them with barely a nod or salute coming from any direction. And I myself was now moving pretty slowly, encumbered by my new petticoats and skirts, bows, scarves, and shoes made for anything but feet. It was hard to argue that these clothes weren't designed for anything but absolute debilitation.

We entered a tent lit by a single oil lamp. There was a chair and a table with a bottle of wine, a wide camp bed. I was excited and I was frightened, but Santa Ana was as patient with seduction as he was with the Alamo. He exuded desire and patience. He talked about how beautiful I was and every time I spoke he remarked on my intelligence. He poured wine. He kissed the air. He touched me and my softest parts, which were in different places than they used to be, hardened and rose to his touch. He made me feel like I wanted him more than he wanted me, and he did it by making me feel like he wanted me more than I wanted him.

But may the Great Everywhere Spirit help me, because I don't know where I got the strength or the impulse, I thought that something good should come out of my virgin sacrifice. Nonetheless, my last direct plea to Santa Ana, for the lives in the Alamo, had accomplished absolutely nothing. I figured maybe that the great general, being such a poetical type, might be better influenced by an appeal to history and metaphor. I accepted a glass of wine from him and led him to the bed.

"Before I give myself to you, my Popoca, I want to tell you a story," I said.

"A short and seductive story?" said Santa Ana.

"It is about seduction," I said. "Have you heard of Arabia?"

"Of course," he said. "How have you heard of Arabia?"

"Because there are things that pass from one soul to another," I whispered to him. "Even through time."

"I think you're speaking of India, little Mixtli," said the President of Mexico.

"Maybe India, too, my President," I said. "In Arabia, long ago, there was a great sultan," I said.

"A king," said Santa Ana.

"An emperor," I said. "Who was betrayed by his wife. And so, out of hatred and fear of all women, he decreed that each night he would only sleep with a virgin, and in the morning, to insure her fidelity, she would be beheaded."

"Like slaying a baby after its baptism," said my President.

"You might call it a metaphor for the plight of all women," I said to him. "Though I would not."

"No?"

"I am not sophisticated enough."

"You are beautiful, smart and funny. I would not call it such a metaphor," said Santa Ana, "because it portrays me in a bad light."

"You are smart and funny, as well, my President. The Sultan had a brother who had the most beautiful daughter in all the land, a girl who knew all the ancient stories of Arabia. When she came of age she insisted to her father that she should not be excluded from the plight of other women. Her father reluctantly agreed, and mournfully he permitted her to submit herself to the grand Sultan. But on the night of their consummation, the young princess began telling the Sultan a story which was so entertaining and endless that each night the Sultan went to sleep holding the girl in his arms, waking up in the morning feeling holy and refreshed and anxious for the story to continue the next night."

"I see, little one," said the great Commander-in-Chief of Mexico.

"After a thousand and one nights, when the story ended, the Sultan forgave all women and married the princess."

"And so," said Santa Ana, "if I am so entertained, I shall become a faithful husband and save the prisoners at Goliad because I have forgotten about them."

I kissed him then, on the forehead and then the lips.

"Tell me the story, Mixtli," he said to me.

And I did. The first one is a story about a merchant who accidentally kills a jinni's son by throwing away a date pit. The jinni is about to kill him, but the merchant convinces him to listen to a story first. That's how it goes, on and on. I might repeat it here had I another lifetime, but you can go read it yourself.

Santa Ana laughed and cried out loud during my rendition of that thing.

When I was done he held my face in his hands. "You are the most amazing!" he said. Then he fucked me. In the morning he ordered the execution of Fannin and all the men at Goliad.

# 64

BY THE TIME THE ARMY reached González I was on "Ali Baba and the Forty Thieves" and Santa Ana was awaking as refreshed as a sultan in Arab heaven, blissfully restored by stories and sex, which says something for the kind of man he was. Across Texas, the Anglo settlers abandoned everything, scourging their fields and barns, killing their livestock, burning food crops, tobacco crops, cotton storehouses and putting the ax to their mills and spinning wheels and gins. It was an abomination and waste incomprehensible to the Mexicans who contended to the end they weren't making war on settlers or farmers. Sure, Santa Ana had executed a thousand or so prisoners, but those men had been combatants, barely a one born in Texas. Besides, Mexicans had been executing prisoners since before time. Near the end of their empire the Aztecs didn't even fight real battles. They'd declare war on some vassal or another, meet them in a field and trade prisoners—of course they took a lot more than they gave—then they took those prisoners back to town and sliced their hearts out up on top that pyramid of theirs. Like I said before, it was a big honor.

One of the big mistakes that North American Anglos made when dealing with the Mexicans was that they treated them like they were some aberrant kind of Spaniard. The majority of Mexicans were Indians. City Indians maybe, but Indians nonetheless. And if the people running the show were of mixed

Spanish blood, well, as influence goes, the Spanish of Mexico became a lot more Mexican than the Mexicans ever became Spanish. So for all the yack about international European what-not policies during Santa Ana's war against the Texians, in the end Mexico was not a European country and the war, so to speak, wasn't a war between anybody, but a rebellion inside Mexican borders led by men who weren't Mexican and never planned to be. Given that, it was being fought by Mexican rules. Combatants, if they lost, got killed. But citizens and colonists, whatever their race or origin, were left alone.

So all that burning and abandoning and scourging didn't make a damn bit of sense to anybody on the Mexican side. These Mexican soldiers were some of the most unlikely conquerors in the world. They'd stand around in the ruins of some burned down farmhouse and start weeping over a broken spinning wheel or some child's toy. I don't know, maybe they were thinking of home. They could talk forever about these Texians and their foolishness and bravery and what a pity it was that we had to fight a war. Of course if they caught one they might flay him alive before getting all weepy about it later.

On the Texian side, it was that old European thing: if we can't have it, then nobody can. In the meantime, you burn the bridges and leave the conquering army nothing to live on. But this wasn't Russia in the winter, either. There was still plenty of game out there if you had time to hunt it, not that anybody did. Everybody was too busy rolling cannons and fording rivers and pitching and unpitching tents to take care of the necessities. Not that I had to work hard. Besides telling stories and making love, I spent my time sitting around in a dress inside a wagon or a tent. Though that evening after we hit González, I borrowed some pants and a shirt from some Zapotec boys from Oaxaca and slipped out with them and caught a parcel of rabbits. I was heading for Santa Ana's tent back at the end of the line, two fresh rabbits strung over my shoulder, when who did I see offering mass at the back of a gilded wagon but the Great Crooked Inquisitor!

It was just my Coyote nature to go over there and test his prescience, which I was on my way over to do, when I spied somebody else behind the wagon, none other than my mentor from Mexico City, Sor María Juana. For the moment I forgot who I was, which, of course, was debatable enough, when the three women who Sor María Juana was speaking to backed away at the sight of me, making the sign of the cross.

"What frightens these women, little boy-girl?" Sor María Juana said to me.

For a moment I thought she saw through me, but then remembered that I was dressed in borrowed Zapotec men's clothes.

"Maybe because I am the mistress of the emperor," I said.

"How does that make you different from the women in the hospital wagons?"

"They work by the hour for different people," I said. "I work for the same person every minute."

"A more common fate than you might imagine," she said. "Though I imagine, too, that his mistresses are less common than his wives." Having been Santa Ana's mistress herself, I didn't expect a fond welcome from her, but I felt a bond to her now greater than the fantasies of my boyhood infatuations.

"So you are our Mary Magdalene," said Sor María Juana.

"I prefer a comparison to Shahrazād," I said.

"Few of us get to live out our preferences," said she.

Well Sor María Juana was never one much to show her cards, though I guess I, myself, held a few to my chest, too. I turned to the women she'd been speaking to and offered them my rabbits. Some of the women who followed the camp were young enough and pretty enough, though poor, so that the officers, when they visited them, brought camp stores, or even wild game like these hares. But these women were middle-aged. Most likely widowed by the war down in Zacatecas, their villages and families destroyed, they followed the military train, helping the wounded, cooking, or trading sexual favors to the lower of rank. This was their last shot at survival. Without the war they'd end up begging somewhere. They were reluctant, but food is food.

"The Great Emperor's surprise dinner," I said to Sor María. "He won't miss it."

I stashed those men's clothes for future use and returned to Santa Ana's wagon to don my ribbons and bows for dinner. The emperor liked undressing me almost as much as he liked slipping in under my dress, both of which required full attire. It began to rain that night, and rain pounded at the top of his canvas tent. I told him that I'd caught him two rabbits for dinner that night, but that I'd given them to the good sister who aided the women camp followers.

"She is an interesting woman," said the great general. "But you should not give away my rabbits."

"Wasn't she a poet?" I said.

"Did she tell you that?"

When I didn't say anything he grabbed me hard and brought me to him. "If you were not small and soft you would be threatening," he said. "Don't find things out. It won't bring you power, but it could kill you."

"I'm threatening?"

He put his hands in my hair and kissed me. It was too forceful and I didn't like it. Then he suddenly backed away. "The Pope himself ordered her excommunication," he said.

"For sleeping with the President?" I said.

He laughed. "Don't make me hate you," he said. "I might be flattered, if I truly thought you jealous." He turned. "Besides, I was not President then. She was banished because her poems, her letters, secret ones," he paused, "threatened the Church."

"How can you threaten the Church?" I said.

"How can you threaten the Emperor?" He put his hand out to me. "How do you think so much power is held, and kept, little one?"

"Where I am from, power is not held or kept."

"And where are you from, Mixtli, another world?"

"Yes," I whispered.

His eyes narrowed. "If I had not interceded and brought Sor María Juana on this war, she would be dead."

"There is some good company on both sides of this war," I said softly, going to him, "and some bad company on both sides."

Santa Ana raised his arms. "I shall never forget my vacation in Tejas!" he exclaimed, bringing me to him. There was a feeling he gave me, I couldn't help it, call it my feminine side, but I melted under his touch. "Tomorrow, Mixtli," he whispered, "catch me two more rabbits."

For the next few weeks as we chased the Texians across the plains of Texas, it rained and rained. Santa Ana divided his army into three prongs which surged toward the Brazos River, one toward Washington-on-the-Brazos to the north, the next toward San Felipe de Austin, and the third toward Brazoria. Wanting to catch the rebel government in session, and not knowing for certain if they were in Washington or Austin, we followed along between the rear guards of the northern and central armies so the great general could move in either direction when we caught them. He knew that Houston had now vowed to Stephen F. Austin and the Texian congress that he would not let the Mexicans cross the Brazos, and Santa Ana took tremendous pleasure, even as he pushed his beleaguered troops forward across the raging Colorado, in the prospect of sweeping across Texas so quickly that the congress, bogged down on the flooded Brazos river, and not expecting such a quick, Mexican advance, would be caught pants down. Had he not already surprised them by crossing the northern Mexican desert in the dead of winter?

The fact was, the Mexicans now had thousands of troops in the field, even if tired and poorly equipped, and by the looks of what we saw in our advance, there were fewer Texians fighting for Texas everyday. Though they couldn't burn their fields in the downpour, everything we passed was wrecked and abandoned and the Mexican officers were already so overburdened with booty that it was sifting down to the infantry. Our scouts returned daily with reports of Texian men fleeing west and east and north, many of them fleeing so fast that they left their wives and kids behind, dragging their wagons of belongings through the mud. When we came upon those women, Santa Ana would interview them and beseech them to return to their ranches and farms, that if they were good Catholics and had no slaves, then they were also good Mexicans and had nothing to fear. Of course, he also promised the same land to his officers.

"You'd take land away from good Mexicans?" I asked him in the privacy of our bed.

He responded that they would not be the first good Mexicans to lose their land. He was softening on the idea of turning Texas into a wasteland buffer zone and thinking more along de la Peña's lines of turning Texas into a military colony. For all his talk of marching all the way to Washington, he sure feared the Americans, almost as much as he feared his own officers who, if he discovered that their men loved them, or they showed an over-abundance of competence, he had them dismissed and sent back to Mexico.

"Why do you do that?" I asked.

"Because it would be a waste to kill them."

When he wasn't drunk, or stoned on opium, then he was crazy. Opium, for Santa Ana, did much the same as it did for his counterpart, General Houston. It kept him sane. At night, in the tent, he'd wait in the light of his lantern as lizards crawled beneath the canvas to escape from the rain. There, armed with a string that he attached to the end of a stick, he made a little noose that he hung over the head of each intruding lizard, placing it slowly and delicately over their heads and snapping them up, only to release them and catch them again. It fascinated him how many times he could catch the same damn lizard with the same trick, pulling it off right in front of their faces.

"They are not so different from the Yankees," he said to me. "They can be surprised again and again."

As we moved across those drenched plains, fording one flooding stream after another with the speed of a tortoise, Mexican boys died of fever and starvation almost as fast as Texians could desert their own. It just made you think about the value of an individual human life and why anybody ever bothered to fight anybody about anything, a discussion I had more than once with my new friend, Sor María Juana.

"Men fight," she said. "That is the world."

"And they're getting better at it," I said.

She paused then, as she was placing a wet cloth on the forehead of a feverish soldier. She looked at me. I knew the look. She recognized something.

"You hide as much as I do," she said.

"It's the refuge of the powerless," I told her.

As I've said before, we didn't have any doctors. The sick and wounded tried to stay in line as long as they could because if they fell they were left for dead or until the women's camp caught up to them, then we did what we could, maybe write their last letter home for them. Fact is, there are a thousand fever-fighting plants you can find right out there on the prairie if you have the time to look: Adder's Tongue, Sticklewort, Blackberry, Five Finger Grass, and I did what I could to point them out to Sor María Juana so she could harvest them as she saw them on the way. Crazy as it is, we started curing some of those boys and sending them back to the front lines. Of course no deed like that goes unpunished, and soon the news my witchcraft reached the ears of the Great Crooked Inquisitor.

"He wishes to interview you," said Sor María Juana.

"Tell him I am too humble for his presence."

"He wonders why you have not come to Communion."

"I'm not Catholic," I said, because I had to say something, so I said something stupid.

She put a finger to her lips. "Everyone in Mexico is Catholic."

"I'm afraid of him," I said.

She turned to me then. She placed her fingertips on my cheek. "Little one," she said. "Everyone sleeps with someone. It is called Original Sin."

"He's suspicious of me," I said to her.

"That is his job. Even the devil will do some good to win souls to the fire."

"Do you believe that?" I said.

"I am a nun."

"Well quit being a nun," I said.

"I cannot divorce my own husband, the Church," said Sor María Juana. "Even more so, I cannot divorce God."

Knowing your place seemed to be the way of the world among the Mexicans, if not all white folks. And the *Histoire du Monde* just didn't have a place for a Coyote. Nonetheless, I made up my mind that I'd have to confront the Great Crooked Inquisitor once again. In fact, I'd see him for Communion the very next morning, right after I got done telling Santa Ana a story about a magic carpet.

# 65

I SUPPOSE I DIDN'T SEE the point of being brave on principle. A person who was brave all the time was a fool. But to be a coward in the face of certain death is downright ignoble. It was something Davy Crockett understood and I admired him for it. There were plenty of Comanche who couldn't make the distinction.

In the morning, after leaving the great general both bodily and intellectually sated, I went off to do my spiritual duty. I slogged through the rain in my finest, getting mud all over the hem of my skirt, and stood at the back of the church wagon. That thing looked something like a big, rolling tabernacle, if you've ever seen a tabernacle, which is a gold house at the center of a Catholic altar where consecrated hosts are kept, a little Jesus house, so to speak. Of course, these priests were the representatives of Christ on earth, according to the Church, and so they could live like little Jesus if they chose, regardless how the big Jesus lived. That was the big head-scratcher about Christianity; it seemed to me that following Jesus somehow involved a more ascetic existence than I generally observed practiced by most Christians. The Great Crooked Inquisitor's wagon was painted in red and gold, a cross on top, a painting on the side panel of a white dove, golden rays emanating from it like rays of the sun. On the other side was painted a white hand with two fingers held together, pointing upward at some glorious clouds. Jesus stood up on the top of one cloud and his mother on another, the flag of Mexico in between. You didn't have to look too close to see that the flag of Mexico had been painted over the flag of Spain and the Virgin of Guadalupe over the Virgen de los Remedios. I guess that explained well enough the survival of the Great Crooked Inquisitor himself. I'd been convinced when I left Mexico City that night of Iturbide's overthrow, bombs and shouts of "Death to the priests!" flying through the air, that the Inquisitor wouldn't see the daylight.

I lowered the back step of the wagon, stepped up, and knocked on his door.

"I have called for no one!" came his voice.

"It is Trinidad Saucedo," I shouted through the door and the rain, "from the side of the President."

It took a moment, but the door swung open. I don't know how it did because there was nobody behind it and the Great White Inquisitor, crookeder and whiter and more ominous than a dead king, sat in his bed, a shelf of wood over his lap like a desk. The sheets of his bed were white, red satin hung from the walls between gold crucifixes, statues of suffering saints, white virgins holding infants and standing on globes or stepping on snakes or both. Behind the Inquisitor's bed, a huge painting of St. George putting the sword to a dragon, and at either side of me, at the door, paintings of huge, white archangels, white robes, white faces, white hands and white wings, golden swords drawn and glorious in the defense of God.

The Inquisitor sat back. He let his breath fill his crooked chest until he sat almost straight. Then he put his left elbow on his desk. He rested his chin on his thumb, two fingers at his cheek and two at his lips.

"The new mistress of the Emperor," he said.

"This wagon doesn't look this big from the outside," I said.

He put out his right hand. "Sit," he said, motioning to a stool at the foot of the bed.

I guided my skirts over the stool. From there, of course, I had to look up at him.

"Where are you from, daughter?" he asked.

"I am an orphan, but surely you know everything about me," I said.

"In fact," he said to me, "I can see through souls and I cannot see through yours."

And that was a good thing. He suspected me enough back when I was me, with a different name.

"The world is slippery, but God is true," said the Inquisitor. "Sister said you are not Catholic."

"Baptize me," I said.

He let a little grin crack through. "You are the consort of the President."

"He's a Catholic, Father," I said.

"I would erase one sin to cover it with a thousand more. Woman is the body of sin." What he was saying was that I existed in Original Sin now, being a heathen, but if he baptized me, I'd be creating new sins on my own all over the place. What's more, it was my fault for sleeping with Santa Ana; there was only one pure woman and that was the Blessed Virgin, so he'd just as well have Santa Ana sleeping with a heathen for the sake of all three of us. Santa Ana wasn't responsible because first he was a man and it was my fault for tempting him, and second he wasn't making me sin because I was currently doomed already, which only goes to show that you can think yourself out of a box or into a sack, it's all the same.

"You are familiar," he said to me, "but the familiarity is impossible unless you are some kind of demon."

The fact was, I was some kind of demon. And being who I was, I figured I'd just show him what kind. I opened my palms and blood poured from them. I took off my shoes and stockings and showed him the bloody sores on my feet. Blood ran onto my dress from a wound that exploded above my left breast. He raised a crucifix between us. And I opened my arms in front of him, just like Jesus.

# 66

I ALWAYS FIGURED Jesus was a Coyote. The surprising thing was that those Christians only had one of them. I later learned that the Hindus had millions. I went back to Santa Ana's tent none the worse for my interview, but for the blood on my clothes. My rustling woke the great emperor up.

"You look disheveled, little one," he said.

"That high priest is a hard man to talk to," I said.

"Ah, the Monsignor, he blesses our path," said Santa Ana, and you could tell he didn't mean a damn word of it.

I got out of my gowns and went to him. "I'm a little worried about the military situation," I said to him.

Santa Ana sat up. "Bed is for love and stories," he said.

So it was after we made love and sat at breakfast that I tried to talk to him again.

"My president," I said, "your army is all divided up. Any branch of it could be attacked and defeated."

"Little Mixtli," he said, "you are a woman and a child. My army is mopping up the countryside. Houston will be pinned down at San Jacinto."

"He has Indian allies everywhere," I said.

"Indians? They fight with twigs. You are suddenly interested in battle strategy?" said Santa Ana.

You hated to pick a side, but somebody was going to win this affair and somebody was going to lose it. "I am the consort of the greatest general on the earth," I said.

"You wish to learn."

"For learning's sake," I said.

He sat back, put down his coffee cup and scrutinized me. "So you can one day become Joan of Arc," he said.

That was another thing these white Christians only had one of, woman warriors, if you didn't count Susannah Dickinson.

"I will tell you of Hannibal," said Santa Ana, and he did. Crossing the Alps, raging around Italy for fifteen years, the whole thing. Of course, having had a Jesuit education in Mexico City and briefly living as an Italian, I knew a little bit about it. But Santa Ana's big point was the Battle of Cumae, where Hannibal let his middle collapse only to surround the Romans with his flanks and massacre them. That's what Santa Ana was doing now, broadly speaking. We were going to plant ourselves in front of Houston with our apparently reduced army and wait for Houston's desperate surprise attack. We'd sound our horns and fall back slowly while the rest of the Mexican army returned and surrounded the Texians, the battle for Texas over. Then Santa Ana would lead his combined forces to the gates of Washington, D.C. Maybe he'd rage around the U.S. for fifteen years the way Hannibal did in Italy, wily as a fox. I didn't mention to my President that Hannibal lost that war.

Anyway, breakfast was over and it was time for some opium and a nap until the big mid-afternoon luncheon.

That's how it went for another week. We scoured the countryside, Texian colonies falling faster than horses in the desert, until we had Houston backed up outside San Jacinto. There Santa Ana planted the remnants of his army and sent out communiqués to the other generals to draw near enough to get to us in a two-hour forced march. Santa Ana even had his army camp with our backs to the river to make us look vulnerable and stupid. The trap was set. But I didn't want to spend the next fifteen years in Santa Ana's stable. Besides, I'm a Coyote. Trouble is my middle name. It was time to visit Sam Houston.

# 67

"COYOTE DONATELLI," screamed Houston. "A ghost!" He was throwing back a mixture of rye and opium, his red hair sprawling out of his wide brimmed hat. Unlike Davy Crockett, Houston actually wore a fringed deerskin jacket, Cherokee style, and beaded moccasins. I wore my white man's suit. If you ever plan on becoming a shaman shape-shifter, always hold onto your last set of clothes. We sat in the center of his tipi.

"Hear what happened at the Alamo?" said Houston. "Goliad?"

"You're trapped. I'm repaying a debt," I said.

"Trapped by what? Two hundred Mayas in pajamas?"

"Has anyone in Texas stopped them?"

"We're not running, we're just tiring them out," said Houston. "Tenderizing them."

"I think you'll find them pretty battle hardened," I said. "And everywhere, not just in front of you."

Houston put down his bottle and covered his face with his hands. "Oh!" he said. "Oh! You make me weep!"

"You're surrounded," I told Houston. "Stephen F. Austin has already abandoned Washington-on-the-Brazos along with everybody else."

"Abandoned the capital," muttered Sam Houston. "Austin is a pansy. A political genius, but a pansy. A pansy genius!"

"Santa Ana expects you to attempt a desperate surprise attack," I said.

"Of course!" said Sam Houston. "So we'll move out at dawn, battle hour, in tight formation."

"He'll fall back."

He raised his arms. It was hard to tell if he was crying or laughing. "We'll face each other in battle formation for days, like Caesar and Vercingetorix!" Suddenly, he sobered and tilted a brow at me. "How do you know all this?"

"Remember, I'm a spy," I said. "It's why you saved my life."

"Not what my Indian friends say," said Houston. "They say you turned yourself into smoke. Ha!"

"You'll never hold this rabble in any battle formation," I said to him.

"Oh, these men! These souls of Texas!" screamed Sam Houston. Now he drank again and groaned. "That's better. That's better." He hunched forward. "A night attack?"

"They'll expect it. Broad daylight, right after their lunch. They all go to sleep. It would be against all battle etiquette for you to attack then."

"Battle etiquette?"

"No battle formation. Just charge in screaming. If you're lucky you'll get to Santa Ana before his reinforcements collapse on your flanks."

"I'll face Santa Ana in the field, *mano a mano*, like Achilles and Hector!"

"I don't think they spoke Spanish," I said to Houston.

"But it could be suicide," Houston cried. "Suicide! Noble suicide!"

"It's your only chance."

"We could just hold out here and wait for Texas to rally around us," whispered Sam Houston. "For the U.S. government to step in."

"Like they did at the Alamo."

"Oh fate!" said Houston, burying his face again. "Destiny or mishap?"

I stood up. "Tomorrow afternoon. I'll make sure the great general is asleep."

# 68

THERE WAS A WAY in which I trusted Houston because he was a madman and madmen are honest, unlike my current lover, Santa Ana, who walked a thin, cold line between the cruel and the ruthless. I even said it to him.

"There is no line there, little one. I am ruthless. You do not make love to a cruel man, but to a ruthless lover."

That was a fine point, but to be honest and not go into detail, he was more a charmer than a lover; some banter, a little romance, then bang. It was all about him.

He took my hand, then stiffened.

"Why do all my lovers smell like Sam Houston?" he said.

Because you can change your shape but not your smell, whiskey and smoke, not Santa Ana's tequila and opium. I should have soaked in the river. I'd made a big mistake.

"I am not his lover," I said.

He turned his back on me. "All women are spies in the house of love," he said. "I always knew."

"Should I join a convent now?"

"If you are so lucky," said Santa Ana. "The Monsignor is an Inquisitor. You will be tortured until you confess to being a witch, then he will baptize you.

Then he will save your new, pure soul by burning you at the stake."

"He is cruel, not ruthless," I said.

"My clever Mixtli," said Santa Ana. "You will tell me your last story tonight."

"I have about nine hundred more stories," I said.

"We shall be ready for Houston at dawn. If he does not attack, I will decide his fate, and yours, after lunch," said my president.

You wouldn't want to call lovemaking what he did to me after that. Then I told him a story about a jinni, trapped in the body of a fish, who gets tricked into granting a poor fisherman three wishes. In the end the fisherman gets tricked and the jinni swallows him.

"No one survives, little Mixtli," mumbled Santa Ana as he wandered towards sleep. "No one."

I got up to take a walk after he became unconscious, but now there were armed guards surrounding the tent.

And you might wonder why I didn't just turn myself into a raven and fly out of there, that being particularly ironic because that was Sam Houston's Cherokee name, the Raven, aside from Big Drunk, but a shape shifter can't just shift at random and at will. To change shapes you have to consolidate a lot of power and it takes some time. You can't just change yourself into anything; there are particular animal spirits you come to know through practice and ritual; for me the raven was one. It takes a lot of power out of you and you have to recover; it can take days or weeks. And you always have to shift back to your original form before you move on to a new one. So I was stuck between Trinidad and Coyote and minute to minute I was still safer as Trinidad Saucedo.

The great general awoke in the middle of the night and readied his troops for Houston's attack. He'd spent a week drilling his army for a slow retreat across the river and now they were ready. He put trumpeters on both his flanks to call in the armies waiting to the north and south to close in and surround the Texians as he drew them in. Now they waited for the dawn. Santa Ana came to his tent and took me by the wrist and dragged me out to the battle line. He held me there with him, in fact, in front of him, a human shield.

"Are you being cruel now or ruthless?" I said.

He said nothing, only tightening his grip.

The red sun broke over the plain behind Houston's army. We waited for hours as the sun rose yellow over the trees and their shadows shrank in the warming air.

"He's not coming," said Santa Ana. He ordered his army to stand down, then ordered his trumpeters to call in the nearby armies after siesta. Then he dragged me into his tent with him. He didn't take his morning opium. He sat clean and sober and watched me.

"I didn't want a massacre," he said. "I wanted a battle."

And that was true enough about him. He'd have allowed half of Texas to pour into the Alamo to get a battle out of it. He'd been really itching to use his Cumae strategy and go down in history as the great military genius he knew himself to be. Now he'd just have to surround Houston and end it.

"We'll bring in the armies," he said, "and then, tomorrow, at dawn, it will be over." He said that almost sadly. It had been a great campaign. He'd suppressed a rebellion, trained peasants into a functioning army, traversed Mexico and Texas driving his enemy before him. Now it was all going to be over, back to the drudgery of running an empire that stretched from Central America to the Canadian border.

But for now, he enjoyed sitting there and watching a young girl sweat under her petticoats while he decided her fate. A death watch. As noon approached he called for two beeves to be slaughtered and soon there was a huge feast. He ordered mescal for all the men. Let them drink this afternoon, then sleep it off, because they'd spend the night preparing for battle. Those boys feasted and drank hard and by afternoon they were all sleeping out the heat of the day. Santa Ana fell asleep with my wrist in his hand, gripped tightly; and however slightly I moved, his fist clenched my wrist harder.

I lay awake beside him. I lay there a long time, watching the sun glare at the top of the tent, then at its sides. Why did I think Houston would attack? He never came to rescue the Alamo. For a month, while Santa Ana ran amok through Texas, all Houston had done was run. Right then he was probably as asleep as Santa Ana, dozing in laudanum dreams of noble suicide or running for president. I'll say one thing for sure, I'd had it with great men, with madmen, with men in general, not that my opinion mattered. In fact, at that moment, I was coming to believe that no opinion mattered, least of all informed ones. I was convinced that Houston had blown his only chance when in the distance I heard shots, and the screams of charging men.

# 69

THE TEXIANS WERE AMONG us before we could even wake up, shooting into our tents, slaughtering drowsy, unarmed Mexicans with Bowie knives. Santa Ana jumped up and ran to the tent entrance, then turned to me. "You are free, little Mixtli," he said. And thanks for nothing. As Trinidad Saucedo I wouldn't be very free among five hundred horny Texian roughnecks, though alone now I had time to make my return as Coyote.

Outside, Sam Houston himself led the charge into our camp, swinging his saber at anything he could reach. He had his horse shot out from under him and he got up and jumped on another. Then he got shot in the thigh and fell off again. Though a thigh wound could be fatal, often they bled out if you didn't get a tourniquet on them right away, Houston staggered to his feet and jumped back on his horse. He was either really brave or drugged out of his mind. Despite the chaos, the Mexican horns cried out underneath the blasts of gunfire and the screams of men, slaughtered and slaughtering: the call for Santa Ana's reinforcements.

The Mexican army did not make an organized retreat as trained, but ran for the river, so if the Texians wanted to shoot them they had to shoot them in the back, and they did. Stories arose later that Santa Ana put on a dress and hid out with the prostitutes or dressed up like a nun and took refuge with the Monsignor, but that was just a lot of Texian nonsense. Santa Ana mounted Cielo de Noche and gathered a few mounted soldiers, rode across the river and rallied the troops who made it across. Some of them turned to fight even though they didn't have guns. The Texians slaughtered the laggards and the wounded who begged for mercy. They didn't get it. They got a gun to the temple or got their throats slit as the Texians screamed "Remember the Alamo!" and "Remember Goliad!" The river ran with blood. To Houston's credit, he tried to stop the slaughter, but it didn't diminish until the Mexican volley roared from the opposite bank.

The Texians made a mad charge for the Mexican line, only to get bogged down in the bloody, rushing river. Even those Brown Bess's could be effective against a line of men slugging through a waist deep, moving current. The ones that made it over were pushed back in hand-to-hand fighting. A bayonet is a match for a Bowie knife, if not better. The Texians fell back and came on again, Houston at first leading the way. When the eyes of those two maniacs, Houston and Santa Ana, met across those lines of dying men, there was a moment when you understood war.

Houston might have got his wish to meet Santa Ana *mano a mano* if he didn't get shot in the shoulder. He fell from his horse again and two of his men dragged him across to the opposite side. He sat there firing a pistol with is good left hand as Deaf Smith loaded guns for him. Santa Ana rode back and forth behind his troops, shouting, sword raised, as Houston, back on a horse again, rode up and down the Texian line, trying to prod them into some kind of organized attack. They came again and were repulsed again. And this went on till dusk approached and Houston figured out that he had much better odds just having his men fire across the river with their Kentucky and Pennsylvania long rifles. Mexican boys began to drop and they didn't have a prayer of hitting anything at that distance with those lousy British antiques they were firing.

When the Texians rolled up a few confiscated Mexican cannons it looked like Houston would have the day, until Almonte and de la Peña showed up on the Mexican right flank, another several hundred fresh soldiers, and armed. But now the light was failing. Houston gathered up his men and withdrew to his camp. Had the Mexican northern flank showed up, he would have been trapped again and out numbered, too, but they didn't. It seems that they'd wandered into Comanche hunting grounds and took down a few too many buffalo. Fat Otter organized a war party from several of the tribes and with over a hundred warriors killed a lot of that army and scattered the rest; I found that out the next day. Now the odds were even and those were not odds that General Santa Ana de López, Emperor of America, liked.

Next morning he rode into Houston's camp with de la Peña at his side. He wore his giant hat with big white feathers on it, looking a lot like some kind of absurd bird. Houston lay under a big cottonwood with his back against the trunk, sipping laudanum, Deaf Smith at his side. Santa Ana dismounted and those two smoked opium for an hour before either one said a word. Apparently they were working something out. In the meantime, the stragglers from the Mexican northern flank began stumbling in and behind them, at the edge of the whole affair, a band of Comanche rode up and stood in a line about a hundred yards away. I tore off my shirt, so at least I'd appear half-way civilized, and jumped on the nearest horse. It was Fat Otter surrounded by the eleven black Comanches, hair flying around their heads like black sunshine, and my love, Morning Star, golden eagle feathers in her flowing, black hair and dressed in battle gear.

"*Quelle surprise!*" I said to them.

"How-how, *carpe diem*," said Fat Otter.

"*Carpe diem*, my ass," I said.

Morning Star removed an eagle feather and put it in my hair. "Now you are not so naked, my husband who defeated the white tribes of two nations by turning himself into maddening smoke."

"Are you making fun of me?" I said to her.

But she only needed to nod toward those two great white chieftains sitting under a tree and smoking opium to make her point. She was right, things looked none too victorious on either side; everywhere a lot of haggard, wounded men. How many men and boys had to die to bring that about is the *histoire* part of the *Histoire du Monde*.

"Wind Sister has returned to us," said Morning Star.

"Because the Coyote turned himself into a ghost and took revenge on Henry Wax Karnes," said Fat Otter.

"I did no such thing."

"He is dead and you are alive. You trapped him in the Alamo. Everyone knows this."

"Everyone knows the wrong thing," I said.

"That is called the truth, Brother," said Fat Otter.

"Since when did you get so wise?" I said. I turned to Morning Star. "I thought you had to be a virgin to run in war."

"All things change, my Coyote. A Coyote, especially, should know."

Regardless, I jumped from my horse to Morning Star's and put my nose beneath her hair at the nape of her neck. Underneath that warrior garb and bone breast plate was the softest creature on earth.

"You'll have to excuse us," I said to Fat Otter and the boys and I kicked that horse into a run. "Love me for an hour and you can hate me the rest of the week," I said to Morning Star. And we made love as only Comanche could, at a dead run across the plains, *kama sutra* on horseback, though then I didn't have those words for it.

# 70

I HAD ONE MORE THING to settle before heading home. I gathered up a half-dozen black Comanche warriors and rode back to the devastated Mexican camp. There I found Sor María Juana and the wagon of the Crooked Inquisitor. Sor María worked with a handful of soldiers who were gathering Mexican corpses and laying them in a line, like putting them to bed. The soldiers looked at us curiously for a moment and then went back to work. They'd seen enough, in fact too much. Black African Comanches just weren't going to upset them. Sor María Juana looked up at us, fearlessly. She was still one gorgeous nun. And if there was anyone besides my mother, Many Powers, who taught me how to be Coyote, intended or not, it was Sor María.

"Roberto," she said, slightly astonished, but not really. "You've grown into a handsome young heathen."

"My good half," I said. "These boys won't hurt you. I just wanted to make sure you were all right."

"Which side did you fight on?"

"I didn't," I said. "I came to get you safely back to Mexico."

"We are already in Mexico, Roberto."

"That would seem to be a matter of dispute. Those two lotus eating generals are working that out right now."

She lowered her head for a moment. "God forgives. God forgives everything."

"Well he better forgive everything, he sure permits everything."

"Even war," she said. "Have you become cynical and savage, too?"

What was there to say? We both had more in common, in terms of Santa Ana anyway, than either of us could admit. If you had to call that cynical, well, maybe the truth was cynical, and maybe savage, too.

"In any case, you've got to leave now. These Texians don't care about nuns."

"They're to be feared more than wild Indians?"

"Indians don't have the word *wild*," I said to her. "Only white people use it."

"We are still teaching each other things," she said.

I dismounted and went to her. I was taller than her now. A man. And she a woman. But I saw my image shiver in her eyes and knew she saw something.

"Is the girl safe?" she asked.

"I would know?"

"Yes, I feel you would." I guess she figured I had more to do with things than you could see *prima facie* or why would I be there?

"She's safe now."

"She showed the Monsignor the wounds of Christ."

"I guess somebody had to do it," I said.

"A miracle," she whispered. "For what purpose?"

I couldn't answer that. I didn't think miracle and purpose belonged in the same sentence.

"These boys can bury their dead," I said. "If you don't leave now, you could get hurt. Killed. Worse."

She turned away, seeming to peer inside the Monsignor's wagon, then looked at me again.

"Honor me," I said.

And she gave me her hand, thin and white; against it my own looked like fire. I helped Sor María Juana into the driver's seat of the wagon.

"Head that way," I said, pointing south, "toward the sun. These boys will follow at a distance and make sure no one molests you until you get behind the Mexican lines."

"Black angels," said Sor María Juana. "I dreamed of them. The Monsignor will be grateful."

"Somehow I doubt that," I said to her.

"Faith changes everything, doubt nothing," said my mentor, Sor María Juana. "*Con Dios*, Roberto O'Donahughe."

So that ended my sojourn with the Mexicans and Texians and their fight over land that neither of them owned. My people greeted my return like a stand of trees greets a deer, not a word said, not in my presence; you don't talk to legends, you tell them, except for Sad Little Dog who was a little bigger dog now.

"I'm glad you survived, so now I have the honor of killing you," he said to me when we met.

"You can join a whole bunch of white people," I said.

Wind Sister kept her pledge to the ghost of Turkey Feathers and remained celibate. She set up a lodge that she kept at the edge of the village. It was impossible to explain to her what transpired between me and Henry Wax Karnes, so I let my myth heal that wound.

"If you were Catholic," I told her, "you could marry your God."

"Does he fuck good?" she said.

Well, there are places you can't go, even if you're a Coyote.

In my lodge I soon had a beautiful daughter who, for lack of a better description, had blonde hair and black eyes.

"You haven't been sleeping with any snakes, have you?" I said to Morning Star.

"Besides you?" she said.

Well who knew how anything happened. Before that girl could walk she could summon lizards and birds and speak several languages. Go ahead, don't believe me.

The black Comanche now had their own tipis and wives and rode out together at the head of war parties. They were known across the plains as Coyote's Black Phantoms and rode with my medicine. They could fire an arrow and catch it before it hit the ground; they could knock down bullets with their shields.

My father, Hermano, it was said, had left Santa Fe for California because he had a dream he'd find rivers of gold there. Free gold, his American dream.

Always Hits got me a new mare, a pinto that the Kiowa stole from the Cheyenne and that he stole from the Kiowa.

"That horse was too easy to steal," I said to him. "It means she's too much trouble and nobody wants her," I said.

"That's your kind of horse," said Hits.

And Many Powers had finished the *Histoire du Monde*. It ended with the death of Napoleon. "I told it to Hits around the fire at night," she said to me. "He said it was just a lot of fucking and fighting, like everywhere else. Why write it down?"

"We're not in it," I said.

"No."

"That's good. We should stay out of it."

"I'm afraid we will be in the next one," my mother said. "As well, I am pregnant with your new brother."

And at that very moment, in the great white world, Mexicans wrote that Santa Ana was the savior of Mexico and Yankees wrote that Sam Houston was the founder of Texas. In truth, after all that fighting, not a damn thing was resolved and just as well. As long as those land grabbing white fools, Yankee and Mexican alike, kept their guns pointed at each other they'd be too busy to think about us. I'd done my work behind the great scene of white man's history, and you know that's true because you don't find me in it. No Comanche was ever going to write down that truth either, because when you did, well, that was the end of it. Tell it to the clouds, the rivers, the stars. So why did I write it down now? It's got something to do with endings.

But in the history of my small world, I made love to Morning Star, had a daughter and then a son, hunted buffalo in the spring and stole Apache horses in the fall. I spent winters under buffalo robes whispering love and holding babies. We had fire and love and stars and it would be that way as long as the rain fell, the grass grew, the buffalo ran, and the wind swept over the plains.

CHUCK ROSENTHAL is the author of seven published novels: the Loop Trilogy, *Loop's Progress*, *Experiments With Life and Deaf*, and *Loop's End*; *Elena of the Stars*; *Avatar Angel, the Last Novel of Jack Kerouac*; *My Mistress, Humanity*; and *The Heart of Mars*. He's the author of a memoir, *Never Let Me Go* and a book of Magic Journalism, *Are We Not There Yet? Travels in Nepal, North India, and Bhutan*. He has just completed another novel, *Ten Thousand Heavens, the Story of Annie and Bird*, and is working on two other books, a book about animal cognition entitled *Pet Me While I Eat* and a non-fiction novel (Magic Journalism), *West of Eden: a Life in 21st Century Los Angeles*. Rosenthal has lived in the west since 1978 and has been studying Native American cultures of California and the Great Plains for two decades. He's traveled and done extensive research throughout Texas and Mexico, and rides and trains horses. He teaches narrative writing and theory for the Syntext program at Loyola Marymount University and lives in Topanga Canyon, outside Los Angeles, California.

## TITLES FROM
# WHAT BOOKS PRESS

### POETRY

Molly Bendall & Gail Wronsky, *Bling & Fringe (The L.A. Poems)*

Kevin Cantwell, *One of Those Russian Novels*

Ramón García, *Other Countries*

Karen Kevorkian, *Lizard Dream*

Gail Wronsky, *So Quick Bright Things*
BILINGUAL, SPANISH TRANSLATED BY ALICIA PARTNOY

### FICTION

François Camoin, *April, May, and So On*

A.W. DeAnnuntis, *Master Siger's Dream*

Katharine Haake, *The Origin of Stars and Other Stories*

Chuck Rosenthal, *Coyote O'Donohughe's History of Texas*

### MAGIC JOURNALISM

Chuck Rosenthal, *Are We Not There Yet? Travels in Nepal, North India, and Bhutan*

### ART

Gronk, *A Giant Claw*
BILINGUAL, SPANISH

LOS ANGELES

*What Books Press books may be ordered from:*
SPDBOOKS.ORG | ORDERS@SPDBOOKS.ORG | (800) 869 7553 | AMAZON.COM

*Visit our website at*
WHATBOOKSPRESS.COM